"But many of the guests in this establishment are more odd than otherwise," said
Jeeves. He gestured toward a break in the mist,
through which Grimes glimpsed lush greenery,
vivid flowers, a veritable jungle. And surely that
was the coughing roar of a lion, followed by the
shrill chattering of disturbed tropical birds. . . .
"Lord Greystoke lives there, sir, with his wife,
the Lady Jane. They have a house in a big tree,
and they consort with *apes*. . . . And the
people next door . . . live in a gamekeeper's
cottage. A Mr. Mellors and a Lady Constance
Chatterley. . . ."

"So I'm not real?" demanded Grimes.

"But you are, sir, otherwise you could never
have come here. . . . But sir, are you an *enduring* product?"

AN *ENDURING PRODUCT*??
COMMODORE JOHN GRIMES??

Well, he has no choice but to find out, in

THE COMMODORE AT SEA

THE COMMODORE AT SEA

BY A. BERTRAM CHANDLER

SF
ace books
A Division of Charter Communications Inc.
A GROSSET & DUNLAP COMPANY
360 Park Avenue South
New York, New York 10010

THE COMMODORE AT SEA

For my favorite wife.

An ACE Book

Cover art by Paul Alexander

First Ace printing: June 1979

2 4 6 8 0 9 7 5 3 1
Manufactured in the United States of America

Hall of Fame

SONYA GRIMES WAS UNPACKING. Grimes watched her contentedly. She was back at last from her galactic cruise, and the apartment was no longer just a place in which to live after a fashion, in which to eat lonely meals, in which to sleep in a lonely bed. It was, once more, home.

She asked lightly, "And have you been good while I've been away?"

"Yes," he replied without hesitation, bending the truth only slightly. There had been that girl on Mellise, of course, but it had all been in the line of duty. A reminiscent grin softened his craggy features. "So good, in fact, that I was given the honorary rank of Admiral on Tharn . . ."

She laughed. "Then I'd better give you something too, my dear. Something I know you'll like . . ." She fell gracefully to her knees beside a suitcase that she had not yet opened, unsnapped and lifted up the lid, plunged a slender hand into a froth of gossamer undergarments. "Ah, here it is. I didn't want it to get broken . . ."

It was a leather case and, although it obviously had been well cared for, it was worn and cracked, was ancient rather than merely old. The Commodore took it carefully from his wife, looked at it

1

with some puzzlement. Its shape was clue enough to what it contained, but Grimes had never guessed that such homely and familiar masculine accessories could ever possess any value other than a strictly utilitarian one.

"Open it!" she urged.

Grimes opened the case, stared in some bewilderment at the meerschaum pipe that was revealed, archaic and fragile in its nest of faded plush.

"There was a little shop in Baker Street," she said, speaking rapidly. "An antique shop. They had this. I knew you'd like it . . ."

"Baker Street . . ." he repeated. "In London? On Earth?"

"Of course, John. And you *know* who lived there . . ."

Yes, thought Grimes. *I know who lived there. And he smoked a pipe, and he wore something called a deerstalker hat. The only trouble is that he never lived at all in real life. Oh Sonya, Sonya, they must have seen you coming. And how much did you pay for . . . this?*

"Think of it," she went on. "Sherlock Holmes's own pipe . . ."

"Fantastic."

"You don't like it?" Neither of them was a true telepath, but each was quick to sense the mood of the other. "You don't like it?"

"I do," he lied. But was it a lie? The thought behind the gift was more important, much more important than the gift itself. "I do," he said, and this time there was no smallest hint of insincerity in his voice. He put the precious pipe down carefully on the coffee table. "But you've brought yourself back, and you're worth more to me than Sherlock Holmes's pipe, or Julius Caesar's blood-stained toga, or King Solomon's mines. Come here, woman!"

"That's an odd-looking weapon you've got, Grimes," remarked Admiral Kravinsky.

The Commodore laughed. "Yes, and there's quite a story attached to it, sir. Sonya bought it for me in London—and you'd think that a woman who holds a commission in the Intelligence Branch of the Survey Service would have more intelligence than to be taken in by phony antiques! This, sir, is alleged to be the actual pipe smoked by the great Sherlock Holmes himself."

"Really?"

"Yes, really. But I'll say this for Sonya, she's got a sense of humor. After I'd explained to her in words of one syllable that Sherlock Holmes was no more than a fictional character she saw the joke, even though it was on her . . ."

"And on you."

"I suppose so. When I think of all the first class London briars that could have been purchased for the same money . . ."

"I'm surprised that you're smoking *that*. After all, a secondhand pipe . . ."

"Sonya's thorough. She took the thing to the nearest forensic laboratory to have it examined. They assured her that it was untouched by human hand—or lip. It's a perfectly good meerschaum, recently manufactured and artificially aged. So she said that she liked to see her husband smoking the most expensive pipe in the Rim Worlds. It's not a bad smoke either . . ."

"Don't drop it," warned the Admiral. "Whatever you do, don't drop it." Then the tolerant smile vanished from his broad, ruddy features. "But I didn't send for you to discuss your filthy smoking habits." He selected a gnarled, black cigar from the box on his desk, lit it. "I've a job for you, Grimes. I've already spoken to Rim Runners' management and arranged for your release for service with the Reserve."

Normally Grimes would have been pleased, but with Sonya just back . . .

"The Federation has a finger in this particular pie as well, Grimes. And as their Commander Sonya Verrill is back in Port Forlorn she may as well go along with you."

Grimes's face cleared.

"And this *will* please you, Commodore. I haven't any warships to spare, and so your beloved *Faraway Quest* will be recommissioned, with you in full command. The selection of personnel will be up to you."

"And what is the job, sir?" asked Grimes.

"A detailed, leisurely investigation of Kinsolving's Planet. We all of us tend to shy away from that ruddy world—but, after all, it is in our back garden. And after those outsiders from Francisco landed there to carry out their odd experiments . . ."

"I was there too," said Grimes.

"Well I bloody well know it. And I had to organize the rescue party. Anyhow, you're our expert on Rim World oddities. Things seem to happen around you rather than to you. If anybody falls through a crack in the continuum the odds are at least a hundred to one that Commodore Grimes, Rim Worlds Naval Reserve, will be lurking somewhere in the background . . ."

"I've been in the foreground too, sir."

"I know, Grimes, I know. But you always survive, and the people with you usually survive. I
had no hesitation in recommending you for
this . . . survey. Yes. I suppose you could call it
that, although what you'll be surveying God
knows."

"Which god?" asked Grimes, remembering vividly what had happened to the expedition from
Francisco.

"Fill me in," ordered Sonya. "Put me in the
picture."

"I wrote to you," said Grimes. "I told you all
about it."

"I never received the letter."

"It must still be chasing you. Well, you know of
Kinsolving's Planet, of course . . ."

"Not as much as I should, my dear. So just make
believe that I've just come out to the Rim, and that
I was never in the Intelligence Branch of the Survey Service. Start from there."

"You have access to all the official reports, including mine."

"I prefer to hear the story in less formal language. I never did care for officialese."

"Very well, then. Now, Kinsolving's Planet. It's
one of the Rim Worlds, and it was colonized at the
same time as the others, but the colonization
didn't stick. There's something . . . odd about the
atmosphere of the place. No, not chemically, or
physically. Psychologically. There are all sorts of
fancy theories to account for it; one of the more
recent is that Kinsolving lies at the intersection of
stress lines; that there the very fabric of space and

time is stretched almost to bursting; and that the boundaries between *then* and *now*, between *here* and *there*, are so thin as to be almost nonexistent. Oh, I know that the same sort of thing has been said often enough about the Rim Worlds in general—but nowhere is the effect so pronounced as on Kinsolving. People just didn't like living on a world where they could never feel sure of *anything*, where there was always the dread at the back of their minds that the Change Winds would reach gale force at any tick of the clock. So, when their suicide rate had risen to an unprecedented level and their nut hatches were crammed to capacity, they got the hell out.

"That was that. And then, a century and a half ago, Galactic Standard, one of the Commission's tramps, *Epsilon Eridani*, made an emergency landing at the spaceport. She had to recalibrate the controls of her Mannschenn Drive and, as you know, that's best done on a planetary surface. It could be that the temporal precession fields set up while this was being done triggered some sort of continuum-warping chain reaction ... Anyhow, a few of the officers were allowed shore leave, and they decided to explore the famous caves, which were not far distant. In these caves are remarkably well-preserved rock paintings, made by the Stone Age aborigines who once lived on Kinsolving. (What happened to *them*, nobody knows. They just vanished, millennia before the first humans landed.) They returned to their ship in quite a dither, reporting that the paint of some of the pictures of various animals was *wet*.

"The Federation's Survey Service finally got to hear about this and sent a small team of investigators, one of them a very well-qualified young lady from the Rhine Institute. They found the rock paintings without any trouble—and found that a new one had been added, one depicting men in the standard spaceman's rig of that period. While they were standing around marveling they were pounced upon by a horde of cavemen and made prisoner.

"But the Rhine Institute's star graduate was equal to the occasion. Telepathy, teleportation, psychokinesis—you name it, she had it. The party escaped with a prisoner of their own, the artist in person. His name was Raul . . .

"And, back on Earth, Raul became a pet of the Rhine Institute himself. He was a very specialized kind of painter. When he drew an animal, that animal was drawn, in the other sense of the word, to within range of the weapons of the hunters. He was also a telepath, and after the Institute had just about sucked him dry he went to Francisco to become chief psionic radio officer of the Deep Space Communications Station on that world. By this time he'd married the wench who'd captured him and, although he wasn't human, strictly speaking, the genetic engineers were able to make certain modifications to his body so that the union was a fruitful one.

"You've been to Francisco, of course. You know how religion is almost a primary industry on that planet. Raul got religion—and became, of all things, a neo-Calvinist, as did all his family. His great-granddaughter fell from grace with a loud thud and became one of the so-called Blossom People . . ."

"So there's a woman mixed up in it!" commented Sonya.

"Look around, my dear, and you'll find a

woman mixed up in almost everything. But where was I? Yes, Clarisse. She rather overdid things—drink, sex, drugs—and was picked up out of the gutter and brought back into the fold. But the neo-Calvinists weren't being charitable. They knew that she had inherited her ancestor's talents, and they knew that certain of the psychedelic drugs amplified these same talents, and so . . ."

"And so?" she echoed.

"And so some perverted genius cooked up a scheme that even now makes me shudder. The idea was that she should be taken to Kinsolving and there, on a suitable mountain top, invoke by her graphic art and magic the God of the Old Testament, in the pious hope that He would provide for the neo-Calvinists a new edition of the Ten Commandments. That bunch of unspeakable wowsers had to get the permission of the Confederacy, of course, before they could land on Kinsolving—and so my lords and masters decided that Commodore Grimes, Rim Worlds Naval Reserve, should go along as an observer . . ."

"You never tell me anything."

"I wrote to you about it. And it's all in the reports that you, as the senior representative of the Survey Service's Intelligence Branch on the Rim Worlds, should have read by now. Besides, I've hardly had a chance to get a word in edgewise since you came home."

"Never mind that. What happened?"

"They set up shop on top of the mountain that they'd decided was the new Sinai. Clarisse, after the proper preparations, painted a picture of a suitably irate-looking, white-bearded deity . . . The trouble was, of course, that so many of those patriarchal gods looked alike. And the Blossom People's religion is a pantheistic one. Cutting a long and sad story short—what we got wasn't Sinai, but Olympus. . ."

There was a long silence. And then, "If I didn't know you, and if I didn't know from personal experience what odd things do happen out on the Rim, I'd say that you'd missed your vocation, that you should be a writer of fairy stories . . . But you assure me that all this is in the reports?"

"It is. And Clarisse is still on Lorn. She married Mayhew. I was thinking that we might have them round tomorrow evening. And they'll be coming with us in the Quest, in any case."

"But what's our expedition supposed to be in aid of?" she demanded. "You're leading it, and I shall be your second-in-command; and two more unlikely people to be involved in any sort of religious research, I can't think of."

The Commodore smiled a little crookedly. "I'll tell you what Kravinsky said to me. 'It boils down to this, Grimes. Both the Confederacy and our big brothers of the Federation think that something should be done about Kinsolving. Nobody is quite sure what. So I'm sending you, with your usual crew of offbeats and misfits, and if you bumble around in your inimitable manner something is bound to happen . . .' "

Sonya grinned back at him. "The man could be right," she said.

Finally—the recommissioning of a long laid up vessel takes time. Faraway Quest, Commodore John Grimes commanding, lifted slowly from Port Forlorn. She was well-manned; Grimes had selected his crew, both spacefaring personnel and civilian scientists and technicians, with care. The officers of all departments were, like the Commodore himself, naval reservists, specialists in navigation and gunnery and engineering: in ship's biochemistry. And there was the Major of Marines—also, as were his men, a specialist. Grimes hoped that the spaceborn soldiers' services would not be needed, but it was good to have them along, just in case. There was Mayhew, one of the few psionic radio officers still on active service, youthful in appearance but old in years; and Clarisse, really beautiful since her marriage and her breakaway from the neo-Calvinists and their severe rules regarding dress and decorum, her hair styling revealing the pointed ears inherited from her nonhuman ancestor. There were the two fat, jolly men from the Dowser's Guild who, even in this day and age, were shunned by the majority of the scientists. There were men and women whose specialty was the measurement of radiation, others whose field was chemistry, organic and inorganic. There were archeologists, and paleontologists, and . . .

"One more specialist, Grimes," Admiral Kravinsky had growled, "and that old bitch of yours won't be able to lift a millimeter . . ."

But a converted freighter, with all space properly utilized, has quite amazing capacity insofar as the carrying of passengers is concerned.

So she lifted, her inertial drive running sweetly and uncomplainingly, with Grimes himself at the controls, all the old skill flowing back into his fingers, the ship an extension of his fit, stocky body, obedient to his will, as were his officers grouped around him in the control room, each in his own chair with his own bank of instruments before him.

She lifted, accelerating smoothly, soaring up to the low cloud ceiling, and through it, breaking out into the steely sunlight of high altitudes, driving up to the purple sky that soon deepened to black, into the darkness where glimmered the few, faint stars of the Rim, where, rising above the gleaming arc that was the sunlit limb of the planet, glowed the misty ellipsoid that was the Galactic Lens.

Sonya, who had traveled vast distances as a passenger, said quietly, "It's good to see this from a control room again."

"It's always good . . ." said Grimes.

Faraway Quest was clear of the atmosphere now, still lifting, and below them the planet presented the appearance of a huge, mottled ball, an enormous flawed pearl lustrous against the black immensities. She was clear of the Van Allen, and Grimes snapped an order. The Senior Communications Office spoke quietly into his intercom microphone. "Attention all! Attention all! There will be a short countdown, from ten to zero. The inertial drive will be shut off, after which there will be a period of free fall, with brief lateral accelerations as trajectory is adjusted." He turned to the Commodore. "Ready, sir?"

Grimes studied the chart tank. "Now!" he said.

"Ten . . ." began the officer. "Nine . . ."

Grimes looked to Sonya, raised his heavy eyebrows and shrugged. She shrugged back, and made even this gesture graceful. She knew, as he knew, that all this formality was necessary only because there were so many civilians aboard.

". . . Zero!"

The irregular, throbbing beat of the inertial drive suddenly ceased and there was brief weightlessness and a short silence. Then there was the hum of the maneuvering gyroscopes, rising to a whine, and centrifugal force gently pressed those in Control to the sides of their chairs. Slowly, slowly, the target star, the Kinsolving sun, drifted across the black sky until the glittering spark was centered in the cartwheel sight, wavered, then held steady. The inertial drive came on again, its broken rumble a bass background to the thin, high-keening of the ever-precessing rotors of the Mannschenn Drive. Ahead, save for the tiny, iridescent spiral that was the target sun, there was only emptiness. Lorn was to starboard; a vast, writhing planetary amoeba that was dropping back to the quarter, that was dwindling rapidly. And out to port was the Galactic Lens, distorted by the temporal precession field of the Drive to the similitude of a Klein flask blown by a drunken glassblower.

Grimes rather wished, as he had often wished before, that somebody would come up with another way of describing it. He doubted if anybody ever would.

This was a far more pleasant voyage than the one that he had made to Kinsolving in the unhappy *Piety*. To begin with, he had Sonya with him. Second, he was in command, and the ship was being run his way. *Faraway Quest* was no luxury liner, but she was warm, comfortable. Her internal atmosphere carried the scents of women's perfume, of tobacco smoke, of good cooking—not that omnipresent acridity of disinfectant. The snatches of music that drifted through her alleyways from the playmasters in the public rooms were anything and everything from grand opera to the latest pop, never the morbid hymns and psalms in which the neo-Calvinists had specialized. He spoke of this to Clarisse. She grinned and said, "You're not with it, Dad. You're just not with it. By our standards this wagon is bitter endsville, just a spaceborne morgue."

He grinned back. "If the best that the Blossom People can do is to resurrect the hip talk of the middle twentieth century, I doubt if you're with it either."

"Every religion," she told him seriously, "uses archaic language in its scriptures and in its rituals." Then she laughed. "I'm not complaining, John. Believe me, I'm not complaining. When I look back to the *Piety*, and Rector Smith and Presbyter Cannan, and that she-dragon of a deaconess, I realize how lucky I am. Of course, I could have been luckier . . ."

"How so?"

"That tall, beautiful redhead of yours could have been left behind."

"To say nothing of that highly capable telepath you're married to."

Her face softened. "I was joking, John. Before I met Ken—before I met him physically, that is—something might have been possible between us. But I'm well content now, and I feel that I owe it all to you. Ken was against our coming on this expedition, but I insisted. I'll do anything I can to aid your . . . researches."

"Even to a repeat performance?"

"Even to a repeat performance."

"I hope it doesn't come to that."

"Frankly, John, so do I."

The voyage was over. *Faraway Quest*, her Mannschenn Drive shut down, her inertial drive ticking over just sufficiently to induce a minimal gravitation field, was falling in orbit about the lonely world, the blue and green mottled sphere hanging there against the blackness. The old charts were out, and the new ones too, made by Grimes himself with the assistance of the officers of *Rim Sword*. "Here," said the Commodore, stabbing a blunt forefinger down onto the paper, "is where the spaceport *was*. There's only a crater there now. Whoever or whatever destroyed *Piety* made a thorough job of it. And here's the city— Enderston it was called—on the east bank of the Weary River . . ."

" 'Where even the weariest river winds some- where safe to sea . . .' " quoted Sonya. "They must have been a cheerful bunch, those first colonists."

"I've already told you that the very atmosphere of the planet engenders morbidity. And there, on the shore of Darkling Tarn, is what was the Sports Stadium, where *Rim Sword* landed. In the ab- sence of any spaceport facilities it's as good a place as any." He turned from the chart to the big screen upon which a magnification of the planet was presented. "You can see it all there—just to the east of the sunrise terminator. That river, with all the S bends, is the Weary, and that lake which looks like an octopus run over by a streamroller is Darkling Tarn. The city's too overgrown for it to show up at this range."

"You're the boss," said Sonya.

"Yes. So I suppose I'd better do something about something." He turned to his executive officer. "Make it landing stations, Commander Williams."

"Landing stations it is, sir."

The officers went to their acceleration chairs, strapped themselves in. In seconds the intercom speakers were blatting, "Secure all for landing stations! Secure all for landing stations! All idlers to their quarters!" And then the maneuvering gyroscopes hummed and whined as the ship was tilted relative to the planet until the surface was directly beneath her. The sounding rockets were discharged as she began her descent, each of them releasing a parachute flare in the upper atmosphere, each of them emitting a long, long streamer of white smoke.

Faraway Quest dropped steadily—not too fast and not too slow. Grimes made allowance for drift and, as the first of the flares was swept west by a jet stream, he applied lateral thrust. Down she dropped, and down, almost falling free, but always under the full control of her master. The picture of the surface on the target screen expanded. The city could be seen now, a huddle of ruins on the river bank, and beside the lake there was the oval of the Stadium, *Eau de Nil* in the midst of the indigo of the older growth. The last of the flares to have been fired was still burning down there, the column of smoke rising almost vertically. The brush among which it had fallen was slowly smoldering.

Grimes shivered. The feeling of *déjà vu* was chillingly uncanny. But he had seen this before. He had been here before—and, save for the different choice of landing site, circumstances had been almost exactly duplicated, even to that luckily unenthusiastic bush fire. And again there was the sensation that supernal forces—malign or beneficent?—were mustering to resist the landing of the ship.

But she was down at last.

There was the gentlest of shocks, the faintest of creakings, the softest sighing of the shock absorbers as the great mass of the vessel settled in her tripodal landing gear. She was down. "Finished with engines!" said Grimes softly. Telegraph bells jangled, and the inertial drive generators muttered to themselves and then were still. She was down, and the soughing of the fans intensified the silence.

Grimes turned in his swivel chair, looked toward the distant mountain peak, the black, truncated cone sharp against the blue sky. "Sinai," Presbyter Cannan had named it. "Olympus," Grimes had called it on his new charts. It was there that the neo-Calvinists had attempted to invoke Jehovah, and there that the old gods of the Greek pantheon had made their disastrous appearance. Grimes hoped that he would never have to set foot upon that mountain top again.

He was not first off the ship; after all, this was no newly discovered planet, this was not a historic first landing of Man. The honor fell to the Major of Marines, who marched smartly down the ramp at the head of his clattering column of space soldiers. He barked orders and the detachment broke up into its component parts, fanning out from the landing site, trampling through the bushes. From somewhere came a sharp rattle of machine-pistol fire. The Commodore was not concerned. He said, "There'll be fresh pork or rabbit on the table in the Marines' mess tonight. Or pigburger or rabbit-burger if the man who fired was too enthusiastic."

"Pigs? Rabbits?" inquired Sonya.

"Descendants of the livestock brought here by the original colonists. They—the pigs, probably —seem to have wiped out most of the indigenous fauna. And, come to that, the hens and the sheep and the cattle." He lit his pipe. "They were, I suppose, the two species best fitted to survive. The pigs with their intelligence, the rabbits with their ability to go underground and to breed . . . like rabbits."

She said, "I could do with some fresh air after weeks of the tinned variety. What's good enough for pigs and rabbits and Marines is good enough for me."

"Just as well that the gallant Major didn't hear you say that. Commander Williams!"

"Sir!" replied the burly Executive Officer.

"Shore leave is in order, as long as a full working watch—and that includes the manning of weaponry—is left aboard the ship at all times. And every party of boffins is to be accompanied by at least one officer or one Marine other rank, armed. Nobody is to go down the ramp without checking out or without wearing his personal transceiver. Apart from that, we'll make this a day of general relaxation. After all, there are no physical dangers on this world. As for the other kind—I doubt if the Federation's Grand Fleet could cope with them."

"Good-oh, Skipper," replied Williams.

Grimes glared at him, then laughed. "I wondered how long it would be before the veneer of your last drill in the Reserve wore off. Anyhow, those are the orders—and just try to remember now and again that this is an auxiliary cruiser of the Rim Worlds Navy, not your beloved *Rim Mamelute*." He closed on a formal note. "The ship is yours, sir, until my return."

"The ship is mine, sir, until your return."

Then Grimes and Sonya went down to their quarters, replaced their light uniform sandals with knee-high boots, strapped on their wrist transceivers, buckled on the belts from which depended their holstered hand weapons. The Commodore was sure that these would never be required but, as leader of the expedition, he could not break the orders that he had issued. It was, he already knew, warm outside; the slate gray shorts and shirts that he and his wife were wearing would be adequate.

They made their way down to the after airlock, checked out with the officer on gangway duty, walked slowly down the ramp. The fresh air was good, and the last traces of smoke from the now dead fire added a pleasant tang to it. The light of the sun, past its meridian and now dropping slowly to the west, was warm on the exposed portions of their bodies. (*I made much better time down than Rector Smith did in his* Piety, thought Grimes smugly. It had been late afternoon when that ship had landed.) And yet there was a chill in the air—psychological rather than physical. There was a chill in the air, and with the scent of green growing things there was a hint of corruption.

Sonya shivered. "There's something . . . wrong," she stated.

"That's why we're here," Grimes told her.

They were met by the Major. He was returning to the ship, seven of his men behind him. Four of them carried the bodies of two large boars, slung on branches; the others were loaded down with rabbits. The young officer saluted cheerfully. "Enemy beaten off, sir, with heavy casualties."

"So I see, Major. But this is more than a hunting party, you know."

"I know, sir. I've set alarms all around the field so that we shall be alerted if anything large and dangerous approaches."

"Good."

Grimes and Sonya walked on, picking their way with care over the tangle of tough vines, making their slow way toward what had once been the Stadium's grandstand, now a terraced, artificial hillock overgrown with flowering creepers. They saw the two dowsers, stumbling about happily with their gleaming divining rods in their hands, trailed by a bored-looking junior officer. They passed a party of the more orthodox scientists setting up a piece of apparatus that looked like a miniature radio telescope. They met Mayhew and Clarisse.

"Do you feel it?" demanded the Psionic Radio Officer. "Do you feel it, sir? None of these others seem to."

"Yes, I feel it. And so does Sonya."

"Like something that has been waiting for us for a long time. Like something getting ready to pounce. But it's not sure that it has the strength anymore . . ."

"Yes . . . I thought myself that the ominous atmosphere wasn't quite so pronounced as when I was here last. What do you think, Clarisse? You were here too."

"I'm not as scared as I was then, John. But there are reasons for that."

"It's pronounced enough for me," said Sonya.

"It's here still," admitted Grimes. "But it could be fading. It could be that this planet has been at the very focus of . . . forces, and now the focus is shifting." He laughed. "We shan't be at all popular if, after our masters have sent us here at enormous expense, nothing happens."

"Frankly," said Clarisse, "I hope nothing does."

Nothing did.

Day followed day, and the parties of scientists spread out from around the landing site, on foot and in *Faraway Quest's* pinnaces. The archeologists grubbed happily in kitchen middens that they discovered on the banks of the lake and the river, penetrated the caves and photographed the famous paintings in a wide range of illuminations. Nothing new was found in the middens, no evidence that would throw any light at all on the disappearance of the aboriginal race. The rock paintings were just rock paintings, the pigments dry and ancient. The dowsers dowsed, and discovered deposits of metals that would be valuable if the planet were ever recolonized, and found oil, and mapped the meanderings of underground streams in desert areas. The other specialists plotted and measured and calculated—and found nothing that could not have been found on any Earth-type planet.

"At least," said Grimes, "we've proven that this world is suitable for resettlement." He, with Sonya and Clarisse and Mayhew, was sitting over after dinner coffee in his comfortable day cabin. "All hands are really enjoying a marvelous outdoor holiday."

"Except us," said Sonya in a somber voice.

"There's a reason for that, my dear. You're sensitive to my moods, as I am to yours. And I had such a scare thrown into me when I was here last that I could never feel at ease on this planet. And Clarisse was more frightened than I was—and with good reason!—and all the time she was in telepathic touch with Mayhew."

"I still say that there's something wrong," insisted Mayhew. "I still say that we should be absolutely sure before we put in a report recommending another attempt at colonization."

Grimes looked at Clarisse. "Would you be willing to repeat that experiment?" he asked.

She replied without hesitation. "Yes. I was going to suggest it. I've talked it over with Ken. And I feel that if I try to call those old gods, rather than the deity of the neo-Calvinists, the results might be better. It could be that it is in their interests that this world be peopled again—this time with potential worshippers."

"Like your Blossom People," said Mayhew, unmaliciously.

"Yes. Like the Blossom People. After all, the slogan *Make Love, Not War*, would appeal to Aphrodite if not to Ares . . ."

Grimes laughed, but without real humor. "All right, Clarisse. We'll arrange it for tomorrow night. And we'll have all hands out of the ship and well scattered just in case Zeus is too handy with his thunderbolts again. Williams has been getting too fat and lazy; it'll do him good to have a job of organization thrown suddenly onto his lap . . ."

Williams enjoyed himself; things had been altogether too quiet for his taste. And then, with the ship quiet and deserted, Grimes, with Sonya and Clarisse and Mayhew, and with a full dozen of assorted scientists, boarded one of the pinnaces, in which the necessary materials had already been stowed.

It was just before sunset when they landed on the smooth, windswept plateau that was the summit of the mountain. A thin, icy wind swept into the little cabin as the door opened. One by one, Grimes in the lead, the members of the party clambered down on to the bare, barren rock, the last ones to emerge handing down the equipment before making their own exits. There was an easel, as before, a floodlight, pots of paint, brushes. There were cameras, still and cinematographic, one of which would transmit a television picture to receivers on the plain below the mountain. There were sound recorders.

Silently, slowly, Mayhew and his wife walked to the center of the plateau, accompanied by Grimes and Sonya, carrying what she would be using. Grimes set up the easel, with its stretched black canvas, and the powerful floodlight. Sonya placed the painting materials at its foot. Mayhew, his thin face pale and anxious, lifted the heavy cloak from Clarisse's shoulders. She stood there as she had stood before, naked save for the brief, rough kilt of animal hide, her arms crossed over her full breasts for warmth rather than from modesty. She looked, thought Grimes (again), as her remote ancestresses on this very world must have looked, was about to practice the magic that they had practiced. Mayhew had produced from a pocket a little bottle and a tiny glass—the psychedelic drug. He filled the glass, held it out to her. "Drink this, my dear," he ordered gently.

She took it from him, drained it, threw it down. It shattered with a crystalline crash, surprisingly loud in spite of the wind. "Your bare feet . . ." muttered Mayhew. He squatted down, carefully picking up the glittering fragments. She did not appear to see what he was doing, stood like a statue when he, on his feet again, laid his free hand on her bare shoulder in an attempted gesture of reassurance and . . . farewell?

He whispered to Grimes, his voice taut with strain and worry, "I can't get through to her. Somebody, something's got hold of her . . ."

The three of them walked back to where the scientists were standing by the pinnace, their recording apparatus set up and ready. And suddenly the sun was gone, and there was only the glare of the floodlight, in which Clarisse was standing. Overhead was the almost empty black sky with its sparse scatter of dim stars, and low to the east was the arc of misty luminescence that was the slowly rising Galactic Lens. The wind could have been blowing straight from intergalactic space.

Conditions were almost the same as they had been on the previous occasion. Almost. It was the human element that was different. This time those on the mountain top were skeptics and earnest inquirers, not true believers. But the feeling of almost unendurable tension was the same.

Hesitantly, Clarisse stooped to the clutter of materials at her feet. She selected a brush. She dipped it into one of the pots, then straightened. With swift, sure strokes she began to paint.

But it was wrong, Grimes realized. It was all wrong. It was white paint that she had used before; this time she was applying a bright, fluorescent pigment to the canvas. A figure was taking shape—that of a tall, slender man in red tights, with a pointed beard, a mocking smile . . . A man? But men do not have neat little goatlike horns growing from their heads; neither do they have long, lissome tails ending in a barbed point . . .

A god?

Pan, perhaps.

No, not Pan. Pan never looked like that.

There was a dreadful crack of lightning close at hand, too close at hand, but the flash was not blue white but a dull, unnatural crimson. There was a choking, sulphurous stench. And then *he* was standing there, laughing; amid the rolling clouds of black smoke, laughing.

Grimes heard one of the scientists almost scream, "What the devil . . . ?"

And the devil advanced, still laughing, his very white and very sharp teeth flashing. His surprisingly elegant right hand stretched out to rest on the Commodore's wrist. "You are under arrest," he said. "And I must warn you that anything you say will be taken down and may be used as evidence."

"By what authority?" Grimes heard Sonya cry. "By what . . . ?"

And then there was darkness deeper than that between the universes, and absolute silence.

*   *   *

How long did the journey last? An eternity, or a fraction of a microsecond? It could have been either.

There was light again; not bright, but dim and misty. There was light, and there was solidity underfoot—and there was still the pressure of that restraining hand on his wrist. Grimes looked down—he was reluctant to look up—and saw what looked like a marble pavement. At last he allowed his eyes slowly to elevate. There were the slim, pointed red shoes, inches from his own. There were the slender yet muscular legs in their skintight scarlet hose. There were the elaborately puffed trunks. There was the scarlet, gold-trimmed doublet . . . Suddenly Grimes felt less frightened. This was the Mephistopheles of fancy dress balls, and of opera, rather than a real and living embodiment of unutterable evil. But when he came to the face his assurance began to ebb. There was a reckless handsomeness, but there was power, too much power, power that would be used recklessly and selfishly.

Behind Grimes a very English voice was saying, "We must congratulate our friend on his speedy arrest, Watson."

A deeper voice replied, "Yes, yes, my dear Holmes. But are we sure that we have the right man? After all, to judge by his uniform, he's an officer, and presumably a gentleman . . ."

Mephistopheles laughed sneeringly. "Well I know the villainies of which so-called gentlemen are capable. But I have carried out my part of the bargain and now I shall return to my own place; it's too infernally cold here for comfort."

There was a flash of dull crimson light, the stench of burning sulphur, and he was gone.

"Turn around, fellow, and let us look at you," ordered the first English voice.

Slowly Grimes turned, and what he saw was no surprise to him. There was the tall man with aquiline features, wearing peculiar garments that he knew were a Norfolk jacket, an Inverness cape and a deerstalker cap. There was the short, stout man with the walrus moustache, formally clad, even to black frock coat and gleaming top hat.

Grimes looked at them, and they looked at him.

Then, "Hand it over, sir," ordered the tall man. "Hand it over and I shall prefer no charges."

"Hand what over?" asked Grimes, bewildered.

"My pipe, of course."

Silently the Commodore drew the leather case from his pocket, placed it in the outstretched hand.

"A remarkable piece of deduction, my dear Holmes," huffed the stout man. "It baffles me how you did it."

"Elementary, my dear Watson. It should be obvious, even to you, that a crime, any crime, cannot take place in the three dimensions of space only. The additional factor, the fourth dimension, time, must always be taken into account. I reasoned that the thief must be somebody living so far in our future that our fictional origin will be forgotten. Then I enlisted the aid of the London branch of the Baker Street Irregulars—those fellows are always absurdly flattered when I condescend to share their dreams! Through them I maintained a round the clock watch on the antique shop that stands where our lodgings used to be. At last it was reported to me that my pipe had been purchased by a red-haired young lady of striking appearance.

I learned, too—once again through the invaluable Irregulars—that she was the wife of one Commodore Grimes, of the Rim Worlds Naval Reserve, and would shortly be returning to her husband, who was resident in a city called Port Forlorn, on a planet called Lorn, one of the Rim Worlds. These Rim Worlds are outside our ambit, but I was able to persuade that learned colleague of yours who dabbles in magic to persuade his . . . er . . . colleague, Mephistopheles, to place his services at my disposal. Between us we were able to lay a very subtle pyschological trap on yet another planet, one with the unlikely name of Kinsolving . . ." Holmes opened the case, took out the pipe, looked at it, sniffed it. His face darkened. "Sir, have you been *smoking* this?"

"Yes," admitted Grimes.

Watson intervened. "It will be a simple matter, Holmes, to sterilize it. Just a jet of steam from a boiling kettle, back in our lodgings . . ."

"Very well, Watson. Let us proceed with the purification rites forthwith."

The two men walked rapidly away, their forms becoming indistinct in the mist. Grimes heard Watson say, "And when I chronicle this case, I shall call it 'The Adventure of the Missing Meerschaum . . .'"

And what about "The Case of the Kidnapped Commodore"? wondered Grimes. But before he could start in pursuit of the great detective and his friend another figure had appeared, blocking his way.

He, too, was English, most respectably dressed in the style of the early twentieth century, in black jacket and trousers with a gray waistcoat, a stiff white collar and a black necktie. He was inclined to stoutness, but the ladies of the servants' hall must often have referred to him—but never in his dignified hearing—as "a fine figure of a man."

He raised his bowler hat, and Grimes had sufficient presence of mind to bring the edge of his right hand to the peak of his cap to return the salute. He said, his voice deferential but far from servile, "Welcome aboard, sir." He contrived to enclose the words between quotation marks.

"Er . . . Thank you."

"Perhaps, sir, you will accompany me. I am the only member of my profession in this place, and so it has become my duty—and my pleasure, sir—to welcome new arrivals and to arrange for their accommodation."

"That's very good of you, er . . ."

"Jeeves, sir. At your service. This way, Commodore—I take it that the braid on your epaulettes still has the same significance as in my time—if you please."

"Where are you taking me?"

"I took the liberty, sir, of arranging for your accommodation at the Senior Service Club. There are other naval gentlemen in residence. There is Admiral—Lord Hornblower, that is. You must have heard of him. And there is Commander Bond—a very likable young gentleman, but not quite my idea of what a naval officer should be. And . . ." a flicker of distaste crossed Jeeves's plump face . . . "a certain Lieutenant Commander Queeg, who somehow appointed himself club secretary. He even tried to have Captain Ahab evicted from the premises. How did he put it?" Jeeves's voice acquired a nasal twang. " 'How can

I run a taut ship with that damned whaling skipper stomping around the decks on his peg leg? He'll be putting that pet whale of his in the swimming bath next. I kid you not.' But the Admiral—he's president; although old Captain Noah is the senior member he's really not much interested in anything—asked my advice. So Commander Bond was ordered to act as a one-man press gang—a form of activity for which he seemed well qualified—and, after Captain Ahab had been pressed into the King's service he was promptly commissioned by Lord Hornblower. As an officer of the Royal Navy he was really more entitled to Club membership—it's a very British institution—than Commander Queeg . . ."

"Very ingenious," commented Grimes.

"I am always happy to oblige, sir." Jeeves raised his hat to a tall woman who had appeared out of the mist, a striking brunette, barefooted, wearing a long white nightgown. "Good morning, Your Ladyship."

She ignored him but concentrated on Grimes. She glared at him from slightly mad, dark eyes, and all the time her hands were making peculiar wringing motions. "Ye havena brought any decent soap wi' ye?" she demanded.

"Soap, madam?"

"Aye, soap, ye lackwitted Sassenach!"

"I'm afraid not. If I'd known that I was coming here . . ."

The woman brushed past him, muttering, "Will nothing wash these white hands?"

"I have tried to help her, sir," said Jeeves, "But I can only do so much. After all, I am not a qualified psychiatrist. But many of the guests in this establishment are more odd than otherwise." He gestured toward a break in the mist, through which Grimes glimpsed lush greenery, vivid flowers, a veritable jungle. And surely that was the coughing roar of a lion, followed by the shrill chattering of disturbed tropical birds . . . "Lord Greystoke lives there, sir, with his wife, the Lady Jane. They have a house in a big tree, and they consort with apes . . . And the people next door, in the next estate—like an English woodland, it is—live in a gamekeeper's cottage. A Mr. Mellors and a Lady Constance Chatterley. You would think that with their mutual love of nature the two couples would be on very friendly terms. But no. Lady Chatterley said to me once when I mentioned it—it was when I had invited her and Mr. Mellors to my quarters for a real English afternoon tea, and we were discussing the Greystokes—'The only nature I'm interested in, Jeeves, is human nature.' " Again he raised his hat. "Good morning, Colonel."

"Who was that?" asked Grimes, staring after the figure in the fringed buckskin shirt, with a revolver slung at each hip.

"Colonel William Cody, sir. I feel sorry for the gentleman. You see, he isn't really one of us. As well as living an actual life on the printed page he was also a flesh and blood person. As I understand it, a New York publishing house of his time commissioned a writer to produce a series of stories about the Wild West, and this writer, instead of creating a character, used one who was already in existence in the flesh and blood world, calling him Buffalo Bill. And this, you will understand, makes him, insofar as *we* are concerned, illegitimate. But he is not the only one. There are the Greek ladies and gentlemen—Helen, and Cassandra, and Odysseus, and Achilles, and Oedipus ... And others. And, of course, there is the Prince, although His Highness claims that he was cribbed from an earlier work of fiction and not from what the flesh and blood people call real life."

"So I'm not real?" demanded Grimes.

"But you are, sir, otherwise you could never have come here. You are, like the rest of us, a creation, a product of the imagination of some gifted writer." He stopped suddenly, and Grimes stopped with him. "But, sir, are you an enduring product?" He walked around the Commodore like a tailor inspecting the fit and cut of a new uniform. "This is indeed unfortunate, sir. Already I detect a hint of insubstantiality ..." He paused, turned to face a newcomer, bowed. "Good morning, Your Highness."

The tall, thin, pale man in formfitting black, with the white lace at throat and cuffs, did not reply to the salutation. Instead he said in a sonorous voice, "To be or not to be, that is the question ..."

"Too right," agreed Grimes.

The Prince of Denmark looked down at the age-mottled skull that he held in his right hand. "Alas, poor Yorick, I knew him well ..." He stared at the Commodore. "But you I do not know." He turned on his heel, strode away.

"Good night, sweet Prince," said Grimes bitterly.

"Do not mind His Highness," said Jeeves. "He has a sardonic sense of humor."

"Maybe he has. But you must have had other ...

characters here who were not, as you put it, enduring products. What happened to them?"

"They . . . faded, sir. There was a young man dressed up in old woman's clothing who called himself 'Charley's Aunt.' He lasted quite a few years, Earth Time, but he's vanished now. And there have been many gentlemen like yourself, spacemen. None of them lasted long."

"But what happens to them? To us?"

"I cannot say, sir. When the last book in which you appeared has crumbled into dust, when your last reader has gone to wherever the flesh and blood people go, what then?"

"There must be some way," muttered Grimes. Then, aloud "All right. I'm scared. I admit it. But my own case is different. All you others came here, I suppose, after the death of your authors. You're immortality—perhaps—for the men who created you. But I was brought here before my time. I was the victim of a plot cooked up—and what more unlikely fellow conspirators could there ever be!—by Sherlock Holmes and Dr. Faustus. And Mephistopheles."

Jeeves laughed quietly. "I knew that Mr. Holmes had lost his pipe. I offered to assist him in its recovery; but he, of course, was too proud to accept my humble services. He always likes to do things his own way. And you, sir, I take it, are the innocent victim."

"You can say that again. I was shanghaied away from my own universe to this . . . limbo . . ."

"We prefer, sir, to call it the Hall of Fame."

"And I'm not the only victim. Back there I've a wife, and a ship . . . I must get back to them."

"I appreciate your anxiety, sir, and I admit that

there could be need for haste. Time is measured differently here than elsewhere, sir, and already you are becoming quite diaphanous . . ."

Grimes held out his hand, looked at it. He could see the marble flooring through skin and flesh and blood and bone.

"Hurry, sir," urged Jeeves.

They hurried. Nonetheless, Grimes retained a confused memory of their nightmarish gallop. Men and women stopped to stare at them; and some of them Grimes recognized; and some were hauntingly familiar; and a very few struck no chords in his memory whatsoever. There were occasional rifts in the eddying mists to afford fleeting glimpses of buildings, and, like the clothing of the people, the architecture was of all historical periods. Turreted Camelot, its towers aflutter with gay pennons, they sped by; and beyond its walls was a barren and dusty plain whereon a solitary knight, a scarecrow figure astride a skeletal horse, tilted at windmills. Then there was Sherwood Forest, where the outlaws in Lincoln green paused in their archery practice to cheer on the two runners.

And for a while there was the shambling monstrosity that lurched along beside them, keeping pace, like a large, unlovely dog trying to make friends. Grimes glanced at this giant, who seemed to have been put together from not quite matching parts pilfered from the graveyard, then looked hastily away, sickened by the sight of him and by the charnel stench that emanated from the crudely humanoid form. Then there was the other monster, the handsome man in nineteenth century dress finery who hovered above them on black bat's wings. Jeeves, who did not suffer from lack of wind, muttered something uncomplimentary about Eastern European aristocracy.

At last there loomed before them the house that was their destination. All high gables it was, and oak beams, with narrow, diamond-paned windows. Set high on the stout, ironbound door was the black, iron knocker—metal cast in the form of an inverted crucifix. Jeeves reached for it, rapped smartly.

Slowly the door creaked open. An old, gray-bearded man peered out at them suspiciously. He was dressed in a rusty black robe upon which cabalistic symbols gleamed with a dull luster and a tall, conical, black hat. His blue eyes were so faded as to be almost white.

He demanded querulously, "Who disturbs my rest?"

"It is I, Jeeves, Herr Doktor . . ."

"And this other? This . . . phantasm?"

"The innocent victim, Dr. Faustus, of the peculiar machinations set in motion by yourself and Mr. Holmes."

"What is done cannot be undone." He glared at Grimes, through Grimes. "And do you cry, 'Oh, Lord, put back Thy Universe, and give me back my yesterday'?"

"I have done so," whispered Grimes. "As who has not?"

"I cannot help you." The door was starting to close.

But Jeeves had inserted a stout, highly polished shoe into the narrowing opening. "Do not forget that I have helped you, Dr. Faustus. Have I not sent patients to you?" He added nastily, "Although

Achilles still limps, and Oedipus still chases after older women . . ."

"My name is Faustus, not Freud," grumbled the old man.

"Furthermore," continued Jeeves, "both you and your partner rely upon me for the supply of the luxuries that were unavailable in your own day and age."

The door opened abruptly. "Come in!" snarled the old doctor.

Inside it was dark, the only light coming from a brazier over which a cauldron bubbled. The room was a large one, but it was so cluttered with a fantastic miscellany of objects that it was hard to move without fouling something. Grimes ducked hastily to avoid striking his head on a stuffed crocodile that hung from the low ceiling, then almost tripped over a beautiful—but woefully inaccurate—celestial globe that stood on the stone floor. He would have tripped had his body been solid, but his shadowy leg passed through the obstacle with no more than the faintest hint of resistance.

Grumbling, the old man shuffled to a bench littered with the apparatus of alchemy. "Chalk . . . " he muttered, "for the pentagram . . . Where did I put it? And the sulphur candles . . ."

"There's no time for that, Doctor. Can't you see? This gentlemen needs help urgently."

"But *He* will not like it if I do not observe protocol."

"*He* won't like it if he has to go thirsty from now on."

"Very well, very well. But I warn you—*He* will be bad tempered."

Dr. Faustus tottered to a low table upon which

stood a large, stuffed owl. He lifted the bird, which was hollow, revealing a jarringly anachronistic telephone. He handed the owl to Jeeves, who regarded it with some distaste, then took the handset from its rest, punched a number.

"Yes," he croaked into the instrument. "At once." There was a pause. "Yes, I know that you always insist that the proper procedure be followed, but Mr. Jeeves says that this is urgent." There was another pause. "You'd better come, unless you want to do without your brandy and cigars . . ."

This time there was no thunder, no crimson lightning, no clouds of black, sulphurous smoke. But Mephistopheles was standing there, his arms folded over his muscular chest, scowling down at Grimes. "Yes?" he demanded shortly. "Yes, my man?"

The Commodore, his voice a barely audible whisper, said, "Take me back to where I belong."

The Commodore stepped silently forward, peered over the writer's shoulder. He read, *He was standing in a ship's cabin. The carpeted deck swayed and lurched under his feet* . . . Then the carpeted deck lurched really heavily. Grimes put out a hand, to the back of the other man's chair, to steady himself.

The writer started violently, exclaimed, "What the hell!" He twisted in his seat, stared at Grimes. His pipe fell from his mouth, clattered to the deck. "No . . ." He said slowly. "No. It can't be. Go away."

"I wish that I could," Grimes told him.

"Then why the hell don't you?"

"You, sir, should know the answer to that question," said Grimes, reasonably enough. He looked curiously at the other man, his . . . creator? His . . . parent? But there was no physical resemblance to himself. He, Grimes, was short and stocky, and his ears were his most prominent facial feature. The writer was tall, with normal enough ears, but too much nose.

"You, sir, should know the answer to that question," repeated Grimes.

"I'm sorry, Commodore, but I don't. Not yet, anyhow." Then, in a tone of forced cheerfulness, "But this is only a silly dream. It must be."

"It's not, Captain." The man's gold-braided epaulettes and the uniform cap, with the scrambled egg on its peak, hanging on a hook just inside the curtained door made this a safe enough guess. "It's not, Captain. Pinch yourself."

"Damn it! That hurt."

"Good. Do you mind if I sit down?" Carefully, Grimes eased himself on to the settee that ran along one bulkhead of the day cabin. He feared at first that he was going to sink through the cushion, but it had substance (or he had substance) and supported him, although only just. He shut his eyes for a moment, trying to dispel the faintness that was creeping over him. It was the result of shock, he realized, of shock and of disappointment. He had expected to find himself aboard his own ship, the old, familiar, tried and trusted *Faraway Quest*, to be welcomed back by his wife. But where was he now? When was he? On Earth, the mother world of humankind? Aboard some sort of surface vessel?

The writer answered the unspoken questions.

He said, "I'll put you in the picture, Commodore. You're aboard the good ship *Kantara*, which same plies between Melbourne and the port of Macquarie, on the wild west coast of Tasmania. We load pyritic ore in Macquarie for Melbourne, and make the return trip (as we are doing now) in ballast. I doubt very much if you have anything like this trade in your day and age, sir. Macquarie's one of those places that you can't get into when you're outside, and that you can't get out of when you're inside. To begin with, the tides are absolutely unpredictable, and it's safe to work the entrance—it's called Hell's Gates, by the way— only at slack water. If you tried to come in against a seven knot ebb you'd be in trouble! And the Inner Bar and the Outer Bar are always silting up, and with strong northwesterlies—which we've been having—Outer Bar breaks badly. I've been riding out a howling westerly gale, keeping well to seaward, as I just don't like being caught on a lee shore in a small, underpowered and underballasted ship. But the wind's backed to the south'ard and is moderating, and the glass is rising, and all the weather reports and forecasts look good. So I'm standing in from my last observed position— P.M. star sights—until I'm just inside the extreme range of Cape Sorell light, and then I'll just stand off and on until daylight, keeping within easy reach of the port. Come the dawn, I'll have a natter with the harbor master on the radio telephone, and as soon as he's able to convince me that conditions are favorable I'll rush in."

"Why bother with the extreme range of the light?" asked Grimes, becoming interested in spite of all his troubles. "You have radar, don't you?"

"I do. I have radar and echo sounder. But my radar gets old and tired after only a few hours' operation, and my echo sounder's on the blink. I've nothing against electronic gadgetry *as long as it can be relied upon.* At the moment, mine can't be." The writer laughed. "But this is crazy. To sit here discussing navigation with a navigator from the distant future! I hope that none of my officers comes in to find me carrying on a conversation with myself!"

"I'm real, Captain. And I'm here. And I think that you should do something about getting me back to where I belong."

"What can *I* do, Commodore? People have said, more than once, that my stories just *happen.* And that's true, you know. Furthermore, I've always given *you* a free hand. Time and time again I've had to make plot changes because *you've* insisted on going your own way."

"So you can't help me . . ."

"I wish that I could. Believe me, I wish that I could. Do you think that I want to be haunted by you for the rest of my life?"

"There could be a way . . ." whispered Grimes. *Yes,* he thought, *there could be a way.* Life in that Hall of Fame would not be at all bad as long as he—and Sonya—were assured of the same degree of permanence as the others: Oedipus Rex, Hamlet, Sherlock Holmes, James Bond . . . He said, "I shan't mind a bit going back to that peculiar Elysium you cooked up as long as my status there is better than that of an ephemeral gate crasher. And, of course, I'd like Sonya with me."

"And just how can I arrange that for you, Commodore?"

"Easily, Captain. All you have to do is write a

best seller, a series of best sellers."

The other man grinned. "It's a pity you can't meet my wife." He gestured toward a peculiarly two dimensional photograph in a frame over the desk. The auburn-haired woman who looked out at them reminded Grimes of Sonya. "That's what she's always telling me."

There was a sharp buzz from the telephone on the desk. The writer picked up the handset. "Master here."

"Third Officer here, sir," Grimes heard faintly. "I've just picked up Cape Sorell light, at extreme range, right ahead . . ."

"Good, Mr. Tallent. Turn her on to the reciprocal course. Yes, keep her on half speed. I'll be right up."

Grimes followed the shipmaster out of the day cabin, up the narrow companionway to the chart-room, out of the glass-enclosed wheelhouse, then out through a sliding door to the wing of the bridge. The night was clear, and the stars (would he ever see them again as more than lights in the sky?) were bright. Astern was the winking, group-flashing light, an intermittent spark on the far horizon. And then the light itself was gone, only a flash recurring at regular intervals marking its position as the lantern dipped below the planet's curvature.

The captain grunted his satisfaction, then turned to stare forward. There was still quite a sea running, the wave crests faintly phosphorescent in the darkness; there was still a stiff breeze, broad on the port bow, but there was no weight to it. The ship was lifting easily to the swell, the motion not at all uncomfortable. The captain grunted again, went back to the chartroom. Grimes looked over his shoulder as he bent over the chart, noted the range circle with Cape Sorell as its center, the dot on it in the middle of its own tiny, penciled circle with the time—2235—along it, and another, cryptic notation, △ 33.5. On the chart, to one side, was a message pad. *Final Gale Warning*, it was headed. "Wind and sea moderating in all areas," read Grimes. "All pressures rising."

The shipmaster was busy now with parallel rulers, pencil and dividers. From the observed position he laid off a course—270° True. With the dividers he stepped off a distance, marked it with a cross and wrote alongside it "0200?" Grimes realized that the officer of the watch had come into the chartroom. He could see the young man, but the young man, it seemed, could not see him.

"Mr. Tallent," said the shipmaster, "we'll stand out to this position, then bring her around to 090 True. All being well, we shall be within comfortable VHF range at daylight, and with any luck at all the Bar will have stopped breaking and we shall have slack water. I'll not write up my night orders yet; I'll see the second officer at midnight before I turn in . . ."

"We should get in tomorrow all right, sir," said the officer.

"Don't be so bloody sure. You can never tell with this bloody place!"

"Good night, sir."

"Good night, Mr. Tallent."

Back in the day cabin, Grimes said, "You can see, Captain, that I have no real existence *here* and *now*. You must try to make me real *somewhere*."

"Or somewhen."

"Or somewhen."

"More easily said than done, Commodore. Especially in the existing circumstances. At the moment of writing I am master of this little rustbucket. Master under God, as Lloyd's puts it. This ship is my responsibility—and you should be able to appreciate that. This evening I was writing just as relaxation, one hand on the keyboard, the other ready to pick up the telephone . . ."

Grimes said, "You take yourself too bloody seriously. This is only a small ship with a small crew on an unimportant trade."

"Nonetheless," the shipmaster told him, "this is my ship. And the crew is my crew. The trade? That's the Company's worry; but, as Master, it's up to me to see that the ship shows a profit."

"And I'm your responsibility too," Grimes pointed out.

"Are you? As I've already said, Commodore, you've proven yourself able to go your own sweet way in any story that I've written. But if I am responsible just bear in mind that I could kill you off as easily as I could swat a fly. More easily. How do you want it? Act of God, the King's enemies, or pirates? Nuclear blast—or a knife between the ribs?"

"You're joking, surely."

"Am I? Has it never occurred to you, Commodore, that a writer gets rather tired of his own pet characters? Sir Arthur Conan Doyle killed off Sherlock Holmes, but had to drag him back to life to please his public. Ian Fleming was becoming more than somewhat browned off with James

Bond when he, himself, kicked the bucket . . ."

Grimes looked toward the photograph over the desk. "But you like Sonya," he said.

"I do. She's too good for you."

"Be that as it may. She's part of my world, my time . . ."

"So?"

"Well, I thought . . ."

The telephone buzzed. The shipmaster picked up the handset. "Yes?"

"The wind's freshening, sir, and it's veered to west."

"Put her back on full speed, Mr. Tallent." The captain got up from his chair, went to the aneroid barometer mounted on the bulkhead. He tapped it. The needle jerked in a counterclockwise direction. "Just what I need," he said. "A bloody secondary."

"What does that mean, Captain?"

"It means, Commodore, that those *Final Gale Warnings* aren't worth the paper that Sparks typed them on. Very often, too often, in these waters the secondary depression is more vicious than the so-called primary."

"What can you do?"

"Stand out. Make offing. Get the hell off this bloody lee shore."

Again the telephone buzzed. "Master here."

"Sir, we've lifted Cape Sorell again . . ."

"Tell the engineers to give her all they've got. I'll be right up."

The ship was lurching, was rolling heavily as she fell away from the wind. She was pounding as her fore part lifted and then slammed back down into the trough. Her screw was racing each time that her stern came clear of the water, and as the propeller lost purchase, so did the rudder. "Sir," complained the helmsman, "the wheel's hard over, but she's not coming back . . ."

"Keep it hard over until she answers," ordered the Master. He was looking into the radar screen. It was not a very good picture. There was spoking, and there was too much clutter. But there, right astern, was the faint outline of the rocky coast, a ragged luminosity. And there were the range circles—and slowly, slowly, the coastline was drifting from the 24 mile to the 20 mile ring. Even Grimes, peering over the other man's shoulder, could appreciate what was happening.

"Mr. Tallent!"

"Sir?"

"Call the Chief Officer. Tell him to flood the afterhold."

"*Flood* the afterhold, sir?"

"You heard me. We have to get the arse down somehow, to give the screw and the rudder some sort of grip on the water."

"Very good, sir."

"She's logging three knots," whispered the Master. "But she's making one knot—*astern*. And that coast is nothing but rocks . . ."

"And flooding the hold will help?" asked Grimes.

"It'd better. It's all I can do."

They went back out to the wing of the bridge, struggling to retain their balance as the wind hit them. Cape Sorell light was brightly visible again, right astern, and even to the naked eye it had lifted well clear of the sea horizon. A shadowy figure joined them there—the Chief Officer, decided Grimes.

"I've got two fire hoses running into the hold, sir. What depth of water do you want?"

"I want 100 tons. Go below and work it out roughly."

"What if the ceiling lifts?"

"Let it lift. Put in your hundred tons."

"Very good, sir."

Another officer came onto the bridge—big, burly, bearded. This must be, realized Grimes, the midnight change of watch. "Keep her as she's going, sir?" he asked.

"Yes. Keep her as she's going, Mr. Mackenzie. She'll be steering better once we get some weight in aft, and racing less. But you might tell the engineers to put on the second steering motor . . ."

"Will do, sir."

The shipmaster made his way back into the wheelhouse, staggering a little as the vessel lurched in the heavy swell. He went to the radar unit, looked down into the screen with Grimes peering over his shoulder. Right astern, the ragged outline of Cape Sorell was touching the twenty mile ring. Slowly the range decreased—slowly, but inexorably.

The Chief Officer was back. "About two foot six should do it, sir."

"Make it that . . ."

Then, gradually, the range was opening again. The range was opening, and the frequent heavy vibrations caused by the racing screw were becoming less. The wind was still shrieking in from the westward, whipping the crests off the seas, splattering them against the wheelhouse windows in shrapnel bursts of spray, but the ship was steering again, keeping her nose into it, clawing away from the rocks that had claimed, over the years, too many victims.

Grimes followed the Master down to the after-deck, stood with him as he looked down a trunk-way into the flooded hold. Swirling in the filthy water were the timbers of the hold ceiling, crashing against the bulkheads fore and aft, splintering themselves against frames and brackets and the hold ladders, self-destroying battering rams driven by the force of the ship's pitching and rolling. There would be damage, even Grimes could see that. There would be damage—and, inevitably, the writing of reports with carbon copies every which way.

Grimes knew this, and he should have had more sense than to attempt to bring up the subject again of his own, private worries.

He said, "This hold flooding seems to have worked . . ."

"Yes."

"Then perhaps, Captain, you could spare the time to discuss the question of returning me to my own place and period . . ."

". . . off!" snarled the shipmaster. "I've more important things on my plate than your troubles . . . Off!"

The screaming wind took hold of Grimes, whirling him away into the darkness. But, before he was gone, he heard the Chief Officer ask his captain, "Who was that sir? I thought I saw somebody standing there with you, a stranger in an odd-looking uniform . . ."

"Just a figment of the imagination, Mr. Briggs. Just a figment of the imagination."

He was standing in his own day cabin, aboard *Faraway Quest*. He was staring at Sonya, and she, her face white under the auburn hair, was staring at him.

"John! You're back!"

"Yes."

"I've been holding the ship, here on Kinsolving, but our lords and masters have been putting the pressure on us to return . . ."

"It wouldn't have mattered," Grimes told her.

"Why not?"

"Because wherever you are, that's where I belong."

He was sitting in his day cabin, trying to relax over a stiff drink. He had brought his ship into port, scurrying in during a lull between two depressions, pumping out after the ballast to compensate for the weight of water in the flooded hold, clearing the Bar without touching. He was overtired and knew that sleep was out of the question. But there was nothing for him to do; his Chief Officer was capably overseeing the pumping out of the flooded compartment and would, as soon as possible, put the necessary repairs in hand.

He thought, *I might as well finish that bloody story.*

He inserted paper into his typewriter, refueled and lit his pipe, began to write. As the final words shaped themselves on the white sheet he looked up at the photograph of the red-haired woman over his desk. *Because wherever you are, that's where I belong . . .*

"And I hope you're satisfied, you cantankerous old bastard," he muttered.

"And it all actually happened . . ." murmured Admiral Kravinsky, indicating the thick report that lay on his desk.

"I . . . I suppose so . . ." said Grimes uncertainly.

"You should know, man. You were there."

"But *where* was *there?*"

"Don't go all metaphysical on me, Grimes." The Admiral selected a gnarled cheroot from the box before him, lit it. In self-defense the Commodore filled and ignited a battered briar pipe. He regretted, he realized, having lost that meerschaum during his last adventure.

Kravinsky regarded the swirling clouds of acrid blue smoke thoughtfully. He said at last, "It was rummy, all the same. Very rummy."

"You're telling *me*," concurred Grimes.

"I think that we shall be leaving Kinsolving severely alone for quite a while. I don't like this business about our just being a figment of the imagination or an imagination of the figment or whatever . . ."

"You don't like it . . ." muttered Grimes.

"All right, all right, my heart fair bleeds for you. Satisfied? And now, Admiral, I have a job for you that should be right up your alley."

"Admiral? Have I been promoted, sir?"

"That'd be the sunny Friday! But, Grimes, I seem to remember that you're an honorary admiral in the Tharn Navy, and that same Navy consists of seagoing surface vessels. The rank, meaningless though it is, should be useful to you when we send you to Aquarius."

"The rank's not meaningless, sir," protested Grimes.

"So much the better, then. On your way, Admiral. Weigh anchor, splice the main brace, heave the lead or whatever it is you seafaring types do when you get under way."

"It should be interesting," said Grimes.

"With you around to complicate matters, it's bound to be."

THE SISTER SHIPS

CAPTAIN JOHN GRIMES stood impassively in the
port wing of his bridge as his ship, the round-
the-world tramp *Sonya Winneck*, slid gently in
toward her berth. But although his stocky body
was immobile his brain was active. He was gaug-
ing speed, distances, the effect of the tide. His
engines were stopped, but the vessel still seemed
to be carrying too much way. He was stemming
the ebb, but, according to the Port Directions there
was sometimes—not always—an eddy, a counter
current along this line of wharfage. In any case, it
would be a tight fit. Ahead of him was *Iron Baron*,
one of the steel trade ships: a huge, beamy brute
with gigantic deck cranes almost capable of lifting her by her own bootstraps. In the berth astern
was the Lone Star Line's *Orionic*, with even more
beam to her than the *Baron*.

"Port!" ordered Grimes. "Hard over!"

"Hard a-port, sir!" replied the quartermaster.

Sonya Winneck was accosting the wharf at a
fairly steep angle now, her stem aimed at a bollard
just abaft *Iron Baron's* stern. Grimes lifted his
mouth whistle to his lips, blew one short, sharp
blast. From the fo'c'sle head came the rattle of
chain cable as the starboard anchor was let go,

then one stroke of the bell to signal that the first
shackle was in the pipe.

Grimes looked aft. *Sonya Winneck's* quarter
was now clear of *Orionic's* bows. "Midships! Slow
astern!"

He heard the replies of the man at the wheel and
the Third Officer. He felt the virbration as the
reversed screw bit into the water. But would slow
astern be enough? He was about to order half
astern, then realized that this was what he was
getting, if not more. The transverse thrust of the
screw threw *Sonya Winneck's* stern to port even
as her headway was killed. Already a heaving line
was ashore forward, and snaking after it the first of
the mooring lines. Aft, the Second Mate was ready
to get his first line ashore.

"Stop her," ordered Grimes. "That will do the
wheel, thank you."

On fo'c'sle head and poop the self-tensioning
winches were whining. Grimes, looking down
from the bridge wing to the marker flag on the
wharf, saw that he was exactly in position. He
made the tranditional "arms crossed above the
head" gesture—*Make her fast as she is*—to the
Chief Officer forward, the Second Officer aft. Then
he walked slowly into the wheelhouse. The Third
Officer was still standing by the engine control
pedestal.

"Finished with engines, Mr. Denham," said
Grimes coldly.

"Finished with engines, sir." The young man
put the lever to that position. There was a jangling
of bells drifting up from below.

"Mr. Denham . . ."

"Sir?" The officer's voice was an almost inaudible squeak. He looked frightened, and, thought Grimes, well he might be.

"Mr. Denham, I am well aware that in your opinion I'm an outsider who should never have been appointed to command of this vessel. I am well aware, too, that in your opinion, at least, your local knowledge far surpasses mine. Even so, I shall be obliged if you will carry out my orders, although you will still have the right, the obligation, in fact, to query them—but not when I'm in the middle of berthing the bloody ship!" Grimes simmered down. "For your information, Mr. Denham, even I realized that slow astern would not be sufficient. I was about to order more stern power, then saw that you had taken matters into your own possibly capable but definitely unqualified hands."

"But, sir . . ."

Grimes's prominent ears had reddened.

"There are no 'buts.' "

"But, sir, I tried to put her to slow astern. The lever jerked out of my hand to full."

"Thank you, Mr. Denham," said Grimes at last. He knew that the young man was not lying. "You'd better see the Engineer, or the Electrician, and get those controls fixed. The next time they might do the wrong thing, instead of the right one."

He went through the chartroom and then down to his quarters. Sonya, who had watched the berthing from the lower bridge, was there waiting for him. She got up from her chair as he entered the day cabin and stood there, tall and slim and graceful. Her right hand snapped up to the widow's peak of her shining auburn hair.

She said, "I salute you, Cap'n. A masterly piece of ship handling."

"Mphm," grunted Grimes.

"But, John, it was like something out of one of your own books." She went to the case on the bulkhead in which were both privately owned volumes and those considered by the Winneck Line to be fit and proper reading for its masters. From the Company's shelf she lifted *The Inter-Island Steamer Express*, by John Grimes. She read aloud, ". . . These captains, maintaining their timetables and berthing and unberthing their big, seagoing passenger ferries in the most appalling weather conditions, were, without doubt, among the world's finest ship handlers . . ."

"The weather conditions this morning aren't appalling," said Grimes. "In any case, that was on Earth. This is Aquarius."

Aquarius, as its name implies, is a watery world.

It lies in toward the center from the Rim Worlds, fifty or so light-years to the galactic east of the Shakespearean Sector. It is Earth-type insofar as gravitation, atmosphere and climate are concerned, but geographically is dissimilar to the "home planet." There are no great land masses; there are only chains of islands: some large, some small, some no more than fly specks on even a medium scale chart. In this respect it is like Mellise, one of the planets of the Eastern Circuit. Unlike Mellise, it possesses no indigenous intelligent life. Men colonized it during the Second Expansion—and, as was the case with most Second Expansion colonizations, it was discovery and settlement by chance rather than by design. Time and time again it happened, that disastrous, often tragic sequence of events. The magnetic storm, the gaussjammer thrown light millennia off course, her pile dead and the hungry emergency diesels gulping precious hydrocarbons to feed power to the Ehrenhaft generators, the long plunge into and through the Unknown; the desperate search for a world, any world, that would sustain human life . . .

Lode Messenger stumbled upon Aquarius and made a safe landing in the vicinity of the North Magnetic Pole. Like all the later ships of her period she carried a stock of fertilized ova, human and animal, a wide variety of plant seeds and an extensive technical library. (Even when the gaussjammers were on regular runs, as Lode Messenger had been, there was always the possibility that their people would finish up as founders of a new colony.) When the planet was rediscovered by Commodore Shakespeare, during his voyage of exploration out toward the Rim, the settlement was already well established. With the Third Expansion it accepted its quota of immigrants, but insisted that all newcomers work for a probationary period in the merchant or fishing fleets before, if they so wished, taking up employment ashore. Somebody once said that if you wanted to emigrate to Aquarius you had to hold at least an "Able-bodied seaman's" papers. This is not quite true, but it is not far from the truth: It has also been said that Aquarians have an inborn dislike and distrust of spaceships but love seagoing ships. This is true.

Grimes, although not an immigrant, was a seaman of sorts. He was on the planet by invitation, having been asked by its rulers—the Havenmaster and the Master Wardens—to write a history of the colony. For that he was well qualified, being acknowledged as the leading maritime historian, specializing in Terran marine history, in the Rim Worlds. His books: *The Inter-Island Steamer Express, The Flag Of The Southern Cross, The Western Ocean Greyhounds, Times of Transition*— had sold especially well on Aquarius, although in the worlds of the Rim Confederacy they were to be found mainly only in libraries, and in very few libraries at that.

And Commodore Grimes, Rim Worlds Naval Reserve, Master Astronaut, was more than just a writer about the sea. He held the rank of admiral — honorary, but salt water admiral nonetheless — in the Ausiphalian Navy, on Tharn. Captain Thornton, the Havenmaster, had said, "Legally speaking, that commission of yours entitles you to a Certificate of Competency as a Master Mariner. Then you can sail in command of one of our ships, to get the real feel of life at sea."

"I'm not altogether happy about it, Tom," Grimes had objected, not too strongly.

"I'm the boss here," Thornton assured him. "And, in any case, I'm not turning you loose until you've been through crash courses in navigation, seamanship, meteorology, cargo stowage and stability."

"I'm tempted . . . " Grimes had admitted.

"Tempted?" scoffed Sonya. "He's just dying to strut his bridge like the ancient mariners he's always writing about. His only regret will be that you Aquarians didn't re-create the days of sail while you were about it."

"Now and again I regret it myself," admitted the Havenmaster. "Fore and aft rig, a diesel auxiliary, electrical deck machinery—there'd be something quite fast enough for some of our trades and economical to boot. But I'm well known as an enemy of progress—progress for its own sake, that is."

"A man after my own heart," said Grimes.

"You're just a pair of reactionaries," Sonya had told them.

I suppose I am a reactionary, Grimes had thought. But he enjoyed this world. It was efficiently run, but it was always recognized that there are things more important than efficiency. There was automation up to a certain point, but up to that certain point only. (But the Havenmaster had admitted that he was fighting a rearguard action to try to keep control of the ships in the hands of the seamen officers . . .) There was a love of and a respect for the sea. It was understandable. From the first beginnings of the colony these people had grown up on a watery world, and the books in their technical library most in demand had been those on shipbuilding, seamanship and navigation. Aquarius was poor in radioactives but rich in mineral oil, so the physicists had never been able, as they have on so many worlds, to take charge. The steam engine and the diesel engine were still the prime movers, even in the air, where the big passenger-carrying airships did the work that on other planets is performed by jet planes and rockets.

The surface ships were, by modern standards, archaic. Very few of them ran to bow thrusters—

and those only ferries, cargo and passenger, to whom the strict adherence to a timetable was of paramount importance, whose masters could not afford to make a leisurely job of backing into a roll-on-roll-off berth and therefore required the additional maneuvering aid. There was some containerization, but it was not carried to extremes, it being recognized that the personnel of the cargo carriers were entitled to leisure time in port. Self-tensioning winches and, for cargo handling, cranes rather than derricks cut down the number of hands required on deck, and engine rooms were almost fully automated, with bridge control for arrival and departure maneuvers.

There were electronic navigational aids aplenty—radar, echometer, loran, shoran, an inertial system, position fixing by artificial satellite — but these the Havenmaster frowned upon, as did most of the senior shipmasters. He quoted from Grimes's own book, *Times Of Transition*, "The electronic wizards of the day, who were not seamen, failed to realize that a competent navigator, armed only with sextant, chronometer and ephemeris, together with a reasonably accurate log, can always fix the position of his ship with reasonable accuracy provided that there is an occasional break in the clouds for an identifiable celestial body to shine through. Such a navigator is never at the mercy of a single fuse . . ."

"And that, John, is what I'm trying to avoid," said Thornton. "Unless we're careful our ships will be officered by mere button pushers, incapable of running a series of P/Ls. Unluckily, not all the Master Wardens think as I do. Too many of them are engineers, and businessmen—and in my

experience such people have far less sales resistance than we simple sailors.''

"And what pups have they been sold?" asked
Grimes.

"One that's a real bitch from my viewpoint, and
probably from yours. You've heard of Elektra?"

"Yes," broke in Sonya. "Carinthian Sector.
Third Expansion colonization." She grinned a little unkindly. "It's a planet where the minimum
qualification for immigration is a doctorate in one
of the sciences, preferably physics. But they have
to let in occasional chemists, biologists and the
like to keep the dump habitable."

"And they have quite a few, now, with degrees
in salesmanship," went on the Havenmaster.
"One of them was here a few years back."

"And he sold you this female pup," said
Grimes.

"He did that. The Purcell Navigator. It's named,
I suppose, after its inventor. It's a sealed box, with
the gods know what sort of mess of memory fields
and the like inside it. It's hooked up to all the
ship's electronic navigational gear: gyro compass,
radar, echometer, loran, shoran . . . Just name a pie
and it's got a finger in it. Or a tentacle. It knows just
where the ship is at any given second. If you ask it
nicely it might condescend to tell you."

"You don't like it," said Grimes.

"I don't like it. To begin with, some of the
shipowners—and this is a private enterprise
planet, remember—feel that now the bridge can
be automated to the same extent as the engine
room, with just one man, the Master, in charge,
snoring his head off on the chartroom settee and
being awakened by an alarm bell just in time to

rub the sleep out of his eyes and take his ship into port. But that's not the worst of it. Now the Institute of Marine Engineers is saying, 'If navigation is only a matter of pushing buttons, we're at least as well qualified as deck officers.' "

"I've heard that often enough," said Grimes. "Even in space."

"Does anybody know how these Purcell Navigators work?" asked Sonya.

"No. One of the terms of sale is that they must be installed by technicians from the world of manufacture, Elektra. Another is that they must not, repeat not, be tampered with in any way. As a matter of fact the Chief Electrician of the Carrington Yard did try to find out what made one tick. He was lucky to lose only a hand."

"It seems," said Grimes, "that I came here just in time."

"What do you mean, John?"

"Well, I shall be able to enjoy the last of the old days, the good old days, on Aquarius, and I shall have the material for a few more chapters to my *Times Of Transition*."

"He likes being morbid," said Sonya. "Almost as much as he likes being reactionary."

"Mphm," grunted Grimes. "Old-fashioned sounds better."

He got up from his chair, walked soundlessly over the carpeted floor to the bookshelves that formed a space divider in the huge, circular room that was called the Havenmaster's Lookout. He stared at the rows of books, most of them old (but in recent printings), only a few of them new. And they were *real* books, all of them, not spools of microfilm. There were the standard works on the

old arts of the seaman, hopelessly out of date
on most worlds, but not (yet) on this one.
Brown, Nicholl, Norie, Riesenberg . . . Lecky . . .
Thomas . . . And the chronicles of the ancient
explorers and navigators: Hakluyt, Dampier,
Cook, Flinders, Bligh . . . Then there were the
novels: Conrad (of course), McFee, Monsarrat,
Herman Wouk, Forester . . . Grimes's hand went
out to Melville's *Moby Dick,* and he rememberd
that odd Hall of Fame to which he had been
whisked from the mountaintop on Kinsolving,
and felt regret that he had not been able to meet
Lieutenant Commander Queeg, Admiral
Hornblower and Captain Ahab. (Were there any
white whales in the Aquarian seas?)

He turned, saw that his wife and Captain
Thornton had risen from their own seats, were
standing staring out through the huge window
that formed the entire outer wall of the Lookout
that, in its turn, was the top level of the two
thousand foot high Havenmaster's Control Tower.
Above it was only the mast from which sprouted
antennae, radar scanners, anemometers and the
like, that was topped by the powerful, group-
flashing Steep Island light.

Grimes walked slowly to join Sonya and his
host, gazed out through the clear glass into the
darkness. At regular intervals the beam of the
light, a sword of misty radiance, swept overhead.
Far to the south, a loom of luminescence on the
distant sea horizon, was Port Stellar, and to east
and west, fainter still, were other hazy luminosi-
ties, island cities, island states. Almost directly
below was a great passenger liner, from this
height no more than a gaudy, glittering insect

crawling over the black carpet of the sea.

In spite of the insulation, the soundproofing, the thin, high whine of the wind was evident.

Sonya shivered. "The winds of change are blowing," she whispered.

"A seaman should be able to cope with the wind," said the Havenmaster. Then, to Grimes, "I wonder how you'll cope, John? I've arranged for you to take over *Sonya Winneck* at Port Stellar tomorrow."

"I'll get by," said Grimes.

"He always does," said Sonya. "Somehow."

Grimes fell in love with *Sonya Winneck* from the very start. She was, of course, his first sea command; nonetheless, she made an immediate appeal to the eye, even to the eye of one who, for all his admiral's commission, had very little practical knowledge of oceangoing ships. The lady was a tramp, but the tramp was also a lady.

Five hundred feet long overall, she was, with a seventy-foot beam. Bridge and funnel—the latter scarlet, with a black top and two narrow black bands—were amidships. Her upperworks and deck cranes were white, her hull green with a yellow ribbon. The boot-topping was red.

There is more to a ship than outward appearance, however. And Grimes, himself a shipmaster of long standing, knew this as well as the most seasoned master mariner on the oceans of Aquarius. But she had, he discovered, a fair turn of speed, her diesel-electric drive pushing her through the water at a good twenty knots. She was single screw, with a right-handed propeller. Her wheelhouse and chartroom reminded him almost of the spaceships that he was accustomed to command, but the electronic gadgetry was not unfamiliar to him after the sessions he had put in on the various simulators in the Havenmaster's Control Tower. The only thing that he did not like was the Purcell Navigator squatting like a sinister octopus in its own cage abaft the chartroom. Oh, well, he would make sure that his young gentlemen had no truck with the electronic monster. He hoped.

"I don't like it either," said the tall, skinny, morose Captain Harrell, whom Grimes was relieving. "But it works. Even I have to admit that. It works."

Then Harrell led Grimes down to the big, comfortable day cabin where the two wives—Mrs. Harrell very dumpy and mousy alongside the slender Sonya—were waiting. The Harrells' baggage, packed and ready to be carried ashore, was against one bulkhead. On a table stood bottles and glasses, a bowl of cracked ice. The officers came in then, neat in their slate gray shirt-and-shorts uniforms, their black, gold-braided shoulderboards, to say good-bye to their old captain, to greet their new one. There was Wilcox, Chief Officer, a burly, blond young (but not too young) giant. There was Andersen, the Second, another giant, but red-haired. There was Viccini, the Third, slight and dark. And Jones, the Engineer, a fat, bald man who could have been any age, came up to be introduced, and with him he brought Mary Hales, the Electrician, a fragile, silver-headed little girl who looked incapable of changing a fuse. Finally there came Sally Fielding, Stewardess-Purser, plump and motherly.

Glasses were charged. "Well, Captain," began Harrell. "Or should I say Commodore, or Admiral?"

"Captain," Grimes told him.

"Well, Captain, your name's on the Register and the Articles. You've signed the Receipt for Items Handed Over. You've a good ship, and a good team of officers. Happy sailing!"

"Happy sailing," everybody repeated.

"Thank you, Captain," replied Grimes. "And I'm sure that we all wish you an enjoyable leave."

"And how are you spending it, Mrs. Harrell?" asked Sonya.

"We've a yacht," the other woman told her. "Most of the time we shall be cruising around the Coral Sea."

"A busman's holiday," commented Grimes.

"Not at all," Harrell told him, grinning for the first time. "There'll just be the two of us, so there'll be no crew problems. And no electronic gadgetry to get in my hair either."

"Happy sailing," said Grimes, raising his glass.

"Happy sailing," they all said again.

And it was happy sailing at first.

It did not take Grimes long to find his feet, his sea legs. "After all," he said to Sonya, "a ship is a ship is a ship . . ." He had been afraid at first that his officers and crew would resent him, an outsider appointed to command with no probationary period in the junior grades—but there hung about him the spurious glamour of that honorary admiral's commission, and his reputation as a maritime historian earned him respect. *Sonya Winneck's* people knew that he was on

Aquarius to do a job, a useful job, and that his sailing as master of her was part of it.

Sonya enjoyed herself too. She made friends with the other women aboard: with Mary Hales, with Sally Fielding, with the darkly opulent Vanessa Wilcox, who had joined just before departure from Port Stellar, with Tessa and Teena, the Assistant Stewardesses, with the massive Jemima Brown who was queen of the beautifully mechanized galley. This shipboard life—*surface* shipboard life—was all so new to her, in spite of its inevitable resemblances to life aboard a spaceship. There was so much to see, so much to inquire into . . .

The weather was fine, mainly, with warm days and nights with just sufficient chill to provide a pleasant contrast. Grimes played with the sextant he had purchased in Port Stellar, became skilled in its use, taking altitude after altitude of the sun, of the planet's two moons, of such stars, planets and artificial satellites as were visible at morning and evening twilight. His officers watched with a certain amusement as he plotted position after position on the working chart, congratulated him when these coincided with those for the same times shown on the chart that was displayed on the screen of the Purcell Navigator. And they, he was pleased to note, tended to ignore that contraption, consulting it only when there was a wide variance between positions taken by two observers.

A shipmaster, however, is more than a navigator. Pilotage was not compulsory for the majority of the ports visited by *Sonya Winneck*, although in each one of them pilots were available. Grimes had taken a pilot sailing from Port Stellar, but after the six-day run between that harbor and Tallisport decided to try to berth the ship himself. After all, he had spent hours in the simulator and, since joining his ship, had read Ardley's *Harbor Pilotage* from cover to cover.

This book, a standard, Terran, twentieth century work on the handling and mooring of ships, had been given him by the Havenmaster, who had said, "You should find this useful, John. Ardley was one of the authorities of his time. One thing I like about him—he says that anchors are there to be used. For maneuvering, I mean . . ." He laughed, then added, "But don't go making too much of a habit of it. It annoys chief officers!"

And so, having made a careful study of the large scale chart, the plan and the "sailing directions," Grimes stood in to Tallisport shortly after sunrise. The wheel was manned, the engines on stand by. According to the Tide Tables it was just two hours after first high water, which meant that *Sonya Winneck* would be stemming the ebb on her way in. (But, Wilcox had told him, complications were bound to crop up in this river harbor. All wharfage was on the western bank of the river, on the starboard hand entering—and to berth starboard side to is to risk damage in a vessel with a right-handed single screw, especially when the master is an inexperienced ship handler. Sometimes, however, an eddy, a countercurrent, set strongly along the line of wharfage, giving the effect of flood tide. If this eddy were running—and only visual observation when approaching the berth would confirm this or not—Grimes would be able to bring the ship's head to starboard, letting go the

starboard anchor to stub her around, and then ease
her alongside, port side to, with the anchor still on
the bottom.)

Grimes stood into Tallisport. With his naked
eye he could now see the Main Leads, two white
towers, nicely in line. He told the Harbor Quartermaster to steer for them, to keep them right
ahead. Yes, and there was the breakwater to port,
with its red beacon . . . The red beacon was abeam
now, and *Sonya Winneck* was sweeping into the
harbor in fine style.

"Hadn't you better reduce speed, sir?"
suggested the Third Officer.

"Mphm. Thank you, Mr. Viccini. Better make it
slow—no, dead slow."

"Dead slow, sir."

The rhythmic thudding of the diesel generators
was unchanged, but there was a subtle diminu-
tion of vibration as the propeller revolutions decreased. The Main Leads were still ahead, but
coming abeam to starboard were the two white
obelisks that were the Leads into the Swinging
Basin. "Port ten degrees," ordered Grimes. Would
it be enough? Then he saw the ship's head swinging easily, heard the clicking of the gyro repeater.
"Midships. Steady!"

He went out to the starboard wing of the bridge,
looked aft. The Swinging Basin Leads were coming into line astern nicely. "Steady as you go!" he
called.

Now *Sonya Winneck* was creeping up the last
navigable reach of the river. To starboard was the
line of wharfage, and behind it the clumps of
greenery, spangled with blossoms like jewels, the
white-walled houses, all clean and bright in the

morning sun. But Grimes had no eye for scenery; he was too new to the game. Through his binoculars he studied the quay at which he was to berth, the furthest up river. Beyond it was a mess of dredging equipment, all part and parcel of the port expansion plan. Which side to would it be? He had still to make up his mind.

"Sir," said the Third Officer.

"Yes?"

"It doesn't look as though the eddy, the countercurrent is running, sir."

"What makes you think that, Mr. Viccini?"

The young man pointed to the small craft—a yacht, two fishing vessels—past which they were sliding. Their upstream moorings were bar taut, their downstream lines hanging in bights. "Mphm," grunted Grimes. So it was ebb all over the river. He made up his mind. "Tell the Chief and Second Officers it will be starboard side to. Tell Mr. Wilcox to have his port anchor ready."

He came to starboard, lined the ship's head up on the up river end of the wharf. With his mouth whistle he blew one short, sharp blast. The chain cable of the port anchor rattled out through the pipe, the grip of the flukes in the mud acted as a brake. *Sonya Winneck* was still making way, but with the ebb against her and the drag of the anchor she was almost stopped.

This, thought Grimes, *is easy*, as he nosed in toward his berth.

But there was an eddy after all, and as soon as the ship was well inside it she was swept upstream toward the dredges, buoys and pipelines. "Hard a-starboard!" Grimes ordered. The anchor was still holding, luckily, and it acted as a fulcrum, checking the upstream motion of the stem while the stern was free to swing. The vessel was broadside on to the line of the river now, still appraching the wharf, but head on.

"Swing her, sir," suggested Viccini. "Get a headline ashore and tell the linesmen to run it to the down river end of the berth . . ."

Yes, thought Grimes, *it'll work. It'd better . . .*

A heaving line snaked ashore from the fo'c'sle head, was caught by one of the waiting linesmen. He and another man ran with it to the post indicated by the Chief Officer. Then the self-tensioning winch, whining, took the weight. Belatedly Grimes thought that he had better stop the engines, had better go astern before the ship's stem crashed through the wharf stringer. But the order had been anticipated. *A good lad, Viccini . . .* he thought. *But he'd better not make a habit of this sort of thing.*

Now *Sonya Winneck's* bows were being pulled downriver against the countercurrent, her stern still only a few feet from the stringer, the stern swinging in easily. "Stop her," Grimes ordered. She was alongside now, with the very gentlest of impacts, and the leading hand of the mooring gang was shouting up that she was in position.

Grimes filled and lit his pipe. "Make fast fore and aft," he said. "That'll do the wheel. Finished with engines." And then, "Mr. Viccini, I appreciate your help. Don't get me wrong. I like an officer to show initiative. But I think you should try to remember there's only one Master on the bridge."

"But, sir . . ."

"That's all right, Mr. Viccini. You did the right

things, and I appreciate it. I'll try to do the right things myself in future."

Probably the Third Officer would have made a full explanation to Grimes during the day, but as soon as the gangway was out the Winneck Line's local agent came aboard with the mail, and among it was a letter saying that Viccini was to be paid off to commence his annual leave and would be relieved that morning by a Mr. Denham.

Sonya Winneck continued her steady, round-the-planet progress, rarely straying north or south of the tropics. The met. screen in the chartroom rarely showed indications of disturbed weather conditions, and when it did these were invariably hundreds of miles from the ship's track. It was, Mr. Wilcox said to Grimes, the sort of weather you sign on for. The days and the nights passed pleasantly. At sea, there was sunbathing, swimming in the ship's pool that, when inflated, occupied all the foredeck between the forward and after cranes of the main hatch, deck golf and, in the evenings, a variety of games or a wide selection of programs on the playmasters installed throughout the accommodation. In port, the day's business over, there was so much to see, so much to do. There was *real* swimming from sunwashed, golden beaches, and surfing; and now and again Grimes was able to hire a small sailing yacht for the day and found this sport much more enjoyable than on the lakes of Lorn, where there was wind enough but it was always bitter. There were the waterfront taverns—and both Grimes and Sonya loved seafood. The Terran lobster, prawn, oyster and herring had all done well in the Aquarian seas, and there were the local delicacies: the sand crawlers, which were something like Earth's trilobites must have been, the butterfly fish and the sea steaks.

It was, for both of them, a holiday, but for Sonya it was a holiday that palled in time. It was all right for Grimes, he had his navigation to play with, his pilotage and, when he got around to it, research to carry out on the projected history and a chapter or so of it to write. His wife, however, was becoming bored.

It was a longish run between Lynnhaven and Port Johnson, all of seven days. During it Sonya found stacks of magazines in one of the lockers in the ship's office, back numbers of the *Merchant Shipping Journal*, dating back for years. She brought a pile of them up to the master's day cabin. She said, "These could be useful to you, John." Grimes picked one up, leafed through it. "Mphm. All rather dry stuff. At the moment I'm trying to get the essential *feel* of this planet."

"But they're full of information."

"So's a dictionary."

She said, "Suppose I go through them, making notes of anything that might be useful to you . . ."

"That," he told her, "is very sweet of you, Sonya."

She made a grimace at him, then settled down with the supply of factual reading matter. Everything was there: specifications of new tonnage, sales, breakings up, wrecks, strandings, collisions, courts of inquiry. These latter were of interest to her. She could see how, time and time again, the unfortunate Master was given only seconds to decide what to do, while learned judges, counsel and marine assessors had weeks to decide what should have been done. And then, as she read on, nagging hints of some sort of pattern began to form in her mind, her trained mind. After all, she had been an intelligence officer, and a good one, in the Federation's Survey Service.

It seemed to her that the Winneck Line ships were getting into more than their fair share of trouble, with Lone Star Line running a close second. She knew little about the Lone Star Line, although she had seen their ships often enough in various ports and, with Grimes, had been a guest aboard a few of them for drinks and meals. They were well-run, well-maintained vessels. She could speak with more authority regarding the Winneck Line; *Sonya Winneck* was typical of their newer tonnage. There wasn't the same spit and polish as in the Lone Star, but there was a very real efficiency.

She read again the details of one of the collision cases. *Olga Winneck* had been bound up the Great Muddy River to Steelport, *Suzanne Winneck* had been outbound. The ships had passed each other — or had attempted to pass each other — in Collier's Reach, the navigable channel in that locality being both deep and wide. Suddenly *Olga Winneck* had taken a sheer to port and, in spite of the efforts of both Masters to avert collision, had struck *Suzanne Winneck* on her port quarter, holing her so badly that she was obliged to return to dock for repairs.

There was the transcription of evidence:

Mr. Younghusband (counsel for Havenmaster's Office): Can you tell me, Mr. Margolies, what orders were given by Captain Hazzard?

Mr. Margolies (Third Officer of *Olga Winneck*):
Yes, sir. The Master ordered, "Hard
a-starboard! Stop engines! Full astern!"

Mr. Younghusband: And were these orders carried out?

Mr. Margolies: Of course, I at once put the controls to full astern.

Mr. Younghusband: And what about the wheel?
Quartermasters have been known to put the
helm the wrong way, especially in an
emergency.

Mr. Margolies: The quartermaster put the wheel
hard to starboard.

Mr. Younghusband: And did you look at the rudder indicator? It has been suggested that
steering gear failure was a cause of the collision.

Mr. Margolies: Yes, I looked. The pointer was hard
over to starboard.

And so it went on. It was established finally that
both Masters had done all the right things, although Captain Hazzard should have realized
that a delay was inevitable when switching directly from full ahead to full astern. It was thought
that a tidal eddy had been responsible for the
collision. The court recommended that ships
passing in Collier's Reach keep each well to their
own sides of the channel, also that speed be reduced.

That was one case. There were others, and
Sonya made notes, drew up tables. There had
been collisions in narrow channels and in the
open sea. Some had been in clear weather, some in
conditions of reduced visibility. The causes were

various: tidal eddies, steering gear failure, radar breakdown and, inevitably, errors of judgment. And the Winneck Line and the Lone Star Line were having more than their fair share of marine casualties . . . It was odd, she thought. Odd. There was something rotten in the state of Aquarius.

She asked Grimes if she could browse through the ship's files of correspondence. He said, "Of course. They aren't top secret." She found the one labeled *Damage Reports*. It wasn't especially bulky. But its contents were interesting.

"Sir, (she read)

I regret to have to report that whilst berthing this morning at No. 3 Inner East, Port Kantor, the stem of the vessel came into heavy contact with the starboard side of the Lone Star Line's *Canopic*. Damage to *Sonya Winneck* was superficial only—please see enclosed sketch—but that to the other ship was considerable and, I am informed by *Canopic's* master, will necessitate dry-docking.

I entered the harbor at 0545 hrs., standing in on the Main Leads. When clear of the breakwaters I reduced to dead slow and altered course to port, steering for the shore end of No. 3 Jetty. Visibility was good, wind was ENE at about 10 knots, tidal influence, it being just after low water slack, was negligible.

When my bridge was just abeam of *Canopic's* stern, however, *Sonya Winneck* took a sudden sheer to port. I at once ordered a hard a-starboard, stopped the engines and ordered full astern. Also I signaled to the Chief Officer to let go the starboard anchor, but unfortunately it jammed in the pipe, and was released too late to have any effect. In spite of the application of full starboard rudder and full stern power, contact occurred at 0555 hrs.

It is possible that I underestimated the force of the wind while standing in to my berth, but, even so, find it hard to account for the sudden sheer to port . . .''

But *Sonya Winneck* was sometimes at the receiving end.

"Sir,

I have to report that this afternoon, at 1327 hrs., the vessel was struck by the Company's *Elizabeth Winneck*, which same was proceeding down river, bound for sea. Unfortunately, it being Saturday afternoon, with no work in progress, no officers were on deck at the time of the contact, and the Company's gangway watchman was at his place of duty, at the head of the gangway, on the inshore side of the vessel.

Damage, fortunately, was not extensive and all above the waterline. My Chief Officer's report is enclosed herewith. No doubt you will be hearing from Captain Pardoe of *Elizabeth Winneck* . . .''

There were several more letters, some going into great detail, others composed on the good old principle of "least said, soonest mended." With two exceptions the other ships concerned were units of either the Winneck or the Lone Star fleets. One of the exceptions was the contact with *Iron Duchess*. On that occasion Captain Harrell, Grimes's predecessor, had been trying to berth his ship during a howling gale. The other occasion was a collision with a ferry steamer in Carrington Harbor, with fortunately no loss of life.

So, Sonya wondered, just what was the connection between the Winneck Line and the Lone Star Line? She borrowed from the Chief Officer's office the bulky *Aquarian Registry* in which was listed comprehensive details of all the commercial shipping of the planet. Against the name of each ship were the lines of information: tonnage, gross, net and deadweight; propulsion; speed; length overall, length between posts, breadth . . . And builders.

She looked up her namesake first. She had been built by the Carrington State Dockyard. She looked up *Canopic*. Her builders were Varley's Dockyard, in Steelport. She looked up *Elizabeth Winneck*—another Varley's job. So it went on. The majority of the collisions had occurred between ships constructed at those two yards.

And what about the contact that her husband, Grimes, had so narrowly averted, that time coming into Newhaven? What was the name of the ship that he had almost (but not quite) hit? *Orionic* . . . She looked it up. Carrington State Dockyard. She murmured, "All us Carrington girls must stick together . . ."

"What was that?" demanded Grimes, looking up from his book.

"Just a thought," she told him. "Just a passing thought."

"Mphm."

"Do ships *really* have personalities?" she asked.

He grinned. "Spacemen and seamen like to kid themselves that they do. Look at it this way. You're bringing a ship in—a spaceship or a surface ship—and you've failed to allow for *all* the factors affecting her handling. Your landing or berthing isn't up to your usual standard. But you kid yourself, and your officers, that it wasn't your fault. You say, 'She was a proper little bitch, wasn't she? Wouldn't do a thing right . . .' But you were the one who wasn't doing a thing right.''

She said, "I've handled ships too."

"I know, my dear. I've seen you do it. Your landing technique is a little too flashy for my taste."

"Never mind that now. I'm talking about surface ships. Is there any reason to believe, John, that two ships built to the same design, but in different yards, would have conflicting personalities?"

Grimes was starting to get annoyed with his wife. "Damn it all," he expostulated, "spacemen's superstitions are bad enough! But I'm surprised that you, of all people, should pay any heed to seamen's superstitions."

"But are they superstitions? Couldn't a machine absorb, somehow, something of the personalities of the people who built it, the people who handle it?"

"Hogwash," said Grimes.

"If that's the way you feel about it . . ." She slumped in her deep chair, struck a cigarillo on her thumbnail, put it to her mouth, looked at her husband through the wreathing smoke. "All right. Before you get back to your precious research, what do the initials P N mean?"

"In what context?"

Sonya nudged with a slim, sandaled foot the bulky *Aqaurian Registry*, which lay open on the deck in front of her. "It's printed against the names of some of the ships, the newer ships—but only those built by the Carrington State Dockyard or Varley's."

"P . . . N . . ." muttered Grimes. "P . . . N . . . ? We

can ask the Mate, I suppose . . ."

"But you don't like to," she scoffed. "You're the Captain, you know everything."

"Almost everything," he qualified smugly. The ship lurched suddenly, and Grimes knew the reason. When last he had been on the bridge he had been slightly perturbed by the chart presented in the met. screen, televised from one of the weather satellites. Ahead of *Sonya Winneck* was a deepening depression, almost stationary. He had considered altering course to try to avoid it—but, after all, he had a big, powerful ship under his feet, well found, stoutly constructed. And, he had thought, he would not like to be remembered on this world as a fair weather sailor. Even so, he saw in his mind's eye that chart—the crowded isobars, the wind arrows with their clockwise circulation. Now the heavy swell running outward from the center, like ripples from a pebble dropped into a pond, was beginning to make itself felt. He looked at the aneroid barometer on the bulkhead. The needle had fallen ten millibars since he had last set the pointer, two hours ago.

He said, "I fear we're in for a dirty night."

She said, "It's what you're paid for."

He grunted, got up from his chair, went up to the bridge by the inside companionway to the chartroom. He looked at the instruments over the chart table. According to the Chernikeeff Log, speed through the water had already dropped by half a knot. The barograph showed a fairly steep fall in pressure. The met. screen, set for the area through which the ship was passing, showed a chart almost identical with the one that he had last seen.

He went out to the bridge. The sky was mainly overcast now, with the larger of the two Aquarian moons, almost full, showing fitfully through ragged breaks in the cloud. There was high altitude wind, although it had yet to be felt at sea level. But the swell seemed to be increasing.

Young Mr. Denham, the Third Officer, came across from the wing of the bridge. He said, rather too cheerfully, "Looks like a blow, sir."

"We can't expect fine weather all the time," Grimes told him. He stood with his legs well apart, braced against the motion of the ship. He wondered if he would be seasick, then consoled himself with the thought that both the actual Lord Nelson and the fictional Lord Hornblower had been afflicted by this malady.

Mr. Denham — since Grimes had torn that strip off him regarding the unauthorized engine movements he had tended to overcompensate— went on chirpily, "At this time of the year, sir, the revolving storms in these waters are unpredictable. In theory the center should be traveling east, away from us, but in practice it's liable to do anything."

"Oh?"

"Yes, sir. I remember one when I was in the old *Sally—Sara Winneck*, that is. Captain Tregenza tried to outmaneuver it; we had a pile of deck cargo that trip, teak logs from Port Mandalay. But it was almost as though it had a brain of its own. Finally it sat right on top of us and matched speed and course, no matter which way we steered. We lost all the cargo off the foredeck, and the wheelhouse windows were smashed in . . ."

Cheerful little swine . . . thought Grimes. He

stared ahead into the intermittently moonlit night, at the long swell that was coming in at an angle to the ship's course. Sonya Winneck's bows lifted then dipped, plunging into and through the moving dune of water. They lifted again, and a white cascade poured aft from the break of the fo'c'sle, spangled with jewels of luminescence. Grimes said, "Anyhow, we have no deck cargo this trip."

"No, sir."

He remained on the bridge a while longer. There was nothing that he could do, and he knew it. The ship was far from unseaworthy, capable of riding out a hurricane. There was ample sea room; the Low Grenadines were many miles to the north of her track. And yet he felt uneasy, could not shake off a nagging premonition. Something, he somehow knew, was cooking. But what, when and where?

At last he grunted, "You know where to find me if you want me. Good night, Mr. Denham."

"Good night, sir."

Back in his quarters his uneasiness persisted. He told Sonya that he would sleep on the settee in his day cabin, so as to be more readily available in the event of any emergency. She did not argue with him; she, too, felt a growing tension in the air. It could have been that she was sensitive to his moods but, she told him, she didn't think so. She quoted, *"By the pricking of my thumbs something wicked this way comes."*

He laughed. "A tropical revolving storm is not wicked, my dear. Like any other manifestation of the forces of nature it is neither good nor evil."

She repeated, "Something wicked this way comes."

They said good night then, and she retired to the bedroom and he disposed himself comfortably on the settee. He was rather surprised that sleep was not long in coming.

But he did not enjoy his slumber for more than a couple of hours. A particularly violent lurch awakened him, almost pitched him off his couch. He switched on a light, looked at the aneroid barometer. The needle was down another twenty millibars. And, in spite of the well-insulated plating of the accommodation, he could hear the wind, both hear and feel the crash of the heavy water on deck. He thrust his feet into his sandals and, clad only in his shorts (Master's privilege) went up to the bridge. He found the Second Officer—it was now the middle watch—in the wheelhouse, looking ahead through the big clear view screen. Grimes joined him. When his eyes became accustomed to the semi-darkness he could see that the wind was broad on the starboard bow; he could see, too, that with each gust it was veering, working gradually around from southeast to south. *Southern Hemisphere,* he thought. *Clockwise circulation, and the low barometer on my left hand . . .* Now that he had something to work on he might as well avoid the center with its confused, heavy seas. "Bring her round to starboard easily," he told the Second Officer. "Bring wind and sea ahead."

"Wind and sea ahead, sir." The officer went to the controls of the autopilot. Grimes watched the bows swinging slowly, then said, "That should do, Mr. Andersen."

"Course one three five now, sir."

Grimes went back into the chartroom, looked down at the chart, busied himself briefly with parallel rulers and dividers. He grunted his satisfaction. This new course took him even further clear of the Low Grenadines, that chain of rocky islets that were little more than reefs. There was nothing to worry about.

He was aware that Sonya was standing behind him; there was a hint of her perfume, the awareness of her proximity. He said without turning around, "Passengers not allowed on the bridge."

She asked, "Where are we?"

He indicated with the points of the dividers the penciled cross of the position, the new course line extending from it. "I'm more or less, not quite heaving to. But she's easier on this heading, and it pulls her away from the eye of the storm."

She said, "There's a lot to be said for spaceships. They don't pitch and roll. When you're in your virtuous couch you're not slung out of it."

"We take what comes," he told her.

"We haven't much option, have we?"

Then they went below again, and she made coffee, and they talked for awhile, and eventually Grimes settled down to another installment of his broken night's sleep.

The next time he awakened it was by the insistent buzzing of the bridge telephone, which was in his bedroom. He rolled off the settee, stumbled through the curtained doorway. Sonya, looking rather hostile, lifted the instrument off its rest, handed it to him.

"Master here," said Grimes into the mouthpiece.

"Second Officer, sir. There's a Mayday . . ."

"I'll be right up."

The Second Mate was in the chartroom, plotting positions on the chart. He straightened as Grimes came in, turned to speak to him. "It's *Iron Warrior*, sir. One of their big bulk carriers. She's broken down, lying in the trough, and her cargo's shifted. Zinc concentrates."

"Not good. Where is she?"

The young man stood away from the chart so that Grimes could see, indicated the other ship's position with the point of a pencil. "Here, sir. Just twenty miles south of the Low Grenadines. And she reports a southerly gale, the same as we're getting."

"Not good," said Grimes again. "Not good at all. She'll be making leeway, drifting . . ." Swiftly he measured the distance between *Sonya Winneck's* last recorded position—electronic navigation had its good points!—and that given by the disabled ship. One hundred and fifty nautical miles . . . And *Sonya Winneck* would have to turn, putting the wind right aft. With her high superstructure this should mean a marked increase of speed . . . Suppose she made twenty knots over the ground . . . Twenty into one hundred and fifty . . . Seven and a half hours . . . He looked at the chartroom clock. Oh three thirty . . .

"Put your standby man on the wheel, Mr. Andersen," he ordered. "I'm bringing her round manually."

He went out into the wheelhouse. Both moons were down, but the sky had cleared. Overhead the scattered stars were bright; and bright, too, were the living stars thrown aloft and back in the sheets of spray each time that the ship's prow crashed down to meet the racing seas. Grimes stood there, waiting, hoping for a lull, however brief. He glanced behind him, saw that the wheel was manned and that Andersen was standing beside the helmsman.

He looked ahead again. It seemed to him that the pitching of the ship was a little less pronounced, that sea and swell were a little less steep. "Port," he ordered. "Easily, easily . . ." He heard the clicking of the gyro-repeater as the ship's head started to come round. And then he saw it, broad on the starboard bow, a towering cliff of water, white capped, a freak sea. "Hard a-port!" Grimes shouted. "Hard over!"

She responded beautifully, and the clicking of the repeater was almost one continuous note. She responded beautifully, but not quite fast enough. The crest of the dreadful sea was overhanging the bridge now, poised to fall and smash. Still she turned, and then she heeled far over to port, flinging Grimes and the Second Officer and the helmsman into an untidy huddle on that side of the wheelhouse. She shuddered as the tons of angry water crashed down to her poop, surged forward along her decks, even onto the bridge itself. There was a banging and clattering of loose gear, cries and screams from below. But miraculously she steadied, righted herself, surging forward with only a not very violent pitching motion.

Somehow Grimes got to his feet, disentangling himself from the other two men. He staggered to the untended wheel, grasped the spokes. He looked at the repeater card. Three two oh . . .

Carefully he applied starboard rudder, brought the lubber's line to the course that had been laid off on the chart, three three five. He saw that Andersen and the seaman had recovered their footing, were standing by awaiting further orders.

"Put her back on automatic," he told the Second Officer. "On this course." He relinquished the wheel as soon as this had been done. "Then take your watch with you and make rounds through the accommodation. Let me know if anybody's been hurt."

"Who the hell's rocking the bloody boat?" It was Wilcox, the Chief Officer. Then, as he saw Grimes by the binnacle, "Sorry, sir."

"It's an emergency, Mr. Wilcox. A Mayday call. *Iron Warrior*, broken down and drifting on to the Low Grenadines. We're going to her assistance."

"What time do you estimate that we shall reach her, Captain?"

"About eleven hundred hours."

"I'd better start getting things ready," replied the Mate.

Grimes went back into the chartroom, to the transceiver that had been switched on as soon as the auto-alarm had been actuated by the Mayday call. "*Sonya Winneck* to Ocean Control, Area Five," he said.

"Ocean Control to *Sonya Winneck*. I receive you. Pass your message."

"I am now proceeding to the assistance of *Iron Warrior*. Estimated time of visual contact ten thirty hours, Zone Plus Seven."

"Thank you, *Sonya Winneck*. *Pleiaidic* cannot be in the vicinity until thirteen hundred hours at the earliest. Please use Channel Six when working

Iron Warrior. Call me on Sixteen to keep me informed. Over."

He switched to Channel Six. "*Sonya Winneck* to *Iron Warrior* . . ."

"*Iron Warrior* here, *Sonya Winneck*." The other Captain's voice, was, perhaps, a little too calm.

"How are things with you, *Iron Warrior*?"

"Bloody awful, to be frank. A twenty degree list, and my boats and rafts smashed on the weather side. Estimated rate of drift, two knots."

"I should be with you in seven hours," said Grimes. "I shall try to take you in tow."

"We'll have everything ready, Captain."

"Good. We shall be seeing you shortly. Over and standing by."

Wilcox had come into the chartroom. He said, "Everybody's been informed, sir. The Chief reckons that he can squeeze out another half knot."

"Anybody hurt when she went over?"

"Only minor lacerations and contusions, sir."

"Such as this," announced Sonya, who had joined the others in the chartroom, putting a cautious hand up to the beginnings of a black eye. "But it's in a good cause."

Iron Warrior was not a pretty sight.

She lay wallowing in a welter of white water, like a dying sea beast. The seas broke over her rust-colored hull in great explosions of spray, but now and again, during brief lulls, the extent of the damage that she had sustained could be made out. She was a typical bulk carrier, with all the accommodation aft, with only a stumpy mast right forward and her mainmast growing out of her funnel, and no cargo gear but for one crane on the poop for ship's stores and the like. That crane, Grimes could see through his binoculars, was a twisted tangle of wreckage. That would explain why the Warrior's Captain had not used oil to minimize the effect of breaking waves; probably the entrance to the storerooms was blocked. And there must be some other reason why it had not been possible to pump diesel fuel overside—even though a mineral oil is not as effective as vegetable or animal oil it is better than nothing. The side of the bridge seemed to be stove in, and under the boat davits dangled a mess of fiberglass splinters.

Beyond her—and not far beyond her, a mere three miles—was the black, jagged spine of Devlin's Islet, dead to leeward. It seemed more alive, somehow, than the stricken ship, looked like a great, malevolent sea monster creeping nearer and ever nearer through the boiling surf toward its dying prey.

Grimes was using oil, a thin trickle of it from his scuppers, wads of waste soaked in it thrown overside to leeward. Luckily there had been plenty of it in Sonya Winneck's storerooms—fish oil for the preservation of exposed wire ropes, a heavy vegetable oil for the treatment of wooden decks and brightwork. It was beginning to have effect; the thin, glistening surface film was a skin over the water between the two ships, an integument that contained the sea, forcing some semblance of form upon it. The swell was still there—heavy, too heavy—but the waves were no longer breaking, their violence suppressed.

Aft, Andersen and his men were standing by the

rocket gun. The heavy insurance wire was already flaked out ready for running, its inboard end taken not only around both pairs of bitts—these, in a ship with self-tensioning winches, were rarely used for mooring, but there was always the possibility of a tow—but also around the poop house. The sisal messenger was coiled down handy to the line-throwing apparatus.

On the bridge, Grimes conned his ship. She was creeping along parallel to *Iron Warrior* now, at reduced speed. She was making too much leeway for Grimes's taste; unless he was careful there would be two wrecks instead of only one. Too, with the swell broad on the beam *Sonya Winneck* was rolling heavily, so much so that accurate shooting would be impossible. But the necessary maneuvers had been worked out in advance. At the right moment Grimes would come hard to port, presenting his stern to the *Iron Warrior*. Andersen would loose off his rocket, aiming for a point just abaft the break of the other ship's fo'c'sle head, where men were already standing by. They would grab the light, nylon rocket line, use it to pull aboard the heavier messenger, use that to drag the end of the towing wire aboard, shackling it to the port anchor cable. After that, it would be plain sailing (Grimes hoped). He would come ahead slowly, slowly, taking the weight gently, trying to avoid the imposition of overmuch strain on either vessel. Slowly but surely he would pull the wounded *Warrior* away from the hostile fortifications. (*Come off it, Grimes*, he told himself sternly. *Don't be so bloody literary.*)

"Hard a-port!" he ordered.

"Hard a-port, sir!" The clicking of the repeater

was audible above the shrieking of the wind.

"Ease her ... Midships ... Steady! Steady as you go!"

Sonya Winneck hung there, her stern a bare two cables from the side of *Iron Warrior*. Grimes thought, *I cut that rather too close. But at this range it'll be impossible for Andersen to miss.* To the Third Officer, at the radar, he called, "Are we opening the range?"

"Slowly, sir."

It was time that Andersen got his rocket away. The ship was not pitching too badly; firing at just the right moment should not be difficult. As long as the missile passed over the target it would be a successful shot. Grimes went out to the wing of the bridge to watch. The air scoop dodger deflected the wind, throwing it up and over, so it was not too uncomfortable away from the wheelhouse.

Andersen fired—and at precisely the wrong moment the ship's head fell off heavily to starboard. The rocket streaked through the air, arcing high, a brief orange flare against the gray, ragged clouds, a streamer of white smoke, and behind it the fluorescent yellow filament of the nylon line. Inevitably it missed, finally splashing to the sea well forward of and beyond *Iron Warrior's* bows.

Grimes didn't see it drop. He stormed into the wheelhouse, bawled at the helmsman, "What the hell do you think you're playing at?"

"It's the wheel, sir," The man's voice was frightened. "It turned in my hands. I can't budge it!"

The ship was coming round still, turning all the time to starboard. The gale force wind and her own engines were driving her down on to the helpless *Warrior*. "Stop her!" ordered Grimes. "Full astern!"

Denham was still at the radar, so Wilcox jumped to the engine controls. He slammed the lever hard over to the after position. Still the ship was making headway—but, at last, slowing. She stopped at last, her stem scant feet from *Iron Warrior's* exposed side. Grimes could see the white faces of her people as they stared at him, as they watched, in horrified disbelief, this rescuer turned assassin.

Sonya Winneck was backing away now, her stern coming up into the wind. She was backing away, but reluctantly. Wilcox shouted, "Denham, come and give me a hand! I can't keep this bloody handle down!"

Grimes dragged his attention away from the ship he had so nearly rammed to what was happening on his own bridge. Both the Chief and Third Officer—and Wilcox was a big, strong man—were having to exert all their strength to keep the metal lever in its astern position. It was jerking, forcing itself up against their hands.

Sonya—who until now had been keeping well out of the way—grabbed him by the arm. "Tell the Chief to put the engine controls on manual!" she screamed. "I know what's happening!"

"What's happening?"

"No time now to tell you. Just put her on manual, and get Lecky up here!"

Grimes went to the telephone, rang down to the engineroom. "Manual control, your end, Mr. Jones," he ordered. "Keep her on full astern until I order otherwise. And send Miss Hales up to the bridge. At once."

Thankfully, Wilcox and Denham released their painful grip on the bridge control lever. On the console the revolution indicator still showed maximum stern power. Ahead, the distance between the two ships was fast diminishing. From the VHF transceiver came a frightened voice, "What's happening, *Sonya Winneck?* What's happening?"

"Tell him," said Grimes to Denham, "that we're having trouble with our bridge controls. We'll get a line aboard as soon as we can."

Wilcox, watching the indicator, yelled, "She's stopped! The bitch is coming ahead again!"

Sonya said urgently. "There's only one thing to do, John. Shut off the Purcell Navigator. *Iron Warrior* has P N against her name in the Registry—and she was built by Varley's." She turned to Mary Hales, who had just come onto the bridge. "Mary, switch off that bloody tin brain, or pull fuses, or something—but *kill it!*"

The pretty little blonde was no longer so pretty. On one side of her head the hair was charred and frizzled, and her smooth face was marred by an angry burn. "We've been trying to," she gasped. "The Chief and I. It won't let us."

"She's coming astern again," announced Wilcox. "She's . . . No, she's stopped . . ."

"Watch her, Mr. Wilcox," ordered Grimes. He ran with his wife and the Electrician to the house abaft the chartroom in which the Purcell Navigator lived. It squatted there sullenly on its four stumpy legs, the dials set around its spherical body glaring at them like eyes. From its underside ran armored cables, some thick and some thin— that one leading aft and down must be the main power supply, the ones leading into the wheelhouse and chartroom would be connected to various controls and navigational equipment. On the after bulkhead of the house was a switchboard and fuse box. Mary Hales went straight to this, put out her hand to the main switch. There was a sudden, intense violet flare, a sharp crackling, the tang of overheated metal. The girl staggered back, her blistered hands covering her eyes. "That's what happened to the engineroom switchboard!" she wailed. "It's welded itself in the On position!" Then, using language more seamanlike than ladylike, she threw herself at the fuse box. She was too late—but perhaps this was as well. Had she got the lid open she would have been blinded.

Still cursing softly, she grabbed a spanner from her belt. Her intention was obvious; she would unscrew the retaining nut holding the main supply lead firmly in its socket. But an invisible force yanked the tool out of her hand, threw it out of the open door.

Grimes watched, helpless. Then he heard Sonya snarling, "Do something. Do something, damn you!" She thrust something into his right hand. He looked down at it. It was the big fire ax from its rack in the chartroom. He got both hands about the haft, tried to swing up the head of the weapon, staggered as the magnetic fields which now were the machine's main defense tugged at it. But he lifted the ax somehow, brought it crashing down—and missed his own right foot by a millimeter. Again he raised the ax, straining with all his strength, and again struck at the thick cable. The ship lurched heavily, deflecting his aim, and, fantastically, the magnetic deflection brought the head back to its target. The armored cable writhed away from the blow, but not in time, not enough.

The keen edge bit home, in a coruscation of violet sparks. And Mary Hales, with a smaller ax that she had found somewhere, was chopping away, sobbing and cursing; and Sonya was jabbing with a heavy screwdriver at the thing's "eyes"—and so, at last, it died.

And so it died, damaged beyond its built-in powers of self-regeneration. (Mary Hales made sure of that.) And so Grimes was able to get a line aboard *Iron Warrior*, and the *Warrior's* people got the towing wire shackled onto their anchor cable, and slowly, slowly but surely, the crippled ship was dragged to safety, away from the avidly waiting fangs and talons of Devlin's Islet; the rocky teeth and claws that, when the tow finally commenced, had been less than half a mile distant.

The Purcell Navigator was dead, and its last flares of energy had destroyed or damaged much more than itself. The gyro-compass and the autopilot were inoperative (but the ship had a magnetic compass and hand steering). Loran and radar were burned out, inertial navigator and echometer were beyond repair, even the Chernikeeff Log was useless. But Grimes was not worried. He had sextant, chronometer, ephemeris and tables—and the great navigators of Earth's past had circled their globe with much less in the way of equipment. In the extremely unlikely event of his not knowing where he was he could always ask *Iron Warrior* for a fix—but he did not think that he would have to do so.

He did, however, urge the *Warrior's* Master to put his own Purcell Navigator out of commission, explaining why in some detail. Then he went to

the house abaft the chartroom where, under the
direction of Mary Hales, Wilcox and his men were
loosening the holding down bolts, disconnecting
the cables that had not already been cut. (There
might still be a flicker of life in the thing, some
capability of self-repair.) He watched happily as
the Mate and three brawny ratings lifted the
spherical casing from the deck, staggered with it
out the door.

"What shall we do with it, sir?" asked the Mate.

"Give it a buoyancy test," ordered Grimes. He
followed the men to the side rail of the bridge,
watched as they tipped it over. It sank without a
trace.

Grimes was relieved of his command in Long-
haven, after the successful completion of the tow,
and flown back to Steep Island, accompanied by
Sonya. Neither he nor his wife felt very strong
when they boarded the airship—the crews of both
Sonya Winneck and *Iron Warrior* had united in
laying on a farewell party more enthusiastic than
restrained. ("You must be glad to see the back of
us," Sonya had remarked at one stage of the pro-
ceedings.) Even so, old and tired as he was feeling,
Grimes had insisted on seeing the airship's captain so as to be assured that the craft was not fitted
with a Purcell Navigator. Then, he and his wife
went to their cabin and collapsed into their bunks.

Steep Island, although not officially an airport,
had a mooring mast, so a direct flight was possible. When the time came for Grimes and Sonya to
disembark they were feeling better and, in fact,
had been able to put the finishing touches to their
report.

Captain Thornton, the Havenmaster, welcomed them warmly but was obviously anxious to hear what they had to tell him. In minutes only they were all seated in the Havenmaster's Lookout and Thornton was listening intently as they talked.

When they were finished, he smiled grimly. "This is good enough," he said. "It's good enough even for the Council of Master Wardens. I shall issue orders that those infernal machines are to be rendered inoperative in every ship fitted with them, and that no more are to be put aboard any Aquarian vessel. Then we make arrangements to ship them all back to where they came from."

Grimes was surprised, and said so. He was used to having his recommendations adopted eventually, but in most cases there was a lot of argument first.

Thornton laughed. "What you've said is what I've been saying, John, for months. But nobody listens to me. I'm just a reactionary old shellback. But you, sir, as well as being a well-known maritime historian, have also one foot—at least—in what to us is still the future. You're a master astronaut, you hold the rank of commodore in the Space Navy of your Confederacy. They'll listen to you, when they won't listen to me."

"It's Sonya they should listen to," Grimes said. "She's a spacewoman *and* an intelligence officer. She tied the loose ends together."

"But it was all so obvious," she said smugly. "Two yards, and two yards only, on this planet licensed to fit the Purcell Navigator: Varley's and the Carrington State Dockyard. Two . . . sororities? Yes, two sororities of ships, the Varley Sisterhood and the Carrington Sisterhood, each hating the other. Limited intelligence, but, somehow, a strong, built-in spite, and also a strong sense of self-preservation. That much, I think, was intended by those electronic geniuses on Elektra— and possibly more, but I'll come to that later.

"Anyhow, if a Carrington sister saw a chance of taking a swipe at a Varley sister without much risk of damage to herself she'd take it. And *vice versa*. Hence all the collisions, and all the minor berthing accidents. Now and again, of course, the sense of self-preservation worked to everybody's benefit . . ." She smiled at he husband rather too sweetly. "I know of at least one bungled berthing where everything, almost miraculously, came right in the end . . ."

"But what's behind it all?" asked the Havenmaster. "You're the Intelligence Officer. Is it, do you think, intentional on somebody's part?"

"I don't know, Tom. I'd have to snoop around on Elektra to find out, and I doubt if the Elektrans would let me. But try this idea on for size . . . What if the Elektrans want to make Aquarius absolutely dependent upon them?"

"It could be . . ." mused Thornton. "It could be . . ." He went up, walked to the bookshelves, took out a book, opened it. It was Grimes's own *Times Of Transition*. The Havenmaster leafed through it to find the right place. He read aloud, " 'And so was engendered a most unseamanlike breed of navigator, competent enough technicians whose working tools were screwdrivers and voltmeters rather than sextants and chronometers. Of them it could never be said *Every hair a ropeyarn, every fingernail a marlinespike, every* drop of blood pure Stockholm tar. They were servants to rather than masters of their machines, and ever they were at the mercy of a single fuse . . .' " He shut the book with a slam. He said, "It can't happen here."

"Famous last words," scoffed Sonya, but her voice was serious.

"It mustn't happen here," said Grimes.

THE MAN WHO SAILED THE SKY

IT WAS FORTUNATE, Sonya always said, that the Federation Survey Service's *Star Pioneer* dropped down to Port Stellar, on Aquarius, when she did. Had not transport back to the Rim Worlds, although it was by a roundabout route, become available it is quite possible that her husband would have become a naturalized Aquarian citizen. Seafaring is no more (and no less) a religion than spacefaring; be that as it may, John Grimes, Master Astronaut, Commodore of the Rim Confederacy's Naval Reserve, Honorary Admiral of the Ausiphalian Navy and, lately, Master Mariner, was exhibiting all the zeal of the new convert. For some months he had sailed in command of an Aquarian merchantman and, although his real job was to find out the cause of the rapidly increasing number of marine casualties, he had made it plain that insofar as his own ship was concerned he was no mere figurehead. Although (or because) only at sea a dog watch, he was taking great pride in his navigation, his seamanship, his pilotage and his ship handling.

"Damn it all," he grumbled to Sonya, "if our lords and masters wanted us back they'd send a ship for us. I know that *Rim Eland* isn't due here for another six weeks, on her normal commercial voyage—but what's wrong with giving the Navy a spot of deep space training? The Admiralty could send a corvette . . ."

"You aren't all that important, John."

"I suppose not. I'm only the Officer Commanding the Naval Reserve, and the Astronautical Superintendent of Rim Runners . . . Oh, well—if *they* don't want me, there're some people who do."

"What do you mean?" she asked sharply.

"Tom told me that my Master Mariner's Certificate of Competency and my Pilotage Exemption Certificates are valid for all time. He told me, too, that the Winneck Line will give me another appointment as soon as I ask for it. There's just one condition . . ."

"Which is?"

"That we take out naturalization papers."

"No," she told him. "No, repeat, capitalize, underscore no."

"Why not, my dear?"

"Because this world is the bitter end. I always thought that the Rim Worlds were bad enough, but I put up with them for your sake and, in any case, they've been improving enormously over the past few years. But Aquarius . . . It's way back in the twentieth century!"

"That's its charm."

"For you, perhaps. Don't get me wrong. I enjoyed our voyage in *Sonya Winneck*—but it was no more than a holiday cruise . . ."

"An odd sort of holiday."

"You enjoyed it too. But after not too long a time you'd find the life of a seafaring commercial shipmaster even more boring than that of a spacefaring one. Do you want to be stuck on the surface of one planet for the rest of your life?"

"But there's more variety of experience at sea than there is in space . . ."

Before she could reply there was a tap on the door. "Enter!" called Grimes.

Captain Thornton, the Havenmaster of Aquarius, came into the suite. He looked inquiringly at his guests. "Am I interrupting something?" he asked.

"You are, Tom," Sonya told him. "But you're welcome to join the argument, even though it will be the two of you against me. John's talking of settling down on Aquarius to continue his seafaring career."

"He could do worse," said Thornton.

Sonya glared at the two men, at the tall, lean, silver-haired ruler of Aquarius, at her stocky, rugged husband whose prominent ears, already flushing, were a thermometer of his rising temper. Grimes, looking at her, had the temerity to smile slightly, appreciatively. Like the majority of auburn-haired women she was at her most attractive when about to blow her top.

"What are you grinning at, you big ape?" she demanded.

"You."

Before she could explode Thornton hastily intervened. He said, "I came in with some news that should interest you, both of you. I've just got the buzz that the Federation's *Star Pioneer* is putting in to Port Stellar. I know that you used to be in the Survey Service, John, and that Sonya still holds a Reserve commission, and it could be that you'll be meeting some old shipmates . . ."

"Doubtful," said Grimes. "The Survey Service has a very large fleet, and it's many years since I resigned . . ."

"Since you were asked to resign," remarked Sonya.

"You were still in your cradle, so you know nothing about the circumstances. But there might be some people aboard that Sonya would know."

"We shall soon find out. I have to throw a party for the Captain and officers—and you, of course, will be among the guests."

Grimes knew none of *Star Pioneer's* officers, but Sonya was acquainted with Commander James Farrell, the survey ship's captain. How well acquainted? Grimes felt a twinge of jealousy as he watched them chatting animatedly, then strolled over to the buffet for another generous helping of the excellent chowder. There he was engaged in conversation by two of the *Pioneer's* junior lieutenants. "You know, sir," said one of the, "your name's quite a legend in the Service . . ."

"Indeed?" Grimes felt flattered.

The other young man laughed—and Grimes did not feel quite so smug. "Yes, sir. Any piece of insubordination—justifiable insubordination, of course—is referred to as 'doing a Grimes . . .'"

"Indeed?" The Commodore's voice was cold.

The first young man hastened to make amends. "But I've heard very senior officers, admirals and commodores, say that you should never have been allowed to resign . . ."

Grimes was not mollified. "*Allowed* to resign? It was a matter of choice, my choice. Furthermore . . ." And then he became aware that Sonya, with Commander Farrell in tow, was making her way toward him through the crowd. She was smiling happily. Grimes groaned inwardly. He knew that smile.

"John," she said, "I've good news."

"Tell me."

"Jimmy, here, says that I'm entitled to a free passage in his ship."

"Oh."

"I haven't finished. The Survey Service Regulations have been modified since your time. The spouses of commissioned officers, even those on the Reserve List, are also entitled to a free passage if suitable accommodation is available. *Star Pioneer* has ample passenger accommodation, and she will be making a courtesy call at Port Forlorn after her tour of the Carlotti Beacon Stations in this sector of space . . ."

"We shall be delighted to have you aboard, sir," said Farrell.

"Thank you," replied Grimes. He had already decided that he did not much care for the young Commander who, with his close-cropped sandy hair, his pug nose and his disingenuous blue eyes, was altogether too much the idealized Space Scout of the recruiting posters. "Thank you. I'll think about it."

"We'll think about it," said Sonya.

"There's no mad rush, sir," Farrell told him, with a flash of white, even teeth. "But it should be an interesting trip. Glebe, Parramatta, Wyong and Esquel . . ."

Yes, admitted Grimes to himself, *it could be interesting*. Like Aquarius, Glebe, Parramatta and

Wyong were rediscovered Lost Colonies, settled originally by the lodejammers of the New Australia Squadron. Esquel was peopled by a more or less humanoid race that, like the Grollons, had achieved the beginnings of a technological civilization. Grimes had read about these worlds, but had never visited them. And then, through the open windows of the hall, drifted the harsh, salty smell of the sea, the thunderous murmur of the breakers against the cliff far below.

I can think about it, he thought. *But that's as far as it need go.*

"We'll think about it," Sonya had said—and now she was saying more. "Please yourself, John, but I'm going. You can follow me when *Rim Eland* comes in. If you want to."

"You will not consider staying here on Aquarius?"

"I've already made myself quite clear on that point. And since you're hankering after a seafaring life so badly it'll be better if you make the break *now*, rather than hang about waiting for the Rim Runners' ship. Another few weeks here and it'll be even harder for you to tear yourself away."

Grimes looked at his wife. "Not with you already on the way home."

She smiled. "That's what I thought. That's why I took Jimmy's offer. He is rather sweet, isn't he?"

"All the more reason why I should accompany you aboard his blasted ship."

She laughed. "The old, old tactics always work, don't they?"

"Jealousy, you mean?" It was his turn to laugh. "Me, jealous of that puppy!"

"Jealous," she insisted, "but not of him. Jealous of the Survey Service. You had your love affair with the Service many years ago, and you've gotten over it. You've other mistresses now—Rim Runners and the Rim Worlds Naval Reserve. But I was still in the middle of mine when I came under the fatal spell of your charm. And I've only to say the word and the Service'd have me back; a Reserve Officer can always transfer back to the Active List . . ." She silenced Grimes with an upraised hand. "Let me finish. If I'd taken passage by myself in *Rim Eland* there'd have been no chance at all of my flying the coop. There's so much of you in all the Rim Runners' ships. And the Master and his officers would never have let me forget that I was Mrs. Commodore Grimes. Aboard *Star Pioneer*, with you not there, I'd soon revert to being Commander Sonya Verrill . . ."

Slowly, Grimes filled and lit his pipe. Through the wreathing smoke he studied Sonya's face, grave and intent under the gleaming coronal of auburn hair. He knew that she was right. If he persisted in the pursuit of this new love for oceangoing steamships, she could return to her old love for the far-ranging vessels of the Interstellar Federation's military and exploratory arm. They might meet again sometime in the distant future, they might not. And always there would be the knowledge that they were sailing under different flags.

"All right," he said abruptly. "Better tell your boyfriend to get the V.I.P. suite ready."

"I've already told him," she said. She grinned. "Although as a mere Reserve Commander, traveling by myself, I shouldn't have rated it."

* * *

The last farewells had been said, not without real regrets on either side, and slowly, the irregular throbbing of her inertial drive drowning the brassy strains of the traditional *Anchors Aweigh*, *Star Pioneer* lifted from the Port Stellar apron. Guests in her control room were Grimes and Sonya. Usually on such occasions the Commodore would be watching the ship handling technique of his host, but today he was not. He was looking down to the watery world fast falling away below. Through borrowed binoculars he was staring down at the slender shape that had just cleared the breakwaters of the Port Stellar seaport, that was proceeding seawards on yet another voyage; and he knew that on her bridge *Sonya Winneck's* officers would be staring upward at the receding, diminishing ship of space. He sighed, not loudly, but Sonya looked at him with sympathy. That was yet another chapter of his life over, he thought. Never again would he be called upon to exercise the age-old skills of the seaman. But there were worse things than being a spaceman.

He pulled his attention away from the viewport, took an interest in what was going on in the control room. It was all much as he remembered it from his own Survey Service days—dials and gauges and display units, telltale lights, the remote controls for inertial, auxiliary rocket and Mannschenn Drives, the keyboard of the Gunnery Officer's "battle organ." And, apart from the armament accessories, it was very little different from the control room of any modern merchantman.

The people manning it weren't quite the same as merchant officers; and, come to that, weren't quite the same as the officers of the Rim Worlds Navy. There was that little bit of extra smartness in the uniforms, even to the wearing of caps inside the ship. There were the splashes of fruit salad on the left breast of almost every uniform shirt. There was the crispness of the Captain's orders, the almost exaggerated crispness of his officers' responses, with never a departure from standard Naval terminology. This was a taut ship, not unpleasantly taut, but taut nonetheless. (One of Grimes's shortcomings in the Survey Service had been his inability, when in command, to maintain the requisite degree of tension.) Even so, it was pleasant to experience it once again—especially as a passenger, an outsider. Grimes looked at Sonya. She was enjoying it too. Was she enjoying it too much?

Still accelerating, although not uncomfortably, the ship drove through the thin, high wisps of cirrus. Overhead the sky was indigo, below Aquarius was already visibly a sphere, an enormous mottled ball of white and gold and green and blue—mainly blue. Over to the west'ard was what looked like the beginnings of a tropical revolving storm. And who would be caught in it? Grimes wondered. Anybody he knew? In deep space there were no storms to worry about, not now, although in the days of the lodejammers magnetic storms had been an ever-present danger.

"Secure all!" snapped Commander Farrell.

"Hear this! Hear this!" the Executive Officer said sharply into his microphone. "All hands. Secure for free fall. Report."

Another officer began to announce, "Sick Bay

—secure. Enlisted men—secure. Hydroponics—secure . . ." It was a long list. Grimes studied the sweep second hand of his wristwatch. By this time a Rim Runners' tramp would be well on her way. Quite possibly, he admitted, with some shocking mess in the galley or on the farm deck. ". . . Mannschenn Drive Room—securem Inertial drive room—secure. Auxiliary rocket room—secure. All secure, sir."

"All stations secure, sir," the Executive Officer repeated to the Captain.

"Free fall—execute!"

The throb of the inertial drive faltered and died in midbeat.

"Centrifugal effect—stand by!"

"Centrifugal effect—stand by!"

"Hunting—execute!"

"Hunting—execute!"

The mighty gyroscopes hummed, then whined. Turning about them, the ship swung to find the target star, the distant sun of Glebe, lined it up in the exact center of the Captain's cartwheel sights and then fell away the few degrees necessary to allow for galactic drift.

"Belay gyroscopes!"

"Belay gyroscopes!"

"One gravity acceleration—stand by!"

"One gravity acceleration—stand by!"

"One gravity acceleration—execute!"

"One gravity acceleration—execute!"

The inertial drive came to life again.

"Time distortion—stand by!"

"Time distortion—stand by!"

"Mannschenn Drive—stand by!"

"Mannschenn Drive—stand by!"

"Mannschenn Drive—3 lyps—On!"
"Mannschenn Drive—3 lyps—On!"
There was the familiar thin, high keening of the ever-precessing gyroscopes, the fleeting second (or century) of temporal disorientation, the brief spasm of nausea; and then, ahead, the sparse stars were no longer steely points of light but iridescent, pulsating spirals, and astern the fast diminishing globe of Aquarius could have been a mass of multihued, writhing gases. *Star Pioneer* was falling down the dark dimensions, through the warped continuum toward her destination.

And about time, thought Grimes, looking at his watch again. *And about bloody time.*

Glebe, Parramatta, Wyong . . . Pleasant enough planets, with something of the Rim Worlds about them, but with a flavor of their own. Lost Colonies they had been, settled by chance, discovered by the ships of the New Australia Squadron after those hapless lodejammers had been thrown lightyears off course by a magnetic storm, named after those same ships. For generations they had developed in their own way, isolated from the rest of the man-colonized galaxy. Their development, Commander Farrell complained, had been more of a retrogression than anything else. Commodore Grimes put forward his opinion, which was that these worlds were what the Rim Worlds should have been, and would have been if too many highly efficient types from the Federation had not been allowed to immigrate.

Sonya took sides in the ensuing argument—the wrong side at that. "The trouble with you, John," she told him, "is that you're just naturally against all progress. That's why you so enjoyed playing at being a twentieth century sailor on Aquarius. That's why you don't squirm, as we do, every time that you hear one of these blown away Aussies drawl, 'She'll be right . . .' "

"But it's true, ninety-nine percent of the time." He turned to Farrell. "I know that you and your smart young technicians were appalled at the untidiness of the Carlotti Stations on all three of these planets, at the slovenly bookkeeping and all the rest of it. But the beacons work and work well, even though the beacon keepers are wearing ragged khaki shorts instead of spotless white overalls. And what about the repairs to the one on Glebe? They knew that it'd be months before the spares for which they'd requisitioned trickled down through the Federation's official channels, and so they made do with the materials at hand..."

"The strip patched with beaten out oil drums . . ." muttered Farrell. "Insulators contrived from beer bottles . . ."

"But that beacon works, Commander, with no loss of accuracy."

"But it shouldn't," Farrell complained.

Sonya laughed. "This archaic setup appeals to John, Jimmy. I always used to think that the Rim Worlds were his spiritual home—but I was wrong. He's much happier on these New Australian planets, which have all the shortcomings of the Rim but nary a one of the few, the very few good points."

"What good points are you talking about?" demanded Grimes. "Overreliance on machinery is one of them, I suppose. That's what I liked about

Aquarius, and what I like about these worlds—
the tacit determination that the machine shall be
geared to man, not the other way round . . ."

"But," said Sonya. "The contrast. Every time
that we step ashore it hits us in the eye. Jimmy's
ship, with everything spick and span, every
officer and every rating going about his duties at
the very peak of efficiency—and this city (if you
can call it that) with everybody shambling around
at least half-asleep, where things get done after a
fashion, if they get done at all. It must be obvious
even to an old-fashioned . . . seaman like yourself."

"Aboard a ship," admitted Grimes, "any sort of
ship, one has to have some efficiency. But not too
much."

The three of them were sitting at a table on the
wide veranda of the Digger's Arms, one of the
principal hotels in the city of Paddington, the
capital (such as it was) of Wyong. There were
glasses before them, and a bottle, its outer surface
clouded with condensation. Outside the high sun
blazed down on the dusty street, but it was pleasant enough where they were, the rustling of the
breeze in the leaves of the vines trailing around
the veranda posts giving an illusion of coolness,
the elaborate iron lace of pillars and railing con-
tributing its own archaic charm.

A man came in from outside, removing his
broad-brimmed hat as soon as he was in the shade.
His heavy boots were noisy on the polished
wooden floor. Farrell and Sonya looked with
some disapproval at his sun-faded khaki shirt, the
khaki shorts that could have been cleaner and
better pressed.

"Mrs. Grimes," he said. "How yer goin'?"

"Fine, thank you, Captain," she replied coldly.

"How's tricks, Commodore?"

"Could be worse," admitted Grimes.

"An' how's the world treatin' you, Commander?"

"I can't complain," answered Farrell, making it sound like a polite lie.

The newcomer—it was Captain Dalby, the Port Master—pulled up a chair to the table and sat down with an audible *thump*. A shirt-sleeved waiter appeared. "Beer, Clarry," ordered Dalby. "A schooner of old. An' bring another coupla bottles for me friends." Then, while the drinks were coming, he said, "Your Number One said I might find you here, Commander."

"If it's anything important you want me for," Farrell told him, "you could have telephoned."

"Yair. Suppose I could. But yer ship'll not be ready ter lift off fer another coupla days, an' I thought the walk'd do me good . . ." He raised the large glass that the waiter had brought to his lips. "Here's lookin' at yer."

Farrell was already on his feet. "If it's anything serious, Captain Dalby, I'd better get back at once."

"Hold yer horses, Commander. There's nothin' you can do till you get there."

"Get where?"

"Esquel, o' course."

"What's wrong on Esquel?"

"Don't rightly know." He drank some more beer, taking his time over it. "But a signal just came in from the skipper of the *Epileptic Virgin* that the Esquel beacon's on the blink."

"*Epsilon Virginis*," corrected Farrell automatically. Then—"But this could be serious . . ."

"Nothin' ter work up a lather over, Commander. It's an unwatched beacon, so there's no need to worry about the safety of human personnel. An' it's not an important one. Any nog who can't find his way through this sector o' space without it ain't fit ter navigate a plastic duck across a bathtub!"

"Even so . . ." began Farrell.

"Sit down and finish your beer," said Grimes.

"Yer a man after me own heart, Commodore," Dalby told him.

"Did the Master of *Epsilon Virginis* have any ideas as to what might have happened?" asked Sonya.

"If he had, Mrs. Grimes, he didn't say so. Mechanical breakdown, earthquake, lightnin'—you name it." He grinned happily at Farrell. "But it suits me down ter the ground that you're here, Commander. If you weren't, I'd have ter take me own maintenance crew to Esquel an' fix the bloody thing meself. I don't like the place, nor its people . . ." He noticed that Sonya was beginning to look at him in a rather hostile manner. "Mind yer, I've nothin' against wogs, as long as they keep ter their own world an' I keep ter mine."

"So you've been on Esquel?" asked Sonya in a friendly enough voice.

"Too right. More'n once. When the beacon was first installed, an' three times fer maintenance. It's too bleedin' hot, for a start. It just ain't a white man's planet. An' the people . . . Little, gibberin' purple monkeys—chatter, chatter, chatter, jabber, jabber, jabber. Fair gets on yer nerves. I s'pose their boss cockies ain't all that bad when yer get ter know 'em—but they know what side their bread's buttered on an' try ter keep in our good books. If they hate our guts they don't show it. But the others—the lower classes I s'pose you'd call 'em—do hate our guts, an' they do show it."

"It often is the way, Captain," said Sonya. "Very often two absolutely dissimilar races are on far friendlier terms than two similar ones. I've never been to Esquel, but I've seen photographs of the natives and they're very like Terran apes or monkeys; and the apes and monkeys are our not so distant cousins. You and your men probably thought of the Esquelians as caricatures in very bad taste of human beings, and they thought of you in the same way."

"Yair. Could be. But I'm glad it's not me that has ter fix the beacon."

"Somebody has to," said Farrell virtuously.

Star Pioneer was on her way once more, driving along the trajectory between Wyong and Esquel, her inertial drive maintaining a normal one standard gravity acceleration, her Mannschenn Drive set for cruising temporal precession rate. Farrell had discussed matters with Grimes and Sonya and with his own senior officers. All agreed that there was no need for urgency; the Esquel beacon was not an essential navigational aid in this sector of space; had it been so it would have been manned.

There was, of course, no communication with the world toward which the ship was bound. The Carlotti beacons are, of course, used for faster-than-light radio communication between distant ships and planets, but the one on Esquel was a direction finding device only. A team of skilled technicians could have made short work of a conversion job, rendering the beacon capable of the transmission and reception of FTL radio signals — but there were no human technicians on Esquel. Yet. Imperialism has long been a dirty word; but the idea persists even though it is never vocalized. The Carlotti beacon on Esquel was the thin end of the wedge, the foot inside the door. Sooner or later the Esquelian rulers would come to rely upon that income derived from the rental of the beacon site, the imports (mainly luxuries) that they could buy with it; and then, not blatantly but most definitely, yet another planet would be absorbed into the Federation's economic empire.

There was conventional radio on Esquel, but *Star Pioneer* would not be able to pick up any messages while her time and space warping interstellar drive was in operation, and not until she was within spitting distance of the planet. There were almost certainly at least a few Esquelian telepaths—but the Survey Service ship was without a psionic radio officer. One should have been carried; one had been carried, in fact, but she had engineered her discharge on Glebe, where she had become wildly enamored of a wealthy grazier. Farrell had let her go; now he was rather wishing that he had not done so.

The *Pioneer* fell down the dark dimensions between the stars, and life aboard her was normal enough. There was no hurry. Unmanned beacons had broken down before, would do so again. Meanwhile there was the pleasant routine of a ship of war in deep space, the regular meals, the card-playing, the chess and what few games of a more physically demanding nature were possible in the rather cramped conditions. Sonya was enjoying it, Grimes was not. He had been too long away from the spit and polish of the Survey Service. And Farrell—unwisely for one in his position—was starting to take sides. Sonya, he not very subtly insinuated, was his breed of cat. Grimes might have been once, but he was no longer. Not only had he resigned from the finest body of astronauts in the galaxy, known or unknown, but he had slammed the door behind him. And as for this craze of his for—of all things!— seamanship . . . Grimes was pained, but not surprised, when Sonya told him, one night, that aboard this ship he was known as the Ancient Mariner.

Ahead, the Esquel sun burgeoned; and then came the day, the hour and the minute when the Mannschenn Drive was shut down and the ship reemerged into the normal continuum. She was still some weeks from Esquel itself, but she was in no hurry—until the first messages started coming in.

Grimes sat with Sonya and Farrell in the control room. He listened to the squeaky voice issuing from the transceiver. "Calling Earth ship . . . Calling any Earth ship . . . Help . . . Help . . . Help . . ."

It went on and on without break, although it was obvious that a succession of operators was working a more or less regular system of reliefs at the microphone. Farrell acknowledged. It would be minutes before the radio waves carrying his voice reached the Esquelian receiver, more minutes for a reply to come back. He said, as they were waiting for this, that he hoped that whoever was making the distress call had more than one transceiver in operation.

Abruptly the gibbering plea for unspecified aid ceased. A new voice came on the speaker. "I talk for Cabarar, High King of Esquel. There has been . . . revolution. We are . . . besieged on Drarg Island. Cannot hold out . . . much longer. Help. You must . . . help."

There was a long silence, broken by Farrell. "Number One," he ordered, "maximum thrust."

"Maximum thrust, sir." Then, into the intercom, "All hands to acceleration couches! Maximum thrust!"

The backs of the control room chairs fell to the horizontal, the leg rests lifted. The irregular beat of the inertial drive quickened, maddening in its noisy nonrhythm. Acceleration stamped frail human bodies deep into the resilient padding of the couches.

I'm getting too old for this sort of thing, thought Grimes. But he retained his keen interest in all that was going on about him. He heard Farrell say, every word an effort, "Pilot . . . Give me . . . data . . . on . . . Drarg . . ."

"Data . . . on . . . Drarg . . . sir . . ." replied the Navigator.

From the corner of his eye Grimes could see the young officer stretched supine on his couch, saw the fingers of his right hand crawling among the buttons in the arm rest like crippled white worms. A screen came into being overhead, a Mercator map of Esquel, with the greens and yellows and browns of sprawling continents, the oceanic blue. The map expanded; it was as though a television camera was falling rapidly to a position roughly in the middle of one of the seas. There was a speck there in the blueness. It expanded, but not to any extent. It was obvious that Drarg was only a very small island.

The map was succeeded by pictorial representations of the beacon station. There were high, rugged cliffs, with the sea foaming angrily through the jagged rocks at the waterline. There was a short, spidery jetty. And, over all, was the slowly rotating antenna of the Carlotti beacon, an ellipsoid Mobius strip that seemed ever on the point of vanishment as it turned about its long axis, stark yet insubstantial against the stormy sky.

Farrell, speaking a little more easily now, said, "There's room on that plateau to land a boat—but to put the ship down is out of the question . . ."

Nobody suggested a landing at the spaceport. It must be in rebel hands; and those same rebels, in all probability, possessed at least a share of Earth-manufactured weapons and would be willing to use them against the Earthmen whose lackeys their rulers had been. *Star Pioneer* was armed, of course—but too active participation in other people's wars is frowned upon.

"You could land on the water," said Grimes. "To leeward of the island."

"I'm not a master mariner, Commodore," Farrell told him rather nastily. "But this is *my* ship, and I'm not hazarding her. We'll orbit about Esquel and send down a boat."

I hope that one boat will be enough, thought Grimes, not without sympathy. *The mess isn't of your making, Jimmy boy, but you'll have to an-*

*swer the "please explains." And as human beings
we have some responsibility for the nongs and
drongoes we've been propping up with Terran
bayonets—or Terran credits, which have been
used to purchase Terran bayonets or their present
day equivalent.*

"Whatever his shortcomings," commented
Sonya, "High King Cabrarar used his brains. He
knew that if the beacon ceased functioning
there'd be an investigation . . ."

"And better us to make it," said Farrell, "than
Dalby and his bunch of no hopers."

"Why?" asked Grimes coldly.

"We're disciplined, armed . . ."

"And if you'll take my advice, Commander,
you'll not be in a hurry to use your arms. The top
brass is apt to take a dim view of active intervention in outsiders' private squabbles."

"But Cabrarar . . ."

". . . *was* the Federation's blue-eyed boy. His
kingdom now is limited to one, tiny island. I've no
doubt that your lords and masters are already considering dickering with whatever new scum
comes to the top."

"Sir . . ." One of the officers was trying to break
into the conversation.

"Yes, Mr. Penrose?"

"A signal, sir, from Officer Commanding Lindisfarne Base . . ."

The young man crawled slowly and painfully to
where his captain was stretched out on the acceleration couch, with a visible effort stretched out
the hand holding the flimsy. Farrell took it, managed to maneuver it to where his eyes could focus
on it.

After a long pause he read aloud, "Evacuate King Cabrarar and entourage. Otherwise do nothing, repeat nothing, to antagonize new regime on Esquel."

"As I've been saying," commented Grimes. "But at least they're exhibiting some faint flickers of conscience."

Shortly thereafter Farrell ordered a half hour's reduction of acceleration to one G, a break necessary to allow personnel to do whatever they had to do essential to their comfort. Grimes and Sonya — she with some reluctance — left the control room and retired to their own quarters.

Star Pioneer was in orbit about Esquel. Free fall, after the bone-crushing emergency acceleration, was a luxury—but it was not one that Commander Farrell and those making up the landing party were allowed to enjoy for long. Farrell had decided to send down only one boat—the pinnace. There was insufficient level ground on the island for more than one craft to make a safe landing. He had learned from King Cabrarar that the rebels had control of the air, and that their aircraft were equipped with air-to-air missiles. An air-spacecraft hovering, awaiting its turn to land, would be a tempting target—and effective self-defense on its part could easily be the beginnings of a nasty incident.

The deposed monarch and his party comprised three hundred beings, in terms of mass equivalent to two hundred Earthmen. In addition to its crew the pinnace could lift fifty men; so four rescue trips would be necessary. While the evacuation was in process a small party from the ship would remain on the island, deciding what in the way of stores, equipment and documents would be destroyed, what lifted off. Sonya had volunteered to be one of the party, pointing out that she was the only representative of the Intelligence Branch of the Survey Service in the ship, Reserve commission notwithstanding. Too, Esquelian was one of the many languages at her command; some years ago it had been intended that she visit Esquel, at the time of the installation of the Carlotti beacon, but these orders had been canceled when she was sent elsewhere on a more urgent mission. So, even though she had never set foot on the planet, she could make herself understood and—much more important—understand what was being said in her hearing.

Grimes insisted on accompanying his wife. He was an outsider, with no standing—but, as he pointed out to Farrell, this could prove advantageous. He would have more freedom of action than *Star Pioneer's* people, not being subject to the orders of the distant Flag Officer at Lindisfarne Base. Farrell was inclined to agree with him on this point, then said, "But it still doesn't let me off the hook, Commodore. Suppose you shoot somebody who, in the opinion of my lords and masters, shouldn't have been shot . . . And suppose I say, 'But, sir, it was Commodore Grimes, of the Rim Worlds Naval Reserve, who did the shooting . . .' What do *they* say?"

"Why the bloody hell did you let him?" replied Grimes, laughing. "But I promise to restrain my trigger finger, James."

"He's made up his mind to come," Sonya said. "But not to worry. After all his playing at being a

merchant sea captain he'll not know one end of a
gun from the other . . ."

So, with the landing party aboard, the pinnace
broke out of its bay and detached itself from the
mother ship. The young lieutenant at the controls
was a superb boat handler, driving the craft down
to the first tenuous wisps of atmosphere, then
decelerating before friction could overheat the
skin. Drarg Island was in the sunlit hemisphere,
the sky over which was unusually clear—so clear
that there was no likelihood of mistaking the
smoke from at least two burning cities for natural
cloud. Navigation presented no problems. All
that the officer had to do was to home on a continuous signal from the transmitter on the island.
Grimes would have liked to have played with the
bubble sextant and the ephemerides—produced
by Star Pioneer's navigator just in case they would
be needed—that were part of the boat's equipment, but when he suggested so doing Sonya gave
him such a scornful look that he desisted.

There was the island: a slowly expanding speck
in the white-flecked sea. And there, a long way to
the westward, were two airships, ungainly dirigible balloons. They must have seen the pinnace on
her way down, but they made no attempt to intercept; a blimp is not an ideal aircraft in which to
practice the kamikaze technique. But, remarked
Farrell, they would be reporting this Terran intervention to their base. The radio operator found
their working frequency and Sonya was able to
translate the high-pitched squeakings and gibber-
ings.

"As near as I can render it," she reported,
"they're saying, 'The bastard king's bastard

friends have come . . .' In the original it's much more picturesque." The operator turned up the gain to get the reply. " 'Keep the bastards under observation,' " said Sonya. Then, " 'Use Code 17A . . .' "

"They can use any code they please," commented Farrell. "With what weaponry there is on this world, the island's impregnable. It'll be more impregnable still after we've landed a few of our toys."

"Never underrate primitive peoples," Grimes told him. He dredged up a martime historical snippet from his capacious memory. "In one of the wars on Earth—the Sino-Japanese War in the first half of the twentieth century—a modern Japanese destroyer was sent to the bottom by the fire of a concealed battery of primitive muzzle-loading cannon, loaded with old nails, broken bottles and . . . horseshoes for luck . . ."

"Fascinating, Commodore, fascinating," said Farrell. "If you see any muzzle-loaders pointed our way, let me know, will you?"

Sonya laughed unkindly.

Grimes, who had brought two pipes with him, took out and filled and lit the one most badly in need of a clean.

They dropped down almost vertically on to the island, the lieutenant in charge of the pinnace making due allowance for drift. As they got lower they could see that the elliptical Mobius strip that was the antenna of the Carlotti beacon was still, was not rotating about its long axis. Draped around it were rags of fabric streaming to leeward in the stiff breeze. It looked, at first, as though somebody had improvised a wind sock for the benefit of the landing party—and then it was obvious that the fluttering tatters were the remains of a gasbag. A little to one side of the machinery house was a crumpled table of wickerwork and more fabric, the wreckage of the gondola of the crashed airship. Some, at least, of the refugees on the island must have come by air.

Landing would have been easy if the Esquelians had bothered to clear away the wreckage. The lieutenant suggested setting the pinnace down on top of it, but Farrell stopped him. Perhaps he was remembering Grimes's story about that thin-skinned Japanese destroyer. He said, "There's metal there, Mr. Smith—the engine, and weapons, perhaps, and other odds and ends. We don't want to go punching holes in ourselves . . ."

So the pinnace hovered for a while, vibrating to the noisy, irregular throb of her inertial drive, while the spidery, purple-furred humanoids on the ground capered and gesticulated. Finally, after Sonya had screamed orders at them through the ship's loudhailer, a party of them dragged the wreckage to the edge of the cliff, succeeded in pushing it over. It plunged untidily down to the rocks far below. There was a brilliant orange flash, a billowing of dirty white brown smoke, a shock wave that rocked the pinnace dangerously. There must have been ammunition of some kind in that heap of debris.

Farrell said nothing. But if looks could have killed, the King, standing aloof from his loyal subjects, distinguishable by the elaborate basket-work of gold and jewels on his little, round head, would have died. Somebody muttered, "Slovenly bastards . . ." Grimes wondered if the rebels were any more efficient than the ruling class they had deposed, decided that they almost certainly must be. It was such a familiar historical pattern.

The pinnace grounded. The noise of the intertial drive faded to an irritable mumble, then ceased. Farrell unbuckled his seat belt, then put on his cap, then got up. Sonya — who was also wearing a uniform for the occasion — did likewise. Somehow, the pair of them conveyed the impression that Grimes had not been invited to the party, but he followed them to the airlock, trying to look like a duly accredited observer from the Rim Worlds Confederacy. The airlock doors, inner and outer, opened. The Commodore sniffed appreciatively the breeze that gusted in, the harsh tang of salt water that is the same on all oceanic worlds. His second sniff was not such a deep one; the air of the island was tainted with the effluvium of too many people cooped up in far too small a space.

The ramp extended. Farrell walked slowly down it, followed by Sonya, followed by Grimes, followed by two ratings with machine pistols at the ready. The King stood a few yards away, watching them, surrounded by his own officers, monkeylike beings on the purple fur of whose bodies gleamed the golden ornaments that were badges of rank.

Stiffly (reluctantly?) Farrell saluted.

Limply the King half raised a six-fingered hand in acknowledgement. The rings on his long fingers sparkled in the afternoon sunlight. He turned to one of the staff, gibbering.

The being faced Farrell, baring yellow teeth as

he spoke. "His Majesty say, why you no come earlier?"

"We came as soon as we were able," said Farrell.

There was more gibbering, unintelligible to all save Sonya. Then— "His Majesty say, where big ship? When you start bomb cities, kill rebels?"

Farrell turned to face his own people. He said, "Take over, please, Commander Verrill. You know the language. You might be able to explain things more diplomatically than me. You know the orders."

"I know the orders, Commander Farrell," said Sonya. She stepped forward to face the King, speaking fluently and rapidly. Even when delivered by her voice, thought Grimes, this Esquelian language was still ugly, but she took the curse off it.

The King replied to her directly. He was literally hopping from one splayed foot to the other with rage. Spittle sprayed from between his jagged, yellow teeth. The elaborate crown on his head was grotesquely awry. He raised a long, thin arm as though to strike the woman.

Grimes pulled from his pocket the deadly little Minetti automatic that was his favorite firearm. Viciously, Farrell knocked his hand down, whispering, "Hold it, Commodore! Don't forget that we represent the Federation . . ."

"You might," snarled Grimes.

But the King had seen the show of weapons; Grimes learned later that the two spacemen had also made threatening gestures with their machine pistols. He let his arm fall to his side. His clawed fingers slowly straightened. At last he spoke again—and the unpleasant gibbering was less high-pitched, less hysterical.

Sonya translated. "His Majesty is . . . disappointed. He feels that he has been . . . betrayed."

"Tell his Majesty," said Farrell, "that my own rulers forbid me to take part in this civil war. But His Majesty and those loyal to him will be transported to a suitable world, where they will want for nothing."

Grimes tried to read the expression on the King's face. Resignation? Misery? It could have been either, or both. Then his attention was attracted by the glint of metal evident in the crowd behind the deposed monarch. He saw that most of the Esquelians were armed, some with vicious-looking swords, others with projectile weapons, archaic in design, but probably effective enough. He doubted if any of the natives would be able to fly the pinnace—but a human pilot might do what he was told with a knife at his throat.

Farrell spoke again. "Tell His Majesty, Commander Verrill, that if he has any ideas about seizing my pinnace he'd better forget 'em. Tell him that those odd-looking antennae poking out from their turrets are laser cannon, and that at the first sign of trouble this plateau will be one big, beautiful barbecue. Tell him to look at that bird, there . . ." he pointed . . . "over to the eastward." He raised his wrist to his mouth, snapped an order into the microphone.

After Sonya finished her translation, everybody looked at the bird—if bird it was. It was a flying creature of some kind, big, with a wide wing span. It was a carrion eater, perhaps, hovering to leeward of the island in the hope of a meal. It died suddenly in a flare of flame, a gout of greasy smoke. A sparse sprinkling of smoldering fragments drifted down to the surface of the sea.

There was an outburst of squealing and gibbering. The Esquelians, with quite advanced armaments of their own at the time of Man's first landing on their world, had never, until now, been treated to a demonstration of the more sophisticated Terran weaponry. But they were people who knew that it is not the *bang* of a firearm that kills.

"His Majesty," said Sonya, "demands that he and his people be taken off this island, as soon as possible, if not before." She grinned. "That last is a rather rough translation, but it conveys the essential meaning."

"I am happy to obey," replied Farrell. "But he and his people will have to leave all weapons behind."

There was more argument, and another demonstration of the pinnace's firepower, and then the evacuation was gotten under way.

It had been intended, when the beacon was established on Drarg Island, that the island itself should serve as a base for some future survey party. The rock was honeycombed with chambers and tunnels, providing accommodation, should it be required, for several hundred humans. At the lowest level of all was the power station, fully automated, generating electricity for lights and fans as well as for the Carlotti beacon. The refugees had been able to live there in reasonable comfort—and in considerable squalor. Grimes decided that, as soon as things quietened down, he would get Sonya to inquire as to whether or not the flush toilet had been invented on Esquel. In spite of the excellent ventilation system, the stench was appalling.

But it was necessary for Sonya, at least, to go down into those noisome passages. In spite of the King's protests, Farrell had ordered that no property be lifted from the island; his orders were to save life, and life only. There were tons, literally, of gold and precious stones. There were tons of documents. These latter were, of course, of interest, and Sonya was the only member of *Star Pioneer's* party able to read them. And so, accompanied by Grimes and two junior officers, she went into the room in which the papers had been stacked, skimmed through them, committing those that she thought might be important to microfilm. Now and again, for the benefit of her helpers, she translated. "This," she told them, "seems to be the wages sheet, for the palace staff . . . No less than fourteen cooks, and then fifty odd scullions and such . . . And a food taster . . . And a wine taster . . . And, last of all, and the most highly paid of the lot, a torturer. He got twice what the executioner did . . ." She passed the sheet to the Ensign who was acting as photographer, picked up the next one. "H'm. Interesting. This is the pay list for the Royal Guard. The Kardonar—roughly equivalent to Colonel—got less than the Third Cook . . ."

"This could be just yet another Colonels' Revolt," commented Grimes. He looked at his watch, which had been adjusted to local time. "Midnight. Time we had a break. This stink is getting me down."

"You can say that again, sir," agreed one of the Ensigns.

"All right," said Sonya at last. "I think we've skimmed the cream down here."

"*Cream?*" asked Grimes sardonically.

They made their way up the winding ramps, through the tunnels with their walls of fused rock, came at last to the surface. The plateau was brightly illumined by the floodlights that Farrell's men had set up. The pinnace was away on a shuttle trip, and only a handful of natives remained, huddling together for warmth in the lee of the beacon machinery house. The King, Grimes noted sardonically, was not among them; obviously he was not one of those captains who are last to leave the sinking ship. He was quite content to let Farrell be his stand in.

The Commander walked slowly to Grimes and Sonya. "How's it going, Commander Verrill?" he asked.

"Well enough," she replied. "We've enough evidence to show that this was a thoroughly corrupt regime."

"Physically, as well as in all the other ways," added Grimes. "This fresh air tastes good! How are you off for deodorants aboard *Star Pioneer*, Commander Farrell?"

"Not as well as I'd like to be, Commodore. But I'll put the bulk of the passengers in deep freeze, so it shouldn't be too bad." He looked up at the sky. "It'll be a while before the pinnace is back. Perhaps, sir, you might like a look at some of the surface craft that these people came out to the island in. There's a half dozen of them at the jetty; rather odd-looking contraptions . . ."

"I'd like to," said Grimes.

Farrell led the way to the edge of the plateau, to a stairway, railed at the seaward edge, running down the cliff face to a sheltered inlet in which was a short pier. Moored untidily alongside this were six sizable boats, and there was enough light from the floods at the cliff top for Grimes to make out details before he and the others commenced their descent.

"Yes, I'd like a closer look," he said. "Steam, I'd say, with those funnels. Paddle steamers. Stern-wheelers. Efficient in smooth water, but not in a seaway . . ."

He led the way down the stairs, his feet clattering on the iron treads. He said, "I'd like a trip in one of those, just to see how they handle . . ."

"Out of the question, Commodore," laughed Farrell.

"I know," said Grimes; as Sonya sneered, "You and your bloody seamanship!"

They stepped from the stairway on to the concrete apron, walked across it to the foot of the jetty. Grimes stopped suddenly, said, "Look!"

"At what?" demanded Sonya.

"At that craft with the red funnel . . . That's smoke, and a wisp of steam . . . She's got steam up . . ."

Farrell's laser pistol was out of its holster, and so was Sonya's. Grimes pulled his own Minetta out of his pocket. Cautiously they advanced along the pier, trying to make as little noise as possible. But the natives who erupted from the tunnel at the base of the cliff were completely noiseless on their broad, bare feet and, without having a chance to use their weapons, to utter more than a strangled shout, the three Terrans went down under a wave of evil-smelling, furry bodies.

Grimes recovered slowly. Something hard had

hit him behind the right ear, and he was suffering from a splitting headache. He was, he realized, propped in a sitting posture, his back against a wall of some kind. No, not a wall—a bulkhead. The deck under his buttocks had a gentle rolling motion, and—his head was throbbing in synchronization — there was the steady *chunk, chunk, chunk* of a paddle wheel. Grimes tried to lift his hands to his aching head, discovered that his wrists were bound. So were his ankles.

He heard a familiar voice. "You and your bloody boats!"

He opened his eyes. He turned his head, saw that Sonya was propped up beside him. Her face, in the light of the flickering oil lamp, was pale and drawn. She muttered sardonically, "Welcome aboard, Commodore." Beyond her was Farrell, trussed as were the other two. Nonetheless, he was able to say severely, "This is no time for humor, Commander Verrill."

"But it is, James," she told him sweetly.

"What . . . what happened?" asked Grimes.

"We were jumped, that's what. It seems that a bunch of the loyalists—quote and unquote— suffered a change of mind. They'd sooner take their chances with the rebels than on some strange and terrifying planet . . ."

"Better the devil you know . . ." said Grimes.

"Precisely."

"But where do *we* come in?" asked the Commodore.

"They had to stop us from stopping them from making their getaway," explained Farrell, as though to a mentally retarded child.

"There's more to it than that, James," Sonya told

him. "There's a radio telephone of some kind in the compartment forward of this. Battery powered, I suppose. Not that it matters. Our friends have been arranging a rendezvous with a rebel patrol craft. They've made it plain that they're willing to buy their freedom, their lives. And the price is . . ."

"Us," completed Grimes. "What's the current market value of a full Commander in the Survey Service these days. Farrell? I've no doubt that the rebels will wish to show a profit on the deal."

"And how many laser cannon, complete with instruction manuals, is the Confederacy willing to pay for you, Commodore?" asked Commander Farrell.

"Shut up!" snapped Sonya.

The cabin was silent again, save for the creaking of timbers, the faint thudding of the engines, the chunk chunk, chunk of the paddle. And then, audible in spite of the intervening bulkhead, there was the high-pitched gibbering, in bursts, that, in spite of the strange language, carried the sense of "over," "roger" and all the rest of the standard radio telephone procedure.

Sonya whispered, "As far as I can gather, hearing only one end of the conversation, the patrol craft has sighted this tub that we're in. We've been told to heave to, to await the boarding party . . ." As she spoke, the engines and the paddle wheel slowed, stopped.

There was comparative silence again. Grimes strained his ears for the noise of an approaching stern-wheeler, but in vain. There was, he realized, a new mechanical sound, but it came from overhead. Then it, too, ceased. He was about to speak when there was a loud *thud* from the deck outside, another, and another . . . There was an outbreak of excited gibbering. Shockingly, there were screams, almost human, and three startlingly loud reports.

Abruptly the cabin door slammed open. Two Esquelians came in. There was dark, glistening blood on the fur of one of them, but it did not seem to be his own. They grabbed Grimes by the upper arms, dragged him roughly out on deck, jarring his lower spine painfully on the low sill of the door. They left him there, went back in for Sonya, and then Farrell.

Grimes lay where they had dropped him, looking upward. There were lights there, dim, but bright against the black sky, the sparse, faint stars. As his eyes grew accustomed to the darkness he could make out the great, baggy shape of the dirigible balloon, the comparative rigidity of the gondola slung under it. While he was trying to distinguish more details a rope was slipped about his body and he was hoisted aloft, like a sack of potatoes, by a creakingly complaining hand winch.

"And what now, Commodore? What now?" asked Farrell. By his tone of voice he implied, *You've been in far more irregular situations than me . . .*

Grimes chuckled. "To begin with, we thank all the odd gods of the galaxy that real life so very often copies fiction . . ."

Sonya snarled, "What the hell are you nattering about?"

Grimes chuckled again. "How often, in thrillers, have the baddies tied up the goodies and then carelessly left them with something sharp or abrasive to rub their bonds against . . .?"

"You aren't kidding?" she asked. Then—"And since when have you been a goodie?"

"You'd be surprised . . ." Grimes swore then, briefly and vividly. The sharp edge in the wicker-work of which the airship's car was constructed had nicked his wrist quite painfully. He grunted, "But in fiction it's usually much easier . . ."

He worked on, sawing away with his bound hands, even though his wrists were slippery with blood. He was afraid that one of the airship's crew would come into the cabin to look at the prisoners, but the four Esquelians in the control room at the forward end of the gondola seemed fully occupied with navigation and, presumably, the two who were aft were devoting all their time to the engine of the thing.

Hell! That rope was tough—tougher than the edge against which he was rubbing it, tougher than his skin. Not being able to see what he was doing made it worse. He began to wonder if the first result that he would achieve would be the slitting of an artery. He had never heard of that happening to a fictional hero; but there has to be a first time for everything. Sonya whispered, very real concern in her voice, "John! You're only hurting yourself! Stop it, before you do yourself some real damage!"

"It's dogged as does it!" he replied.

"John! It's not as though they're going to kill us. We're more value to them alive than dead!"

"Could be," he admitted. "But I've heard too many stories about samples from the bodies of

kidnap victims being sent to their potential ran-
somers to speed up negotiations. Our furry
friends strike me as being just the kind of businessmen who'd stoop to such a practice!"

"After the way in which they slaughtered the
crew of the steamboat," put in Farrell, "I'm inclined to agree with the Commodore."

"The vote is two against one," said Grimes. And
then the rope parted.

He brought his hands slowly round in front of
him. There was a lamp in the cabin, a dim, incandescent bulb, and by its feeble light he could see
that his wrists were in a mess. But the blood was
dripping slowly, not spurting. He was in no immediate danger of bleeding to death. And he
could work his fingers, although it seemed a long
time before repeated flexings and wrigglings rendered them capable of use.

He started on the rope about his ankles then. He
muttered something about Chinese bowlines, Por-
tuguese pig knots and unseamanlike bastards in
general. He complained, "I can't find an end to
work on." Then, with an attempt at humor,
"Somebody must have cut it off!"

"Talking of cutting . . ." Sonya's voice had a
sharp edge to it. "Talking of cutting, if you can get
your paws on to the heel of one of my shoes . . ."

Yes, of course, thought Grimes. Sonya was in
uniform, and the uniform of a Survey Service
officer contained quite a few concealed weapons.
Sophisticated captors would soon have found
these, but the Esquelians, to whom clothing was
strange, had yet to learn the strange uses to which
it could be put. Without overmuch contortion
Grimes was able to get his hand around the heel of

his wife's left shoe. He twisted, pulled—and was armed with a short but useful knife. To slash through his remaining bonds was a matter of seconds.

The Esquelian came through into the cabin from forward just as Grimes was getting shakily to his feet. He was wearing a belt, and from this belt depended a holster. He was quick neither on the draw nor the uptake, but the Commodore was half crippled by impeded circulation to his ankles and feet. The native got his pistol—a clumsy revolver—out before Grimes was on him. He fired two shots, each of them too close for comfort, one of them almost parting the Commodore's close-cropped hair.

Grimes's intention—he told himself afterward — had been to disable only, to disarm. It was unfortunate, perhaps, that the airship at that moment dived steeply. The Earthman plunged forward in a staggering run, the knife held before him, stabbing deep into the furry chest. The Esquelian screamed shrilly as a disgustingly warm fluid gushed from his body over Grimes's hands, tumbled to the deck. As he fell, Grimes snatched the pistol. He was more at home with firearms than with bladed weapons.

Surprisingly it fitted his hand as though made for him—but there is parallel evolution of artifacts as well as of life forms. Holding it, almost stumbling over the body of the dead native, Grimes continued his forward progress, coming into the control cabin. It was light in there, wide windows admitting the morning twilight. Gibbering, the three Esquelians deserted their controls. One of them had a pistol, the other two matched knives from a handy rack. Grimes fired, coldly and deliberately. The one with the revolver was his first target, then the nearer of the knife wielders, then his mate. At this range, even with an unfamiliar weapon with a stiff action, a man who in his younger days had been a small arms specialist could hardly miss. Grimes did not, even though he had to shoot one of the airmen twice, even though the last convulsive stab of a broad-bladed knife missed his foot by a millimeter.

He did not know whether or not the gun that he had been using was empty; he did not bother to check. Stooping, he quickly snatched up the one dropped by the dead pilot. It had never been fired. He turned, ran back into the cabin. He was just in time. One of the engineers was just about to bring a heavy spanner crashing down on Sonya's head but was thrown back by the heavy slug that smashed his own skull.

Saying nothing, Grimes carried on aft. The other engineer was dead already, killed by the first wild shot of the encounter. Grimes thought at first that the loud dripping noise was being made by his blood. But it was not. It came from the fuel tank, which had been pierced by a stray bullet. Before Grimes could do anything about it, the steam turbine ground to a halt.

The sun was up. It was a fine morning, calm insofar as those in the disabled airship were concerned, although the whitecaps on the sea were evidence of a strong breeze. To port was the coastline: rugged cliffs, orange beaches, blue green vegetation inland, a sizable city far to the south'ard. It was receding quite rapidly as the

aircraft, broadside on to the offshore wind, scud-
ded to leeward.

The bodies of the airmen had been dragged into
the cabin in which the Terrans had been impris-
oned. Farrell and Sonya had wanted to throw
them overside, but Grimes had talked them out of
it. From his historical researches he knew
something—not much, but something—about
the handling of lighter-than-air flying machines.
Until he had familiarized himself with the controls of this brute, he had no intention of dumping
ballast.

He had succeeded in fixing the ship's position.
In the control room there was a binnacle, and
there were sight vanes on the compass. There
were charts, and presumably the one that had
been in use at the time of the escape was the one
that covered this section of coast. The compass
was strange; it was divided into 400 degrees, not
360. The latitude and longitude divisions on the
chart were strange, too, but it wasn't hard to work
out that the Esquelians worked on 100 minutes to
a degree, 100 degrees to a right angle. There was a
certain lack of logic involved—human beings,
with their five-fingered hands, have a passion for
reckoning things in twelves. The Esquelians,
six-fingered, seemed to prefer reckoning by tens.
Even so, compass, sight vanes and charts were a
fine example of the parallel evolution of artifacts.

There was the compass rose, showing the varia-
tion (Grimes assumed) between True North and
Magnetic North. There was that city to the south.
There were two prominent mountain peaks, the
mountains being shown by what were obviously
contour lines. Grimes laid off his cross bearings,

using a roller, ruler and a crayon. The cocked hat was a very small one. After fifteen minutes he did it again. The line between the two fixes coincided with the estimated wind direction. And where would that take them?

Transferring the position to a small scale chart presented no problems. Neither did extending the course line. The only trouble was that it missed the fly speck that represented Drarg Island by at least twenty miles, regarding one minute on the latitude scale as being a mile. Sonya, recruited in her linguistic capacity, confirmed that the (to Grimes) meaningless squiggles alongside the dot on the chart did translate to "Drarg."

The trouble was that the unlucky shot that had immobilized the airship's engines had also immobilized her generator. There were batteries—but they were flat. (During a revolution quite important matters tend to be neglected.) The radio telephone was, in consequence, quite useless. Had there been power it would have been possible to raise the party on the island, to get them to send the pinnace to pick them up when the aircraft was ditched, or, even, to tow them in.

"At least we're drifting away from the land," said Farrell, looking on the bright side. "I don't think that we should be too popular if we came down ashore." He added, rather petulantly, "Apart from anything else, my orders were that there was to be no intervention . . ." He implied that all the killing had been quite unnecessary.

"Self-defense," Grimes told him. "Not intervention. But if you ever make it back to Lindisfarne Base, James, you can tell the Admiral that it was the wicked Rim Worlders who played hell with a big stick."

"We're all in this, Commodore," said Farrell stiffly. "And this expedition is under *my* command, after all."

"This is no time for inessentials," snapped Sonya. She straightened up from the chart, which she had been studying. "As I see it, they'll sight us from the island, and assume that we're just one of the rebel patrol craft. They might try to intercept us, trying to find out what's happened to us. On the other hand . . ."

"On the other hand," contributed Farrell, "my bright Exec does everything by the book. He'll insist on getting direct orders from Lindisfarne before he does *anything*."

"How does this thing work?" asked Sonya. "Can you *do* anything, John? The way that you were talking earlier you conveyed the impression that you knew something about airships."

Grimes prowled through the control compartment like a big cat in a small cupboard. He complained, "If I had power, I could get someplace. This wheel here, abaft the binnacle, is obviously for steering. This other wheel, with what looks like a crude altimeter above it, will be for the altitude coxswain. The first actuates a vertical steering surface, the rudder. The second actuates the horizontal control surfaces, for aerodynamic lift . . ."

"I thought that in an airship you dumped ballast or valved gas if you wanted to go up or down," said Sonya.

"You can do that, too." Grimes indicated toggled cords that ran down into the control room from above. "These, I *think*, open valves if you pull them. So we can come down." He added grimly, "And we've plenty of ballast to throw out if we want to get upstairs in a hurry."

"Then what's all the bellyaching about?" asked Farrell. "We can control our altitude by either of two ways, and we can steer. If the rudder's not working we can soon fix it."

Grimes looked at him coldly. "Commander Farrell," he said at last, "there is one helluva difference between a free balloon and a dirigible balloon. This brute, with no propulsive power, is a free balloon." He paused while he sought for and found an analogy. "She's like a surface ship, broken down, drifting wherever wind and current take her. The surface ship is part of the current if she has neither sails nor engines. A balloon is part of the wind. We can wiggle our rudder as much as we like and it will have no effect whatsoever . . ." Once again Grimes tried to find a seamanlike analogy—and found something more important. He whispered, "Riverhead . . ."

"Riverhead?" echoed Farrell. "What's that, Commodore?"

"Shut up, James," murmured Sonya. "Let the man think."

Grimes was thinking, and remembering. During his spell of command of Sonya Winneck, on Aquarius, he had been faced with an occasional knotty problem. One such had been the delivery of a consignment of earth-moving machinery to Riverhead, a new port miles inland—equipment which was to be used for the excavation of a swinging basin off the wharfage. The channel was deep enough—but at its upper end it was not as wide as Sonya Winneck was long. However, everything had been arranged nicely. Grimes was to come alongside, discharge his cargo and then, with the aid of a tug, proceed stern first down river until he had room to swing in Carradine's Reach. Unfortunately the tug had suffered a major breakdown so that Sonya Winneck, if she waited for the repairs to be completed, would be at least ten days, idle, alongside at the new wharf.

Grimes had decided not to wait and had successfully dredged down river on the ebb.

He said slowly, "Yes, I think we could dredge..."

"Dredge?" asked Farrell.

Grimes decided that he would explain. People obey orders much more cheerfully when they know that what they are being told to do makes sense. He said, "Yes. I've done it before, but in a surface ship. I had to proceed five miles down a narrow channel, stern first . . ."

"But you had engines?"

"Yes, I had engines, but I didn't use them. I couldn't use them. Very few surface ships, only specialized vessels, will steer when going astern. The rudder, you see, must be in the screw race. You must have that motion of water past and around the rudder from forward to aft . . .

"The dredging technique is simple enough. You put an anchor on the bottom, not enough chain out so that it holds, but just enough so that it acts as a drag, keeping your head up into the current. You're still drifting with the current, of course, but not as fast. So the water is sliding past your rudder in the right direction, from forward, so you can steer after a fashion."

"It works?"

"Yes," said Sonya. "It works all right. But with all the ear bashing I got before and after I was inclined to think that John was the only man who'd ever made it work."

"You can do it here?" asked Farrell.

"I think so. It's worth trying."

The hand winch was aft, in the engine compartment. To dismount it would have taken too much time, so Grimes had the rope fall run off it, brought forward and coiled down in the control room. To its end he made fast four large canvas buckets; what they had been used for he did not know, nor ever did know, but they formed an ideal drogue. Farrell, using the spanner that had been the dead engineer's weapon, smashed outward the forward window. It was glass, and not heavy enough to offer much resistance. Grimes told him to make sure that there were no jagged pieces left on the sill to cut the dragline. Then, carefully, he lowered his cluster of buckets down toward the water. The line was not long enough to reach.

Carefully Grimes belayed it to the base of the binnacle, which fitting seemed to be securely mounted. He went back forward, looked out and down. He called back, over his shoulder, "We have to valve gas . . ."

"Which control?" asked Sonya.

"Oh, the middle one, I suppose . . ."

That made sense, he thought. One of the others might have an effect on the airship's trim, or give it a heavy list to port or starboard. *And so,* he told himself, *might this one.*

He was aware of a hissing noise coming from overhead. The airship was dropping rapidly, too rapidly. "That will do!" he ordered sharply.

"The bloody thing's stuck!" he heard Sonya call. Then, "I've got it clear!"

The airship was still falling, and the drogue made its first contact with the waves—close now, too close below—skipping over them. The line tightened with a jerk and the flimsy structure of the gondola creaked in protest. The ship came round head to wind, and an icy gale swept through the broken window. The ship bounced upward and there was a brief period of relative calm, sagged, and once again was subjected to the atmospheric turbulence.

"Ballast!" gasped Grimes, clinging desperately to the sill. It seemed a long time before anything happened, and then the ship soared, lifting the drogue well clear of the water.

"Got rid . . . of one . . . of our late friends . . ." gasped Farrell.

"Justifiable, in the circumstances," conceded Grimes grudgingly. "But before we go any further we have to rig a windscreen . . . I saw some canvas, or what looks like canvas, aft . . ."

"How will you keep a lookout?" asked Farrell.

"The lookout will be kept astern, from the engine compartment. That's the way that we shall be going. Now give me a hand to get this hole plugged."

They got the canvas over the empty window frame, lashed it and, with a hammer and nails from the engineroom tool kit, tacked it into place. Grimes hoped that it would hold. He discovered that he could see the surface of the sea quite well from the side windows, so had no worries on that score. Before doing anything else he retrieved the crumpled chart from the corner into which it had blown, spread it out on the desk, made an estimation of the drift since the last observed position, laid off a course for Drarg Island. Once he had the ship under control he would steer a reciprocal of this course, send Sonya right aft to keep a lookout astern, with Farrell stationed amidships to relay information and orders. First of all, however, there was more juggling to be done with gas and ballast.

Grimes descended cautiously, calling instructions to Sonya as he watched the white-crested waves coming up to meet him. The drogue touched surface—and still the ship fell, jerkily, until the buckets bit and held, sinking as they filled. There was a vile draft in the control room as the wind whistled through chinks in the makeshift windshield.

"All right," ordered Grimes. "Man the lookout!"

The others scrambled aft, while the Commodore took the wheel. He knew that he would have to keep the lubber's line steady on a figure that looked like a misshapen, convoluted 7, saw that the ship's head was all of twenty degrees to starboard off this heading. He applied port rudder, was surprised as well as pleased when she came round easily. He risked a sidewise glance at the altimeter. The needle was steady enough—but it could not possibly drop much lower. The instrument had not been designed for wave hopping.

He yelled, hoping that Farrell would be able to hear him, "If you think we're getting too low, dump some more ballast!"

"Will do!" came the reply.

He concentrated on his steering. It was not as easy as he thought it would be. Now and again he had taken the wheel of *Sonya Winneck*, just to get the feel of her—but her wheel could be put over with one finger, all the real work being done by the powerful steering motors aft. Here it was a case of Armstrong Patent.

But he kept the lubber's line on the course, his arms aching, his legs trembling, his clothing soaked with perspiration in spite of the freezing draft. He wished that he knew what speed the airship was making. He wanted a drink, badly, and thought longingly of ice-cold water. He wanted a smoke, and was tempted. He thought that the airship was helium filled, was almost certain that she was helium filled, but dared take no risks. But the stem of his cold, empty pipe between his teeth was some small comfort.

Faintly he heard Sonya call out something.

Farrell echoed her. "Land, ho!"

"Where away?" yelled Grimes over his shoulder, his pipe clattering unheeded to the deck.

"Astern! To port! About fifteen degrees!"

Carefully, Grimes brought the ship round to the new course. She held it, almost without attention on his part. There must, he thought, have been a shift of wind.

"As she goes!" came the hail. "Steady as she goes!"

"Steady," grunted Grimes. "Steady . . ."

How much longer? He concentrated on his steering, on the swaying compass card, on the outlandish numerals that seemed to writhe as he watched them. *How much longer?*

He heard Sonya scream, "We're coming in fast! Too low! The cliffs!"

"Ballast!" yelled Grimes.

Farrell had not waited for the order, already had

the trap in the cabin deck open, was pushing out another of the dead Esquelians, then another. The deck lifted under Grimes's feet, lifted and tilted, throwing him forward onto his now useless wheel. A violent jerk flung him aft, breaking his grip on the spokes.

After what seemed a very long time he tried to get to his feet. Suddenly Sonya was with him, helping him up, supporting him in his uphill scramble toward the stern of the ship, over decking that canted and swayed uneasily. They stumbled over the dead bodies, skirting the open hatch. Grimes was surprised to see bare rock only a foot or so below the aperture. They came to the engineroom, jumped down through the door to the ground. It was only a short drop.

"We were lucky," said Grimes, assessing the situation. The airship had barely cleared the cliff edge, had been brought up short by its dragline a few feet short of the Carlotti beacon.

"Bloody lucky!" Farrell said. "Some Execs would have opened fire first and waited for orders afterward . . ."

His Executive Officer flushed. "Well, sir, I thought it might be you." He added, tactlessly, "After all, we've heard so many stories about Commodore Grimes . . ."

Farrell was generous. He said, "Excellent airmanship, Commodore."

"Seamanship," corrected Grimes huffily.

Sonya laughed—but it was with him, not at him.

The voyage between Esquel and Tallis, where the King and his entourage were disembarked, was not a pleasant one. Insofar as the Terrans were concerned, the Esquelians stank. Insofar as the Esquelians were concerned, the Terrans stank— and that verb could be used both literally and metaphorically. Commander Farrell thought, oddly enough, that the King should be humbly grateful. The King, not so oddly, was of the opinion that he had been let down, badly, by his allies. Grimes, on one occasion when he allowed himself to be drawn into an argument, made himself unpopular with both sides by saying that the universe would be a far happier place if people did not permit political expediency to influence their choice of friends.

But at last, and none too soon, *Star Pioneer* dropped gently down to her berth between the marker beacons at Tallisport, and the ramp was extended, and, gibbering dejectedly, the Esquelians filed down it to be received by the Terran High Commissioner.

Farrell, watching from a control room viewport, turned to Grimes and Sonya. He said thankfully, "My first order will be 'Clean ship.' And there'll be no shore leave for anybody until it's done."

"And don't economize on the disinfectant, Jimmy," Sonya told him.

THE RUB

Slowly Grimes awakened from his nightmare.

It had been so real, too real, and the worst part of it was always the deep sense of loss. There was that shocking contrast between the dreary life that he was living (in the dream) and the rich and full life that he somehow knew that he should be living. There was his wife—that drab, unimaginative woman with her irritating mannerisms—and that memory of somebody else, somebody whom he had never met, never would meet, somebody elegant and slim, somebody with whom he had far more in common than just the physical side of marriage, somebody who knew books and music and the visual arts and yet evinced a deep appreciation of the peculiar psychology of the spaceman.

Slowly Grimes awakened.

Slowly he realized that he was not in his bedroom in the Base Commander's quarters on Zetland. He listened to the small, comforting noises: the irregular throbbing of the inertial drive, the sobbing of pumps, the soughing of the ventilation syste, the thin, high whine of the Mannschenn Drive unit. And there was the soft, steady breathing of the woman in the bed with him. (That other one snored.)

But—such was the impression that his dream had made upon him—he had to be sure. (All cats are gray in the dark.) Without too much fumbling, he found the stud of the light switch on his side of the bed. His reading lamp came on. Its light was soft, subdued—but it was enough to wake Sonya.

She looked up at him irritably, her lean face framed by the auburn hair that somehow retained its neatness, its sleekness, even after sleep. She demanded sharply, "What is it, John?"

He said, "I'm sorry. Sorry I woke you, that is. But I had to be sure."

Her face and voice immediately softened. "That dream of yours again?"

"Yes. The worst part of it is knowing that you are somewhere, somewhen, but that I shall never meet you."

"But you did." She laughed with him, not at him. "And that's your bad luck."

"My good luck," he corrected.

"*Our* good luck."

"I suppose that we could have done worse . . ." he admitted.

Grimes was awakened again by the soft chiming of the alarm. From his side of the bed he could reach the service hatch in the bulkhead. He opened it, revealing the tray with its silver coffee service.

"The usual?" he asked Sonya, who was making a lazy attempt to sit up in bed.

"Yes, John. You should know by this time."

Grimes poured a cup for his wife—black, unsweetened—then one for himself. He liked sugar, rather too much of it, and cream.

"I shall be rather sorry when this voyage is over," said Sonya. "Jimmy is doing us well. We shouldn't be pampered like this in an *Alpha* Class liner."

"After all, I am a Commodore," said Grimes smugly.

"Not in the Survey Service, you aren't," Sonya told him.

In that dream, that recurring nightmare, Grimes was still an officer in the Federation's Survey Service. But he had never gotten past Commander, and never would. He was passing his days, and would end his days, as commanding officer of an unimportant base on a world that somebody had once described as a planetwide lower middle class suburb.

"Perhaps not," Grimes admitted, "but I pile on enough Gees to be accorded V.I.P. treatment aboard a Survey Service ship."

"You do? I was under the impression that it was because of me that Jimmy let us have the V.I.P. suite."

"Not you. You're only a mere Commander, and on the Reserve list at that."

"Don't be so bloody rank conscious!"

She took a swipe at him with her pillow. Grimes cursed as hot coffee splashed onto his bare chest. Then, "I don't know what your precious Jimmy will think when he sees the mess on the sheets."

"He'll not see it—and his laundrobot won't worry about it. Pour yourself some more coffee, and I'll use the bathroom while you're drinking it." Then, as she slid out of the bed, "And go easy on the sugar. You're getting a paunch . . ."

Grimes remembered the fat and slovenly Commander of Zetland Base.

Commander James Farrell, the Captain of *Star Pioneer*, prided himself on running a taut ship. Attendance at every meal was mandatory for his officers. As he and Sonya took their seats at the captain's table, Grimes wondered how Farrell would cope with the reluctance of middle watch keepers aboard merchant vessels to appear at breakfast.

All of *Star Pioneer's* officers were here, in their places, except for those actually on duty. Smartly uniformed messgirls circulated among the tables, taking orders, bringing dishes. Farrell sat, of course, at the head of his own table, with Sonya to his right and Grimes to his left. At the foot of the table was Lieutenant Commander Malleson, the Senior Engineering Officer. There was little to distinguish him from his captain but the badges of rank. There was little to distinguish any of the officers one from the other. They were all tall young men, all with close-cropped hair, all with standardized good looks, each and every one of them a refugee from a Survey Service recruiting poster. *In my young days*, thought Grimes, *there was room for individuality* . . . He smiled to himself. *And where did it get me? Oh you bloody tee, that's where.*

"What's the joke, John?" asked Sonya. "Share it, please."

Grimes's prominent ears reddened. "Just a thought, dear." He was saved by a messgirl, who presented the menu to him. "Nathia juice, please. Ham and eggs—sunny-side up—to follow, with just a hint of French fries. And coffee."

"You keep a good table, Jimmy," Sonya said to Farrell. Then, looking at her husband, "Rather too good, perhaps."

"I'm afraid, Sonya," Farrell told her, "that our meals from now on will be rather lacking in variety. It seems that our Esquelian passengers brought some local virus aboard with 'em. The biologists in the first survey expeditions found nothing at all on Esquel in any way dangerous to human life, so perhaps we didn't take the precautions we should have done when we embarked the King and his followers. Even so, while they were on board their excretory matter was excluded from the ship's closed ecology. But after they were disembarked on Tallis the plumbing wasn't properly disinfected . . ."

Not a very suitable topic of conversation for the breakfast table, thought Grimes, sipping his fruit juice.

"So?" asked Sonya interestedly.

"So there's been a plague running its course in the 'farm.' It's just been the tissue culture vats that have been affected, luckily. We could make do indefinitely on yeasts and algae—but who wants to?" He grinned at Grimes, who was lifting a forkload of yolk-coated ham to his mouth. "Who wants to?"

"Not me, Captain," admitted Grimes.

"Or me, Commodore. The beef's dead, and the pork, and the chicken. The quack says that the lamb's not fit for human consumption. So far the mutton seems to be unaffected, but we can't even be sure of that."

"You'll be able to stock up when we get to Port Forlorn," said Grimes.

"That's a long way off." Farrell looked steadily at Grimes as he buttered a piece of toast. "I've a job for you, Commodore."

"A job for me, Commander Farrell?"

"Yes, you, Commodore Grimes. By virtue of your rank you represent the Rim Worlds Confederacy aboard this vessel. Kinsolving's Planet, although no longer colonized, is one of the Rim Worlds. I want to put down there."

"Why?" asked Grimes.

"Correct me if I'm wrong, Commodore, but I understand that the original settlers introduced Earth-type flora and fauna, some of which have not only survived, but flourished. It's not the flora that I'm interested in, of course—but I've heard that there are the descendants of the original rabbits, pigs, cattle and hens running wild there."

"No cattle," Grimes told him. "And no hens. Probably the pigs did for 'em before they could become established."

"Rabbit's a good substitute for chickens," said Farrell.

"Jimmy," reproved Sonya, "I do believe that you like your tummy."

"I do, Sonya, I do," said the young man.

"And so do I," said Lieutenant Commander Malleson, who until now had been eating in dedicated silence.

"But I don't like Kinsolving," grumbled Grimes. "And, in any case, we shall have to get permission to land."

"You will get it, John," said Sonya firmly.

Later that ship's morning, Farrell discussed the proposed landing on Kinsolving with Grimes and Sonya.

"Frankly," he told them, "I'm glad of an excuse to visit the planet. Not so long ago the Survey Service released a report on the three expeditions, starting off with that odd wet paint affair . . ."

"That was over a hundred and fifty years ago," said Grimes.

"Yes. I know. And I know, too, that you've been twice to Kinsolving—the first time as an observer with the neo-Calvinists, the second time in command of your own show . . ."

"And both times," admitted Grimes, "I was scared. Badly."

"You don't frighten easily. Commodore, as well I know. But what actually did happen? The official reports that have been released to the likes of us don't give much away. It was hinted—no more, just hinted—that the neo-Calvinists tried to call up the God of the Old Testament, and raised the entire Greek pantheon instead. And you, sir, attempted to repeat the experiment, and got tangled with a Mephistopheles, straight out of Gounod's *Faust*."

"Cutting extraneous cackle," said Grimes, "that's just what did happen."

"What I'm getting at, Commodore, is this. Were your experiences objective or subjective?"

"That first time, Commander, the neo-Calvinists' ship, *Piety*, was destroyed, as well as her pinnaces. Their leaders—the Presbyter, the Rector, the Deaconess and thirteen others, men and women—completely vanished. That was objective enough for anybody. The second time—*I* vanished."

"I can vouch for that," stated Sonya.

"But you came back. Obviously."

"More by luck than judgment." Grimes laughed, without humor. "When you do a deal with the Devil it's as well to read the small print."

"But at no time was there any actual physical harm to anybody."

"There could have been. And we don't know what happened to the neo-Calvinist boss cockies . . ."

"Probably being converted to hedonism on Mount Olympus," said Sonya.

"But we don't know."

Farrell grinned. "And aren't those very words a challenge to any officer in the Survey Service? You used to be one of us yourself, sir, and Sonya is still on our Reserve list. Kinsolving is almost directly on the track from Tallis to Lorn. I have a perfectly valid excuse to make a landing. And even in these decadent days . . ." He grinned again at the Commodore . . . "my Lords Commissioners do not discourage initiative and zeal on the part of their captains."

Reluctantly, Grimes grinned back. It was becoming evident that Farrell possessed depths of character not apparent on first acquaintance. True, he worked by the book—and had Grimes done so he would have risen to the rank of Admiral in the Survey Service—but he was also capable of reading between the lines. A deviation from his original cruise pattern—the evacuation of the King and his supporters from Esquel—had brought him to within easy reach of Kinsolving; he was making the most of the new circumstances. Fleetingly Grimes wondered if the destruction of the ship's fresh meat supply had been intentional rather than accidental, but dismissed the thought. Not even he, Grimes, had ever done a thing like that.

"Later," said Farrell, "if it's all right with you, sir, we'll go over the official reports, and you can fill in the gaps. But what is it that makes Kinsolving the way it is?"

"Your guess is as good as anybody's, Commander. It's just that the atmosphere is . . . odd. Psychologically odd, not chemically or physically. A terrifying queerness. A sense of impending doom . . . Kinsolving was settled at the same time as the other Rim Worlds. Physically speaking, it's a far more desirable piece of real estate than any of them. But the colonists lost heart. Their suicide rate rose to an abnormal level. Their mental institutions were soon overcrowded. And so on. So they pulled out.

"The reason for it all? There have been many theories. One of the latest is that the Kinsolving system lies at some intersection of . . . of stress lines. Stress lines in *what*? Don't ask me. But the very fabric of the continuum is thin, ragged, and the dividing lines between *then* and *now*, *here* and *there*, *what is* and *what might be* are virtually nonexistent . . ."

"Quite a place," commented Farrell. "But you're willing to visit it a third time, sir?"

"Yes," agreed Grimes after a long pause. "But I'm not prepared to make a third attempt at awakening ancient deities from their well-earned rest. In any case, we lack the . . . I suppose you could call her the medium. She's on Lorn, and even if she were here I doubt if she'd play."

"Good. I'll adjust trajectory for Kinsolving, and then we'll send Carlottigrams to our respective lords and masters requesting permission to land. I don't think that they'll turn it down."

"Unfortunately," said Grimes, but the faint smile that lightened his craggy features belied the word.

Slowly, cautiously Farrell eased *Star Pioneer* down to the sunlit hemisphere of Kinsolving, to a position a little to the west of the morning terminator. Grimes had advised a landing at the site used by the Confederacy's *Rim Sword* and, later, by his own *Faraway Quest*. The destruction of the neo-Calvinists' *Piety* had made the spaceport unusable. This landing place was hard by the deserted city of Enderston, on the shore of the Darkling Tarn. It had been the Sports Stadium.

Conditions were ideal for the landing. The sounding rockets, fired when the ship was descending through the first tenuous fringes of the atmosphere, had revealed a remarkable absence of turbulence. The parachute flares discharged by them at varying altitudes were falling straight down, each trailing its long, unwavering streamer of white smoke.

Grimes and Sonya were in the control room. "There's Enderston," the Commodore said, "on the east bank of the Weary River. We can't see much from this altitude; everything's overgrown. That's the Darkling Tarn . . ." With a ruler that he had picked up he pointed to the amoebalike glimmer of water among the dull green that now was showing up clearly on the big approach screen. "You can't miss it. That fairly well-defined oval of paler green is the Stadium . . ."

The inertial drive throbbed more loudly as Farrell made minor adjustments and then, when the Stadium was in the exact center of the screen, settled down again to its almost inaudible muttering.

At Farrell's curt order they all went to their acceleration chairs, strapped themselves in. Grimes, with the others, watched the expanding picture on the screen. It was all so familiar, too familiar, even to the minor brush fire started by the last of the parachute flares. And, as on the previous two occasions, there was the feeling that supernatural forces were mustering to resist the landing of the ship, to destroy her and all aboard her.

He looked at Farrell. The young Captain's face was pale, strained—and this, after all, was a setting down in almost ideal conditions. There were not, it is true, any ground approach aids. But neither was there wind, or cloud, or clear air turbulence. And Survey Service officers were trained to bring their ships down on worlds with no spaceport facilities.

So Farrell was feeling it too. The knowledge made Grimes less unhappy. *Now you begin to know what it's like, Jimmy boy,* he thought smugly.

But she was down at last.

There was almost no shock at all, and only an almost inaudible complaint from the ship's structure, and a faint sighing of shock absorbers as the great mass of the vessel settled in the cradle of her tripodal landing gear. She was down. "Secure main engines," ordered Farrell at last. Telegraph bells jangled sharply, and the inertial drive generators muttered to themselves and then were still. She was down, and the silence was intensified by the soft soughing of the ventilation fans.

Grimes swiveled in his chair, gazed out through the viewport toward the distant mountain peak, the black, truncated cone hard and sharp against the pale blue sky. "Sinai," Presbyter Cannon had named it. "Olympus," Grimes had labeled it on his new charts of the planetary surface. But that name was no longer apt. On its summit the neo-Calvinists had attempted to invoke Jehovah—and Zeus had answered their call. On its summit Grimes had tried to invoke the gods of the Greek pantheon—and had been snatched into an oddly peopled Limbo by Mephistopheles himself.

This time on Kinsolving the Commodore was going to be cautious. Wild horses—assuming that there were any on this planet, and assuming that they should be possessed by such a strange ambition—would not be able to drag him up to the top of the mountain.

Nonetheless, Grimes did revisit the mountaintop, taken there by the tamed horsepower of *Star Pioneer's* pinnace rather than by wild horses. Nothing happened. Nothing could happen unless Clarisse, descendant of the long dead artist-magicians, was there to make it happen. There was nothing to see, except the view. All that remained of the two disastrous experiments was a weathered spattering of pigments where the witch girl's easel had stood.

Everybody visited the famous caves, of course, and stared at and photographed the rock paintings, the startlingly lifelike depiction of beasts and their hunters. And the paint was dry, and the paintings were old, even though some faint hint of their original magic still lingered.

Even so, this was an uneasy world. Men and women never walked alone, were always conscious of something lurking in the greenery, in the ruins. Farrell, reluctant as he was to break the Survey Service's uniform regulations, issued strict orders that everybody ashore on any business whatsoever was to wear a bright, scarlet jacket over his other clothing. This was after two hunting parties had opened fire upon each other; luckily nobody was killed, but four men and three women would be in the sick bay for days with bullet wounds.

Grimes said to Farrell, "Don't you think it's time that we were lifting ship, Captain?"

"Not for a while, Commodore. We have to be sure that the new tissue cultures will be successful."

"That's just an excuse."

"All right, it's just an excuse."

"You're waiting for something to happen."

"Yes. Damn it all, Commodore, this sensation of brooding menace is getting me down; it's getting all of us down. But I want to have something definite to report to my Lords Commissioners . . ."

"Don't pay too high a price for that fourth ring on your sleeve, James."

"It's more than promotion that's at stake, sir, although I shall welcome it. It's just that I hate being up against an enemy that I can't see, can't touch. It's just that I want to accomplish something. It's just that I don't want to go slinking off like a dog with his tail between his legs."

"The original colony did just that."

"But they . . ." Farrell stopped abruptly.

"I'll finish it for you, James. But they were only civilians. They weren't wearing the Survey Service badge on their caps, Survey Service braid on their sleeves or shoulders. They weren't disciplined. And how long do you think your ship's discipline is going to stand up to the strain, gold braid and brass buttons notwithstanding?"

"For long enough."

Sonya broke in. "This is Jimmy's show, John. He makes the decisions. And I agree with him that we should stay on Kinsolving until we have something to show for our visit."

"Thank you, Sonya," said Farrell. Then, "You must excuse me. I have things to attend to."

When the young man had left their cabin, Sonya turned to her husband. "You're getting too old and cautious, John. Or are you sulking because you're not running things?"

"I don't like this world, my dear. I've reasons not to."

"You're letting it get you down. You look as though you haven't slept for a week."

"I haven't. Not to speak of."

"Why didn't you let me know?"

"It's so damned silly. It's that bloody nightmare of mine—you know the one. Every time I shut my eyes it recurs."

"You should have told me."

"I should have done." He got slowly to his feet. "Probably some good, healthy exercise will make me sleep better. A long walk . . ."

"I'll come with you."

She fetched from the wardrobe the scarlet jackets that they had been given. Grimes took from a drawer his deadly little Minetti, put it in one pocket, a spare clip of cartridges in the other. Heavier handguns and miniaturized transceivers they would collect from the duty officers at the airlock.

Within a few minutes they were walking down the ramp to the path that had been hacked and burned and trodden through the encroaching greenery, the trail that led to the ruined city.

It was early afternoon. The sun was still high in the pale sky, but the breeze, what there was of it, was chilly. And the shadows, surely, were darker here than on any other world that Grimes had ever visited, and seemed to possess a life of their own. But that was only imagination.

They walked steadily but carefully, watching where they put their feet, avoiding the vines and brambles that seemed deliberately to try to trip them. On either side of the rough track the vegetation was locked in silent, bitter warfare: indigenous trees and shrubs, importations from Earth and other worlds, and parasites upon parasites. In spite of the overly luxuriant growth the overweening impression was of death rather than of life, and the most readily identifiable scent on the chill air was that of decay.

They came to the outskirts of the city, picking their way over the tilted slabs of concrete, thrust up and aside by root and trunk, that had once been a road. Once the buildings between which it ran had been drably utilitarian; now the madly proliferating and destructive ivy clothed them in somber, Gothic splendor. An abandoned ground car, the glass of its headlights by some freak of circumstances unobscured, glared at them like a crouching, green-furred beast.

Grimes tried to imagine what this place had been like before its evacuation. Probably it had been very similar to any sizable town on Lorn, or Faraway, Ultimo or Thule—architecturally. But there had been one difference, and a very important one. There had been the uncanny atmosphere, that omnipresent premonition of . . . Of . . . ? That fear of the cold and the dark, of the Ultimate Night. Other cities on other worlds had their haunted houses; here every house had been haunted.

He said, "The sooner young Farrell lifts ship off this deserted graveyard, the better."

"At least it's not raining," Sonya told him, with an attempt at cheerfulness.

"Thank the odd gods of the galaxy for one small mercy," grumbled Grimes.

"Talking of odd gods . . ." she said.

"What about them?"

"Sally Veerhausen, the Biochemist, told me that there's a very odd church on a side street that runs off the main drag."

"Oh?"

"Yes. It's to the right, and it's little more than an alley, and you turn into it just before you get to a tall tower with a latticework radio mast still standing on top of it . . ."

"That it there, to the right?"

"Must be. Shall we investigate?"

"What is there to investigate?" he asked.

"Nothing, probably. But I seem to recall a period when you exhibited a passion for what you referred to as freak religions. This could be one to add to your collection."

"I doubt it," he told her.

But after a few minutes' careful walking they were turning off the main street, making their way along an alley between walls overgrown with the ubiquitous ivy that had been brought to the world by some long dead, homesick colonist.

The church was there.

It was only a small building, a masonry cube with its angles somehow and subtly wrong. And it was different from its neighbors. Perhaps the stone, natural or synthetic, from which it had been constructed possessed some quality, physical or chemical, lacking in the building materials in more general use. Its dull gray facade was unmarked by creeper, lichen or moss. Its door, gray like the walls, but of metal, was uncorroded. Over the plain rectangle of the entrance were the embossed letters in some matte black substance— TEMPLE OF THE PRINCIPLE.

Grimes snorted almost inaudibly. Then, "What Principle?" he demanded. "There have been so many."

"Perhaps," said Sonya seriously, "the greatest and most mysterious one of all."

"The Golden Way? The greatest, I admit . . ."

"No. Sally got her paws onto such records as still exist—the vaults in the city hall kept their contents quite intact—and found out that there was a cult here that worshipped, or tried to worship, the Uncertainty Principle . . ."

"Mphm. Could have been quite a suitable religion for this world. Inexplicable forces playing hell with anything and everything, so, if you can't lick 'em, join 'em."

"Or get the hell out."

"Or get the hell out. But—who knows?—this freak religion might just have worked. Shall we go inside?"

"Why not?"

The door opened easily, too easily. It was almost as though they had been expected. But this, Grimes told himself, was absurd thinking. The officers from the ship who had found this place must have oiled the hinges. And had they done something about the lighting system too? It should have been dark inside the huge, windowless room, but it was not. The gray, subtly shifting twilight was worse than darkness would have been. It accentuated the wrongness of the angles where wall met wall, ceiling and floor. It seemed to concentrate, in a formless blob of pallid luminescence, over the coffin-shaped altar that stood almost in the middle of the oddly lopsided hall. *Almost* in the middle . . . Its positioning was in keeping with the rest of the warped geometrics of this place.

"I don't like it," said Grimes. "I don't like it at all."

"Neither do I," whispered Sonya.

Yet neither of them made any attempt to retreat to the comparative light and warmth and sanity of the alley outside.

"What rites did they practice?" whispered the Commodore. "What prayers did they chant? And to *what*?"

"I'd rather not find out."

But still they did not withdraw, still, hand in hand, they advanced slowly toward the black altar, the coffin-shaped . . . coffin-shaped? No. Its planes and angles shifted. It was more of a cube. It was more than a cube. It was . . .

Grimes, knew, suddenly, what it was. It was a tesseract. And he knew, too, that he should never have come again to this world. Twice he had visited Kinsolving before, and on the second occasion had become more deeply involved than on the first. Whatever the forces were that ruled this planet, he was becoming more and more attuned to them.

And this was the third time.

"John!" he heard Sonya's distant voice. "John!"

He tightened the grasp of his right hand, but the warmth of hers was no longer within it.

"John . . ."

It was no more than a fading whisper.

"John . . ."

"Grmph . . ." He didn't want to wake up. Full awareness would mean maximum appreciation of his nagging headache. His eyes were gummed shut, and he had the impression that small and noisome animals had fought and done other things inside his mouth.

"John!"

Blast the woman, he thought.

"JOHN!" She was shaking him now.

He flailed out blindly, felt one fist connect with something soft, heard a startled gasp of pain. "Never touch an officer," he enunciated thickly. " 'Gainst regulations."

"You . . . You *hit* me. You brute."

"Own fault."

"Wake up, damn you!"

He got his eyes open somehow, stared blearily at the plump, faded woman in the shabby robe who was staring down at him with distaste.

Who are you? he demanded silently. *Who are you?* The memory of someone slim, sleek and elegant persisted in his befuddled brain. Then—*Where am I? Who am I?*

"You've got a job to do," the woman told him in a voice that was an unpleasant whine. "You'd better get your stinking carcass out of that bed and start doing it. I like to go on eating, even if you don't."

A starvation diet would do you the world of good, he thought. He said, "Coffee."

"Coffee *what?* Where's your manners?"

"Coffee, please."

She left him then, and he rolled out of the rumpled bed. He looked down with distaste at his sagging drinker's paunch, then got to his feet and walked unsteadily to the bathroom. He was surprised at the weakness he felt, the near nausea, the protests of a body allowed to degenerate into a state of general unfitness. It all seemed worng. Surely he had always taken pride in maintaining himself in good condition.

He stood under the shower, and gradually the mists cleared from his brain. In a little while John Grimes, Officer Commanding the Zetland Base, passed over Commander, would be ready to begin his dreary day.

Nobody quite knew why the Federation maintained a base on Zetland. Once, a long time ago, the planet had been strategically important when it seemed possible that the Federation and the expanding Shaara Empire might clash, but the Treaty of Danzenorg, respected by both cultures, had neatly parceled up the entire galaxy into spheres of influence. True, there were other spacefaring races who belonged neither to the Federation nor the Empire, but their planets were many, many light years distant from Zetland and their trade routes passed nowhere near this world.

There was a base on Zetland. There always had been one; there always would be one. The taxpayer had bottomless pockets. There were spaceport facilities, of a sort. There were repair facilities, also of a sort. There was a Carlotti beacon, which was an absolutely inessential part of the navigational network in this sector of space, and relay station. The whole setup, such as it was, could have been run efficiently by a lieutenant junior grade, with a handful of petty officers and ratings. But a base commander must have scrambled egg on the peak of his cap. The Commander of a base like Zetland is almost invariably on the way up or the way down.

Commander John Grimes was not on the way up.

Nonetheless, he did have that scrambled egg on the peak of his cap. There was also a smear of egg yolk at the corner of his mouth, and a spatter of it on the lapel of his jacket. His enlisted woman driver, waiting for him in the ground car outside the Base Commander's bungalow, looked at him with some distaste—apart from anything else, she had been there for all of twenty minutes—clambered reluctantly out of the vehicle (her legs, noted Grimes, were too thick and more than a little hairy) and threw him a salute that almost, but not quite, qualified as "dumb insolence." Grimes returned it contemptuously. She opened the rear door of the car for him. He got in, thanking her as an afterthought, sagged into the seat. She got back behind the controls, clumsily stirred and prodded the machine into reluctant motion.

It was only a short drive to the military spaceport. The Commander thought, as he had thought many times before, that he should walk to his office rather than ride; the exercise would do him good. But somehow he never felt up to it. He stared unseeingly through the dirty windows. The view was as it always was: flat fields with an occasional low farmhouse, uninteresting machines trudging through the dirt on their caterpillar treads sowing or reaping or fertilizing the proteinuts which were Zetland's only export—and that only to worlds too poverty-stricken to send anything worthwhile in exchange. Ahead was the base—administration buildings, barracks, control tower and the lopsided ellipsoid that was the Carlotti beacon, slowly rotating.

The car rolled over the concrete apron, jerked to a halt outside the control tower. The girl driver got out clumsily, opened the Commander's door. Grimes got out, muttered, " 'K you."

She replied sweetly, "It was a pleasure, sir."

Saucy bitch, thought Grimes sourly.

He did not take the elevator to his office on the top level of the tower. Thoughts about his lack of physical fitness had been nagging him all morning. He used the stairs, taking them two at a time at first. He soon had to abandon this practice. By the time that he reached the door with BASE COMMANDER on it in tarnished gilt lettering he was perspiring and out of breath and his heart was hammering uncomfortably.

Ensign Mavis Davis, his secretary, got up from her desk as he entered the office. She was a tall woman, and very plain, and old for her junior rank. She was also highly efficient, and was one of the few persons on this world whom Grimes liked.

"Good morning, Commander," she greeted him, a little too brightly.

"What's good about it?" He scaled his cap in the general direction of its peg, missed as usual. "Oh, well, it's the only one we've got."

She said, holding out a message flimsy, "This came in a few minutes ago . . ."

"Have we declared war on somebody?"

She frowned at him. She was too essentially good a person to regard war as a joking matter. "No. It's from *Draconis*. She's making an unscheduled call here . . ."

A Constellation Class cruiser, thought Grimes. *Just what I need* . . . He asked, "When is she due?"

"Eleven hundred hours this morning."

"*What?*" Grimes managed a grin. "The fleet's in port, or almost in port, and not a whore in the house washed . . ."

"That's not funny, Commander," she said reprovingly.

"Indeed it's not, Mavis," he agreed. Indeed it wasn't. He thought of the huge cruiser, with all her spit and polish, and thought of his own, slovenly, planet-based command, with its cracked, peeling paint, with dusty surfaces everywhere, with equipment only just working after a fashion, with personnel looking as though they had slept in their uniforms—as many of them, all too probably, had. He groaned, went to the robot librarian's console, switched on. "Fleet List," he said.

"*Draconis*. Name of commanding officer."

"Yes, sir." The mechanical voice was tinny, absolutely unhuman. "Captain Francis Delamere, O.G.C., D.C.O., F.M.H. . . ." Grimes switched off.

Frankly Delamere, he thought. *A lieutenant when I was a two and a half ringer. A real Space Scout, and without the brains to come in out of the rain, but a stickler for regulations. And now he's a four ring captain . . .*

"John . . ." There was sympathy in the Ensign's voice.

"Yes, Mavis?"

She was abruptly businesslike. "We haven't much time, but I issued orders in your name to get the place cleaned up a bit. And the Ground Control approach crew are at their stations, and the beacons should be in position by now . . ."

Grimes went to the wide window. "Yes," he said, looking down at the triangle of intensely bright red lights that had been set out on the gray concrete of the apron, "they are. Thank you."

"Do you wish to monitor G.C.A.?"

"Please."

She touched a switch, and almost immediately there was the sound of a crisply efficient voice. "*Draconis* to Zetland Base. E.T.A., surface contact, still 1100 hours. Is all ready?"

"All ready, *Draconis*," came the reply in accents that were crisp enough.

"Just one small thing, John," said Mavis. She stood very close to him, and with a dampened tissue removed the flecks of egg yolk from the corner of his mouth, from his uniform. "Now, let 'em all come," she declared.

"Let 'em all come," he echoed.

He rememberd a historical romance he had read

recently. It was about a famous English regiment whose proud epitaph was, *They died with their boots clean.*

Living with your boots clean can be harder.

Draconis was heard long before she was seen, the irregular throb of her inertial drive beating down from beyond the overcast. And then suddenly, she was below the cloud ceiling, a great, gleaming spindle, the flaring vanes of her landing gear at her stern. Grimes wondered if Francis Delamere were doing his own pilotage; very often the captains of these big ships let their navigating officers handle the controls during an approach. He thought smugly that this was probably the case now; when Delamere had served under Grimes he had been no great shakes as a ship handler.

Whoever was bringing the cruiser down, he was making a good job of it. Just a touch of lateral thrust to compensate for the wind, a steady increase of vertical thrust as altitude diminished, so that what at first had seemed an almost uncontrolled free fall was, at the moment of ground contact, a downward drift as gentle as that of a soap bubble.

She was tall, a shining metallic tower, the control room of her sharp stem well above the level of Grimes's office. Abruptly her inertial drive was silent. "Eleven oh oh oh seven . . ." announced Mavis Davis.

"Mphm," grunted Grimes.

He retrieved his cap from the floor, let the Ensign, who had found a clothes brush somewhere, brush its crown and peak. He put it on. He said to the girl, "Look after the shop. I have to go visiting." He left his office, took the elevator down to ground level. He was joined by the Base Supply Officer, the Base Medical Officer and the Base Engineering Officer. All three of them, he noted, looked reasonably respectable. Grimes in the lead, they marched out to the ramp that was just being extended from *Draconis's* after airlock.

It was good to be boarding a ship again, thought Grimes, even one commanded by a man who had once been his junior and who was now his senior. As he climbed the ramp he threw his shoulders back and sucked in his belly. He returned the salute of the junior officer at the airlock smartly and then, followed by his own officers, strode into the elevator cage. The woman operator needed no instructions; in a very few seconds the party from the base was being ushered into the Captain's day room.

"Ah," said Delamere, "Commander Grimes, isn't it?" He had changed little over the years; his close-cropped hair was touched with gray, but he was as boyishly slim and handsome as ever. The four gold rings gleamed bravely on each sleeve, and the left breast of his uniform was gaudy with ribbons. "Welcome aboard, Commander."

"Thank you, Captain." Grimes had no intention of addressing the other as "sir."

"You're putting on weight, John," said the Specialist Commander who was one of the group of officers behind Delamere.

"Maggie!"

"Commander Lazenby," said the Captain stiffly, "this touching reunion can be deferred until such time as the Base Commander and I have discussed business."

"Aye, aye, sir," snapped Margaret Lazenby, just a little too crisply.

Delamere glared at her, John Grimes looked at her wistfully. She hadn't put on weight. She had hardly changed since they had been shipmates in the census ship *Seeker*. Her red hair gleamed under her cap, her figure was as slim and trim as ever. But . . .

But she was not the slender, auburn-haired woman who haunted his dreams.

"Commander Grimes," said Delamere. Then, more loudly, "Commander Grimes!"

"Yes, Captain?"

"Perhaps we can get the introductions over with, and then you and I can get down to business."

"Certainly, Captain. This is Lieutenant Commander Dufay, the Base Medical Officer. Lieutenant Danby, Supplies. Lieutenant Roscoe, Engineering."

Delamere introduced his own people, and then the specialist officers went below, leaving the Captain to conduct business with Grimes.

"A drink, Commander?"

"Please, Captain. Gin, if I may."

"You may. Sit down, Grimes." Delamere poured the drinks, took a chair facing the other. "Down the hatch."

"Down the hatch."

The Captain grinned. "Well, Grimes, I don't seem to have caught you with your pants down. Frankly, I was rather hoping I would . . ."

"What do you mean?"

"I haven't forgotten that bad report you put in on me . . ."

"It was truthful," said Grimes. "You were a lousy ship handler." Then, "By the way, who brought *Draconis* in?"

"None of your business," snapped Delamere, an angry flush on his face. After a second or so he continued. "For your information, Grimes, an economy wave is sweeping the Service. There is a cutting out of deadwood in progress. Certain ships, *Draconis* among them, have been selected by our lords and masters to make the rounds of bases such as this one, and to report upon them. My last call was at Wuggis III. The Base Commander who was in charge is now on the retired list. His G.C.A. was in such a state that I was obliged to use the commercial spaceport."

"How nice for you," commented Grimes.

The Captain ignored this. "I'm giving you fair warning, Commander. You'd better be prepared. For the purposes of this exercise a state of war is deemed to exist. *Draconis* has limped into your base with 75% casualties, including all technical officers. These same technical officers are, even now, arranging a simulation of extensive damage. The Mannschenn Drive, for example, will require a new governor and will have to have its controls recalibrated. Only one inertial drive unit is functional, and that is held together with spit and string. My laser cannon are burned out. My yeast, algae and tissue culture vats contain only slimy, dead messes utterly unfit for human—or even unhuman—consumption." He laughed. "All the parts that have been removed from machinery and weapons are, of course, securely locked in my storerooms, where your people won't be able to get their greasy paws on them. *You*, Grimes, starting from scratch, using your people, your workshops, starting from scratch, will have to bring *Draconis* back to a state of full fighting efficiency, as soon as possible if not before."

"Then I'd better get cracking," said Grimes. He got to his feet, glanced briefly and regretfully at his almost untouched glass. It was good liquor, far better than any that could be obtained locally—but, even now, he was rather fussy about whom he drank with.

"You'd better," agreed Delamere. "Oh, you haven't finished your drink Commander."

"Your ship's in such a sorry, simulated state," Grimes told him, "that we'll make believe that you need it yourself."

He forgot to salute on the way out.

"I knew something like this would happen," complained Marian tearfully. "What shall we do, John? What can we do? A commander's pension is not much."

"Too right it isn't." He looked thoughtfully at the half inch of oily gin remaining in his glass, brought it to his mouth and swallowed it, gagging slightly. He reached for the bottle, poured himself another generous shot.

"You drink too much," flared his wife.

"I do," he agreed, looking at her. She was almost passable when alcohol had dimmed the sharp edges of his perception. He murmured:

> *"Malt does more than Milton can*
> *To Justify God's ways to Man . . ."*

"What?"

"Housman," he explained. "A poet. Twentieth century or thereabouts."

"Poetry!" she sneered contemptuously. "But what are you doing about Captain Delamere? He was such a nice young man when he was one of your officers, when we were all happy at Lindisfarne Base . . ."

"Yes, Franky was always good at sucking up to captains' and commodores' and admirals' wives."

"But you must have done something to him, John. Couldn't you apologize?"

"Like hell," growled Grimes. "Like adjectival, qualified hell."

"Don't swear at me!"

"I wasn't swearing."

"You were thinking it."

"All right, I was thinking it." He finished his drink, got up, put on his cap. "I'd better get down to the ship to see what sort of mess my butterfly-brained apes are making of her."

"What difference will your being there make?"

"I'm still Commander of this bloody base!" he roared.

He looked back at her briefly as he reached the door, felt a spasm of pity. She was such a mess. She had let herself go. (As he had let himself go.) Only faint traces remained of the attractive Ensign Marian Hall, Supply Branch, whom he, on the rebound, had married. Physically there was no longer any attraction. Mentally there was— nothing. She read only trash, was incapable of intelligent conversation, and could never join Grimes in his favorite pastime of kicking ideas around to see if they yelped. He wondered how things would have worked out if he and Maggie

Lazenby had made a go of things. But to have Maggie here, on this world, at this juncture was too much.

He walked to the military spaceport. The night was mild, not unpleasant in spite of the wisps of drizzle that drifted over the flat landscape. Now and again Zetland's twin moons appeared briefly in breaks in the clouds, but their light was faint and pallid in comparison to the glare of the working floods around *Draconis*.

He tramped slowly up the ramp to the airlock, returned the salute of the O.O.D., one of Delamere's men. The elevator was unmanned—but, after all, the ship had suffered heavy simulated casualties, so ratings could not be spared for nonessential duties. He went first to the "Farm." The vats had been cleaned out, but the stink still lingered. The cruiser's Biochemist had carried out his "sabotage under orders" a little too enthusiastically. He exchanged a few words with Lieutenant Commander Dufay, in charge of operations here, then went down a couple of decks to the inertial drive room. He looked at the confusion without understanding it. Roscoe and his artificers had bits and pieces scattered everywhere. It was like a mechanical jigsaw puzzle.

"She'll be right, Commander," said the Engineer Lieutenant. He didn't seem to be convinced by his own words. Grimes certainly wasn't.

"She'd better be right," he said.

Somebody else was using the elevator, so he decided to take the companionway up to Control—he *did* know more than a little about navigational equipment—rather than wait. His journey took him through Officers' Country. He was not altogether surprised when he was accosted by Commander Lazenby.

"Hi, John."

"Hi, Maggie."

"Are you busy?"

He shrugged. "I should be."

"But we haven't seen each other for years. Come into my dogbox for a drink and a yarn. It's all right—the Boy Wonder's being wined and dined by the Governor in Zeehan City."

"He might have told me."

"Why should he? In any case, he's on the Simulated Casualty List. He's probably awarded himself a posthumous Grand Galactic Cross."

"With golden comets."

"And a platinum spiral nebula." She laughed. "Come in, John. Take the weight off your feet." The door to her day cabin opened for her. "This is Liberty Hall. You can spit on the mat and call the cat a bastard."

"You haven't changed, Maggie," he said ruefully, looking at her. "I wish . . ."

She finished it for him. "You wish that you'd married me instead of that little commissioned grocer's clerk. But you were always rather scared of me, John, weren't you? You were afraid that you, a spacehound pure and simple, wouldn't be able to cope with me, a qualified ethologist. But as an ethologist I could have seen to it that things worked out for us."

She sat down on her settee, crossing her slim, sleek legs. Her thin, intelligent face under the red hair was serious. He looked at her wistfully. He murmured—and it was as much a question as a statement—"It's too late now."

"Yes. It's too late. You've changed too much. You did the wrong thing, John. You should have resigned after that court martial. You could have gone out to the Rim Worlds to make a fresh start."

"I wanted to, Maggie. But Marian—she's incurably Terran. She made it quite plain that she'd not go out to live among the horrid, rough colonials. As far as she's concerned, everywhere there's a Survey Service Base there's a little bit of Old Earth, with society neatly stratified. Mrs. Commander is just a cut above Mrs. Lieutenant Commander, and so on down." He fumbled for his pipe, filled and lit it. "She had the idea, too, that My Lords Commissioners would one day forgive me and that she'd finish up as Mrs. Admiral Grimes . . ."

"My heart fair bleeds for you both," she said drily. "But mix us drinks, John. You'll find the wherewithal in that locker."

"For you?"

"The same as always. BVG, with just a touch of lime."

There was a hologram over the grog locker, a little, brightly glowing window onto another, happier world. It was a beach scene: golden sand, creamy surf, blue sea and sky, and the golden brown bodies of the naked men and women.

Grimes asked, "Do you still spend your long leaves on Arcadia, Maggie?"

"Too right I do. It's the only possible planet for an ethologist who takes the 'Back To Nature' slogan seriously."

"You look happy enough in this hologram . . ." Grimes inspected the three-dimensional picture more closely. "Who is that with you?"

"Peter Cowley. He's a Senior Biochemist with Trans-Galactic Clippers."

"No. Not *him*. The woman."

She got up to come to stand beside him. "Oh, her. That's Sonya Verrill. Yet another of the Commanders with whom the Survey Service is infested. She's Intelligence. Do you know her?"

Grimes stared at the depiction of the nude woman. She was like Maggie Lazenby in many ways, her figure, her coloring, her facial features, could almost have been her sister. He looked more closely. There should be a mole on her left hip. There was.

"Do you know her?" asked Maggie again.

"Yes . . . No . . ."

"Make your mind up."

I don't know her, thought Grimes. *I have never met her. But I have dreamed about her. I thought it was Maggie in my dreams, a somehow different Maggie, but she hasn't a mole anywhere on her body . . .*

He said, "No, I don't know her. But she *is* like you, isn't she?"

"I can't see any resemblance. You know, she was almost going to call here; she's sculling around this neck of the woods in one of those little, fully automated armed yachts. Some hush-hush Intelligence deal. But when she heard that this was one of the Boy Wonder's ports of call she decided to play by herself somewhere."

"Has *he* met her?" asked Grimes, feeling absurdly jealous.

"Yes. They do not, repeat not, like each other."

"Then there must be some good in her," said Grimes, with a quite irrational surge of relief.

"Never mind her. What about me? I'm thirsty."

"All right, all right," said Grimes, mixing the drinks.

When he got home Marian was waiting up for him.

"You've been drinking," she accused him.

"And so, to coin a phrase, what?"

"I don't mind that so much. But you've been with that . . . bitch, that Maggie Lazenby."

"I had a couple of drinks with her, that was all."

"Don't lie to me!"

"I'm not lying."

No, he wasn't lying. Maggie, in her woman's way, had offered him more than a drink, but he had turned it down. Even now he was not sure why he had done so. Or he was sure, but would not admit it to himself. It was all so crazy, so utterly crazy. He had been loyal to a woman whom he had never met, whose hologram he had seen for the first time, in Maggie's day cabin.

"After all I've done for you, and you going sniffing around that carroty alley cat. You're no good, you're just no good. You never were, and you never will be . . ."

Grimes brushed past her, into the living room, the Service severity of which had been marred by his wife's tasteless attempts at interior decoration.

"Say something, damn you! Say something, you waster. Haven't you even the guts to defend yourself?"

The telephone buzzed urgently. Grimes went to it, flipped down the switch. The screen came alive and the plain, almost ugly face of Mavis Davis looked out at him. "Commander, there's an emergency . . ."

"Yes?" *And what was it? Had his fumbling repair squads wreaked some irreparable damage upon the cruiser? He'd better start packing his bags.*

"A Mayday."

"Who?" he demanded. "Where?"

"The armed yacht *Grebe*. In solar orbit between Zetland and Freiad." She rattled off coordinates. "Meteor swarm. Extensive hull and machinery damage. Loss of atmosphere. Orbit decaying."

"Mavis, send a car for me. At once."

"Wilco, Commander."

"And what can you do?" his wife sneered. "Captain Delamere's got a cruiser and hundreds of really efficient men and women. What have you got?"

"Out of my way!" he snarled.

"John! You can't go. I forbid you!" She clung to his sleeve but, brutally, he shook her off. She followed him for a little way as he strode out of the house, along the dark road, then gave up. "John!" she called. "John!"

The lights of the car were ahead, approaching rapidly. It passed him, turned, braked. Mavis Davis was driving. He got in beside her.

She said, as she restarted the vehicle. "*Husky*?"

Of course, it had to be the base's space tug *Husky*. Delamere's cruiser was out of commission and the tug at the civilian spaceport was, Grimes knew, undergoing annual survey. *Husky* was the only ship on Zetland capable of getting upstairs in a hurry.

And she was Grimes's toy, his pet. She was more than a toy, much more. In her he could feel the satisfaction of real command, or symbiosis with his ship. She was the only piece of equipment on the base in absolutely first class condition—and Grimes and Mavis, working with their own hands, had kept her so. She was referred to as "the Old Man's private yacht."

"I told Petty Officer Willis to warm her up," said Mavis.

"Good girl."

"Can . . . Can I come with you?"

"I'd like you to." She was a clerical officer, trained as such, but she should have been an engineer. She possessed the inborn skills, the talents and a keen mathematical mind. Often she had accompanied Grimes on his short jaunts outside the atmosphere. "You know the little bitch better than anybody else on the base."

"Thank you, John."

The car screamed on to the apron, circled the great, useless, floodlit hulk of *Draconis*. *Husky* was in her own berth, tucked away behind the workshops, a dull metal ovoid standing in her tripodal landing gear like a gray egg in an egg-cup. A circle of yellow light marked her airlock door.

As the car stopped Grimes heard a noise in the sky. It was a jet, coming in fast. The shriek of its exhaust varied in pitch as its turret drive was used first to brake and then to ease the aircraft to a vertical touchdown. The aircraft slammed to the concrete just a few feet from the car.

A man jumped out of the cabin, confronted Grimes. It was Delamere, still in his mess dress, starched white linen, black bow tie, tinkling miniatures and all.

"Is she ready?" he demanded.

"Yes, Captain. I'll have her up and away as soon as the airlock's sealed."

"You aren't taking her up, Grimes. I am." Delamere grinned whitely. "Life's been a little too dull lately."

"Like hell you're taking her up, Delamere. This is my base, and my tug."

"And I am your superior officer, Grimes. You'd better not forget it."

"You're not likely to let me, are you? But this is a rescue operation—and I know how to handle a ship."

"Out of my way, you insolent bastard!"

Grimes swung clumsily, but with all his weight behind the blow, and the weight of all the years of misery and frustration. Delamere wasn't as fit as he looked. Grimes's fist sank deep into his midriff, under the black silk cummerbund. The air was expelled from the Captain's lungs in an explosive *oof!* He sat down hard and abruptly. He gasped something about striking a superior officer, about mutiny.

"Willis," Grimes called to the Petty Officer, who had appeared in the airlock, "drag the Captain clear of the blast area. I'm going to use the auxiliary rockets. And keep clear yourself."

"But, sir . . ."

"You don't want to be up with me on a charge of mutiny. Get out of here, and take the Captain with you. That goes for you too, Mavis."

"Like hell it does!"

Grimes paused briefly. He could manage the tug singlehanded, but with rescue operations involved it would be asking for trouble. He grabbed Mavis by her bony shoulder. "Scream!" he whispered. "I'm dragging you aboard by force!"

She screamed, shrieked, "Let go of me!" From where Delamere was sprawled the struggle would

look convincing enough. And then they were in
the airlock, and as the door shut Grimes saw that
Willis already had Delamere well clear. The
Commander hurried up to the little control room
while Mavis went to the engines. He plumped
down into the pilot's chair and, as he strapped
himself in, cast an experienced eye over the
telltale lights. REACTION DRIVE—READY. IN-
ERTIAL DRIVE—READY. MANNSCHENN
DRIVE—STAND BY.

His fingers found the firing studs in the arm of
his chair. He said into the microphone hanging
before him, "Secure all. Secure all for blast off."

Mavis's voice came in reply. "All secure, Captain."

"Then—*blast!*" almost shouted Grimes.

He pressed the button, and *Husky* screamed
upstairs like a bat out of hell.

There was only one person aboard the crippled
Grebe, a woman. Her voice was faint, almost inco-
herent. She was in her suit, she said. She had a
broken arm, and possible internal injuries. She
thought that she would be able to ship a new air
bottle when the one in use was exhausted . . .

"Can you actuate your Carlotti transceiver?"
demanded Grimes urgently.

"I . . . I think so . . ."

"Try. I'm going to switch to Mannschenn Drive.
I'll home on your Carlotti."

"Mannschenn Drive?" asked Mavis, who had
come up to Control.

"Yes. I want to be there in minutes, not days,
and the Mannschenn Drive's the only way. I know
it's risky, but . . ."

It *was* risky, to operate the Drive in a planetary system with its tangle of gravitational and magnetic fields, but it had to be done. Grimes jockeyed the free-falling *Husky* around on her gyroscope, lining her up on the faint signals from the survivor's suit radio. He started the Drive. There was the usual second or so of disorientation in space and time, and then, astern of them, Zetland assumed the appearance of a writhing, convoluted ball of luminous gas, and ahead and to starboard the sun became an iridescent spiral. Grimes paid no attention. He heard the faint voice from his own Carlotti speaker—"Carlotti on."

"Can you fix it so that it sends a continuous note? Turn up the gain . . ."

"Wilco."

A faint, continuous squeal came from the speaker.

Good. Grimes watched the quivering antenna of his Carlotti direction finder and communicator, the ellipsoid Mobius strip that was rotating slowly about its long axis. He restarted the inertial drive and then, with lateral thrust, using the antenna as a compass needle, headed the tug directly for the distant wreck. He pushed the inertial drive control to full ahead. The irregular throbbing shook the little ship. "Mavis," he said, "see if you can coax a few more revs out of the bone shaker . . ."

"I'll try," she told him, and was gone.

A fresh voice came from the speaker. It was Delamere. "Grimes. Captain Delamere calling ex-Commander Grimes. Do you read me?"

"Loud and clear, Delamere. Get off the air. I'm busy."

"Grimes, I order you to return at once. Ensign Davis, I authorize you to use force if necessary to overcome the mutineer and to assume command of *Husky*."

Grimes watched the antenna. It showed a continual drift of the target in a three o'clock direction. The wreck was in orbit, of course. He would have to allow for that. He did so, applying just the right amount of lateral thrust.

"Grimes! Ensign Davis! Do you hear me?"

Damn the man. So far the antenna was keeping lined up on the signal from the disabled *Grebe*, but with the base transmitting at full power it was liable to topple at any second.

"Grimes! Ensign Davis!"

"Grimes here. I can't give any orders, but I can appeal to those of you in the Carlotti room. This is a rescue operation. I'm homing on *Grebe's* Carlotti beacon. There's a woman out there, in the wreck, and she can't last much longer. Please get off the air, and stay off."

He was never to know what happened, but he thought he heard the sound of a scuffle. He thought he heard a voice—Maggie's voice— whisper, "Pull the fuse!"

He transferred his attention to the spherical tank of the mass proximity indicator. Yes, there it was, a tiny, glowing spark, barely visible. It was drifting fast in toward the center of the globe. Too fast? Not really. For a collision to occur, two vessels must occupy the same space at the same time, and as long as *Husky's* Mannschenn Drive was operating she was in a time of her own. But—talking of time—he didn't want to waste any. "Mavis," he said into the intercom mike, "when I put her on full astern I *want* full astern. No half measures."

"You'll get it," she assured him.

The spark was brighter now, crossing one concentric ring after another. Grimes adjusted the scale of the indicator, pushing the target back to the outermost circle. Still it drove in. Grimes adjusted the scale again, and again, and once more. Target spark merged with the bead of luminosity that represented *Husky*. For a microsecond there was an uncanny sensation of merging—not of ships, but of two personalities. "Mannschenn Drive—off!" snapped Grimes, executing his order. "Inertial drive—full astern!"

The ship shuddered, striving to tear herself apart. Colors sagged down the spectrum as the ever-precessing gyroscopes of the Mannschenn Drive were braked to a halt—but outside the viewports the stars, vibrating madly, still looked as they had done while the drive was in operation.

"Stop all!" muttered Grimes, jerking the lever to its central position.

And there, scant feet away, rotating slowly about some cockeyed axis, was the torn, buckled hull of the space yacht *Grebe*.

Mavis Davis came up to Control while Grimes was putting on his suit. She was bleeding slightly from an abrasion on her forehead. Like many another plain woman she was beautiful in conditions of emotional and physical stress. Before she lowered the helmet onto his shoulder she kissed him. It was a brief contact, but surprisingly warm. Grimes wished that it could have been longer.

She said, "Good-bye. It's been nice knowing you, John."

"What the hell's this, Mavis?"

She grinned lopsidedly. "I have my fey moments—especially when somebody is playing silly buggers with the Mannschenn Drive . . ." Then she was securing the helmet and further speech was impossible.

Grimes collected what tools he would require on his way down to the airlock. When the outer door opened he found that he could almost step across to *Grebe*. He pushed himself away from his own little ship, made contact with the hull of the other with the magnetic soles of his boots and palms of his gloves. He clambered over her like a clumsy, four-legged spider. He soon discovered that it would be impossible to open *Grebe's* airlock door. But it didn't matter. A few feet away from it was a hole large enough for him to crawl through.

He said into his helmet microphone, "I'm here."

The faint voice that replied, at long last, held an oddly familiar astringent quality. "And about time."

"I came as quickly as I could. Where are you?"

"In the control room."

Grimes made his way forward, using cutting torch and crowbar when he had to. When he found her she was in the pilot's chair, held there by the seat belt. Moving feebly, she contrived to swivel to look at him. *Husky's* floods were on, glaring through the viewports, but her face, inside the helmet, was in shadow.

She said, "I hate to have to admit it, but you're right, John."

"What do you mean?"

"What you always say when you deliver yourself of one of your diatribes against automation. 'Never put yourself at the mercy of a single fuse.' My meteor shield might as well have not been there, and by the time the alarm sounded it was too late to do anything . . ."

He was beside her now, holding her, cursing the heavy suits that were between them.

"Sonya, I've got to get you out of here. Aboard *Husky*." He fumbled with the strap that held her.

"Too . . . late." She coughed, and the sound of it, telling of fluid-filled lungs, was terrifying. "Too . . . late. I hung on as long . . . as I could. Start . . . Mannschenn Drive. Should be some . . . power . . . in batteries . . ."

"Sonya! I'm getting you out of here!"

"No. No! Start . . . Drive . . ."

But he persisted in trying to unstrap her. Summoning her last reserves of strength she pushed him away. He lost contact with the deck, drifted away from her. Her clutched at something—a lever?—that moved in his hand.

He did not hear the Drive starting; there was no air in the ship to carry the sound. But he felt the vibration as its rotors stirred into life, was aware that the harsh light of *Husky's* floods had deepened from white to a sullen red. Around him, around Sonya, the universe lost its substance. But he was solid still, as she was, and her hand was firm in his.

And . . .

She was saying, "We found each other again. We found each other again . . ."

Grimes looked at her, looked at her a long time, dreadfully afraid that she would vanish. He held her hand tightly. Then, but cautiously, he stared around him at the temple. It seemed to have lost its alien magic. It was just a large, featureless room with the dimensions of a cube. On the floor, annoyingly off center, was a block of black stone in the shape of a coffin.

He said, "That dream . . . If it was a dream . . ."

She said, "There is a fourth rate Survey Service Base on Zetland . . ."

He said, "The last I heard of Delamere he'd been kicked upstairs to become a deskbound commodore . . ."

She said, "Damn your silly dream. Forget about it."

"I'll try," he promised. And then, unbidden, familiar words formed themselves in his mind. He said them aloud:

"To sleep, perchance to dream . . .
    Ay, there's the rub . . ."

Something about the emphasis he used made her ask, "What's the rub, John?"

"What *is* the dream? *That* or *this*?"

"What does it matter?" she asked practically. "We just make the best of what we've got." Then, as they walked out of the drab temple, "Damn! My ribs are still hurting!"

SPARTAN PLANET

BY A. BERTRAM CHANDLER

SF
ace books
A Division of Charter Communications Inc.
A GROSSET & DUNLAP COMPANY
360 Park Avenue South
New York, New York 10010

SPARTAN PLANET

Copyright © 1969 by A. Bertram Chandler

For Susan, whose idea it was.

An ACE Book

First Ace printing: June 1979

2 4 6 8 0 9 7 5 3 1
Manufactured in the United States of America

Chapter One

THERE WAS THAT sound again—thin, high, querulous, yet audible even above the rhythmic stamp and shuffle of the dance that beat out through the open windows of the Club. It sounded as though something were in pain. Something was.

Brasidus belched gently. He had taken too much wine, and he knew it. That was why he had come outside—to clear his head and, he hoped, to dispel the slight but definitely mounting waves of nausea. The night air was cool, but not too cool, on his naked body, and that helped a little. Even so, he did not wish to return inside just yet.

He said to Achron, "We may as well watch."

"No," replied his companion. "No. I don't want to. It's . . . dirty, somehow . . ." Then with a triumphant intonation he delivered the word for which he had been groping. "Obscene."

"It's not. It's . . . natural." The liquor had loosened Brasidus' tongue; otherwise he would never have dared to speak so freely, not even to one who was, after all, only a helot. "It's we who're being obscene by being unnatural. Can't you see that?"

"No, I can't!" snapped Achron pettishly. "And I don't want to. And I thank Zeus, and his priesthood, that *we* don't have to go through what that brute is going through."

"It's only a scavenger."

"But it's a sentient being."

"And so what? I'm going to watch, anyhow."

Brasidus walked briskly to where the sound was coming from, followed reluctantly by Achron. Yes, there was the scavenger, struggling in the center of the pool of yellow light cast by a streetlamp. The scavenger—or scavengers . . . Had either of the young men heard of Siamese twins, that would have been the analogy to occur to them—a pair of Siamese twins fighting to break apart. But the parallel would not have been exact, as one of the two linked beings was little more than half the size of the other.

Even in normal circumstances the scavengers were not pretty animals, although they looked functional enough. They were quadrupedal, with cylindrical bodies. At one end they were all voracious mouth, and from the other end protruded the organs of excretion and insemination. They were unlovely but useful, and had been encouraged to roam the streets of the cities from time immemorial.

Out on the hills and prairies and in the forests, their larger cousins were unlovely and dangerous, but they had acquired the taste for living garbage.

"So . . . messy," complained Achron.

"Not so messy as the streets would be if the beasts didn't reproduce themselves."

"There wouldn't be the same need for reproduction if you rough hoplites didn't use them as javelin targets. But you know what I'm getting at, Brasidus. It's just that I . . . it's just that some of us don't like to be reminded of our humble origins. How would *you* like to go through the budding process, and then have to *tear* your son away from yourself?"

"I wouldn't. But we don't have to, so why worry about it?"

"I'm not *worrying*." Achron, slightly built, pale, blond, looked severely up into the rugged face of his dark, muscular friend. "But I really don't see why we have to watch these *disgusting* spectacles."

"You don't have to."

The larger of the scavengers, the parent, had succeeded in bringing one of its short hind legs up under its belly. Suddenly it kicked, and as it did so it screamed, and the smaller animal shrieked in unison. They were broken apart now, staggering over the cobbles in what was almost a parody of a human dance. They were apart, and on each of the rough, mottled flanks was a ragged circle of glistening, raw flesh, a wound that betrayed by its stench what was the usual diet of the lowly garbage eaters. The stink lingered even after the beasts, rapidly recovering from their ordeal, had scurried off, completing the fission process, in opposite directions.

That was the normal way of birth on Sparta.

Chapter Two

THAT WAS THE normal way of birth on Sparta—but wherever in the universe there is intelligence there are also abnormalities.

Achron looked at his wristwatch, the instrument and ornament that marked him as something more than a common helot, as almost the social equal of the members of the military caste. He said, "I have to be getting along. I'm on duty at the crèche at 2400 hours."

"I hope you enjoy the diaper changing and the bottle feeding."

"But I do, Brasidus. You know that I do." His rather high voice dropped to a murmur. "I always feel that one or two of them might be . . . yours. There are a couple in this new generation that have your nose and eyes."

Brasidus put a large, investigatory and derisory hand to his face. "Impossible. I've still got them."

"Oh, you know what I mean."

"Why not keep a lookout for your own offspring, Achron?"

"It's not the same, Brasidus. In any case, it's not often I'm called upon to contribute . . ."

The two friends walked back to the Club House, but did not go farther inside than the cloakroom.

Brasidus watched Achron slip into his tunic and sandals, then, on an impulse, Brasidus followed suit. Somehow he was no longer in the mood for the dance, and his prominent nose wrinkled a little at the acrid smell of perspiration, the sweet-sour reek of vomit and spilled wine that drifted into the anteroom from the main hall. The thudding of bare feet on the polished floor, in time to the drums and the screaming, brassy trumpets, usually excited him, but this night it failed to do so, as even did the confused shouting and scuffling that told him that the inevitable brawl had just broken out. On other occasions he had hurled himself gleefully into the press of struggling, sweating naked bodies—but this, too, had lost its attraction for him.

More and more he was feeling that there was something missing, just as there had been something missing when he had been a guest at Achron's club. He had thought, at the time, that it was the boisterous good fellowship, the hearty food and the strong, rough wine. Now he had stated himself with all of these, but was still unsatisfied.

He shrugged his heavy shoulders, then tugged the hem of his tunic down to its normal midthigh position. He said, "I'll stroll down to the crèche with you, Achron. I don't feel like going back to the barracks just yet. And, anyhow, tomorrow's my free day."

"Oh, thank you, Brasidus. But are you sure? Usually you hate to leave while there's any wine left in the jars."

"Just don't feel like any more drinking or dancing. Come on."

It was dark outside the building. The sky, although clear, was almost starless, and Sparta had no moons. The widely spaced streetlamps on their fluted columns seemed to accentuate the blackness rather than to relieve it, and the glimmering white pillars of street-fronting buildings appeared to be absorbing rather than reflecting what little light there was. In their shadows there was furtive movement, but it was no more than the scavengers going about their appointed tasks. Then, overhead, there was the drone of engines.

Brasidus stopped abruptly, laid a detaining hand on Achron's upper arm. He looked up, staring at the great, shadowy bulk that drove across the night sky, its course set for the blinking beacon atop the Acropolis, its tiers of ports strings of luminous beads, its ruby and emerald navigation lights pendants at the end of the necklace.

Achron said impatiently, "Come on. I don't want to be late clocking in. It's only the night mail from Helos. You must have seen it dozens of times."

"At least," agreed Brasidus. He fell into step again beside his companion. "But . . ."

"But you always wanted to join the Air Navy yourself, Brasidus. But you're too big, too heavy. A pity." There was a hint of spite in Achron's voice.

Brasidus recognized it, but ignored it. He murmured, "And there are even better things to be than an airman. I've often wondered why we didn't build any more spaceships after we colonized Latterhaven, why we allowed the Latterhaveneers to have the monopoly of the trade between the two worlds. We should own and operate our own spaceships."

Achron laughed unkindly. "And what chance
do you think you'd have of being a spaceman?
Two ships are *ample* for the trade, and the spice
crop's only once a year. What would you do between voyages?"

"We could . . . explore."

"Explore?" Achron's slim arm described an arc
against the almost empty sky. "Explore *what*?
And on the other side of the world there's the
Lens—and we all know that it's no more—or
less—than a vast expanse of incandescent gases."

"So we've been told. But . . . I've managed an
occasional talk with the Latterhaven spacemen
when I've been on spaceport guard duty, and *they*
don't think so."

"*They* wouldn't. Anyhow, you could be a lot
worse things than a soldier—and in the Police
Battalion of the Army at that. And as far as the
possibility or otherwise of other worlds is concerned, I'd sooner listen to our own priests than to
that atheistical bunch from Latterhaven."

They were almost at the creche now, a huge,
sprawling adjunct to the still huger temple. Its
windows glowed with soft yellow light, and
above the main doorway, in crimson neon,
gleamed the insignia of the State Parenthood Service, the red circle from which, at an angle, a
barbed arrow jutted up and out. Brasidus wondered, as he had wondered before, how the crèche
had come to take for its own the symbol of Ares,
the God of War. It was, he supposed, that the
highest caste into which a child could grow was,
after the priesthood, the military. Then he
thought about his own alleged parenthood.

"These babies like me . . ." he said abruptly.

"Yes, Brasidus?"

"I . . . I think I'll come in with you, to see for myself."

"Why not? It's outside visiting hours—not that anybody does ever visit—but you're a police officer. Old Telemachus at the desk won't know if you're on duty or not."

Telemachus, bored by his night duty, welcomed the slight deviation from normal routine. He knew Brasidus slightly but, nonetheless, insisted that he produce his identity card. Then he asked, his wrinkled head protruding turtle-like from his robes, "And what is the purpose of your visit, Sergeant? Has some criminal taken refuge within our sacred precincts?"

"Achron tells me that two of his charges might be . . . mine."

"Ah. *Potential* criminals." The old man cackled at his own humor. "But seriously, Sergeant, it is a great pity that more of our citizens do not evince greater interest in their sons. Even though the direct physical link was abolished ages ago, there should still be responsibility. Yes. Responsibility. Before I was asked to resign from the Council, I succeeded in having the system of regular visiting hours introduced—not that anybody has taken advantage of them . . ."

"Phillip will be waiting for his relief," broke in Achron sulkily.

"So he will. But it will not hurt that young man to be kept waiting. Do you know, at the 2200-hours feed he failed to ensure that the bottles were at the correct temperature! I could hear Doctor Heraklion carrying on, even out here. Luckily the Doctor came into the ward at just the right time." Telemachus added spitefully, "I honestly think that Phillip will make a better factory hand than a children's nurse.''

"Is the correct temperature so important, sir?" asked Brasidus curiously. "After all, we can eat hot things and cold things, and it never seems to do us any harm.''

"But we are fully developed, my dear boy. The children are not. Before the priests learned how to improve upon nature, a child, up to quite an advanced age, would be getting his nourishment directly from the father's bloodstream. So—can't you see?—these immature digestive organs must be coddled. They are not ready to handle what we should consider normal food and drink.''

"Phillip will be in a bad temper," complained Achron. "I hate him when he's that way.''

"All right then, you can relieve your precious Phillip. Are you sure you don't want to stay on for a talk, Brasidus?''

"No, thank you, Telemachus.''

"Off you go, then. And try not to make any arrests.''

Brasidus followed his friend through long corridors and then into the softly lighted ward where he was supposed to be on duty. They were met at the door by Phillip, a young man who, save for his dark coloring, was almost Achron's twin. He glowered at his relief. "So you've condescended to show up at last. I should give you something to help you to remember to get here on time.''

"Do just that," said Brasidus roughly.

Phillip stared insolently at the Sergeant and sneered, "A pity you brought your *friend* with you. Well, I'm off, dearie. It's all yours, and you're welcome to it.''

"What about the handover procedure?" demanded Achron sharply.

"What is there to hand over? Fifty brats, slumbering peacefully—until they all wake up together and start yelling their heads off. Thermostat in the dispenser's on the blink, so you'll have to check bottle temperatures before you break out rations for the little darlings. Clean nappy bin was replenished before the change of watch—or what *should* have been the change of watch. I'm off."

He went.

"Not really suitable for this profession, is he?" asked Achron softly. "I sometimes think that he doesn't *like* children." He gestured toward the double row of white cots. "But who couldn't love them?"

"Not you, obviously."

"But come with me, Brasidus. Leave your sandals by the door and walk softly. I don't want them woken." He tiptoed on bare feet over the polished floor. "Now," he whispered, "I'll show you. This is one of them." He paused at the foot of the crib, looked down lovingly.

And Brasidus looked down curiously. What he saw was just a bud, a baby, with a few strands of wispy black hair plastered across the overlarge skull, with unformed features. The eyes were closed, so he could not tell if there were any optical resemblance between himself and the child. The nose? That was no more than a blob of putty. He wondered, as he had often, how Achron and the other nurses ever told their charges apart. Not that it much mattered, not that it would matter until the boys were old enough for aptitude tests—and by that time all characteristics, psychological and physiological, would be well developed.

"Isn't he *like* you?" murmured Achron.

"Um. Yes."

"Don't you feel . . . proud?"

"Frankly, no."

"Oh, Brasidus, how *can* you be so insensitive?"

"It's a gift. It goes with my job."

"I don't believe you. Honestly, I don't. But quiet. Heraklion's just come in."

Brasidus looked up and saw the tall white-robed figure of the Doctor at the end of the aisle. He bowed stiffly, and the salutation was returned. Then Heraklion beckoned. Remembering to walk softly, the young man made his way between the rows of cots.

"Brasidus, isn't it?" asked Heraklion.

"Yes, Doctor."

"What are you doing here, Sergeant?"

"Just visiting, with Achron."

"I really don't approve, you know. Our charges are very . . . delicate. I shall appreciate it if you don't go wandering all over the building."

"I shan't be doing that, Doctor."

"Very well. Goodnight to you, Sergeant."

"Goodnight to you, Doctor."

And as he watched the tall, spare figure of Heraklion striding away along the corridor, Brasidus, the policeman in his makeup suddenly in the ascendant, asked himself, *What is* he *hiding?*

And then the first of the babies awoke, and almost immediately after the other forty-nine of them. Brasidus bade a hasty farewell to Achron and fled into the night.

Chapter Three

THERE WAS AN odd, nagging suspicion at the back of Brasidus's mind as he walked slowly through the almost deserted streets to the police barracks. Normally he would have been attracted by the sounds of revelry that still roared from the occasional Club—but the mood that had descended upon him earlier still had not left him, and to it was added this new fretting surmise. Crime was not rare on Sparta, but it was usually of a violent nature and to cope with it required little in the way of detective ability. However, crime against the state was not unknown—and the criminals were, more often than not, highly placed officials, better educated and more intelligent than the commonalty. There was a certain smell about such malefactors—slight, subtle, but evident to the trained nose.

Brasidus possessed such an organ, and it had twitched at the odor that lingered about Doctor Heraklion.

Drugs? Could be—although the man himself did not appear to be an addict. But, in his position, he would have access to narcotics, and the peddlers had to get their supplies from somebody.

Even so, Brasidus was reluctant to pass his suspicions on to his superiors. To begin with, there was no proof. Secondly—and this was more important—he had witnessed what had happened, more than once, to overzealous officers who had contrived to trample on the toes of the influential. To present his captain with a *fait accompli*, with all the evidence (but of *what?*) against Heraklion neatly compiled, would be one thing, would almost certainly lead to promotion. To run to him with no more than the vaguest of suspicions, no more than a hunch, actually, could well result in permanent banishment to some dead-end hamlet in the bush.

Nonetheless, an investigation *could* bring rewards and, if carried out discreetly and on his own time, would not be too risky. After all, there was no law or regulation to debar any citizen from entry to the crèche. Now and again, at the instigation of members like Telemachus, the Council had attempted to encourage visits, although with little success. Perhaps a sudden access of parental feeling would look suspicious—but calling to see a friend, one of the children's nurses, would not. Too, Achron himself might have noticed something odd, might even be induced to remember and to talk about it.

"What's biting you, Sergeant?" asked the bored sentry on duty at the barracks gate.

Brasidus started. "Nothing," he said.

"Oh, come off it!" The man who had served with Brasidus for years and was shortly due for promotion himself, could be permitted liberties. "Anybody'd think you had a solid week's guard duty ahead of you, instead of your free day." The sentry yawned widely. "How was the dance, by the way? It's unlike you to be back so early, especially when you've a morning's lay-in for recuperation."

"So-so."

"Any good fights?"

"I don't know. There seemed to be one starting just as I left."

"And you didn't join in? You must be sickening for something. You'd better see a doctor."

"Maybe I'd better. Good night, Leonidas—or should it be good morning?"

"What does it matter to you? You'll soon be in your scratcher."

On his way to his sleeping quarters Brasidus had to pass the duty sergeant's desk. That official looked up as he approached. "Oh, Brasidus . . ."

"I'm off duty, Lysander."

"A policeman is never off duty—especially one who is familiar with the routine for spaceport guard duties." He consulted a pad on his desk. "You, with six constables, are to present yourself at the port at 0600 hours. The men have already been checked off for the duty, and arrangements have been made to have you all called. You'd better get some sleep."

"But there's no ship due. Not for months."

"Sergeant Brasidus, you and I are policemen. Neither of us is an expert on astronautical matters. If the Latterhaveneers decide to send an unscheduled ship, and if the Council makes the usual arrangements for its reception, who are we to demand explanations?"

"It seems . . . odd."

"You're a creature of routine, Brasidus. That's your trouble. Off with you now, and get some sleep."

Once he had undressed and dropped onto the hard, narrow bed in his cubicle he did, rather to his surprise, fall almost at once into a dreamless slumber. And it seemed that only seconds had elapsed when an orderly called him at 0445 hours.

A cold shower completed the arousing process. He got into his black and silver uniform tunic, buckled on his heavy sandals and then, plumed helmet under his arm, made his way to the mess hall. He was the first one there. He looked with some distaste at the already laid table—the crusty bread, the joints of cold meat, the jugs of weak beer. But he was hungry, and pulled up a form and began his meal. As he was eating, the six constables of his detail came in. He nodded in greeting as they muttered sullenly, "Morning, Sergeant." Then, "Don't waste any time," he admonished. "They'll be waiting for us at the spaceport."

"Let 'em wait," growled one of the latecomers. He threw a gnawed bone in the general direction of the trash bucket, missed.

"That's enough from you, Hector. I hear that there's a vacancy for village policeman at Euroka. Want me to recommend you?"

"No. Their beer's lousier even than this, and they can't make wine."

"Then watch your step, that's all."

The men got slowly to their feet, wiping their mouths on the back of their hands, halfheartedly dusting the crumbs from the fronts of their tunics. They took their helmets from the hooks on the wall, put them on, then filed slowly from the mess hall to the duty sergeant's desk. He was waiting for them, already had the armory door unlocked. From it he took, one by one, seven belts, each with two holsters. *So*, thought Brasidus, *this is an actual spaceship landing.* Staves and short swords were good enough for ordinary police duties. As the belts were being buckled on, the duty sergeant produced the weapons to go with them. "One stun gun," he muttered, passing them out. "One projectile pistol. To be used only in extreme urgency. But you know the drill, Sergeant."

"I know the drill, Sergeant," replied Brasidus.

"We should," grumbled Hector, "by this time."

"I'm telling you," explained the duty sergeant with ominous patience, "so that if you do something silly, which is all too possible, you won't be able to say that you weren't told not to do it." He came out from behind the desk, inspected the detail. "A fine body of men, Sergeant Brasidus," he declaimed sardonically. "A credit to the Army. I don't think. But you'll do, I suppose. There'll be nobody there to see you but a bunch of scruffy Latterhaven spacemen."

"What if they aren't from Latterhaven?" asked Brasidus. He was almost as surprised by his question as was the duty sergeant.

"Where else can they be from? Do you think that the gods have come all the way from Olympus to pay us a call?"

But if the gods came, it would be, presumably, on the wings of a supernal storm. It would not be a routine spaceship arrival—routine, that is, save for its unscheduled nature.

The men were silent during the ride to the spaceport.

Air-cushioned, the police transport sped smoothly over the cobbled streets of the city, the rough roads of the countryside. Dawn was not far off and already the harpies were uttering their raucous cries in the branches of the medusa trees. One of the birds, its wings whirring about its globular body, swept down from its perch and fluttered ahead of the driver's cab, squawking discordantly. The vehicle swerved. Hector cursed, pulled his projectile pistol, fired. The report was deafening in the still air. The harpy screamed for the last time and fell, a bloody tangle of membrane and cartilage, by the side of the road.

"Was that necessary, hoplite?" asked Brasidus coldly.

"You heard what Sergeant Lysander told us, Sergeant." The man leered. "This was an emergency."

Only a bird, thought Brasidus. *Only a stupid bird. Even so . . . He asked himself, Am I getting soft? But I can't be. Not in this job. And in all my relationships I'm the dominant partner.*

The spaceport was ahead now, its latticework control tower looming starkly against the brightening yellow of the eastern sky. Atop the signal mast there was flashing the intense green light that warned of incoming traffic. A ship was due. *Latterhaven Venus* or *Latterhaven Hera*? And what would either of them be doing here off season?

The car halted at the main gates, sitting there on the cloud of dust blown up and around it by its ducts. The guard on duty did not leave his box, merely actuated the mechanism that opened the gateway, waved the police through. As they drove to the Spaceport Security Office, Brasidus saw that the inner barrier was being erected on the concrete apron. He noticed, too, that only one conveyor belt had been rigged, indicating that there would be very little cargo either to load or to discharge. That, at this time of the year, made sense. But why should the ship be coming here at all?

They were outside the office now. The car stopped, subsided to the ground as its fans slowed to a halt. The constables jumped out, followed Brasidus into the building. To meet them there was Diomedes—corpulent, pallid, with a deceptively flabby appearance—the security captain. He returned Brasidus' smart salute with a casual wave of his pudgy hand. "Ah, yes. The guard detail. The usual drill, Sergeant. You're on duty until relieved. Nobody, Spartan or spaceman, to pass through the barrier either way without the Council's written authority." He glanced at the wall clock. "For your information, the ship is due at 0700 hours. You may stand down until 0650."

"Very good, sir. Thank you, sir," snapped Brasidus. "If I may ask, sir, which of the two ships is it?"

"You may ask, Sergeant. But I'm just Security. Nobody ever tells me anything." He relented slightly. "If you must know, it's neither of the two regular ships. It's some wagon with the most unlikely name of *Seeker III.*"

"Not like the Latterhaveneers to omit the name of their precious planet," muttered somebody.

"But, my dear fellow, the ship's not from Latterhaven. That's the trouble. And now, Sergeant, if you'll come with me I'll try to put you into the picture. It's a pity that nobody's put me into it first."

Chapter Four

THE SHIP THAT was not from Latterhaven was no more than a glittering speck in the cloudless morning sky when Diomedes, followed by Brasidus and the six hoplites, marched out from the office onto the apron, to the wire mesh barrier that had been erected to define and enclose the strange vessel's landing place. It was no more than a speck, but it was expanding rapidly, and the rhythmic beat of the inertial drive, faint to begin with, was becoming steadily louder.

Old Cleon, the port master, was there, his long white hair streaming out in the breeze. With him were other officials, one of whom carried a portable transceiver. Brasidus could overhear both ends of the conversation. He learned little; it was no more than the exchange of messages to be expected with standard landing procedure. Cleon himself did not seem to be very interested. He turned to Diomedes. "Most unprecedented!" he complained. "Most unprecedented. Had it not been for the Council's direct orders I should have refused permission to land."

"It's not a very large ship," said Diomedes, squinting upwards.

"Large enough. Too large, for an intruder.

Those rebels on Latterhaven might have let us know that they've discovered and colonized other habitable planets."

"They, too, must have a security service," said Diomedes.

"Secrets, secrets! How can I run a spaceport when nobody ever tells me anything? Answer me that, Captain!"

"Descending under full control, to area designated," reported the man with the transceiver.

Diomedes turned to his men. "I've told Sergeant Brasidus all that I know, and he's passed it on to you. So keep alert. We're not expecting any hostile action—but be ready for it. That's all."

Brasidus checked the freedom of his weapons in their holsters. The others followed his example.

Lower dropped the ship, lower. Even with nothing against which to measure her, it could be seen that she was small—only half the size, perhaps, of *Latterhaven Venus* or *Latterhaven Hera*. The gold letters embossed on her side were now readable. "SEEKER III." (And what, wondered Brasidus, of *Seeker I* and *Seeker II*?) And above the name there was a most peculiar badge or symbol. A stylized harpy it looked like—a winged globe surmounted by a five-pointed star. It was nothing like the conventional golden rocker worn on Latterhaven uniforms.

The ship came at last between the waiting men and the rising sun, casting a long, chill shadow. The throbbing of its engines made speech impossible. And then, suddenly augmenting their beat, there was the drone of other machinery. Slowly, majestically, no less than six of the great airships of the Spartan Navy sailed over the spaceport and then, in line ahead, circled the landing field. Their arrival was clearly not fortuitous. Should *Seeker's* crew attempt any hostile action they, and their ship, would be destroyed by a shower of high-explosive bombs—as would be, Brasidus realized, the military ground party and the port officials. The same thought must have occurred to Diomedes. The portly captain looked even unhappier than usual and muttered, "Nobody ever tells me *anything*."

With a crunch of metal on concrete the ship landed, an elongated ovoid quivering on her vaned landing gear, in spite of its bulk somehow conveying the impression that the slightest puff of wind could blow it away. Then, as the engines were shut down, it ceased to vibrate, settled down solidly. There was a loud *crack* and a jagged fissure appeared in the scarred concrete of the apron. But the strange vessel was not especially heavy. The initial damage had been caused by a clumsy landing of *Latterhaven Hera*, and Cleon, with months in which to make the necessary repairs, still hadn't gotten around to it.

Slowly an airlock door toward the stern of the ship opened. From it, tonguelike, an extensible ramp protruded, wavered, then sought and found the ground. There were beings standing in the airlock chamber. Were they human? Brasidus had read imaginative stories about odd, intelligent life-forms evolved on other planets—and, after all, this ship could be proof that there were more habitable planets than Sparta and Latterhaven in the universe. Yes, they seemed to be human. Nevertheless, the Sergeant's hands did not stray far from the butts of his holstered weapons.

Somebody was coming down the ramp, a man whose attire bore no resemblance to the carelessly informal rig of the Latterhaven spacemen. There was gold on his visored cap, and a double row of gold buttons on his odd tunic, and bands of gold on the sleeves of it. His black trousers were not the shapeless coverings worn for warmth and protection in the hill country, but were shaped to his legs and sharply creased. His black, highly polished footwear afforded him complete coverage—*and must be*, thought Brasidus, wriggling his toes, *extremely uncomfortable.* He reached the ground, turned and made a gesture toward the open doorway. Another man came out of the airlock, followed the first one to the ground. He, although his uniform was similar, was dressed more sensibly, with a knee-length black kilt instead of the constricting trousers.

But was it a man, or was it some kind of alien? Brasidus once again recalled those imaginative stories, and the assumption made by some writers that natives of worlds with thin atmospheres would run to abnormal (by Spartan standards) lung development. This being, then, could be deformed, or a mutant, or an alien. Somebody muttered, "What an odd-looking creature!"

Walking with calm deliberation the two men approached the barrier. The one with the trousered legs called, "Anybody here speak English?" He turned to his companion and said, "That was a silly question to which I should get a silly answer. After all, we've been nattering to them on RT all the way in."

"We speak Greek," answered Diomedes.

The spaceman looked puzzled. "I'm afraid that I don't. But your English is very good. If you don't mind, it will have to do."

"But we have been speaking Greek all the time."

"Something odd here. But skip it. Allow me to introduce myself. I am Lieutenant Commander John Grimes, Interstellar Federation Survey Service. This lady is Doctor Margaret Lazenby, our ethologist . . ."

Lady, thought Brasidus. *Then he must be a member of some other race. The Ladies? I wonder where they come from. . . . And such odd names—Johngrimes, Margaretlazenby. But the Latterhaveneers go in for odd names, too.*

Diomedes was making his own self-introduction. "I am Diomedes, Captain of Spaceport Security. Please state your business, Johngrimes."

"I've already done so. And, as you must know, I received clearance to land."

"Then state your business again, Johngrimes."

"All right. We're carrying out the census in this sector of space. Of course, your cooperation isn't compulsory, but it will be appreciated."

"That is a matter for the King and his Council, Lieutenant Commander."

"We can wait. Meanwhile, I'd like to comply with all the usual regulations and clear my ship inwards. I'm ready to receive the officers from Port Health and Customs as soon as you like."

"We have no need for them here, Lieutenant Commander Johngrimes. My orders are that you and your crew stay on your side of the barrier until such time as you lift off."

The strange-looking man was talking to the

spaceship commander in a high, angry voice. "But this is impossible, Commander. How can we carry out any sort of survey in these conditions? They distinctly told us that we could land—and now they turn their spaceport into a prison camp just for our benefit. Do something, Commander."

Brasidus saw the Captain's prominent ears redden. Nonetheless, he replied mildly enough, "But this is their world, Miss Lazenby. We're only guests."

"Guests? Prisoners, you mean. A wire barrier around us, and a fleet of antique gasbags cruising over us. Guests, you say!"

Strange, thought Brasidus, how this peculiar-looking spaceman appears attractive when he's in a bad temper, while poor Achron and his like just get more and more repulsive. . . . And why do I compare him to Achron and the others? A finer bone structure, perhaps, and a more slender body—apart from that shocking deformity—and a higher voice?

"Quiet, please!" The owner of the shocking deformity subsided. Johngrimes turned again to the barrier. "Captain Diomedes, I request that you get in touch with some higher authority. I am here on Federation business."

"What federation?" asked Diomedes.

"You don't know? You really don't know?"

"No. But, of course, I'm Security, so nobody ever tells me anything."

"What a bloody planet," murmured Margaret-lazenby. "What a bloody planet!"

"That will do, Peggy," admonished Johngrimes.

And how many names do these people have?

Brasidus asked himself. Through the wire mesh of the barrier he stared curiously at the Lady. *He must be some sort of alien,* he thought. And yet . . . Margaretlazenby, suddenly conscious of his stare, blushed, then returned his gaze in a cool, appraising manner that, fantastically, brought the blood flooding to the skin of his own face.

Chapter Five

BRASIDUS FLUSHED AS he met the spaceman's appraising—and somehow approving—stare. He heard him murmur to his captain, "Buy that one for me, Daddy," and heard Johngrimes' reply, "Peggy, you're incorrigible. Get back on board at once."

"But I *am* the ethologist, John."

"No need to get wrapped up in your work. Get back on board."

"Yes, sir. Very good, sir. Aye, aye, sir."

He looked at Brasidus for a long, last time and then turned with a flounce of kilts. The movement of his hips and full buttocks as he mounted the ramp was disturbing.

"Now, perhaps," said the Commander, "we can get down to business. I may be old-fashioned, but I've never cared much for a mixed crew."

"So it's true, Lieutenant Commander," Diomedes said. "So you aren't from Latterhaven."

"Of course not. We shall be calling there after we've finished here. But tell me, what made the penny drop so suddenly?" He grinned. "Or should I have said 'obol'?"

"You speak strangely, Johngrimes. What do you mean?"

"Just a figure of speech. Don't you have automatic vendors? No? What I meant was this: Why should my mention of a mixed crew suddenly convince you that my claim that this is a Federal ship is correct?"

Diomedes did not answer at once. He glared around at Cleon and his aides, at Brasidus and his men. He growled, "You all of you have ears—unluckily. You all of you have heard far too much. But you will not speak of it. To anybody. I need not remind you of what has happened in the past to men who have breached Security." He turned back to the space captain. "Your arrival here, Lieutenant Commander, has rather upset our notions of cosmogony. It is now a matter for the Council—and for the Council only."

"But why *did* the penny drop?" persisted Johngrimes.

"Because you have brought evidence that there is more than one intelligent race in the universe. At first we thought that your Margaretlazenby was deformed—on this world, of course, he would have been exposed immediately after birth—and then you told us that you have a mixed crew."

The Commander stared at Diomedes incredulously. He said at last, "Of course, it has been said more than once, not altogether in jest, that they aren't really human. . . . But tell me, Captain Diomedes, do you actually mean what I think you mean? Haven't you anybody like her on your planet?"

"Like *what*, Lieutenant Commander?"

"Like her. Like Doctor Lazenby."

"Of course not. We are all human here. As we should be, Sparta being the birthplace of the human race."

"You really mean that?"

"Of course," replied Diomedes.

But does he? wondered Brasidus, who had worked with the Security Captain before.

"And you have no . . . ?" began the spaceman, then pulled himself up abruptly. Brasidus recognized the signs. *Find out all you can, but give nothing away yourself.*

"We have no what?" prompted Diomedes.

Johngrimes made a quick recovery. "No Immigration, no Customs, no Port Health?"

"I've already told you that, Lieutenant Commander. And I've already told you that you and your crew must remain confined to your ship."

"Then perhaps you would care to come aboard, Captain Diomedes, to talk things over."

"Not by myself—and not unarmed."

"You may bring one man with you," said Johngrimes slowly. "But both of you will leave your weapons this side of the barrier."

"We could board by force," said Diomedes.

"Could you? I think not. *Seeker* may be carrying out the Census, but she's still a frigate, with a frigate's armament. In a matter of seconds we could sweep this field—*and* the sky over the field—clear of life. This is not a threat, merely a statement of fact." The words carried conviction.

Diomedes hesitated. "Very well," he said at last. He looked up to the circling airships as though for reassurance, shook his head doubtfully. He addressed Cleon, "Port Master, please have your radioman inform the Flight Admiral of my movements." He turned to Brasidus, "Sergeant, you may come with me. Leave Leading Hoplite Hector in charge."

Brasidus got close enough to Diomedes so that he could speak in a low, urgent whisper. "But, sir, the standing orders . . . the passes, to be signed by a member of the Council . . ."

"And who do you think drew up those standing orders, Sergeant? *I* am Security." Diomedes unlocked the gate with a key from his belt pouch. "Come with me."

"Your weapons," reminded Johngrimes.

Diomedes sighed, unbuckled his belt with its two holstered pistols, passed it to one of the men. Brasidus followed suit. The Sergeant felt naked, far more so than when stripped for the dance or for field sports. He knew that he still retained one weapon in the use of which he was, as were all members of the police branch of the Army, superbly trained—his body. But he missed those smooth, polished wooden butts that fitted so snugly into his hands. Even a despised sword or spear would have been better than nothing.

Ahead of them, Johngrimes was walking briskly toward the open airlock door, toward the foot of the ramp. Diomedes and Brasidus followed. They could see, as they neared the vessel, that the odd excrescences on its skin were gun turrets, that from at least two of them slender barrels were trained upon them, following them, that from others heavier weapons tracked the circling airships.

Johngrimes was taking no chances.

Although he had been often enough on spaceport guard duties, this was the first time that Brasidus had been aboard a spaceship; usually it was only Diomedes who boarded visiting vessels.

Mounting the ramp, the Sergeant eyed professionally the little group of officers waiting just
inside the airlock. They all carried sidearms, and
they all looked competent enough. *Even so,*
thought Brasidus, *they'll not be able to use their
pistols, for fear of hitting each other. The knee to
the groin, the edge of the hand to the neck . . .*

"Better not," said Diomedes, reading his subordinate's face.

"Better not," said Johngrimes, turning back to
look at the pair of them. "An incident could have
unfortunate—for your planet—repercussions."

Better not, thought Brasidus.

Soldierlike, he approved the smartness with
which the spacemen saluted their commander.
And soldierlike, he did not like the feel of a deck
under his feet instead of solid ground. Nonetheless, he looked about him curiously. He was disappointed. He had been expecting, vaguely, vistas
of gleaming machines, all in fascinating motion,
banks of fluorescing screens, assemblages of intri-
cate instruments. But all that there was was a little
metal-walled room, cubical except for the curvature of its outer side, and beyond that another
little room, shaped like a wedge of pie with a bite
out of its narrow end.

But there must be more to the ship than this.

An officer pressed a button on the far, inwardly
curved wall of the inside room. A door slid aside,
revealing yet another little compartment, cylindrical this time. Johngrimes motioned to his
guests—*or hostages?* Diomedes (but he was familiar with spaceships) entered this third room
without any hesitation. Apprehensively Brasidus

followed him, with Johngrimes bringing up the rear.

"Don't worry," said Diomedes to Brasidus. "This is only an elevator."

"An . . . an elevator?"

"It elevates you. Is that correct, Lieutenant Commander?"

"It is, Captain Diomedes." Johngrimes turned to Brasidus. "At the moment, we are inside the axial shaft—a sort of hollow column running almost the full length of the ship. This cage that we've just entered will carry us up to my quarters. We never use it, of course, in free fall—only during acceleration or on a planetary surface."

"Do you have machines to do the work of your legs, sir?"

"Why not, Sergeant?"

"Isn't that . . . decadent?"

The spaceship commander laughed. "Men have been saying that ever since the first lazy and intelligent bastard invented the wheel. Tell me, did you march out from the city to the spaceport, or did you ride?"

"That's different, sir," said Brasidus lamely.

"Like hell it is." Johngrimes pressed a button. The door slid shut. And almost immediately Brasidus experienced an odd, sinking sensation in his stomach. He knew that the cage was in motion, felt that it was upward motion. Fascinated, he watched the lights flashing in succession on the panel by the door—and almost lost his balance when the elevator slowed to a stop.

The door slid open again, revealing a short stretch of alleyway. Still there were no machines, no instruments—but the air was alive with the subdued murmur of machinery.

Brasidus had likened the ship to a metallic tower, but this was not like being inside a building. It was like being inside a living organism.

Chapter Six

"COME IN," SAID Johngrimes, pushing a button that opened another sliding door. "As a very dear friend of mine used to say, this is Liberty Hall. You can spit on the mat and call the cat a bastard."

"Cat?" asked Brasidus, ignoring an admonitory glare from Diomedes. "Bastard? What are they?" He added, "It's the second time you've used that last word, sir."

"You must forgive my Sergeant's unmannerly curiosity, Lieutenant Commander," said Diomedes.

"A healthy trait, Captain. After all, you are both policemen." He smiled rather grimly. "So am I, in a manner of speaking. . . . But sit down, both of you."

Brasidus remained standing until he received a grudging nod from his superior. Then he was amazed by the softness, by the comfort of the chair into which he lowered himself. On Sparta such luxury was reserved for the aged—and only for the highly paced aged at that, for Council members and the like. This lieutenant commander was not an old man, probably no older than Brasidus himself. Yet here he was, housed in quarters that the King might envy. The room in which Johngrimes was entertaining him and Diomedes was not large, but it was superbly appointed. There were the deep easy chairs, fitted with peculiar straps, there was a wall-to-wall carpet, indigo in color, with a deep pile, there were drapes, patterned blue, that obviously concealed other doorways, and there were pictures set on the polished paneling of the walls. They were like no paintings or photographs that Brasidus had ever seen. They glowed, seemingly, with a light of their own. They were three-dimensional. They were like little windows on to other worlds.

Brasidus could not help staring at the one nearest to him. It could have been a typical scene on his own Sparta—distant, snow-capped peaks in the background, blue water and yellow sand, then, in the foreground, the golden-brown bodies of naked athletes.

But . . .

Brasidus looked more closely. Roughly half of the figures were human—and the rest of them were like this mysterious Margaretlazenby. So that was what he must look like unclothed. The deformity of the upper part of the body was bad enough; that of the lower part was shocking.

"Arcadia," said Johngrimes. "A very pleasant planet. The people are enthusiastic nudists—but, of course, they have the climate for it."

"We," said Diomedes, turning his attention to the picture from the one that he had been studying, a bleak, mountain range in silhouette against a black sky, "exercise naked in all weathers."

"You would," replied Johngrimes lightly.

"So," went on Diomedes after a pause, "this Margaretlazenby of yours is an Arcadian." He got to his feet to study the hologram more closely. "H'm. How do they reproduce? Oddly enough, I have seen the same deformation on the bodies of some children who have been exposed. Coincidence, of course."

"You Spartans live up to your name," said Johngrimes coldly.

"I don't see what you mean, Lieutenant Commander. But no matter. I think I begin to understand. These Arcadians are a subject race—intelligent but nonhuman, good enough to serve in subordinate capacities, but temperamentally, at least, unqualified for full command."

"Doctor Lazenby was born on Arcadia. It's a good job she's not here to listen to you saying that."

"But it's true, isn't it? H'm. What amazes and disgusts me about this picture is the way in which humans are mingling with these . . . these aliens on terms of apparent equality."

"I suppose you could look at it that way."

"Here, even though we are all Men, we are careful not to be familiar with any but privileged helots. And these Arcadians are *aliens*."

"Some time," said Johngrimes, "I must make a careful study of your social history. It should be fascinating. Although that is really Peggy's job."

"Peggy?"

"Doctor Lazenby."

"And some time," said Diomedes, "I must make inquiries as to your system of nomenclature. I have heard you call this Margaretlazenby by his rank and profession, with the first part of his name missing. And I have heard you call him Peggy."

Johngrimes laughed. "I suppose that it is rather confusing to people who have only one name apiece. *We* have at least two—the surname, or family name . . ."

"But there is only one family. The State."

"On Sparta, perhaps. But let me finish, Captain Diomedes. We have the family name, which, with us, comes last, although some human races put it first. Then we have one, if not more, given name. Then we have nicknames. For example, Margaret, one word, Lazenby, one word. Peggy—which for some obscure reason is a corruption of Margaret. Of course, she could also be called Maggie or Meg. Or Peg. In my own case—John Grimes. But that 'John' can be changed to 'Jack' or 'Johnnie' by people who really know me."

"Like Theo for Theopompus," contributed Brasidus.

"Yes. Some of our nicknames are curtailments, like Margie or Margo for Margaret."

"How many names *has* that being got?" exploded Diomedes.

"I've heard her called other things—and called her them myself. But you wouldn't know what a bitch is, would you?"

"Doubtless some exotic beast you've run across on your travels. But, Lieutenant Commander, you keep on using these odd pronouns—'she' and 'her.' Are they confined to Arcadians?"

"You could say that." Grimes seemed to be amused by something. "Now, gentlemen, may I offer you refreshment? The sun's not yet over the yardarm, but a drop of alcohol won't kill us. Or would you rather have coffee?"

"Coffee? What's that?"

"Don't you have it here? Perhaps you would like to try some now."

"If you partake with us," said Diomedes cautiously.

"But of course." Grimes got to his feet, went to

his desk, picked up a telephone. "Pantry? Captain here. I'd like my coffee now, please. Large pot, with all the trimmings. Three cups."

He took an oddly shaped wooden...instrument(?) off the desk top, stuffed a hollow bowl at the end of it with what looked like a dried brown weed, put the thin stem in his mouth, applied a flame from a little metal contraption to the open top of the bowl. He inhaled with apparent pleasure, then expelled from the between his lips a cloud of fragrant fumes. "Sorry," he said, "do you smoke?" He opened an ornamental box, displaying rows of slim cylinders obviously rolled from the brown weed.

"I think that one strange luxury will be enough for one day, Lieutenant Commander," said Diomedes, to Brasidus' disappointment.

The door to the outside alleyway opened. A spaceman came in, by his uniform not an officer, carrying a large silver tray on which rested a steaming silver pot, a silver jug and a silver bowl filled with some white powder, and also three cups of gleaming, crested porcelain each standing in its own little plate. But it was not the tray at which Diomedes and Brasidus stared; it was at the bearer.

He was obviously yet another Arcadian.

Brasidus glanced from him to the picture, and back again. He realized that he was wondering what the spaceman would look like stripped of that severe, functional clothing.

"Milk, sir? Sugar?" the man was asking.

"I don't think that they have them on this planet, Sheila," said Grimes. "There's quite a lot that they don't have."

Chapter Seven

SLOWLY DIOMEDES AND Brasidus made their way
down the ramp from the airlock. Both were silent,
and the Sergeant, at least, was being hard put to
sort and to evaluate the multitude of new impressions that had crowded upon him. The coffee—
could it be a habit-forming drug? But it was good.
And that burning weed the fumes of which Lieutenant Commander Grimes had inhaled with such
enjoyment. And the un-Spartan luxury in which
Grimes lived—luxury utterly unsuitable for a
fighting man. And this Interstellar Federation, an
officer of whose navy—although it was called the
Survey Service—he claimed to be.

And those oddly disturbing Arcadians (if they
were Arcadians)—the doctor Lazenby, the
steward Sheila, and one or two more whom the
Spartans had glimpsed on their way ashore . . .

They were out of earshot of the ship now, halfway between the airlock and the gate, outside
which Hector and the other hoplites had stiffened
to attention. Diomedes said, "Come to my office,
Sergeant. I want to talk things over with you.
There's a lot that I don't understand, but much of it
strengthens my suspicions."

"Of whom, sir? This Lieutenant Commander
Grimes?"

"No. He's just a spaceman, the same as Captain Bill and Captain Jim of the Venus and the Hera. If his service prefers to tack a double-barreled label on him, that's his worry. Oh, I want to find out where the ship *is* from and what's the *real* reason for its visit, but my main suspicions are much nearer home."

They passed through the gate, opened for them and locked after them by Hector, Old Cleon approached them, was brushed off by Diomedes. They continued their march to the office, although in the case of Diomedes it was more of a waddle.

"In my job," went on the Security Captain, buckling on his pistol belt as he walked, "I'm no respecter of persons. I shouldn't be earning my pay if I were." He gestured upwards. "Flight Admiral Ajax up there, for example. He holds his rank—and his life—only because I do not choose to act yet. When I do . . ." He closed his pudgy fist decisively and suggestively. "You're an ambitious man, Brasidus. And an intelligent one. I've had my eye on you for some time. I have been thinking of asking to have you transferred to Security. And when Diomedes *asks*, people hurry to oblige him."

"Thank you, sir."

"With promotion to lieutenant, of course."

"Thank you, sir."

"Think nothing of it. I need a young assistant for the . . . the legwork." He smiled, showing all his uneven, discolored teeth, obviously pleased with the expression that he had just coined. "The legwork," he repeated.

The two men entered the Spaceport Security

Office, passed through into Diomedes' private room. At the Captain's order, Brasidus sat down. The chair was hard, comfortless, yet he felt far happier on it than he had felt in the luxury of Lieutenant Commander Grimes' day cabin. Diomedes produced a flagon of beer, two mugs. He poured. "To our . . . partnership," he said.

"To our partnership, sir."

"Now, *Lieutenant* Brasidus, what I am saying to you is strictly confidential. I need not remind you of the consequences to yourself if you abuse my confidence. To begin with, I played along with this man Grimes. I asked the silly questions that he'd assume that I would ask. But I formed my own conclusions."

"And what were they, sir?"

"Oh, I'm not telling you yet, young Brasidus. I could be wrong—and I want your mind to remain uninfluenced by any theories of mine. But they tie in, they tie in. They tie in with the most heinous crime of all—treason to the State. Now, tell me, who're the most powerful men on Sparta?"

"The most powerful man is the King, sir."

Diomedes' thin eyebrows lifted, arching over his muddy eyes. "Is he? But no matter. And I said 'the most powerful men.' "

"The Council, sir."

"H'm. Could be. *Could* be. But . . ."

"What are you driving at, sir?"

"What about the doctors, our precious medical priesthood? Don't they control the birth machines? Don't they decide who among the newly born is to live, and who, to die? Don't they conduct the fatherhood tests? Don't they say, in effect, that there shall be so many members of the military caste, so many helots—*and so many doctors?*"

"Yes. That's so, sir. But how could they be traitors?"

"Opportunity, dear boy. Opportunity. Opportunity for a betrayal of the principles upon which our State was founded. Frankly, although I have long harbored suspicions, I did not really think that it was possible until the man Grimes landed here with his ship and his mixed crew. Now I realize the evil spell that can be exerted by those . . . creatures."

"What creatures?" demanded Brasidus as impatiently as he dared.

"The Arcadians? Yes—that's as good a name as any." He refilled the mugs. "Now, I have to make my report and my recommendations to the Council. When Grimes made his first psionic contact with the spaceport authorities, before he reentered normal Space Time, he requested permission to land and to take a census, and also to carry out ecological and ethological surveys. Ethology, by the way, is the science of behavior. I learned that much, although I've been making use of its principles for years. Later he confirmed this by normal radio—psionic reception at this end was rather garbled as our telepaths were completely unfamiliar with so many new concepts.

"As you well know, after your many spells of spaceport guard duty, it has always been contrary to Council policy to allow visiting spacemen to mingle with our population. But I shall recommend that in this case an exception be made, arguing that Grimes and his men are quite harmless, also that the Federation—yes, I'm afraid that there *is* one—is obviously powerful and might take offense if its servants are not hospitably received.

"My real reason for the recommendation I shall keep to myself."

"And what is it, sir?"

"When a pot boils, Brasidus, all sorts of scum comes to the top. A few . . . Arcadians running around on Sparta might well bring the pot to the boil. And who will get scalded? *That* is the question."

"You don't like the doctors, Captain?"

"That I do not. I am hoping that those whom I suspect of treason will be forced to act—and to act rashly."

"There *is* something suspicious about them—or about some of them." Briefly, but omitting nothing, Brasidus told Diomedes of his encounter with Heraklion in the crèche. "He was hiding something," he concluded. "I am sure of that."

"And you're ideally situated to find out what it was, Brasidus." Diomedes was thoughtful. "This is the way that we shall play it. Officially you are still a sergeant in the Police Battalion. Your pay will be made up, however, to lieutenant's rates out of Security funds. You will be relieved of spaceport guard duties. You will discover, in fact, that your captain will be allowing you considerable free time—free insofar as *he* is concerned. As far as *I* am concerned, it will not be so free. Off duty, you will be able to visit your friend Achron at the crèche. I already knew of your friendship with him, as a matter of fact—that was one of the reasons why I was considering having you transferred to my Branch. One of the nurses might have been a better recruit—but their loyalties are so unreliable. On duty, you will act as escort to Lieutenant Commander Grimes and his officers.

"And you will report to me everything—and I mean *everything*—you learn."

"And what shall I learn, sir?"

"You'll be surprised. It could be that I shall be, too." He picked up the telephone on his desk, ordered his car brought round to the office. Then he said to Brasidus, "Give Hector his instructions. He can carry on until relieved. Then you can ride with me back to the city."

Chapter Eight

BACK IN THE city, Diomedes had his driver proceed directly to the police barracks. There, with no trouble, he obtained an interview with Brasidus' commanding officer. Brasidus, sitting on the hard bench outside the captain's office, wondered what was being said about him. Then the door opened and he was called in.

He looked at the two men confronting him—the squat, somehow squalid Diomedes, the tall, soldierly Lycurgus. Diomedes looked smugly satisfied, Lycurgus, resentful. There could be no doubt as to how things had gone—and, suddenly, Brasidus hoped that he would not regret this change of masters.

"Sergeant—or should I say Lieutenant?" growled Lycurgus. "I think that you already know of your transfer. Officially, however, you are still a sergeant and you are still working for me. Your real orders, however, will come from Captain Diomedes." He paused, then went on, "You are relieved from duty until 0800 hours tomorrow morning, at which time you are to report to the spaceport." He turned to Diomedes. "He's all yours, Diomedes."

"Thank you, Lycurgus. You may accompany me, Brasidus."

They left the office. Diomedes asked, "And when is your friend Achron on duty again, young man?"

"He has the midnight to 0600 shift for the rest of this week, sir."

"Good. Then I propose that you spend the rest of the day at leisure; after all, this was supposed to be your free time, wasn't it? Get some sleep this evening before midnight—you might visit Achron again then. Of course, you will report to me at the spaceport tomorrow morning. I have no doubt that I shall be able to persuade the Council to accede to Lieutenant Commander Grimes' requests, so you will be required for escort duties."

"And when I visit Achron, sir? Am I to carry out any investigations?"

"Yes. But cautiously, cautiously. Find out what you can without sticking your neck out. But I must leave you now. I have to report to my lords and masters." His sardonic intonation left no doubt in Brasidus' mind as to who was the real lord and master.

Brasidus went to the mess hall for a late and solitary luncheon of bread, lukewarm stew and beer. Then, conscious of his new (but secret) rank and his new responsibilities, he decided to visit the library. There were books, of course, in the recreation hall of the barracks, but these were mainly works of fiction, including the imaginative thrillers that were his favorite reading. (But none of the writers had imagined monsters so fantastic as these Arcadians—fantastic because of similarities to as well as differences from normal humankind.) He was in uniform still, but that did not matter. However, there was his belt, with its holstered pistols. He went to the desk sergeant to turn it in.

"Keep it, Brasidus," he was told. "Captain Lycurgus said that you were on instant call as long as the spaceship's in port."

It made sense—just as the regulation forbidding the carrying of firearms when not on duty made sense; they might be used in a drunken brawl at one of the Clubs. However, Brasidus always felt happier when armed and so did not inquire further. He went out into the street, his iron-tipped sandals ringing on the cobbles. He stood on the sidewalk to watch a troop of armored cavalry pass, the tracks of the chariots striking sparks from the paving, the gay pennons whipping from the slender radio masts, the charioteers in their plumed helmets standing tall and proud in their turrets.

Cavalry in the city. The Council must be apprehensive.

Brasidus continued his walk when the chariots had gone by. He strode confidently up the wide stone steps to the white-pillared library entrance, but inside the cool building diffidence assailed him. An elderly man behind a big desk surveyed him disapprovingly, his gaze lingering on the weapons. "Yes, Sergeant?" he demanded coldly.

"I . . . I want to do some reading."

"Unless you've come here to make an arrest, that's obvious. What sort of reading? We do have a thriller section." He made "thriller" sound like a dirty word.

"No, not thrillers. We've plenty of those in our own recreation hall. History."

The bushy white eyebrows lifted. "Oh. Historical thrillers."

"No. Not thrillers." Brasidus was finding it hard to keep his temper. "History."

The old man did not get up from his seat, but turned and pointed. "Through there, Sergeant. That door. If you want to take a book out, you'll have to sign for it and pay a deposit, but there are tables and benches if you want to read on the premises."

"Thank you," said Brasidus.

He went through the door, noted the sign "HISTORICAL SECTION" above it. He stared at the book-lined walls, not knowing where to begin. He walked to the nearer shelves, just inside the doorway, the clatter of his uniform sandals on the marble floor drawing disapproving glares from the half dozen or so readers seated at the tables. But they were only helots, by the looks of them, and their feelings did not matter.

He scanned the row of titles. *A History of Sparta,* by Alcamenes. That would do to start with. He pulled it from its place on the shelf, carried it to a vacant table, sat down. He adjusted the reading lamp.

Yes, he had been lucky in his random choice. This seemed to be a very comprehensive history—starting, in fact, in prehistorical days. The story it told should not have been new to Brasidus. After all, he had been exposed to a normal education. But he had not paid much attention to his teachers; he had known that he was destined to be a soldier. So, apart from the study of past campaigns, of what value was education to him?

But here it all was. The evolution of a biped from a big-headed quadruped, with forelimbs modified to arms and hands. The slow, slow beginnings of civilization, of organized science. And then, at last, the invention of the birth machine by Lacedaemon, the perfection of the technique by which the father's seed could be brought to maturity apart from his body. No longer hampered by the process of budding, men went ahead by leaps and bounds. Aristodemus, the first King of Sparta, organized and drilled his army and navy, subjugated the other city-states, imposed the name of his capital upon the entire planet, although (even to this day, as Brasidus knew) there were occasional armed revolts.

And there were the scientific advancements. The mechanical branch of the priesthood advanced from aeronautics to astronautics and, under Admiral Latterus, a star fleet was launched, its object being the colonization of a relatively nearby planet. But Latterus was ambitious, set up his own kingdom, and with him he had taken the only priests who knew the secret of the interstellar drive. After many generations the people of Latterhaven—as Latterus' colony had been called—revisited Sparta. A trade agreement was drawn up and signed, complying with which the Latterhaveneers sent two ships every year, bringing various manufactured goods in exchange for shipments of the spices that grew only on Sparta.

Impatiently Brasidus turned to the index. Interstellar Federation. No. Not listed. Interstellar ships, interstellar drive, but no Federation. But that would have been too much to expect. Latterhaven had a history, but its people kept it to themselves. This Admiral Latterus had his ships and, no doubt, one planet had not been enough for him. He had his birth machines—and, even though Brasidus was no biologist, he was sure that it would be possible to accelerate production. The natural way—intercourse between two beings and, possibly, each one budding—was slow and wasteful. Suppose that *all* the seed were utilized. Then how long would it take to build up teeming populations on a dozen worlds?

Terra, for example.

And Arcadia?

No. Not Arcadia.

But *were* the Arcadians humans? Could they be the result of a malfunction of the birth machine set up on their planet? If this was the case, how could they, with their obvious physical deficiencies, reproduce?

Brasidus looked up Arcadia in the index. It was not, of course, listed.

He put Alcamenes' book back on the shelf, went out to see the old librarian. "Have you," he asked, "anything on the Interstellar Federation? Or on a world called Arcadia?"

"I told you," huffed the ancient man, "that it was fiction you wanted. Science fiction, at that."

"Suppose I told you that there *is* an Interstellar Federation? Suppose I told you that there are, at present, Arcadians on Sparta?"

"I'd say, young man, that you were quite mad—if it wasn't for your uniform. And it's not that I'm afraid of *that*, or of the guns you wear into my library. It's because that I know—as who doesn't?—that a strange unscheduled ship has made a landing at the spaceport. And you're a sergeant in the Police Battalion of the Army, so you know more about what's going on than we poor scholars." He cackled. "Go on, Sergeant. Tell me more. I am always willing to acquire new knowledge."

"What rumors have you heard?" asked Brasidus. After all, he was a Security officer now and might as well start acting like one.

"They say that this ship's a battleship—and, with the Air Navy hanging over the spaceport like a bad smell and the streets full of cavalry, it could well be. They say that the President of Latterhaven has demanded our instant surrender. They say, too, that the ship's not from Latterhaven at all, that it's manned by robots with twin turrets on their chests from which they shoot lethal rays."

"They must be functional . . . " mused Brasidus, "I suppose."

"What must be?" demanded the librarian.

"Those twin turrets. Good day to you."

He clanked out through the wide doorway, down the stone steps.

Chapter Nine

BRASIDUS WALKED BACK to his barracks, thinking over what he had read and what the librarian had told him. It all tied in—almost. But how did it tie in with Diomedes' suspicions of the medical priesthood? Perhaps tonight he would be able to find something out.

In the mess hall he partook of an early evening meal—and still his active brain was working. The spices exported to Latterhaven were a luxury, so much so that they were used but rarely in Spartan cookery. *And you can say that again,* Brasidus told himself, chewing viciously on his almost flavorless steak. Obviously they were also a luxury on the other planet; otherwise why should the Latterhaveneers find it worthwhile to send two ships every year for the annual shipment? But what *did* the Latterhaveneers bring in return for the spices? Manufactured goods. But *what* manufactured goods?

Brasidus, as a spaceport guard, had watched the Latterhaven ships discharging often enough. He had seen the unmarked wooden crates sliding down the conveyor belts into the waiting trucks, had vaguely wondered where these same trucks were bound when, escorted by police chariots, they had left the spaceport. He had made inquiries once, of one of the charioteers whom he knew slightly. "We just convey them into the city," the man had told him. "They're unloaded at that big warehouse—you know the one, not far from the crèche. Andronicus Imports."

And what did Andronicus import?

Diomedes might know.

Finishing his meal, Brasidus wandered into the recreation hall. He bought a mug of sweet wine from the steward on duty, sat down to watch television. There was the news first—but there was no mention of the landing of *Seeker III*. Fair enough. The Council had still to decide what to say about it as well as what to do about it. The main coverage was of the minor war in progress between Pharis and Messenia. Peisander, the Messenian general, was something of an innovator. Cleombrotus of Pharis was conservative, relying upon his hoplites to smash through the Messenian lines, and his casualties, under the heavy fire of the Messenian archers, were heavy. There were those who maintained that the bow should be classed as a firearm and its use forbidden to the ordinary soldiery, those not in the Police Battalion. Of course, if the hoplites, with their spears and swords, got loose among the archers, there would be slaughter. Against that, the archers, lightly armored, far less encumbered, could run much faster. The commentator, hovering above the battlefield, made this same comment, and Brasidus congratulated himself upon his grasp of military principles.

Following the news came a coverage of the games at Helos. Brasidus watched the wrestling bouts for a while, then got up and left the hall. After all, the games were no more than a substitute for war—and war, to every Spartan worth his salt, was the only sport for a man. Nonlethal sports were only for helots.

Finding the duty orderly, the Sergeant gave instructions to be called at 2330 hours.

He was almost at the crèche when he saw a slight form ahead of him. He quickened his pace, overtook the other pedestrian. As he had thought it would be, it was Achron.

The nurse was pleased to see him. He said, "I rang the barracks, Brasidus, and they told me that you were on duty all day."

"I was, but I'm off the hook now."

"You were at the spaceport, weren't you? Is it true that this ship is from *outside*, with a crew of monsters?"

"Just a ship," Brasidus told him.

"But the *monsters*?"

"What monsters?"

"Horribly deformed beings from outer space. *Mutants*."

"Well, Diomedes and myself were entertained on board by the commander, and he's human enough."

"More than you can say for Diomedes," commented Achron spitefully. "I used to like him *once*, but not any more. Not after what he *did*."

"What did he do?"

"I'll tell you sometime. Are you coming in, Brasidus?"

"Why not?"

"Telemachus will be pleased. He was saying to

me what a fine example you are to the average
Spartan."

"Back again, Sergeant?" the old man greeted
him. "I shall soon think that you would welcome
a return to the bad old days of budding."

"Hardly," said Brasidus, trying to visualize the
difficulties that would be experienced in the use
of weapons when encumbered by undetached offspring.

"And were you out at the spaceport today,
Brasidus?"

"Yes."

"What are they *really* like, these monsters?"

"Captain Diomedes bound us all to secrecy."

"A pity. A pity. If you were to tell me what you
saw, it would never go beyond the walls of this
building."

"I'm sorry, Telemachus. You'll just have to wait
until the news is released by the Council."

"The Council." The old man laughed bitterly.
"In my day there were men of imagination serving
on it. But now . . . " He looked up at the wall clock.
"Well, in you go. Phillip is waiting for his relief.
He was most unpleasant when he discovered that
I had detained you this time yesterday."

Brasidus followed his friend to the ward where
he was on duty. This time Phillip was in a better
mood—and he, too, tried to pump the Sergeant
about the day's events at the spaceport. Finally he
gave up and left the two friends. As before,
Brasidus allowed himself to be led to the sons who
might be his own. Yet again he was unable to
detect any real resemblance. And then—it was
what he had been waiting for—all the babies
awoke.

He retreated hastily, as any normal man would have done, leaving Achron to cope. But he did not go to the door by which he had entered, but to the farther doorway. He waited there for a minute or so, thinking that Doctor Heraklion or one of his colleagues might be attracted by the uproar—but, after all, such noises were common enough in the crèche.

But neither Heraklion nor anybody else appeared in the long, dimly lit corridor, and Brasidus decided to venture further afield. He was barefooted, so could walk silently. He was wearing a civilian tunic, which was advantageous. Should anybody who did not know him see him, his appearance would be less likely to cause alarm than if he was in uniform.

Cautiously he advanced along the corridor. His own was the only movement. If there were any sounds, he could not hear them for the bawling behind him. On either side of the corridor there were numbered doors. Storerooms? Laboratories? Cautiously he tried one. It was locked.

He continued his prowl. It was a long corridor, and he did not wish to get too far from the ward —yet this was a golden opportunity to find something out. He came to a cross passageway, hesitated. He saw that a chair was standing just inside the left-hand passage. Presumably it had just been evacuated—there was a book open, face down, on the seat, a flagon and a mug beside it. A guard? If so, not a very good one. No doubt he had some pressing reason for deserting his post—but he would never have done so, at no matter what cost to personal dignity, had he been a member of the military caste. A helot, then—or even a doctor?

Heraklion? Brasidus did not know what the man's hours of duty were, but they could coincide with or overlap Achron's.

He picked up the book, looked at the title, *Galactic Spy*, by Delmar Brudd. Yet another of those odd double names. He turned to the title page, saw that the novel had been published by the Phoenix Press, Latterton, on the planet of Latterhaven. So this was a sample of the manufactured goods exported by that planet. But why should these books not be put into general circulation? If it were a question of freight, large editions could easily be printed here on Sparta.

He was suddenly aware that a door was opening. He heard someone say, "I must leave you, dear. After all, it is my turn for sentry duty."

A strange voice replied. It was too high-pitched, held an odd, throaty quality. Yet it was oddly familiar. What—*who*—did it remind Brasidus of? Even as he slid silently back around the corner—but not before he had replaced the book as he had found it—he had the answer. It sounded like the voice of the Arcadian, Margaret Lazenby. It was certainly not the voice of any native of Sparta.

Still, Brasidus was reluctant to retreat. He continued to peer around the corner, ready to jerk back in a split second. "I prefer you to the others, Heraklion," the Arcadian was saying.

"I'm flattered, Sally. But you shouldn't have come to me. It's very dangerous. If Orestes found that I'd deserted my post, there'd be all hell let loose. And besides . . ."

"Besides what?"

"Only last night—or, rather, yesterday morning—that revolting young pansy Achron had his boyfriend with him in the ward—and this same boyfriend is a police sergeant. A dumb one, luckily. Even so, we have to be careful."

"Buy why, Heraklion, why? You're priests as well as doctors. You control this planet. It would be easy for you to engineer a rough parity of the numbers of men and women—and then just let Nature take its course."

"You don't understand . . ."

"That's what you're always saying. But you saw to it that we were educated and drew some far-fetched analogy between ourselves and the hetaerae of ancient Greece. I know that we're petted and pampered—but only within these walls. We've never seen outside them. Is that how women live on Latterhaven, on Terra, on all the Man-colonized plaents?"

"You don't understand, Sally."

"No. Of course not. I'm only a woman. And it's obvious that you don't want me, so I'm getting back to my own quarters. To the *harem*." This final word, dripping contempt, was strange to Brasidus.

"As you will."

"And the next time you come to *me*, I shall be busy."

The door opened properly, but still Brasidus did not withdraw his head. The couple who emerged from the storeroom or whatever it was had their backs to him. The shorter of the pair was dressed in a brief, black tunic woven from some transparent material. His lustrous, auburn hair hung to his smooth, gleaming shoulders and his rounded buttocks gleamed through the flimsy garment. He walked with a peculiarly provocative

swing of the hips. Brasidus stared after him—and
so, luckily, did Heraklion. Before the doctor could
turn, Brasidus withdrew, hurried silently back
along the corridor. There were no shouts, no pursuit. The only noise came from the ward, where
Achron—*and what was a pansy?*—still had not
pacified his charges.

Conquering his repugnance, Brasidus went in.
"Can I help?" he asked the nurse.

"Oh, you're still here, Brasidus. I thought you'd
have run away *ages* ago. Bring me some bottles
from the dispenser, will you? You know how."

Brasidus obeyed. While he was so engaged,
Doctor Heraklion strode through the doorway.
"Really, Sergeant," he snapped, "I can't have this.
This is the second time that you've come blunder-
ing in here, disturbing our charges. I shall have to
complain to your superior."

"I'm sorry, Doctor."

"That isn't good enough, Sergeant. Leave,
please. At once."

Brasidus left. He would gain nothing by staying
any longer. And perhaps he should telephone
Diomedes to tell him what he had learned. But
what had he learned? That there was a nest of
Arcadian spies already on Sparta? Spies—or infiltrators? Infiltrators—and the doctors working in
collusion with them?

And how did that tie in with the visit of *Seeker
III*, a vessel with Arcadians in its own crew?

Very well indeed, Brasidus told himself. *Very
well indeed.*

He rang Diomedes from the first telephone
booth he came to, but there was no answer. He
rang again from the barracks, and there was still

no answer. He looked at the time, shrugged his shoulders, went to his cubicle and turned in.

While he was having his breakfast, prior to going out to the spaceport, Captain Lycurgus sent for him. "Sergeant," he said, "I've received a complaint. About you. From Doctor Heraklion, at the crèche. In future, leave his nurses alone in duty hours."

"Very good, sir."

"And one more thing, Brasidus . . ."

"Yes, sir?"

"I shall pass the Doctor's complaint on to Captain Diomedes. I understand that he gives you your real orders these days."

Chapter Ten

DIOMEDES SENT HIS car round to the barracks in the morning to pick up Brasidus. It was another fine day, and the drive out to the spaceport was pleasant. The driver was not disposed to talk, which suited Brasidus. He was turning over and over in his mind what he would tell Diomedes and was wondering what conclusions Diomedes would draw from the events in the crèche. Meanwhile, there was the morning air to enjoy, still crisp, not yet tainted by the pungency from the spice fields on either side of the road.

Above the spaceport the ships of the Air Navy still circled and, as the car neared the final approaches, Brasidus noted that heavy motorized artillery as well as squadrons of armored cavalry had been brought up. Whatever John Grimes had in mind, the Police Battalion would be ready for him. But Brasidus did not regret that he had not, as a recruit, been posted to a mechanized unit. A hoplite such as himself was always fully employed, the armored cavalry, but rarely, the artillery, almost never.

The main gates opened as the car, without slackening speed, approached them. The duty guard saluted smartly—the vehicle rather than himself, Brasidus guessed. There was a spectacular halt in a column of swirling dust outside the Security office. Diomedes was standing in the doorway. He sneezed, glared at the driver, withdrew hastily into the building. Brasidus waited until the dust had subsided before getting out of the car.

"That Agis!" snarled the Captain as he sketchily acknowledged Brasidus' salute, "I'll have him transferred to the infantry!"

"I've seen him do the same when he's been driving you, sir."

"Hmph! That's different, young man. Well, he got you here in good time. Just as well, as I've instructions for you."

"And I've a report for you, sir."

"Already, Brasidus? You've wasted no time." He smiled greasily. "As a matter of fact, I've already had a call from Captain Lycurgus, passing on a complaint from Doctor Heraklion. What did you learn?"

Brasidus, who possessed a trained memory, told his superior what he had seen and heard. Diomedes listened intently. Then he asked, "And what do you think, Brasidus?"

"That Arcadians were already on Sparta before Seeker landed, sir."

"Arcadians? Oh, yes. The twin-turreted androids. Did you hear that rumor, too? And how do you think they got here?"

"There could have been secret landings, sir. Or they could have been smuggled in aboard Latterhaven Venus and Latterhaven Hera."

"And neither of these theories throws Security in a very good light, does it? And the smuggling one rather reflects upon the spaceport guards."

"They needn't be smuggled in as adults, sir. Children could be hidden in some of those crates discharged by the Latterhaven ships. They could be drugged, too, so that they couldn't make any noise."

"Ingenious, Brasidus. Ingenious. But I've been aboard the *Venus* and the *Hera* often enough and, believe me, it would be impossible for either ship to carry more than her present complement. Not even children. They're no more than cargo boxes with a handful of cubicles, cells that we should consider inadequate for our criminals, perched on top of them."

"The cargo holds?"

"No. You can't have a man—or a child—living in any confined space without his leaving traces."

"But they didn't just . . . *happen*, sir. The Arcadians, I mean."

"Of course not. They either budded from their fathers or came out of a birth machine." Diomedes seemed to find this amusing. "No, they didn't just happen. They were either brought here or came here under their own power. But *why?*"

"Heraklion seemed to *like* the one that he was with last night. It was . . . unnatural."

"And what were *your* feelings toward him? Or *it?*"

Brasidus blushed. He muttered, "As you said yourself, sir, these beings possess a strange, evil power."

"So they do. So they do. That's why we must try to foil any plot in which they're engaged." He looked at his watch. "Meanwhile, my own original plan still stands. The Council has approved my suggestion that *Seeker's* personnel be allowed to leave their ship. Today you will, using my car and driver, escort Lieutenant Commander Grimes and Doctor Lazenby to the city, where an audience with the King and the Council has been arranged for them. You will act as guide as well as escort, and—you are armed—also as guard."

"To protect them, sir?"

"Yes. I suppose so. But mainly to protect the King. How do we know that when they are in his presence they will not pull a weapon of some kind? You will be with them; you will be situated to stop them at once. Of course, there will be plenty of my own men in the Council Chamber, but you would be able to act without delay if you had to."

"I see, sir."

"All right. Now we are to go aboard the ship to tell them that everything has been organized."

A junior officer met them in the airlock, escorted them up to the commander's quarters. Grimes was attired in what was obviously ceremonial uniform—and very hot and uncomfortable it must be, thought Brasidus. Professionally he ran his eye over the spaceman for any evidence of weapons. There was one, in full sight, but not a very dangerous one. It was a sword, its hilt gold-encrusted, in a gold-trimmed sheath at his left side. More for show than use, was Brasidus' conclusion.

John Grimes grinned at his two visitors. "I hate this rig," he confided, "but I suppose I have to show the flag. Doctor Lazenby is lucky. Nobody has ever gotten around to designing full dress for women officers."

There was a tap at the door and Margaret

Lazenby entered. He was dressed as he had been the previous day, although the clothing itself, with its bright braid and buttons, was obviously an outfit that was worn only occasionally. He said pleasantly, "Good morning, Captain Diomedes. Good morning, Sergeant. Are you coming with us, Captain?"

"Unfortunately, no. I have urgent business here at the spaceport. But Brasidus will be your personal escort. Also, I have detailed two chariots to convoy you into the city."

"*Chariots?* Oh, you mean those light tanks that we've been watching from the control room."

"*Tanks?*" repeated Diomedes curiously. "A tank is something you keep fluids in."

"There are tanks *and* tanks. Where we come from, a tank can be an armored vehicle with caterpillar tracks."

"And what does 'caterpillar' mean?"

Grimes said, "Over the generations new words come into the language and old words drop out. Obviously there are no caterpillars on Sparta, and so the term is meaningless. However, Captain Diomedes, you are welcome to make use of our microfilm library; I would suggest the *Encyclopedia Galactica.*"

"Thank you, Lieutenant Commander." Diomedes looked at his watch. "But may I suggest that you and Doctor Lazenby proceed now to your audience?"

"And will the rest of my crew be allowed ashore?"

"That depends largely upon the impression that you make upon the King and his Council."

"Where's my fore-and-aft hat?" muttered

Grimes. He got up, went through one of the curtained doorways. He emerged wearing an odd, gold-braided, black cloth helmet. He said, "Lead on, MacDuff."

"It should be 'Lay on, MacDuff,' " Margaret Lazenby told him.

"I know, I know."

"And who is MacDuff?" asked Diomedes.

"He's dead. He was the Thane of Cawdor."

"And where is Cawdor?"

Grimes sighed.

Brasidus, although he could not say why he did so, enjoyed the ride to the city. He, Grimes and Margaret Lazenby were in the back seat of the car, with the Arcadian (it was as good a label as any) sitting between the two humans. He was stirred by the close proximity of this strange being, almost uncomfortably so. When Margaret Lazenby leaned across him to look at a medusa tree swarming with harpies, he realized that those peculiar fleshy mounds, which even the severe uniform could not hide, were deliciously soft. So much for the built-in weapon theory. "What fantastic birds!" exclaimed the Arcadian.

"They are harpies," said Brasidus.

"Those round bodies do look like human heads, don't they? They could be straight out of Greek mythology."

"So you have already made a study of our legends?" asked Brasidus, interested.

"Of course." Margaret Lazenby smiled. (His lips against the white teeth were very red. Could it be natural?) "But they aren't just your legends. They belong to all Mankind."

"I suppose they do. Admiral Latterus must have carried well-stocked libraries aboard his ships."

"Admiral Latterus?" asked Margaret Lazenby curiously.

"The founder of Latterhaven. I am surprised that you have not heard of him. He was sent from Sparta to establish the colony, but he made himself King of the new world and never returned."

"What a beautiful history," murmured the Arcadian. "Carefully tailored to fit the facts. Tell me, Brasidus, did you ever hear of the Third Expansion, or of Captain John Latter, master of the early timejammer *Utah*? Come to that, did you ever hear of the First Expansion?"

"You talk in riddles, Margaret Lazenby."

"And you and your world are riddles that must be solved, Brasidus."

"Careful, Peggy," warned John Grimes.

The Arcadian turned to address his commander—and, as he did so, Brasidus was acutely conscious of the softness and resilience of the rump under the uniform kilt. "They'll have to be told the truth some time, John—and I'm sure that Brasidus will forgive me for using him as the guinea pig for the first experiment. But I am a little drunk, I guess. All this glorious fresh air after weeks of the canned variety. And look at those houses! With architecture like that, there should be *real* chariots escorting us, not these hunks of animated ironmongery. Still, apart from his sidearms, Brasidus is dressed properly."

"The ordinary hoplites," said Brasidus with some pride, "those belonging to the subject city-states, are armed only with swords and spears."

"They didn't have wristwatches in ancient

Sparta," Grimes pointed out.

"Oh, be practical, John. He could hardly wear an hourglass or a sundial on his arm, could he?"

"It's . . . phony," grumbled Grimes.

"It should be as phony as all hell, but it's not," Margaret Lazenby told him. "I wish I'd known just how things are here, though. I'd have soaked up Hellenic history before we came here. . . . What are those animals, Brasidus? They look almost like a sort of hairless wolf."

"They are the scavengers. They keep the streets of the city clean. There is a larger variety, wild, out on the hills and plains. They are the wolves."

"But that one, there. Look! It's Siamese twins. It seems to be in pain. Why doesn't somebody do something about it?"

"But why? It's only budding. Don't you reproduce like us—or like we used to, before Lacedaemon invented the birth machine?" He paused. "But I suppose you have birth machines, too."

"We do," said Grimes—and Margaret Lazenby reddened. It was obviously a private joke of some kind.

"The glory that was Greece, the grandeur that was Rome," murmured the Arcadian after a long pause. "But this isn't—forgive me, Brasidus— quite as glorious as it should be. There's a certain . . . untidiness in your streets. And this absence of women seems . . . odd. As I recall it, the average Greek housewife was nothing much to write home about, but the hetaerae must have been ornamental."

"Did they have hetaerae in Sparta?" asked Grimes. "I thought that it was only in Athens."

We do have hetaerae in Sparta, Brasidus thought but did not say, recalling what he had seen and heard in the crèche. Sally (another queer name!) had admitted to being one. But what were hetaerae, anyhow?

"They had women," said Margaret Lazenby. "And some of them must have been reasonably good-looking, even by our standards. But Sparta was more under masculine domination than the other Greek states."

"Is that the palace ahead, Brasidus?" asked Grimes.

"It is, sir."

"Then be careful, Peggy. Watch your step—and your tongue."

"Aye, aye, Cap'n."

"And I suppose that you, Brasidus, will report everything that you've heard to Captain Diomedes?"

"Of course, sir."

"And so he should," Margaret Lazenby said. "When it gets around, these pseudo-Spartans might realize all that they are missing."

"And is the fact that they're missing it grounds for commiseration or congratulation?" asked Grimes quietly.

"Shut up!" snapped his officer mutinously.

Chapter Eleven

IT WAS NOT the first time that Brasidus had been inside the palace, but, as always, he was awed (although he tried not to show it in front of the foreigners) by the long, colonnaded, high-ceilinged halls, each with its groups of heroic statuary, each with its vivid murals depicting scenes of warfare and the chase. He marched along beside his charges (who, he was pleased to note, had fallen into step), taking pride in the rhythmic, martial clank of the files of hoplites on either side of them, the heralds, long, brazen trumpets already upraised, ahead of them. Past the ranks of Royal Guards—stiff and immobile at attention, tiers of bright-headed spears in right alignment—they progressed. He realized, with disapproval, that John Grimes and Margaret Lazenby were talking in low voices.

"More anachronisms for you, Peggy. Those guards. Spears in hand—and projectile pistols at the belt . . ."

"And look at those murals, John. Pig-sticking — those animals aren't unlike boars — on motorcycles. But these people do have good painters and sculptors."

"I prefer my statues a little less agressively masculine. In fact, I prefer them nonmasculine.''

"You would. I find them a pleasant change from the simpering nymphs that are supposed to be decorative on most planets.''

"You would.''

Brasidus turned his head. "Quiet, please, sirs. We are approaching the throne.''

There was a sharp command from the officer in charge of the escort. The party crashed to a halt. The heralds put the mouthpieces of their instruments to their lips, sounded a long, discordant blast, then another. From a wide, pillared portal strode a glittering officer. "Who comes?'' he demanded.

In unison the heralds chanted, "John Grimes, master of the star ship Seeker. Margaret Lazenby, one of his officers.''

"Enter, John Grimes. Enter, Margaret Lazenby.''

Again a command from the leader of the escort, and with a jangle of accouterments, the march resumed, although at a slower pace. Through the doorway they passed, halted again. There was another prolonged blast from the heralds' trumpets, a crash of grounded spear butts.

There was the King, resplendent in gold armor (which made the iron crown somehow incongruous), bearded (the only man on Sparta to be so adorned), seated erect on his high, black throne. There, ranged behind him on marble benches, was the Council—the doctors in their scarlet robes, the engineers in purple, the philosophers in black, the generals in brown and the admirals in blue. There was a small group of high-ranking helots—agronomists robed in green, industrialists in gray. All of them stared curiously at the men from the ship, from whom the guards had fallen away. But, Brasidus noted, there was more than curiosity on the faces of the scarlet-robed doctors as they regarded Margaret Lazenby. There was recognition, puzzlement and . . . guilt?

Grimes, at heel-clicking attention, saluted smartly.

"You may advance, Lieutenant Commander," said the King.

Grimes did so, once again drawing himself to attention when within two paces from the throne.

"You may relax, John Grimes. At ease." There was a long pause, then, "We have been told that you come from another world—another world, that is, beyond our polity of Sparta and Latterhaven. We have been told that you represent a government calling itself the Interstellar Federation. Assuming that there is such an entity, what is your business on Sparta?"

"Your Majesty, my mission is to conduct a census of the Man-colonized planets in this sector of space."

"The members of our Council concerned with such matters will be able to give you all the information you need. But we are told that you and your officers wish to set foot on this world—a privilege never accorded to the crews of Latterhaven ships. May we inquire as to your motives?"

"Your Majesty, in addition to the census, we are conducting a survey."

"A survey, Lieutenant Commander?"

"Yes, Your Majesty. There are worlds, such as yours, about which little is known. There are worlds—and yours is one of them—about which much more should be known."

"And this Federation of yours" — Brasidus, watching the King's face, could see that he had not been surprised by any of Grimes' answers, that he accepted the existence of worlds other than Sparta and Latterhaven without demur, that even the mention of this fantastic Federation had been no cause for amazement—"it has considerable military strength?"

"Considerable strength, Your Majesty. My ship, for example, is but a small and unimportant unit of our fleet."

"Indeed? And your whereabouts are known?"

"The movements of all vessels are plotted by Master Control."

"And so . . . and so, supposing that some unfortunate accident were to happen to your ship and your crew on Sparta, we might, just possibly, expect a visit from one or more of your big battleships?"

"That is so, Your Majesty."

"And we could deal with them, sire!" interpolated a portly, blue-robed Council member.

The King swiveled around in his throne. "Could we, Admiral Phileus? Could we? We wish that we possessed your assurance. But we do not. It does not matter how and by whom the planets of this Federation were colonized—what does matter is that they own spaceships, which we do not, and even space warships, which even Latterhaven does not. We, a mere monarch, hesitate to advise you upon naval tactics, but we remind you that a spaceship can hang in orbit, clear of the atmosphere—and therefore beyond reach of your airships—and, at the same time, release its shower of bombs upon our cities. Consider it, Phileus." He turned back to Grimes. "So, Lieutenant Commander, you seek permission for you and your men to range unhindered over the surface of our world?"

"I do, Your Majesty."

"Some of our ways and customs may be strange to you. You will not interfere. And you will impart new knowledge only to those best qualified to be its recipients."

"That is understood, Your Majesty."

"Sire!" This time it was one of the doctors. "I respectfully submit that permission to leave this outworld ship be extended only to *human* crew members."

"And what is your reason, Doctor? Let Margaret Lazenby advance so that we may inspect him."

The Arcadian walked slowly toward the King. Looking at his face, Brasidus could see that the being had lost some of his cockiness. But there was a certain defiance there still. *Should this attitude result in punishment ordered by the King,* thought Brasidus, *there will be a large measure of injustice involved.* The major portion of the blame would rest with Grimes who, after all, had so obviously failed to maintain proper disciplinary standards aboard his siip.

Cresphontes, King of All Sparta, looked long and curiously at the alien spaceman. He said at last, "They tell us that you are an Arcadian."

"That is so, Your Majesty."

"And you are a member of a space-faring race."

"Yes, Your Majesty."

"Turn around, please. Slowly."

Margaret Lazenby obeyed, his face flushing.

"So . . ." mused the King. "So . . ." He swiveled in his throne so that he faced the Council. "You have all seen. You have all seen that this Arcadian is smaller than a true man, is more slightly built. Do you think that he would be a match for one of our warriors, or even for a helot? A thousand of these creatures, armed, might be a menace. But . . . " He turned to address Grimes. "How many of them are there in your crew, Lieutenant Commander?"

"A dozen, Your Majesty."

"A mere dozen of these malformed weaklings, without arms. . . . No, there can be no danger. Obviously, since they are members of *Seeker's* crew, they can coexist harmoniously with men. So, we repeat, there is no danger."

"Sire!" It was the doctor who had raised the objection. "You do not know these beings. You do not know how treacherous they can be."

"And do you, Doctor Pausanias? And if you do know, *how do you know?*"

The Councilman paled. He said, lamely, "We are experienced, sire, in judging who is to live and who is not to live among the newborn. There are signs, reliable signs. *She*"—he pointed an accusing finger at Margaret Lazenby—"exhibits them."

"Indeed, Doctor Pausanias? We admit that a child emerging from the birth machine with such a deformed chest would be among those exposed, but how is that deformity an indication of character?"

"It is written in her face, sire."

"In *her* face? Have you suddenly learned a new language, Doctor?"

"Sire, it was a slip of the tongue. *His* face."

"So . . . Face us, Margaret Lazenby. Look at us." The King's right hand went up to and stroked his short beard. "We read no treachery in your countenance. There is a softness, better suited to a children's nurse than to a warrior, but there is courage, and there is honesty."

"Sire!" Pausanius was becoming desperate. "Do not forget that sh—that he is an alien being. Do not forget that in these cases expression is meaningless. A woods boar, for example, will smile, but not from amiability. He smiles when at his most ferocious."

"And so do men at times." The King grinned, his teeth very white in his dark, bearded face. "We become ferocious, and we smile, when councilmen presume to tell us our business." He raised his voice. "Guards! Remove this man."

"But, sire . . ."

"Enough."

There was a scuffle at the back of the chamber as the doctor was hustled out by four hoplites. Brasidus noticed, with grim satisfaction, that none of the man's scarlet-robed colleagues made any move to defend him. He thought, *Crespontes knows where his real strength lies. With us, the military.*

"Lieutenant Commander Grimes!"

"Your Majesty?"

"We have decided that you may carry out your survey. You and your officers and men, both human and Arcadian, may leave your ship—but only as arranged with our Captain Diomedes, and only under escort. Is that quite clear?"

"Quite clear, Your Majesty. We shall see only what we are allowed to see."

"You have made a correct assessment of the situation. And now, as we have matters of import to discuss with out Council, you are dismissed."

Grimes saluted and then, slowly, he and Margaret Lazenby backed from the royal presence. Brasidus accompanied them. Beyond the door to the throne room the escort fell in about them.

As they marched out of the palace to the waiting car, Grimes asked, "Brasidus, what will happen to that doctor? The one who was dragged out of the chamber?"

"He will be beheaded, probably. But he is lucky."

"Lucky?"

"Yes. If he were not a doctor and a councilman, he could have his arms and legs lopped off before being exposed on the hillside with the defective children."

"You're joking, Brasidus!" exclaimed Margaret Lazenby.

"Joking? Of course not."

The Arcadian turned to Grimes. "John, can't we do something?"

Grimes shook his head. "Anything that we could do would mean the death of more than one man. Besides, our strict orders are not to interfere."

"It is expedient," said Margaret Lazenby bitterly, "that one man should die for the good of the people."

"Careful, Peggy. This place may be bugged. Remember that *we* aren't members of the Council."

"Spoken like a true naval officer of these decadent days. I often think that the era of gunboat diplomacy had much to recommend it."

Chapter Twelve

THEY RODE BACK to the spaceport almost in silence. Brasidus realized that the two foreigners had been shocked when told of the probable fate of Pausanius. But why should they be? He could not understand it. Surely on their world, on any word, insolence toward the King himself must result in swift and drastic punishment. To make their reaction even stranger, the doctor had spoken against them, not for them.

They sped through the streets of the city, one chariot rattling ahead of the hovercar, the second astern of it. There were more people abroad now, more sightseers; word must have gotten around that aliens from the ship were at large. Citizen and helot, every man stared with avid curiosity at the Arcadian.

Margaret Lazenby shuddered. He muttered, "John, I don't like this planet at all, at all. I'd have said once that to be one woman in a world of men would be marvelous. But it's not. I'm being undressed by dozens of pairs of eyes. Do you know, I was afraid that the King was going to order me to strip."

"That shouldn't worry an Arcadian," John Grimes told him. "After all, you're all brought up as nudists."

"And I don't see why it should worry him," Brasidus put in, "unless he is ashamed of his deformities."

Margaret Lazenby flared, "To begin with, Sergeant, I'm not deformed. Secondly, the correct pronouns to use insofar as *I* am concered are 'she' and 'her.' Got it?"

"And are those pronouns to be used when talking of the other spacemen who are similarly . . . malformed?" asked Brasidus.

"Yes. But, as a personal favor, will you, please, stop making remarks about the shape of my body?"

"All right." Then he said, meaning no offense, "On Sparta nobody is deformed."

"Not *physically*," remarked Margaret Lazenby nastily, and then it was the Sergeant's turn to lapse into a sulky silence, one that remained unbroken all the rest of the way to the ship.

Brasidus left the spacemen at the barrier, then reported to Spaceport Security. Diomedes was seated in his inner office, noisily enjoying his midday meal. He waved the Sergeant to a bench, gestured toward the food and drink on the table. "Help yourself, young man. And how did things go? Just the important details. I already know that the King has agreed to let Grimes carry out some sort of survey, and I've just received word that Pausanius has lost his head. But what were your impressions?"

Deliberately Brasidus filled a mug with beer. Officers were allowed stronger liquor than the lower-ranking hoplites, even those with the status of sergeant. He rather hoped that the day would soon come when he would be able to enjoy this tipple in public. He gulped pleasurably. Tben he said, "It must be a funny world that they come from. To begin with, they didn't seem to have any real respect for the King. Oh, they were correct enough, but . . . I could sense, somehow, they they were rather looking down on him. And *then* . . . they were shocked, sir, really shocked when I told them what was going to happen to Pausanius. It's hard to credit."

"In my job I'm ready and willing to credit anything. But go on."

"This Margaret Lazenby, the Arcadian. She seems to have a terror of nudity."

"*She*, Brasidus?"

"Yes, sir. She told me to refer to her as 'she.' Do you know, it sounds and feels *right*, somehow."

"Go on."

"You'll remember, sir, that we saw a picture in Lieutenant Commander Grimes' cabin of what seemed to be a typical beach scene on Arcadia. Everybody was naked."

"H'm. But you will recall that in that picture humans and Arcadians were present in roughly equal numbers. To know that one is in all ways inferior is bad enough. To be inferior *and* in the minority—that's rather much. His—or her— attitude as far as this world is concerned makes sense, Brasidus. But how did it come up?"

"She said, when we were driving back through the city, that she felt as though she were being undressed by the eyes of all the people looking at her. (Why should she have that effect on humans? I'm always wondering myself what she is like under her uniform.) And she said that she was afraid that King Cresphontes was going to order her to strip in front of him and the Council."

"Men are afflicted by peculiar phobias, Brasidus. You've heard of Teleclus, of course?"

"The Lydian general, sir?"

"The same. A brave man, a very brave man, as his record shows. But let a harpy get into his tent and he's a glibbering coward." He picked up a meaty bone, gnawed on it meditatively. "So don't run away with the idea that this Arcadian is outrageously unhuman in his—or 'her'—reactions." He smiled greasily. "She may be more human than you dream."

"What are you getting at, sir? What do you know?"

Diomedes waved the bone playfully at Brasidus. "Only what my officers tell me. Apart from that—I'm Security, so nobody tells me anything. Which reminds me, there's something I must tell you. Your little friend Achron has been ringing this office all morning, trying to get hold of you." He frowned. "I don't want you to drop him like a hot cake now that you've acquired a new playmate."

"What new playmate, sir?"

"Oh, never mind, never mind. Just keep in with Achron, that's all. We still want to find out what's going on at the crèche, alien ships or no alien ships. As I've said—and I think you'll agree—it seems to tie in."

"But sir, wouldn't it be simple just to stage a raid?"

"I like my job, Brasidus—but I like the feel of my head on my shoulders much better. The doctors are the most powerful branch of the priesthood. This Pausanius, do you think that the King would have acted as he did if he hadn't known that he, Pausanius, was in bad with his own colleagues? All that happened was that he got himself a public execution instead of a very private one."

"It all seems very complicated, Captain."

"You can say that again, Brasidus." Diomedes tossed his bone into the trash basket. "Now . . ." He picked up a sheaf of crumpled, grease-stained papers from the untidy table. "We have to consider your future employment. You'll not be required for escort duties this afternoon. I shall be arranging his itinerary with Lieutenant Commander Grimes. And tomorrow the bold space commander and his Arcadian sidekick will not be escorted by yourself."

"And why not, sir?"

"Because you'll be working—working with your hands. You've plainclothes experience. You can mix with helots as one of them and get away with it. This afternoon you pay a call on Alessis, who is both an engineer and—but let it go no further—on our payroll. Tomorrow Alessis with a gang of laborers will carry out the annual overhaul of the refrigerating machinery in the Andronicus warehouse. You will be one of the laborers."

"But I don't know anything about refrigeration, sir."

"Alessis should be able to teach you all that a common laborer should know this afternoon."

"But the other helots, sir. They'll know that I'm not a regular member of the gang."

"They won't. Alessis has just recruited green

labor from at least half a dozen outlying villages. You'll be the one big-city boy in the crowd. Oh, this will please you. Your friend Heraklion will not be in the crèche. He has been called urgently to his estate. It seems that a fire of unknown origin destroyed his farm outbuildings."

"Unknown origin, sir?"

"Of course."

"But what has the Andronicus warehouse to do with the crèche?"

"I don't know yet. But I hope to find out."

Brasidus returned to the barracks in Diommedes' car, changed there into civilian clothes. He had been given the address of Alessis' office, walked there briskly. The engineer—a short, compact, man in a purple-trimmed tunic—was expecting him. He said, "Be seated, Lieutenant. And I warn you now that tomorrow, on the job, I shall be addressing you as 'Hey, you!' "

"I'm used to plainclothes work, sir."

"As a helot?"

"Yes. As a helot."

"As a *stupid* helot?"

"If that is what's required."

"It will be. You're going to wander off by yourself and get lost. You'll be tracing the gas-supply main—that will be your story if anybody stumbles on you. I was supposed to be giving you an afternoon's tuition in refrigeration techniques, but that will not be necessary. All I ask of my helots is that they lift when I tell them to lift, put down when I tell them to put down, and so on and so forth. They're the brawn and I'm the brain. Get it?"

"Yes, sir."

"Good. Can you read a plan?"

"I can."

"Splendid." Alessis got up, opened a drawer of his desk and pulled out a large roll of tough paper. He flattened it out. "Now, this is the basement of the Andronicus warehouse. Power supply comes in here," his stubby forefinger jabbed, "through a conduit. Fans here, compressors here—all the usual. The odd chambers are all on the floor above—with the exception of this one. Deep freeze—very deep freeze, in fact."

"There's no reason why it shouldn't be in the basement."

"None at all. And there's no reason why it shouldn't be up one floor, with the other chambers. But it's not its location that's odd."

"Then what is?"

"It's got two doors, Brasidus. One opening into the basement, the other one right at the back. I found this second door, quite by chance, when I was checking the insulation."

"And where does it lead to?"

"That is the question. I think, although I am not sure, that there is a tunnel behind it. And I think that the tunnel runs to the crèche."

"But why?"

Alessis shrugged. "That's what our mutual friend Diomedes wants to find out."

Chapter Thirteen

A BLACK, WINDOWLESS cube, ugly, forbidding, the Andronicus warehouse stood across the cobbled street from the gracefully proportioned crèche complex. To its main door, a few minutes before 0800 hours, slouched the gang of workmen employed by Alessis, among them Brasidus. He was wearing dirty, ill-fitting coveralls, and he was careful not to walk with a military stride, proceeded with a helot's shamble.

The other men looked at him, and he looked at them. He saw a bunch of peasantry from the outlying villages, come to the city to (they vaguely hoped) better themselves. They saw a man like themselves, but a little cleaner, a little better fed, a little more intelligent. There were grunted self-introductions. Then, "You'll be the foreman?" asked one of the workmen.

"No," admitted Brasidus. "He'll be along with Alessis."

The engineer arrived in his hovercar, his foreman riding with him. They got out of the vehicle and the foreman went to the doorway, pressed the bell push set to one side of it. Then he said, "Jump to it. Get the tools out of the car." Brasidus—his years of training were not easily sloughed off—

took the lead, swiftly formed an efficient little working party to unload spanners, hammers, gas cylinders and electrical equipment. He heard the foreman say to his employer, "Who's that new man, sir? We could use a few more like him."

Slowly the door opened. It was thick, Brasidus noted. It appeared to be armored. It looked capable of withstanding a chariot charge, or even the fire of medium artillery. It would have been more in keeping with a fortress than a commercial building. In it stood a man dressed in the gray tunic of an industrialist. That made him a helot, although one of a superior class. Nonetheless, his salutation of Alessis was not that of an inferior to a superior. There could even have been a hint of condescension.

The maintenance gang filed into the building—the engineer and his foreman unhampered, Brasidus and the others carrying the gear. So far there was little to be seen—just a long, straight corridor between featureless metal walls, terminating in yet another door. But it was all so clean, so sterile, impossibly so for Sparta. It reminded Brasidus of the interior of John Grimes' ship, but even that, by comparison, had a lived-in feel to it.

The farther door was heavily insulated. Beyond it was a huge room, crowded with machinery, the use of which Brasidus could only guess. Pumps, perhaps, and compressors, and dozens of white-faced gauges. Nothing was in motion; every needle rested at zero.

"Have you everything you want, Alessis?" asked the industrialist.

"I think so. Nothing's been giving any trouble since the last overhaul?"

"No. I need hardly tell you that the deep freeze is, as always, top priority. But *Hera's* not due for another couple of months."

"Not to worry, what's the hurry?" quipped the engineer. Then, to his foreman, "O.K., Cimon, you can start taking the main compressor down. One of you"—he looked over his workmen carefully as though making a decision—"come with me to the basement to inspect the deep freeze. You'll do, fellow. Bring a hammer and a couple of screwdrivers. And a torch."

Brasidus opened the hatch in the floor for Alessis and then, as he followed the engineer down to the lower level, managed to shut it after himself. It was not difficult; the insulation, although thick, was light. In the basement there was more machinery seeming, thought Brasidus, to duplicate the engines on the floor above. It, too, was silent. And there was the huge, insulated door that he, as instructed by Alessis, opened.

The chamber beyond it was not cooled, but a residual chill seemed to linger in the still air. Physical or psychological? Or psychic? There was . . . something, some influence, some subtle emanation, that resulted in a slight, involuntary shudder, a sudden, prickly gooseflesh. It was as though there were a million voices—subsonic? supersonic? on the verge of audibility—crying out to be heard, striving, in vain, to impart a message. The voices of the dead? Brasidus must have spoken aloud, for Alessis said, "Or the not yet born."

"What do you mean?" demanded Brasidus. "What do you mean?"

"I . . . I don't know, Lieutenant. It seemed that

the words were spoken to me by someone, by *something* outside.''

"But this is only a deep-freeze chamber, sir.''

"It is only a deep-freeze chamber—but it has too many doors.''

"I can't see the second one.''

"No. It is concealed. I found it only by accident. You see that panel? Take your screwdriver and remove the holding screws.''

In spite of his unfamiliarity with power tools, with tools of any kind, Brasidus accomplished the job in a few seconds. Then, with Alessis' help, he pried the insulated panel out from the wall, lifted it to one side. There was a tunnel beyond it, high enough so that a tall man could walk without stooping, wide enough so that bulky burdens could be carried along it with ease. There were pipes and conduits on the roof of the tunnel, visible in the light of the torches.

"An alternative freezing system,'' explained Alessis. "Machinery in the crèche itself. I'm not supposed to know about it. The tunnel's insulated, too—and I've no doubt that when it's in use it can be brought down to well below zero.''

"And what am I supposed to do?'' Brasidus asked.

"You take your orders from Captain Diomedes, not from me. You're supposed to snoop—that's all that I know. And if you *are* caught, I risk my neck by providing you with some sort of a cover story. You thought—and I thought—that all these wires and pipes are supposed to be doing something. As, in fact, they are. Well, you'll find another door at the end, a proper one, and with dogs that can be operated from either side.'' His hand rested briefly on Brasidus' upper forearm. "I don't like this business. It's all too hasty; there's far too much last-minute improvisation. So be careful."

"I'll try," Brasidus told him. He stuck the hammer and the screwdriver into his belt—after all, he was supposed to be a workman, and if it came to any sort of showdown they would be better than no weapons at all—and, without a backward glance, set off along the tunnel.

The door at the far end was easy enough to open, and the screw clamps were well greased and silent. With the thick, insulated valve the slightest crack ajar, Brasidus listened. He could hear nothing. Probably there was nobody on the farther side. He hoped. The door opened away from him into whatever space there was on the other side. It was a pity, as anybody waiting there—the possibility still had not been ruled out—would be hidden from Brasidus as he emerged. But if the door were flung open violently, he would be not only hidden, but trapped.

Brasidus flung the door open violently, catching it just before it could thud noisily against the wall of the corridor.

So far, so good.

But what was there to see? Across the corridor there was yet another door, looking as though it, too, were insulated. And it was locked. To his left stretched a long, long passageway, soft ceiling lights reflected in the polished floor. To his right stretched a long, long passageway, similarly illuminated. On both sides there were doors, irregularly spaced, numbered.

Brasidus stood, silent and motionless, every sense tuned to a high pitch of sensitivity. There was the faintest hint of perfume in the air, merged with other hints—antiseptics, machinery, cooking—noticeable only by reason of its unusualness. A similar fragrance had lingered around Margaret Lazenby. And, remembered Brasidus, around that other Arcadian in this very building—Sally. And, oddly enough, around Heraklion. (Normally the only odors associated with doctors were those of the various spirits and lotions of their trade.)

So, he thought, there are Arcadians here.

So, he told himself, I knew that already.

So what?

His hearing was abnormally keen, and he willed himself to ignore the mutter of his own heartbeats, the susurus of his respiration. From somewhere, faint and faraway, drifted a murmur of machinery. There were voices, distant, and a barely heard tinkle of that silvery laughter he already associated with the Arcadians. There was a whisper of running water, evocative of a hillside rill rather than city plumbing.

He did not want to stray too far from the door, but realized that he would learn little, if anything, by remaining immobile. He turned to his left, mainly because that was the direction from which the Arcadian laughter and the faint splashing sounds were coming. He advanced slowly and cautiously, his hand hovering just clear of the haft of his hammer.

Suddenly a door opened. The man standing there was dressed in a long, soft, enveloping robe. He had long, blonde hair, and the fine features and the wide, red mouth of an Arcadian. There was about him—about her, Brasidus corrected himself—more than just a hint of that disturbing perfume. "Hello," she said in a high, pleasantly surprised voice. "Why, hello! A fresh face, as I live and breath! And what are you doing in this abode of love?"

"I'm checking the refrigeration, sir."

"Sir!" There was the tinkling laughter, amused but not unkind. "Sir! That's a giveaway, fellow. You don't belong here, do you?"

"Why, sir, no."

The Arcadian sighed. "Such a handsome brute—and I have to chase you off. But it's getting on for the time when our learned lovers join us for . . . er . . . aquatic relaxation in the pool. And if they find you wandering around where you shouldn't be . . ." She drew the edge of her hand across her throat in an expressive gesture. "It's happened before—and, after all, who misses a helot? But where did you come from? Of, yes, I see. You could be a refrigeration mechanic. . . . My advice to you is to get back into your hole and to pull it shut after you." Then she said, as Brasidus started to turn to retreat to the tunnel, "No so fast, buster. Not so fast." A slim hand, with red-painted nails, caught his right shoulder to swing him so that he faced her; the other hand came up to rest upon his left shoulder. Her face was very close to his, the lips parted.

As though it were the most natural thing in the world, Brasidus kissed her. *Unnatural,* said a voice in his mind, flatly and coldly. *Unnatural, to mate with a monster from another world, even to contemplate such a sterile coupling. Unnatural. Unnatural.*

But his own arms were about her and he was returning her kiss—hotly, avidly, clumsily. That censor in his mind was, at the moment, talking only to itself. He felt the mounds of flesh on her chest pressing against him, was keenly aware of the softness of her thighs against his own.

Suddenly, somehow, her hands were between their upper bodies, pushing him away. With a twist of her head she disengaged her mouth. "Go, you fool!" she whispered urgently. "Go! If they find you, they'll kill you. Go. Don't worry—I'll say nothing. And if you have any sense, you'll not say anything either."

"But . . ."

"Go!"

Reluctantly, Brasidus went. Just as he closed the door he heard footsteps approaching along the alleyway.

But there was no alarm raised; his intrusion had been undetected.

Back in the deep-freeze chamber, Alessis looked at him curiously. "Have you been in a fight? Your mouth . . . there's blood."

Brasidus examined the back of his investigatory hand. "No," he said. "It's not blood. I don't know what it is."

"But what happened?"

"I don't know," replied Brasidus truthfully. Still he was not feeling the shame, the revulsion that should have been swamping him. "I don't know. In any case, I have to make my reports only to Captain Diomedes."

Chapter Fourteen

"SO IT WAS not the same one that you saw before?" asked Diomedes.

"No, Captain. At least, I don't think so. Her voice was different."

"H'm. There must be an absolute nest of Arcadians in that bloody crèche.... And all ... she did was to talk to you and warn you to make yourself scarce before any of the doctors came on the scene?"

"That was all, Captain."

"You're lying, Brasidus."

"All right." Brasidus' voice was sullenly defiant. "I kissed him, her, it. And it—or she—kissed me back."

"You *what?*"

"You heard me, sir. Your very vague instructions to me were that I should find out all that I could. And that was one way of doing it."

"Indeed? And what did you find out?"

"That these Arcadians, as you have said, exercise a sort of hypnotic power, especially when there is physical contact."

"Hypnotic power? So the touch of mouth to mouth almost put you to sleep?"

"That wasn't the way I meant it, sir. But I did

feel that, if I weren't very careful, I should be doing just what she wanted."

"And what did she want?"

"Do I have to spell it out for you, sir? Oh, I know that intercourse with an alien being must be *wrong*—but that was what she wanted."

"And you?"

"All right. I wanted it, too."

"Brasidus, Brasidus. . . . You know that what you have just told me could get you busted down to helot. Or worse. But in our job, as you are learning, we often have to break the law in order to enforce it."

"As a policeman, sir, I am reasonably familiar with the law. I cannot recall that it forbids intercourse with aliens."

"Not yet, Brasidus. Not yet. But you will recall that contact with the crews of visiting ships is prohibited. And I think that the preliminaries to making love may be construed as contact."

"But are these Arcadians in the crèche crew members of visiting ships?"

"What else can they be? They must have got here somehow." Diomedes looked long and hard at Brasidus, but there was no censure in his regard. "However, I am not displeased by the way in which things are turning out. You are getting to know something about these . . . *things*. These Arcadians. And I think that you are strong enough to resist their lure. . . . Now, what have we for you? This evening, I think, you will visit your friend Achron at the crèche. Keep your eyes and ears open, but don't stick your neck out. Tomorrow I have an assignment for you that you should find interesting. This Margaret Lazenby wishes to

make a sightseeing trip, and she especially asked
for you as her escort."

"Will Lieutenant Commander Grimes be along,
sir?"

"No. He'll be consorting with the top brass.
After all, he is the commander of *Seeker* and, to
use spaceman's parlance, seems to pile on rather
more Gs than the master of a merchantman. . . .
Yes, Brasidus, have yourself a nice visit with your
boyfriend, and then report to me here tomorrow
morning at 0730 hours, washed behind the ears
and with all your brasswork polished."

Brasidus spent the evening with Achron before
the latter reported for duty. It was not the first time
that he had been a guest at the nurse's Club—but it
was the first time that he had felt uncomfortable
there. Apart from his own feelings, it was no different from other occasions. There were the usual
graceful, soft-spoken young men, proud and
happy to play host to the hoplites who were their
visitors. There was the usual food—far better
cooked and more subtly seasoned than that served
in the army messes. There was the usual wine—a
little too sweet, perhaps, but chilled and spar-
kling. There was music and there was dancing—
not the strident screaming of brass and the boom
and rattle of drums, not the heavy thud of bare feet
on the floor, but the rhythmic strumming of lutes
and, to it, the slow gyrations of willowy bodies.

But . . .

But there was something lacking.

But what could be lacking?

"You are very thoughtful tonight, Brasidus,"
remarked Achron wistfully.

"Am I?"

"Yes. You . . . you're not with us, somehow."

"No?"

"Brasidus, I have to be on duty soon. Will you come with me to my room?"

The Sergeant looked at his friend. Achron was a pretty boy, prettier than most, but he was not, he could never be, an Arcadian. . . .

What am I thinking? he asked himself, shocked. *Why am I thinking it?*

He said, "Not tonight, Achron."

"But what is wrong with you, Brasidus? You never used to be like this." Then, with a sort of incredulous bitterness, "It can't be one of the men from the ship, can it? No, not possibly. Not one of those great, hairy brutes. As well consort with one of those malformed aliens they've brought with them!" Achron laughed at the absurdity of the idea.

"No," Brasidus told him. "Not one of the men from the ship."

"Then it's all right."

"Yes, it's all right. But I shall have a heavy day tomorrow."

"You poor dear. I suppose that the arrival of this absurd spaceship from some uncivilized world has thrown a lot of extra work on you."

"Yes. It has."

"But you'll walk with me to the crèche, won't you?"

"Yes. I'll do that."

"Oh, thank you. You can wait here while I get changed. There's plenty of wine left."

Yes, there was plenty of wine left, but Brasidus was in no mood for it. He sat in silence, watching the dancers, listening to the slow, sensuous thrumming. Did the Arcadians dance? And how would *they* look dancing, stripped for performance, the light gleaming on their smooth, golden skins? And why should the mere thought of it be so evocative of sensual imaginings?

Achron came back into the hall, dressed in his white working tunic. Brasidus got up from the bench, walked with him out into the night. The two friends made their way through the streets in silence at first, but it was not the companionable silence to which they had become used. Finally Brasidus spoke, trying to keep any display of real interest out of his voice.

"Wouldn't it be better if you nurses lived in at the crèche? The same as we do in the barracks."

"Then we shouldn't have these walks, Brasidus."

"You could visit me."

"But I don't *like* your barracks. And your Club's as bad."

"I suppose that the cooking could be improved in both. Just who *does* live in at the crèche?"

"All the doctors, of course. And there are some engineers who look after the machinery."

"No helots?"

"No. Of course not." Achron was shocked at the idea.

"Even *we*—but, after all, Brasidus, we are helots—have to live outside. But you know all that. Why are you asking me?"

That was a hard counterquestion to answer. At last Brasidus said, "There have been rumors . . ."

"Rumors of what?"

"Well, it's a very large building. Even allowing for the wards and the birth machine, there must be

ample space inside. Do you think that the staff
doctors and engineers could have . . . friends living with them?"

It was Achron's turn to hesitate. "You could be
right, Brasidus. There are so many rules telling us
that we must not stray away from our wards. Now
that you raise the point, I can see that there has
always been an atmosphere of . . . of secrecy . . ."

"And have you ever seen or heard anything?"

"No."

"And do the staff doctors and engineers have
any friends among the nurses?"

"They wouldn't look as us." Resentment was all
too evident in Achron's voice. "They're too high
and mighty. Keep themselves to themselves,
that's what they do. And their own accommodation, I've heard, the King himself might envy.
They've a heated swimming pool, even. I've never
seen it, but I've heard about it. And I've seen the
food and the wine that come in. Oh, they do themselves well—far better than us, who do all the
work."

"There might be inquiries being made," said
Brasidus cautiously.

"There are always inquiries being made. That
Captain Diomedes wanted me to work for him.
But he's not . . . he's not a gentleman. We didn't get
on. Why should I help him?"

"Would you help me?"

"And how can I, Brasidus?"

"Just look and listen. Let me know of anything
out of the ordinary in the crèche."

"But the doctors can do no wrong," said
Achron. "And even if they did, they couldn't. You
know what I mean."

"In your eyes, you mean?"

"In my eyes," admitted the nurse. "But for you, and only for you, I'll . . . I'll look and listen. Does it mean promotion for you?"

"It does," said Brasidus.

"Are you coming in?" asked Achron as they reached the entrance to the crèche.

"No. I shall have a long and wearing day tomorrow."

"You . . . you don't give me much inducement to help you, do you? If I do, will things be the same between us again?"

"Yes," lied Brasidus.

Chapter Fifteen

BRASIDUS DROVE OUT to the spaceport in the car that had been placed at his disposal. He realized that he was looking forward to what he had told Achron would be a long and wearing day. He enjoyed the freshness of the morning air, looked up with appreciation at the Spartan Navy still, in perfect formation, circling the landing field. But now he did not, as he had done so many times in the past, envy the airmen. He was better off as he was. If he were up there, a crew member of one of the warships, even the captain of one of them, he would not be meeting the glamorous, exotic spacefarers—and most certainly would not, in the course of duty, be spending the entire day with one of the them.

Margaret Lazenby was already ashore, was waiting in Diomedes' office, was engaged in conversation with the Security captain. Brasidus heard his superior say, "I'm sorry, Doctor Lazenby, but I cannot allow you to carry weapons. The cameras and recording equipment—yes. But not that pistol. Laser, isn't it?"

"It is. But, damn it all, Diomedes, on this cockeyed world of yours my going about unarmed degrades me to the status of a helot."

"And the Arcadians are not helots?"

"No. It should be obvious, even to a Security officer. Would a helot hold commissioned rank in the Federation's Survey Service?"

"Then if you possess warrior's status, your being let loose with a weapon of unknown potentialities is even worse insofar as we are concerned." The fat man, facing Margaret Lazenby's glare with equanimity, allowed himself to relent. "All right. Leave your pistol here, and I'll issue you with a stun gun."

"I shall not leave my weapon here. Will you be so good as to put me through to the ship so that I can tell the duty officer to send somebody ashore to pick it up?"

"All right." Diomedes punched a few buttons on his board, picked up the handset, spoke into it briefly, then handed it to the Arcadian. He turned to Brasidus. "So you've arrived. Attention!" Brasidus obeyed with a military crash and jangle. "Let's look at you. H'm, brass not too bad, but your leatherwork could do with another polish. . . . But you're not going anywhere near the palace, so I don't suppose it matters. At ease! Stand easy! In fact, relax."

Meanwhile, Margaret Lazenby had finished speaking into the telephone. She returned the instrument to its rest. She stood there, looking down at the obese Diomedes sprawled in his chair—and Brasidus looked at her. She was not in uniform, but was wearing an open-necked shirt with a flaring collar cut from some soft, brown material, and below it a short kilt of the same color. Her legs were bare, and her slim feet were thrust into serviceable-looking sandals. At her belt was a holstered weapon of unfamiliar design. The cross straps from which depended her equipment — camera, sound recorder, binoculars — accentuated the outthrusting fleshy mounds on her chest that betrayed her alien nature.

She was, obviously, annoyed, and when she spoke it was equally obvious that she was ready and willing to transfer her annoyance to Brasidus. "Well, Brasidus," she demanded. "Seen enough? Or would you like me to go into a song and dance routine for you?"

"I . . . I was interested in that weapon of yours."

"Is that all?" For some obscure reason Brasidus' reply seemed to annoy her still further. And then a junior officer from Seeker came in, and Margaret Lazenby unbuckled the holstered pistol from her belt, handed it to the young spaceman. She accepted the stun gun from Diomedes, unholstered it, looked at it curiously. "Safety catch? Yes. Firing stud? H'm. We have similar weapons. Nonlethal, but effective enough. Oh, range?"

"Fifty feet," said Diomedes.

"Not very good. Better than nothing, I suppose." She clipped the weapon to her belt. "Come on, Brasidus. We'd better get out of here before he has me stripped to a peashooter and you polishing your belt and sandals."

"Your instructions, sir?" Brasidus asked Diomedes.

"Instructions? Oh, yes. Just act as guide and escort to Doctor Lazenby. Show her what you can of the workings of our economy—fields, factories. . . . You know. Answer her questions as long as there's no breach of security involved. And keep your own ears flapping."

"Very good, sir. Oh, expenses . . ."

"Expenses, Brasidus?"

"There may be meals, an occasional drink. . . ."

Diomedes sighed, pulled a bag of coins out of a drawer, dropped it with a clank on to the desk. "I know just how much is in this and I shall expect a detailed account of what you spend. Off with you. And, Doctor Lazenby, I expect you to bring Brasidus, here, back in good order and condition."

Brasidus saluted, then followed the spaceman out through the doorway.

She said, as soon as they were outside the building, "Expenses?"

"Yes, Doctor . . ."

"Call me Peggy."

"I have rations for the day in the car, Peggy, but I didn't think they were . . . suitable. Just bread and cold meat and a flagon of wine from the mess at the barracks."

"And so . . . and so you want to impress me with something better?"

"Why, yes," admitted Brasidus with a certain surprise. "Yes." (And it was strange, too, that he was looking forward to buying food and drink for this alien, even though the wherewithal to do so came out of the public purse. On Sparta every man was supposed to pay for his own entertainment, although not always in cash. In this case, obviously, there could be no reciprocation. *Or could there be?* But it did not matter.)

And then, with even greater surprise, Brasidus realized that he was helping Margaret Lazenby into the hovercar. Even burdened as she was, she did not need his assistance, but she accepted it as her due. Brasidus climbed in after her, took his seat behind the control column. "Where to?" he asked.

"That's up to you. I'd like a good tour. No, not the city—I shall be seeing plenty of that when I accompany John—Commander Grimes—on his official calls. What about the countryside and the outlying villages? Will that be in order?"

"It will, Peggy," Brasidus said. (And why should the use of that name be so pleasurable?)

"And if you'll explain things to me as you drive . . ."

The car lifted on its air cushion in a flurry of dust, moved forward, out through the main gateway, and for the first few miles headed toward the city.

"The spice fields," explained Brasidus with a wave of his hand. "It'll soon be harvest time, and then the two ships from Latterhaven will call for the crop."

"Rather . . . overpowering. The smell, I mean. Cinnamon, nutmeg, almond, but more so. . . . And a sort of mixture of sage and onion and garlic. But those men working in the fields with hoes and rakes, don't you have mechanical cultivators?"

"But why should we? I suppose that machines could be devised, but such mechanical tools would throw the helots out of employment."

"But you'd enjoy vastly increased production and would be able to afford a greater tonnage of imports from Latterhaven."

"But we are already self-sufficient."

"Then what do you import from Latterhaven?" Brasidus creased his brows. "I . . . I don't know,

Peggy," he admitted. "We are told that the ships bring manufactured goods."

"Such as?"

"I don't know." Then he recalled the strange book that he had seen in the crèche. "Books, perhaps."

"What sort of books?"

"I don't know, Peggy. The doctors keep them for themselves. But we turn off here. We detour the city and run through the vineyards."

The road that they were now following was little more than a track, running over and around the foothills, winding through the terraced vineyards on either side. As far as the eye could see the trellises were sagging under the weight of the great, golden fruit, each at least the size of a man's head, the broad, fleshy leaves. Brasidus remarked, "This has been a good year for grapes."

"*Grapes?* Are those things grapes?"

"What else could they be?" Brasidus stopped the car, got out, scrambled up the slope to the nearest vine. With his knife he hacked through a tough stem, then carried the ripe, glowing sphere back to Peggy. She took it, hefted it in her two hands, peered at it closely, sniffed it. "Whatever this is," she declared, "it ain't no grape—not even a grapefruit. Something indigenous, I suppose. Is it edible?"

"No. It has to be . . . processed. Skinned, trodden out, exposed to the air in open vats. It takes a long time, but it gets rid of the poison."

"Poison? I'll take your word for it." She handed the fruit back to Brasidus, who threw it onto the bank. "Oh, I should have kept that, to take to the ship for analysis."

"I'll get it again for you."

"Don't bother. Let the biochemist do his own fetching and carrying. But have you any of the . . . the finished product? You did say that you had brought a flagon of wine with you."

"Yes, Peggy." Brasidus reached into the back of the car, brought up the stone jug, pulled out the wooden stopper.

"No glasses?" she asked with a lift of the eyebrows.

"Glasses?"

"Cups, goblets, mugs—things you drink out of."

"I . . . I'm sorry. I never thought . . ."

"You have a lot to learn, my dear. But show me how you manage when you haven't any women around to exercise a civilizing influence."

"Women?"

"People like me. Go on, show me."

Brasidus grinned, lifted the flagon in his two hands, tilted it over his open mouth, clear of his lips. The wine was rough, tart rather than sweet, but refreshing. He gulped happily, then returned the jug to an upright position. He swallowed, then said, "Your turn, Peggy."

"You can't expect me to drink like that. You'll have to help me."

You wouldn't last five minutes on Sparta, thought Brasidus, not altogether derisively. He turned around in his seat, carefully elevated the wine flagon over Peggy's upturned face. He was suddenly very conscious of her red, parted lips, her white teeth. He tilted, allowing a thin trickle of the pale yellow fluid to emerge. She coughed and spluttered, shook her head violently. Then she gasped, "Haven't the knack of it—although I can manage a Spanish wineskin. Try again."

And now it was Brasidus who had to be careful, very careful. He was acutely aware of her physical proximity, her firm softness. "Ready?" he asked shakily.

"Yes. Fire at will."

This time the attempt was more successful. When at last she held up her hand to signal that she had had enough she must have disposed of at least a third of the flagon. From a pocket in her skirt she pulled a little square of white cloth, wiped her chin and dabbed at her lips with it. "That's not a bad drink," she stated. "Sort of dry sherry and ginger . . . but more-ish. No—that's enough. Didn't you ever hear the saying, 'Candy is dandy, but liquor is quicker'?"

"What is candy?" asked Brasidus. "And liquor is quicker for what?"

"Sorry, honey. I was forgetting that you have yet to learn the facts of life. Come to that, there're quite a few facts of life that I have to learn about this peculiar fatherland of yours. What is home without a mother?" She laughed. "Of course, you're lucky. You don't know *how* lucky. A pseudo-Hellenic culture and nary an Oedipus complex among the whole damn boiling of you!"

"Peggy, please speak Greek."

"Speak English, you mean. But I was using words and phrases that have dropped out of your version of our common tongue." She had slipped a little tablet into her mouth from a tube that she had extracted from her pocket. Suddenly her enunciation was less slurred. "Sorry, Brasidus, but this local tipple of yours is rather potent. Just as well that I brought along some soberer-uppers."

"But why do you need them? Surely one of the pleasures of drinking — the pleasure of drinking — is the effect; the . . . the loosening up."

"And the drunken brawl?"

"Yes," he said firmly.

"You mean that you'd like to . . . to brawl with me?"

Brasidus glimpsed a vivid mental picture of such an encounter and, with no hesitation, said, once again, "Yes."

"Drive on," she told him.

Chapter Sixteen

THEY DROVE ON, through and over the foothills, always climbing, the snowcapped peak of Olympus ever ahead, until, at last, Brasidus brought the car to a halt in the single street of a tiny village that clung precariously to the mountainside.

"Kilkis," he announced. "The tavern here could be worse. We halt here for our midday meal."

"Kilkis." The Arcadian repeated the name, gazed around her at the huddle of low but not ungraceful buildings, and then to the boulder-strewn slopes upon which grazed flocks of slow-moving, dun-colored beasts, many of them almost ready to reproduce by fission. "Kilkis," she repeated. "And how do the people here make a living? Do they take in each other's washing?"

"I don't understand, Peggy."

"Sorry, Brasidus. What are those animals?"

"Goats," he explained. "The major source of our meat supply." He went on, happy to be upon more familiar ground, "The only helots allowed to carry arms are the goatherds—see, there's one by that rock. He has a horn to summon assistance, and a sword, and a spear."

"Odd-looking goats. And why the weapons? Against rustlers?"

"Rustlers?"

"Cattle thieves. Or goat thieves."

"No. Goat raiding is classed as a military operation, and, in any case, none of the other city-states would dare to violate our borders. We have the Navy, of course, and firearms and armored chariots. They do not. But there're still the wolves, Peggy, and they're no respecters of frontiers."

"H'm. Then I think that you should allow your goatherds to carry at least a rifle. Is it a hazardous occupation?"

"It is, rather. But the schools maintain a steady flow of replacements, mainly from among those who have just failed to make the grade as hoplites."

"I see. Failed soldiers rather than passed veterinarians."

They got out of the car and walked slowly into the inn, into a long room with rush-strewn floor, tables and benches, low, raftered ceiling, and a not unpleasant smell of sour wine and cookery. At one end of the room there was an open fire, upon which simmered a huge iron cauldron. The half dozen or so customers—rough-looking fellows, leather-clad, wiry rather than muscular—got slowly to their feet at the sight of Brasidus' uniform, made reluctant and surly salutation. And then, as they got a proper look at his companion, there was more than a flicker of interest on their dark, seamed faces.

"You may be seated," Brasidus told them curtly.

"Thank you, Sergeant," replied one of them, his voice only just short of open insolence.

The taverner—fat, greasy, obsequious—waddled from the back of the room. "Your pleasure, lords?" he asked.

"A flagon of your best wine. And," added Brasidus, "two of your finest goblets to drink it from. What have you to eat?"

"Only the stew, lord. But it is made from a fine, fat young goat, just this very morning cast off from its father. Or we have sausage—well-ripened and well-seasoned."

"Peggy?" said Brasidus, with an interrogative intonation.

"The stew will do very nicely, I think. It smells good. And it's been boiled, so it should be safer . . ."

The innkeeper stared at her. "And may I be so impertinent as to inquire if the lord is from the strange spaceship?"

"You've already done so," Margaret Lazenby told him, then relented. "Yes. I am from the ship."

"You must find our world very beautiful, lord."

"Yes. It is beautiful. And interesting."

Roughly, Brasidus pulled out a bench from a vacant table, almost forced Peggy down onto the seat. "What about that wine?" he growled to the innkeeper.

"Yes, lord. Coming, lord. At once."

One of the goatherds whispered something to his companions, then chuckled softly. Brasidus glared at the men, ostentiously loosened the flap of the holster of his projectile pistol. There was an uneasy silence, and then, one by one, the goatherds rose to their feet and slouched out of the room. The Arcadian complained, "I had my recorder going." She did something to the controls of one of the instruments slung at her side. An amplified voice said loudly, "Since when has the Army been playing nurse to offworld monsters?"

"Insolent swine!"

"Don't be silly. They're entitled to their opinions."

"They're not. They insulted me." Then, as an afterthought, "And you."

"I've been called worse things than 'offworld monster' in my time. And you've ruined their lunchtime session, to say nothing of my chances of making a record of a typical tavern conversation."

Reluctantly, "I'm sorry."

"So you damn well should be."

The innkeeper arrived with a flagon and two goblets. They were mismatched, and they could have been cleaner, but they were of glass, not of earthenware or metal, and of a standard surprising in an establishment such as this. He placed them carefully on the rough surface of the table, then stood there, wine jug in hand, awaiting the word to pour.

"Just a minute," Margaret Lazenby said. She picked up one of the drinking vessels, examined it. "H'm. Just as I thought."

"And what did you think, Peggy?"

"Look," she said, and her pointed, polished fingernail traced the design of the crest etched into the surface of the glass. "A stylized Greek helmet. And under it, easy enough to read after all these years, 'I.T.T.S. DORIC.' "

"I.T.T.S.?"

"Interstellar Transport Commission's Ship."

"But I thought that your ship belonged to the

Interstellar Federation's Survey Service."

"It does."

"But apart from the Latterhaven freighters, no ships but yours have ever called here."

"Somebody must have. But what about getting these . . . these antiques filled?"

Brasidus gestured to the innkeeper, who, after a second's hesitation, filled the Arcadian's glass first. One did not have to be a telepath to appreciate the man's indecision. Here was a sergeant—and a sergeant in the Police Battalion of the Army at that. Here was an alien, in what might be uniform and what might be civilian clothing. Who ranked whom?

Brasidus lifted his goblet. "To your good health, Peggy."

"And to yours." She sipped. "H'm. Not at all bad. Of course, in this setting it should be *retsina*, and there should be *feta* and black olives to nibble . . ."

"You will speak in riddles, Peggy."

"I'm sorry, Brasidus. It's just that you're so . . . so human in spite of everything that I keep forgetting that your world has been in isolation for centuries. But suppose we just enjoy the meal?"

And they did enjoy it. Brasidus realized that his own appreciation of it was enhanced by the Arcadian's obvious delight in the—to her—unfamiliar food and drink. They finished their stew, and then there were ripe, red, gleaming apples—"Like no apples that I've ever seen or tasted," commented Peggy, "but they'll do. Indeed they will"—and another flagon of wine. When they were done, save for the liquor remaining in the jug, Brasidus wiped his mouth on the back of his right hand, watched with tolerant amusement as his companion patted her lips with a little square of white cloth that she brought from one of her pockets.

She said, "That was good, Brasidus." From a packet that she produced from a shoulder pouch she half shook two slim brown cylinders. "Smoke?"

"Is this the same stuff that Commander Grimes was burning in that wooden thing like a little trumpet?"

"It is. Yours must be about the only Man-colonized world that hasn't tobacco. Commander Grimes likes his pipe; I prefer a cigarillo. See— this is the striking end. Just a tap—so. Put the other end in your mouth." She showed him how, then remarked, as she exhaled a fragrant blue cloud, "I hope that the same doesn't happen to us as happened to Sir Walter Raleigh."

"And what did happen?" Brasidus inhaled, then coughed and spluttered violently. He hastily dropped the little cylinder onto his plate. Probably this Sir Walter Raleigh, whoever he was, had been violently ill.

"Sir Walter Raleigh was the Elizabethan explorer who first introduced tobacco into a country called England. He was enjoying his pipe after a meal in an inn, and the innkeeper thought that he was on fire and doused him with a bucket of water."

"This fat flunkey had better not try it on you!" growled Brasidus.

"I doubt if he'd dare. From what I've observed, a sergeant on this planet piles on more Gs than a mere knight in the days of Good Queen Bess." She laughed through the wreathing, aromatic fumes

— then, suddenly serious, said, "We have company."

Brasidus swung round, his right hand on the butt of his pistol. But it was only the village corporal—a big man in slovenly uniform, his leather unpolished, his brass tarnished. His build, his broad, heavy face were indicative of slowness, both physical and mental, but the little gray eyes under the sandy thatch of the eyebrows were shrewd enough.

"Sergeant!" he barked, saluting and stiffening to attention.

"Corporal—at ease! Be seated."

"Thank you, Sergeant."

"Some wine, Corporal?"

The corporal reached out a long arm to one of the other tables, grabbed an earthenware mug, filled it from the flagon. "Thank you, Sergeant. Your health, Sergeant. And yours, sir." He drank deeply and noisily. "Ah, that was good. But, Sergeant, my apologies. I should have been on hand to welcome you and . . ." he stared curiously at the Arcadian. "You and your . . . guest?"

"Doctor Lazenby is one of the officers of the starship Seeker."

"I thought that, Sergeant. Even here there are stories." The man, Brasidus realized, was staring at the odd mounds of flesh that were very obvious beneath the thin shirt worn by the alien.

"They aren't concealed weapons," remarked the Arcadian wryly. "And, in the proper circumstances, they are quite functional."

The corporal flushed, looked away and addressed himself to his superior. "I was absent from the village, Sergeant, as today is Exposure

Day. I had to supervise. But as soon as I was told of your arrival, I hastened back."

"Exposure Day?" asked Margaret Lazenby sharply.

"Yes," Brasidus told her. "One of the days on which the newly born—those newly born who are sickly or deformed, that is—are exposed on the mountainside."

"And what happens to them?"

"Usually the wolves finish them off. But without food or water they'd not last long."

"You're joking." It was an appeal rather than a statement or a question.

"But why should I joke, Peggy? The purity of the race must be maintained."

She turned to the corporal, her face white, her eyes blazing. "You. Had the wolves come when you left the . . . the Exposure?"

"No, sir. But they're never long in hearing the cries and winding the scent."

She was on her feet, pushing her bench away so violently that it toppled with a crash. "Get a move on, Brasidus. If we hurry, we may still be in time."

Brasidus was sickened by her reactions, by her words. Exposure was necessary, but it was not something to take pictures of, to make records of. As well join the scavengers in their filth-eating rounds of the city streets.

"Come on!" she flared.

"No," he said stubbornly. "I'll not help you to make a film that you and your shipmates can gloat over."

"Make a film?" Her voice was incredulous. "You fool. We may be in time to save them."

And then it was Brasidus' turn to experience a wave of incredulity.

Chapter Seventeen

"No!" SAID BRASIDUS.

"*Yes!*" she contradicted him. But, incongru-
ously, it was not the borrowed pistol that she was
leveling at the two men, but a camera. Brasidus
laughed—and then the slim hands holding the
seemingly innocuous instrument twitched ever
so slightly, and from the lens came an almost
invisible flicker of light and, behind the policemen, something exploded. There was a sudden,
acrid stench of flash-boiled wine, of burning
wood.

That deadly lens was looking straight at
Brasidus again.

"Laser," he muttered.

"Laser," she stated.

"But . . . but you were supposed to leave all your
weapons behind."

"I'm not altogether a fool, honey. And, oddly
enough, this *is* a camera, with flash attachment.
Not a very good one, but multipurpose tools are
rarely satisfactory. Now, are you going to drive me
out to the Exposure?"

She'll have to bring along the corporal, thought
Brasidus. *And the two of us should be able to deal
with her.*

And now the deadly camera was in her left hand only, and the borrowed stun gun was out of its holster. She fired left-handed, and at this short range she could hardly miss. The corporal gasped, made one tottering step forward, then crashed untidily to the floor. The belled muzzle swung slightly and she fired again. There was the sound of another heavy fall behind Brasidus. That, he guessed, would be the inkeeper. There would be no telephone calls made to the city for several hours. The goatherds were notorious for their reluctance to assist the forces of law and order.

"Get into the car," she said. "I'll ride behind. And make it snappy."

He walked out of the inn, into the afternoon sunlight, deliberately not hurrying. He consoled himself with the thought that, even though he was falling down on the job as a sergeant of Police, he was earning his keep as a lieutenant of Security. He had been told to find out what made these aliens tick—and he was finding out. In any case, if the wolf packs were as ravenous as usual, there would be nothing left but a scatter of well-gnawed bones.

He climbed into the driver's seat, thought briefly about making a dash for it, then thought better of it. He could never get out of range in time. He heard her clambering in behind him. He wished that he knew which way that so-called camera was pointing—and then he succeeded in catching a glimpse of it in the rear mirror. If the firing stud were accidentally pressed, it would drill a neat, cauterized hole through his head. Or would the water content of his brains explode? In that case, it would not be so tidy.

"Get going," she said. And then, as an after-thought, "I suppose you know the way."

"I know the way," he admitted. The car lifted on its air cushion and proceeded.

"Faster. Faster."

"This is only a goat track," he grumbled. "And this isn't an armored chariot we're riding in."

Even so, deliberately taking the risk of fouling the fan casings on projecting stones, he managed to increase speed. Rather to his disappointment, the vehicle still rode easily, sped over the rough terrain without making any crippling contacts.

And then, ahead of them, seemingly from just over the next rise, sounded the ominous howling and snarling of the wolf pack, and with it, almost inaudible, a thin, high screaming.

"Hurry!" Margaret Lazenby was shouting. "Hurry!"

They were over the rise now. Once before, Brasidus had watched an Exposure, and the spectacle had sickened him, even though he had realized the necessity for it, and appreciated the essential justice of allowing Nature to erase its own mistakes in its own way. But to rescue one or more of these mewling, subhuman creatures— that was unthinkable.

The car was over the rise.

And then it was bearing down on the snarling, quarreling pack, on the carnivores too engrossed in their bloody business to notice the approach of potential enemies. But perhaps they heard the whine of the ducted fans and, even so, remembered that, on these occasions, Men never interfered with them.

The car was sweeping down the slope toward

the melee, and Margaret Lazenby was firing. Brasidus could feel the heat of the discharges, cursed as the hair on the right side of his head crisped and smoldered. But he maintained a steady course nonetheless, and experienced the inevitable thrill of the hunt, the psychological legacy from Man's savage ancestors. Ahead there was a haze of vaporized blood; the stench of seared flesh was already evident. The howling of the pack rose to a frenzied crescendo but the animals stood their ground, red eyes glaring, slavering, crimsoned jaws agape. Then—an evil, gray, stormy tide—they began to surge up the hillside to meet their attackers.

Brasidus was shooting now, the control column grasped in his left hand, the bucking projectile pistol in his right. Between them, he and Margaret Lazenby cleared a path for their advance, although the car rocked and lurched as it passed over the huddle of dead and dying bodies. Then—"Stop!" she was crying. "Stop! There's a baby there! I saw it move!"

Yes, there among the ghastly litter of scattered bones and torn flesh, was a living child, eyes screwed tight shut, bawling mouth wide open. It would not be living much longer. Already two of the wolves, ignoring the slaughter of their companions, were facing each other over the tiny, feebly struggling body, their dreadful teeth bared as they snarled at each other.

Margaret Lazenby was out of the car before Brasidus could bring it to a halt. Inevitably she lost her balance and fell, rolling down the slope, almost to where the two carnivores were disputing over their prey. She struggled somehow to her knees just as they saw her, just as they abandoned what was no more than a toothsome morsel for a satisfying meal. Somehow, awkwardly, she managed to bring her camera-gun into firing position, but the weapon must have been damaged by her fall. She cried out and threw it from her, in a smoking, spark-spitting arc that culminated in the main body of the pack. Even as it exploded in a soundless flare of raw energy she was tugging the borrowed stun gun from its holster.

Once she fired, and once only, and one of the two wolves faltered in the very act of leaping, slumped to the ground. The other one completed its spring and was on her, teeth and taloned hind paws slashing. Brasidus was out of the car, running, a pistol in each hand. But he could not use his guns—animal and alien formed together a wildly threshing tangle, and to fire at one would almost certainly mean hitting the other. But the Arcadian was fighting desperately and well, as yet seemed to be undamaged. Her hands about the brute's neck were keeping those slavering jaws from her throat, and her knee in the wolf's belly was still keeping those slashing claws at a distance. But she was tiring. It would not be long before sharp fangs found her jugular or slashing talons opened her up from breastbone to groin.

Dropping his weapons, Brasidus jumped. From behind he got his own two hands around the furry throat, his own knee into the beast's back. He exerted all of his strength, simultaneously pulled and thrust. The animal whined, then was abruptly silent as the air supply to the laboring lungs was cut off. But it was still strong, was still resisting desperately, was striving to turn so that it could face this fresh enemy. Margaret Lazenby had fallen clear of the fight, was slowly crawling to where she had dropped her pistol.

She never had to use it. Brasidus brought his last reserves of strength into play, heard the sharp snap of broken vertebrae. The fight was over.

He got groggily to his feet, ready to face and to fight a fresh wave of carnivores. But, save for the Arcadian, the squalling child and himself, the hillside was bare of life. There were charred bodies, human and animal, where the laser weapon had exploded; the other wolves, such of them as had survived, must have fled. The stench of burning flesh was heavy in the air.

At a tottering run, Margaret Lazenby was hurrying to the child, the only survivor of the Exposure. More slowly, Brasidus followed, looked down at the little naked body. He said, "It would have been kinder to let it die. What sort of life can it expect with that deformity?"

"Deformity? What the hell do you mean?"

Wordlessly he pointed to the featureless scissure of the baby's thighs.

"Deformity? This, you fool, is a perfectly formed female child."

She got down to her knees and tenderly picked up the infant. And, as she did so, it became somehow obvious that the odd mounds of flesh on her chest, fully revealed now that her shirt had been torn away, were, after all, functional. The baby stopped crying, groped greedily for an erect pink nipple.

Peggy laughed shakily. "No, darling, no. I'm sorry, but the milk bar's not open for business. I'll make up a bottle for you when we get back to the ship."

"So," muttered Brasidus at last, "so it is one of your race."

"Yes."

"And those . . . lumps are where you fission from."

She said, "You've still a lot to learn. And now give me your tunic, will you."

"My tunic?"

"Yes. Don't just stand there, looking as though you've never seen a woman before."

Brasidus silently stripped off his upper garment, handed it to her. He expected that she would put the child back on the ground while she covered her own seminudity. But she did not. Instead, she wrapped the baby in the tunic, cooing to it softly. "There, there. You were cold, weren't you? But Mummy will keep you warm, and Mummy will see that you're fed." She straightened, then snapped in a voice of command, "Take me back to the ship, as fast as all the Odd Gods of the Galaxy will let you!"

Chapter Eighteen

SO THEY DROVE back to the ship swiftly, bypassing Kilkis—Brasidus had no desire to meet again the village corporal—taking roads that avoided all centers of population, however small. Peggy was in the back of the car, making soft, soothing noises to the querulous infant. *Achron*, thought Brasidus sullenly, *would have appreciated this display of paternal solicitude—but I do not.* And what did he feel? Jealousy, he was obliged to admit, resentment at being deprived of the Arcadian's company. Perverts the doctors in the crèche might be, but these aliens could and did exert a dangerous charm. But when it came to a showdown, as now, they had no time for mere humans, lavished their attentions only upon their own kind.

Suddenly the child was silent. The car was speeding down a straight stretch of road, so Brasidus was able to risk turning his head to see what was happening. Peggy had the stopper out of the wine flask, was dipping a corner of her handkerchief into it, then returning the soaked scrap of rag to the eager mouth of the baby. She grinned ruefully as she met Brasidus' stare. "I know it's all wrong," she said. "But I haven't a feeding bottle. Too, it will help if the brat is sound asleep when we get back to the spaceport."

"And why will it help?" demanded Brasidus, turning his attention back to the road ahead.

She said, "It's occurred to me that *we* have probably broken quite a few laws. Apart from anything else, armed assault upon the person of a police officer must be illegal."

"It is. But *you* carried out the armed assault. *We* did not."

She laughed. "Too true. But what about our interference with the Exposure? It will be better for both of us if your boss doesn't know that the interference was a successful one."

"I must make my report," said Brasidus stiffly.

"Of course." Her voice was soft, caressing. "But need it be a *full* report? We got into a fight with the wolf pack—there's too much evidence littered around on the hillside for us to lie our way out of that. I've a few nasty scratches on my back and my breasts."

"So that's what they're called. I was wondering."

"Never mind that now. I've got these scratches, so it's essential that I get back on board as soon as possible for treatment by our own doctor."

"I thought that you were the ship's doctor."

"I'm not. I have a doctorate in my own field, which is not medicine. But let me finish. We had this fight with these four-legged sharks you people call wolves. I fell out of the car, and you jumped out and saved my life, although not before I was mauled a little. And that's near enough to the truth, isn't it?"

"Yes."

"Now, the child. She'll fit nicely into the hamper you brought the provisions in. The poor little tot will be in a drugged stupor by the time we get to the spaceport, so she'll be quiet enough. And with your tunic spread over her, who will know?"

"I don't like it," said Brasidus.

"That makes two of us, my dear. I don't like having to conceal the evidence of actions that, on any world but this, would bring a public commendation."

"But Diomedes will know."

"How can he know? We were there, he was not. And we don't even have to make sure that we tell the same story, exact in every detail. He can question you, but he can't question me."

"Don't be so sure about that, Peggy."

"Oh, he'd like to, Brasidus. He'd like to. But he knows that at all times there are sufficient officers and ratings aboard Seeker to handle the drive and main and secondary armaments. He knows that we could swat your gasbags out of the sky in a split second, and then raze the city in our own good time." There was a long silence. Then, "I'm sorry to have gotten you into quite a nasty mess, Brasidus, but you realize that I had no choice."

"Like calls to like," he replied with bitter flippancy.

"You could put it that way, I suppose, but you're wrong. Anyhow, I'm sure that I shall be able to persuade John—Commander Grimes—to offer you the sanctuary of our ship if you're really in a jam."

"I'm a Spartan," he said.

"With all the Spartan virtues, I suppose. Do you have that absurd legend about the boy who let the fox gnaw his vitals rather than cry out? No matter.

Just tell Captain Diomedes the truth, but not the whole truth. Say that it was all my fault, and that you did your best to restrain me. Which you did—although it wasn't good enough. Say that you saved me from the wolves."

They drove on in silence while Brasidus pondered his course of action. What the Arcadian had said was true, what she had proposed might prevent an already unpleasant situation from becoming even more unpleasant. In saving Peggy's life, he had done no more than his duty; in helping to save the life of the deformed—deformed?—child he, an officer of the law, had become a criminal. And why had he done this? With the destruction of the laser-camera the alien had lost her only advantage.

And why had he *known*, why did he still *know* that his part in the rescue operations had been essentially *right*?

It was this strange awareness of rightness that brought him to full agreement with his companion's propositions. Until now, he had accepted without question the superior intellectual and moral stature of those holding higher rank than himself, but it was obvious that aboard *Seeker* there were officers, highly competent technicians with superbly trained men and fantastically powerful machinery at their command, whose moral code varied widely from the Spartan norm. (Come to that, what about the doctors, the top-ranking aristocrats of the planet, whose own morals were open to doubt? What about the doctors, and their perverse relations with the Arcadians?)

Peggy's voice broke into his thoughts. "She's

sleeping now. Out like a light. Drunk as a fiddler's bitch. I think that we shall be able to smuggle her on board without trouble." She went on, "I appreciate this, Brasidus. I do. I wish . . ." He realized that she must be standing up in the back of the car, leaning toward him. He felt her breasts against the bare skin of his back. The contact was like nothing that he had ever imagined. He growled, "Sit down, damn you. Sit down—if you want this wagon to stay on the road!"

Chapter Nineteen

THEY ENCOUNTERED NO delays on their way back to
the spaceport, but, once they were inside the main
gates, it was obvious that their return had been
anticipated. Diomedes, backed by six armed hoplites, was standing, glowering, outside his office.
A little away from him was John Grimes—and it
was not a ceremonial sword that depended from
his belt but two holstered pistols. And there was
another officer from the ship with him, wearing a
walky-talky headset. The Commander glared at
Brasidus and his companion with almost as much
hostility as did Diomedes.

Diomedes raised an imperious arm. Brasidus
brought the car to a halt. Grimes said something to
his officer, who spoke into the mouthpiece of his
headset. Brasidus, looking beyond the young man
to the ship, saw that the turrets housing her armament were operational, the long barrels of
weapons, fully extruded, waving slowly like the
questing antennae of some giant insect.

"Brasidus." Diomedes' voice was a high-
pitched squeal, a sure sign of bad temper. "I have
received word from the village corporal at Kilkis. I
demand your report—and your report, Doctor
Lazenby—immediately. You will both come into
my office."

"Captain Diomedes," said Grimes coldly, "you have every right to give orders to your own officers, but none whatsoever to issue commands to my personnel. Doctor Lazenby will make her report to me, aboard my ship."

"I have means of enforcing my orders, Commander Grimes."

As one man, the six hoplites drew their stun guns.

Grimes laughed. "My gunnery officer has his instructions, Captain Diomedes. He's watching us from the control room through very high-powered binoculars and, furthermore, he is hearing everything that is being said."

"And what are his instructions, Commander?"

"There's just one way for you to find out, Captain. I shouldn't advise it, though."

"All right." With a visible effort, Diomedes brought himself under control. "All right. I request, then, Commander, that you order your officer to accompany Brasidus into my office for questioning. You, and as many of your people as you wish, may be present."

Grimes obviously was giving consideration to what Diomedes had said. It was reasonable enough. Brasidus knew that, if he were in Grimes' shoes, he would have agreed. But suppose that somebody decided to investigate the contents of that food hamper on the back seat, some thirsty man hopeful that a drink of wine might remain in the flagon. Or suppose that the effects of the alcohol on the presently sleeping baby suddenly wore off.

Margaret Lazenby took charge. She stood up in the back of the car—and the extent of her dishevelment was suddenly obvious. The men stared at her, and Grimes, his fists clenched, took a threatening step toward Brasidus, growling, "You bastard."

"Stop it, John!" The Arcadian's voice was sharp. "Brasidus didn't do this."

"Then who did?"

"Damn it all! Can't you see that I want at least another shirt, as well as medical attention for these scratches? But if you must know, I made Brasidus take me to watch the Exposure."

"So the village corporal told me," put in Diomedes. "And between you, the pair of you slaughtered an entire wolf pack."

"We went too close, and they attacked us. They pulled me out of the car, but Brasidus saved me. And now, Captain Diomedes, I'd like to get back on board as soon as possible for an antibiotic shot and some fresh clothing." Before leaving the car, she stopped to lift the hamper from the back seat, handed it to Grimes' officer.

"What's in that basket?" demanded Diomedes.

"Nothing that concerns you!" she flared.

"I'll decide that," Grimes stated. "Here, Mister Taylor. Let me see."

The officer turned to face his captain, with his body hiding the hamper from Diomedes and his men. It was not intentional—or *was* it? Grimes, his face emotionless, lifted Brasidus' torn tunic from the open top of the wickerwork container. He said calmly, "One wine flagon. About six inches of gnarled sausage. The heel of a loaf of crusty bread. *You* decide, Captain, what may be brought off the ship onto your world, *I* decide what may be brought from your world onto my ship. Mister Taylor, take this hamper to the biochemist so that its contents may be analyzed. And you, Doctor Lazenby, report at once to the surgeon. I'll receive your report later."

"Commander Grimes, I insist that I inspect that hamper." Three of the hoplites stepped forward, began to surround Mister Taylor.

"Captain Diomedes, if any of your men dare to lay hands upon my officer the consequences will be serious."

Diomedes laughed incredulously. "You'd open fire over a mug of wine and a couple of scraps of bread and sausage?"

"Too right I would."

Diomedes laughed again. "You aliens . . ." he said contemptuously. "All right, you can have your crumbs from the sergeants' mess. And I'd like a few words with your Doctor Lazenby as soon as she can spare me the time. And I'll have rather more than a few words with you, Brasidus, *now!*"

Reluctantly Brasidus got out of the car.

"And you let her threaten you with a laser weapon—and, furthermore, one that you had allowed her to carry. . . ."

Brasidus, facing Diomedes, who was lolling behind his desk, said rebelliously, "You, sir, checked her equipment. And she told me herself that the thing did function as a camera."

"All right. We'll let that pass. You allowed her to use a stun gun on the village corporal and the innkeeper, and then you drove her out to the Exposure. Why, Brasidus, did you have to stop at Kilkis, of all villages, on this day, of all days?"

"Nobody told me not to, sir. And, as you know,

the dates of the Exposures are never advertised. You might have been informed, but I was not."

"So you drove her out to see the Exposure. And you got too close. And the wolves attacked you, and pulled her out of the car."

"That is correct, sir."

"Surely she could have used this famous laser-camera to defend herself."

"It was damaged, sir. She had to throw it away in a hurry. It blew up."

"Yes. I've been told that there's an area on the hillside that looks as though some sort of bomb had been exploded." He leaned back in his chair, looked up at the standing Brasidus. "You say that the wolves attacked her. Are you sure that it wasn't you?"

"And why should it have been me, sir?"

"Because it should have been. You let an alien order you around at gun point, and then you ask me why you should have attacked her! And now . . ." the words came out with explosive violence, *"What was in the hamper?"*

"Wine, sir. Bread. Sausage."

"And what was your tunic doing there?"

"I lent it to her, sir, to replace her own shirt."

"So, instead of wearing it, she put it in the hamper."

"The air was warm, sir, when we got down from the mountains. She asked me if she could have it so that the fibers from which it is woven could be analyzed by the . . . the biochemist."

"H'm. All in all, Brasidus, you did not behave with great brilliance. Were it not for the fact that these aliens—or one alien in particular—seem to like you, I should dispense with your services. As it is, you are still useful. Now, just what were this Margaret Lazenby's reactions when she learned of the Exposure?"

Lying, Brasidus knew, would be useless. The village corporal at Kilkis would have made a full report. He said, "She was shocked. She wanted to get to the site in time to rescue the deformed and defective children."

"You were not in time, of course."

"No, sir. We were not in time." He added virtuously, "I made sure of that."

"How, Brasidus?"

"I knew the way, she did not. I was able to make a detour."

The answer seemed to satisfy Diomedes. He grunted, "All right. You may sit down." For a few seconds he drummed on the desktop with his fingertips. "Meanwhile, Brasidus, the situation in the city is developing. Commander Grimes allowed his Arcadians, as well as the human members of his crew, shore leave. There was an unfortunate occurrence in the Tavern of the Three Harpies. An Arcadian, accompanied by a human spaceman, went in there. They got drinking with the other customers."

"Not the sort of place that I'd drink in by choice," Brasidus said, the other's silence seeming to call for some sort of comment.

"They were not so fortunate as to have a guide, such as yourself, to keep them out of trouble." (*You sarcastic swine,* thought Brasidus.) "Anyhow, there was the usual crowd in there. Helots of the laboring class, hoplites not fussy about the company they keep. It wouldn't have been so bad if the two spacemen had just taken one drink and then walked out, but they stayed there, drinking with the locals, and allowed themselves to be drawn into an argument. And you know how arguments in the Three Harpies usually finish."

"There was a fight, sir?"

"Brilliant, Brasidus, brilliant. There was a fight, and the human spaceman was laid out, and the Arcadian was beaten up a little, and then stripped. There was, you will understand, some curiosity as to what her body was like under her uniform."

"That was bad, sir."

"There's worse to follow. At least four hoplites had sexual intercourse with her by force."

"So it is possible, sir, in spite of the malformation."

Diomedes chuckled obscenely. "It's possible, all right. Everybody in the tavern would have had her if the other spaceman hadn't come round and started screaming for help on a little portable transceiver he wore on his wrist. A dozen men from the ship rushed in, real toughs—and I wish that my own personnel could learn *their* techniques of unarmed combat. Then the police condescended to intervene and laid everybody out with their stun guns, and then Commander Grimes, who'd heard about it somehow, came charging into my office threatening to devastate the city, and . . . and . . .

"Anyhow, you can see why I had to handle this Lazenby creature with kid gloves. Even though Grimes admits that his own crew were at fault— he had issued strict orders that no sightseeing party was to consist of fewer than six people—he was furious about the 'rape,' as he called it. You saw how he reacted when he thought that you had

been doing something of the kind. He demanded
that the rapists be punished most severely."

"But they were hoplites, sir, not helots. They
had the right . . ."

"I know, I know. When I need instruction in the
finer points of Spartan law I'll come to you. The
conduct was discourteous rather than criminal.
The culprits will, by this time, have been rep-
rimanded by their commanding officer, and will,
in all probability, be back in the Three Harpies,
telling anybody who cares to listen what intercourse is like with an Arcadian. It is, I gather,
quite an experience. Are you quite sure that you
didn't . . . ?"

"Quite sure, sir."

"That's your story, and you stick to it." Again
there was a pause, and the muffled drumming of
Diomedes' fingers on the top of his desk. Then he
went on, "Even on Sparta we have experienced
occasional mutiny, infrequent rebellion. Tell me,
Brasidus, what are the prime causes of mutiny?"

"Discontent, sir. Overly strict discipline. Un-
just punishments . . ."

"And . . . ?"

"That's about all, sir."

"What about envy, Brasidus?"

"No, sir. We all know that if we show ability we
shall become officers, with all the privileges that
go with rank."

"But what if there's a privilege out of reach to
everybody except a few members of one aristocra-
tic caste?"

"I don't see what you mean, sir."

"Brasidus, Brasidus, what do you use for
brains? What about that nest of Arcadians in the

crèche? What do you suppose the doctors use them for?"

"I . . . I can guess."

"And so they have something that the rest of us haven't. And so"—Diomedes' voice dropped almost to a whisper—"the power that they've enjoyed for so long, for too long, may be broken."

"And you," said Brasidus, "envy them that power."

For long seconds the Captain glared at him across the desk. Then, "All right, I do. But it is for the good of the State that I am working against them."

Perhaps, thought Brasidus. *Perhaps.* But he said nothing.

Chapter Twenty

CLAD IN A LABORING Helot's drab, patched tunic, his feet unshod and filthy, his face and arms liberally besmeared with the dirt of the day's toil, Brasidus sat hunched at one of the long tables in the Tavern of the Three Harpies. There were hoplites there as well as manual workers, but there was little chance that any of them would recognize him. Facial similarities were far from uncommon on Sparta.

He sat there, taking an occasional noisy gulp from his mug and listening.

One of the hoplites was holding forth to his companions. "Yes, it was on this very table that I had him. Or it. Good it was. You've no idea unless you've tried it yourself."

"Must've been odd. Wrong, somehow."

"It was odd, all right. But wrong nohow. This face-to-face business. And those two dirty great cushions for your chest to rest on . . ."

"Is that what they're for?"

"Must be. Pity the doctors can't turn out some of those creatures from their birth machine."

"But they do. Yes. They do."

Everybody turned to stare at the man who had just spoken. He was a stranger to Brasidus, but his voice and his appearance marked him for what he was. This was not the sort of inn that the nurses from the crèche usually frequented—in an establishment such as this they would run a grave risk of suffering the same fate as the unfortunate Arcadian from the ship. "They do," he repeated in his high-pitched sing-song, and looked straight at Brasidus. There was something in his manner that implied, *And you know, too.*

So this was the fellow agent whom Diomedes had told him that he would find in the tavern, the operative to whom he was to render assistance if necessary.

"And what do you know about it, dearie?" demanded the boastful hoplite.

"I'm a nurse . . ."

"That's obvious, sweetie pie."

"I'm a nurse, and I work at the crèche. We nurses aren't supposed to stray from our wards, but . . ."

"But with a snout like yours, you're bound to be nosy," said the hoplite, laughing.

The nurse stroked his overlong proboscis with his right index finger, grinned slyly. "How right you are, dearie. I admit it. I *like* to know what's going on. Oh, those doctors! They live in luxury, all right. You might think that practically all of the crèche is taken up by wards and machinery and the like, but it's not. More than half the building is *their* quarters. And the things they have! A heated swimming pool, even." .

"Decadent," grunted a grizzled old sergeant.

"But nice. Especially in midwinter. Not that I've ever tried it myself. There's a disused storeroom, and this pool is on the other side of its back wall. There're some holes in the wall, where there used to be wiring or pipes or something. Big enough for a camera lens." The nurse fished a large envelope from inside the breast of his white tunic, pulled from it a sheaf of glossy photographs.

"Lemme see. Yes, those are Arcadians, all right. Topheavy, ain't they, when you see them standing up. Wonder how they can walk without falling flat on their faces."

"If they did, they'd bounce."

"Look sort of unfinished lower down, don't they?"

"Let *me* see!"

"Here, pass 'em round, can't you?"

Briefly, Brasidus had one of the prints in his possession. He was interested more in the likeness of the man standing by the pool than in that of his companion. Yes, it was Heraklion, all right, Heraklion without his robe but still, indubitably, the supercilious doctor.

"Must have come in that ship," remarked somebody.

"No," the nurse told him. "Oh, no. They've been in the crèche for *years*."

"You mean your precious doctors have *always* had them?"

"Yes. Nothing but the best for the guardians of the purity of our Spartan stock, dearie. But who are we to begrudge them their little comforts?"

"Soldiers, that's who. It's we who should be the top caste of this world, who should have the first pickings. After all, the King's a soldier."

"But the doctors *made* him, dearie. They made all of us."

"Like hell they did. They just look after the

birth machine. And if there wasn't a machine, we'd manage all right, just as the animals do.''

"We might have to," the nurse said. "I heard two of the doctors talking. They were saying that the people were having it too soft, that for the good of the race we should have to return to the old ways. They're thinking of shutting the machine down."

"What! How can you be a fighting man if you have to lug a child around with you?"

"But you said that we could manage all right without the doctors."

"Yes. But that's different. No, the way I see it is this: These doctors are getting scared of the military, but they know that if most of us are budding we shan't be much good for fighting. Oh, the cunning swine! They just want things all their way all the time instead of for only most of the time."

"But you can't do anything about it," the nurse said.

"Can't we? Who have the weapons and the training to use 'em? Not your doctors, that's for certain. With no more than the men in this tavern, we could take the crèche—and get our paws on to those Arcadians they've got stashed away there."

"More than our paws!" shouted somebody.

"You're talking mutiny and treason, hoplite," protested the elderly sergeant.

"Am I?" The man was on his feet now, swaying drunkenly. "But the King himself had one of the doctors executed. That shows how much *he* thinks of 'em!" He paused, striving for words. They came at last. "Here, on Sparta, it's fair shares for all—excepting you poor damn helots, of course. But for the rest of us, the rulers, it should be share an' share alike. Oh, I know that the colonel gets better pay, better grub an' better booze than I do—but in the field he lives the same as his men, an' all of us can become colonels ourselves if we put ourselves to it, an', come to that, generals. But the colonels an' the generals an' the admirals don't have Arcadians to keep their beds warm. Not even the King does. An' now there's some of us who know what it's like. An' there's some of us who want more of it."

"They're plenty of Arcadians aboard the spaceship," somebody suggested.

"I may be drunk, fellow, but I'm not *that* drunk. The spaceship's a battlewagon, and I've heard that the captain of her has already threatened to use his guns and missiles. No, the crèche'll be *easy* to take."

"Sit down, you fool!" ordered the elderly sergeant. "You got off light after you assaulted the Arcadian spaceman, but he was only a foreigner. Now you're inciting to riot, mutiny, and the gods alone know what else. The police will use more than stun guns on you this time."

"Will they, old-timer? Will they? And what if they do? A man can die only once. What I did to that Arcadian has done something to me, to *me*, do you hear? I have to do it again, even though I get shot for it." The man's eyes were crazy and his lips, foam-flecked. "You don't know what it was like. You'll never know, until you do it. Don't talk to me about boys, or about soft, puling nurses like our long-nosed friend here. The doctors have the best there is, the best that there can ever be, and they should be made to share it!"

"The police . . . " began the sergeant.

"Yes. The police. Now let me tell you, old-timer, that I kept my ears flapping while they had me in their barracks. Practically every man has been called out to guard the spaceport—the *spaceport*, do you hear? That alien captain's afraid that there'll be a mob coming out to take *his* pretty Arcadians by force, and fat old Captain Diomedes is afraid that the space commander'll start firing off in all directions if his ship and his little pets are menaced. By the time that the police get back to the city, every Arcadian in the crèche'll know what a *real* man is like, an' we shall all be tucked up in our cots in our quarters sleeping innocently."

"I didn't see a single policeman on my way here," contributed the nurse. "I wondered why." And then, in spurious alarm, "But you can't. You mustn't. You mustn't attack the crèche!"

"And who says I mustn't? You, you feeble imitation of a . . . a . . ."

He concluded triumphantly, "of an alien monster! Yes, that's a point. All this talk of them as alien monsters. It was only to put us off. But now we *know*. Or some of us know. Who's with me?"

The fools, thought Brasidus, *the fools!* as he listened to the crash of overturned benches, as he watched almost all the customers of the tavern, helots as well as hoplites, jump to their feet.

"The fools," he muttered aloud.

"And you would have been with them," whispered the nurse, "if I hadn't slipped a capsule into your drink." And then Brasidus saw the thin wisp of almost invisible vapor that was still trickling from the envelope in which the photographs had been packed. "I have access to certain drugs," said the man smugly, "and this one is used in our schoolrooms. It enhances the susceptibility of the students."

"Students," repeated Brasidus disgustedly.

"They have a lot to learn, Lieutenant," the nurse told him.

"And so have I. I want to see what happens."

"Your orders were to protect me."

"There's nobody here to protect you from, except that old sergeant. But why wasn't *he* affected?"

"Too old," said the nurse.

"Then you're quite safe."

Brasidus made his way from the tavern out into the street.

Chapter Twenty-One

HE WOULD HAVE retreated to the safety of the inn, but he was given no opportunity to do so. A roaring torrent of men swept along the street, hoplites and helots, shouting, cursing and screaming. He was caught up by the human tide, buffeted and jostled, crying out with pain himself when a heavy, military sandal smashed down on one of his bare feet. He was sucked into the mob, made part of it, became just one tiny drop of water in the angry wave that was rearing up to smash down upon the crèche.

At first, he was fighting only to keep upright, to save himself from falling, from being trampled underfoot. And then—slowly, carefully and, at times, viciously—he began to edge out toward the fringe of the living current. At last he was able to stumble into a cross alley where he stood panting, recovering his breath, watching the rioters stream past.

Then he was able to think.

It seemed obvious to him that Diomedes must have planted his agents in more than one tavern. It was obvious, too, that Diomedes, ever the opportunist, had regarded the unfortunate incident in the Three Harpies as a heaven-sent opportunity for rabble-rousing—and as an excuse for the withdrawal of all police from the city. And that is all that it was—an excuse. It was doubtful, thought Brasidus, that Grimes had demanded protection. The spaceman was quite capable of looking after himself and his own people—and if the situation got really out of hand he could always lift ship at a second's notice.

But there were still puzzling features in the situation. The military police were under the command of General Rexenor, with the usual tally of colonels and majors subordinate to him. Diomedes was only a captain. How much power did the man wield? How much backing had he? Was he—and this seemed more than likely—answerable only to the palace?

The mob was thinning out now; there were only the stragglers half-running, stumbling over the cobblestones. And already the first of the scavengers were emerging from their hiding places, sniffing cautiously at the crumpled bodies of those who had been crushed and trampled. Brasidus fell in with the tattered rearguard, kept pace with a withered, elderly man in rough and dirty working clothes.

"Don't . . . know . . . why . . . we . . . bother . . ." grunted this individual between gasping breaths. "Bloody . . . hoplites . . . 'll . . . be . . . there . . . first. All . . . the . . . bloody . . . pickings . . . as . . . bloody . . . usual."

"What pickings?"

"Food . . . wine . . . Those . . . bloody . . . doctors . . . worse . . . 'n . . . bloody . . . soldiers. . . . Small . . . wonder . . . the . . . King . . . has . . . turned . . . against . . . 'em."

"And . . . the Arcadians?"

"Wouldn't . . . touch . . . one . . . o' . . . them . . . wi'

. . . barge . . . pole. Unsightly . . . monsters."

Ahead, the roar of the mob had risen to an ugly and frightening intensity. There were flames, too, leaping high, a billowing glare in the night sky. The crowd had broken into a villa close by the crèche, the Club House of the senior nursing staff. They had dragged furniture out into the roadway and set fire to it. Some of its unfortunate owners fluttered ineffectually about the blaze and, until one of them had the sense to organize his mates into a bucket party, were treated with rough derision only. And then the crowd turned upon the firemen, beating them, even throwing three of them into the bonfire. Two of them managed to scramble clear and ran, screaming, their robes ablaze. The other just lay there, writhing and shrieking.

Brasidus was sickened. There was nothing that he could do. He was alone and unarmed—and most of the soldiers among the rioters carried their short swords and some them were already using them, hacking down the surviving nurses who were still foolish enough to try to save their property. There was nothing at all that he could do—and he should have been in uniform, not in these rags, and armed, with a squad of men at his command, doing his utmost to quell the disorder.

Damn Diomedes! he thought. He knew, with sudden clarity, where his real loyalties lay—to the maintenance of law and order and, on a more personal level, to his friend Achron, on duty inside the crèche and soon, almost inevitably, to be treated as had been these hacked and incinerated colleagues of his.

The Andronicus warehouse . . .

Nobody noticed him as he crossed the road to that building; the main body of the rioters was attempting to force the huge door of the crèche with a battering ram improvised from a torn-down streetlamp standard. And then, looking at the massive door set in the black, featureless wall of the warehouse, he realized that he was in dire need of such an implement himself. He could, he knew, enlist the aid of men on the fringes of the crowd eager for some violence in which they, themselves, could take part—but that was the last thing that he wanted. He would enter the crèche alone, if at all.

But how?

How?

Overhead, barely audible, there was a peculiar throbbing noise, an irregular beat. He thought, *So the Navy is intervening*, then realized that the sound was not that of an airship's engines. He looked up, saw flickering, ruddy light reflected from an oval surface. And then, in a whisper that seemed to originate only an inch from his ear, a familiar voice asked, "Is that you, Brasidus?"

"Yes."

"I owe you plenty. We'll pick you up and take you clear of this mess. I had to promise not to intervene—I'm just observing and recording— but I'll always break a promise to help a friend."

"I don't want to be picked up, Peggy."

"Then what the hell do you want?"

"I want to get into this warehouse. But the door is locked, and there aren't any windows, and I haven't any explosives."

"You could get your friends to help. Or don't you want to share the loot?"

"I'm not looting. And I want to get into the crèche by myself, not with a mob."

"I wouldn't mind a look inside myself, before it's too late. Hold on, I'll be right with you." Then, in a fainter voice, she was giving orders to somebody in the flying machine. "I'm going down, George. Get the ladder over, will you? Yes, yes, I know what Commander Grimes said, but Brasidus saved my life. And you just keep stooging around in the pinnace, and be ready to come a-runnin' to pick us up when I yell for you. . . . Yes, yes. Keep the cameras and the recorders running."

"Have you a screwdriver?" asked Brasidus.

"*A screwdriver?*"

"If you have, bring it."

"All right."

A light, flexible ladder snaked down from the almost invisible hull. Clad in black coveralls, Peggy Lazenby was herself almost invisible as she rapidly dropped down it. As soon as she was standing on the ground the pinnace lifted, vanished into the night sky.

"What now, love?" she asked. "What now?"

"That door," Brasidus told her, pointing.

"With a *screwdriver?* Are you quite mad?"

"We shall need that later. But I was sure that you'd have one of your laser-cameras along."

"As it happens, I haven't. But I do have a laser pistol—which, on low intensity, is a quite useful electric torch." She pulled the weapon from its holster, made an adjustment, played a dim beam on the double door. "H'm. Looks like a conventional enough lock. And I don't think that your little friends will notice a very brief and discreet fireworks display."

She made another adjustment, and the beam

became thread thin and blinding. There was a brief coruscation of sparks, a spatter of incandescent globules of molten metal.

"That should be it. Push, Brasidus."

Brasidus pushed. There was resistance that suddenly yielded, and the massive valves swung inwards.

Nobody noticed them enter the warehouse—the entire attention of the mob was centered on the door of the crèche, which was still holding. When they were inside, Brasidus pushed the big doors shut. Then he asked, "How did you find me?"

"I wasn't looking for you. We knew about the riot, of course, and I persuaded John to let me take one of the pinnaces so that I could observe the goings-on. Our liftoff coincided with a test firing of the auxiliary rocket drive—even your Captain Diomedes couldn't blame Commander Grimes for wanting to be all ready for a hasty getaway. And the radar lookout kept by your Navy must be very lax—although, of course, our screen was operating. Anyhow, I was using my infrared viewer, and when I saw a solitary figure slink away from the main party, I wondered what mischief he was up to. I focused on him, and, lo and behold, it was you. Not that I recognized you at first. I much prefer you in uniform. Now, what is all this about?"

"I wish that I knew. But the mob's trying to break into the crèche, and I've at least one friend in there whom I'd like to save. Too . . . oh, damn it all, I am a policeman, and I just can't stand by doing nothing."

"What about your precious Diomedes? What

part is he playing in all this?"

"Come on," he snarled. "Come on. We've wasted enough time already." He found the light switch just inside the door, pressed it, then led the way to the hatch in the floor. They went through it, down into the basement, and then to the big chamber. Peggy helped him to open the door, followed him to the far insulated wall. Yes, that was the panel beyond which lay the tunnel—the slots of the screwheads glittered with betraying bright metal.

At the far end of the tunnel the door into the crèche was not secured and opened easily.

Chapter Twenty-Two

IT WAS QUIET in the passageway, but, dull and distant, the ominous thudding of the battering ram could be heard. And there was the sound of crying, faint and faraway, the infants in the wards screaming uncontrollably.

"Which way?" Peggy was asking. "Which way?"

"This way, I think." He set off at a run along the corridor, his bare feet noiseless on the polished floor. She followed at the same pace, her soft-soled shoes making an almost inaudible shuffle. They ran on, past the closed, numbered doors. At the first cross alleyway Brasidus turned right without hesitation—as long as he kept the clangor of forcible entry as nearly ahead as possible, he could not go far wrong.

And then one of the doors opened. From it stepped the tall, yellow-haired Arcadian whom Brasidus had encountered during his first trespass. She was dressed, this time, in a belted tunic, and her feet were shod in heavy sandals. And she carried a knife that was almost a short sword.

"Stop!" she ordered. "Stop!"

Brasidus stopped, heard Margaret Lazenby slither to a halt behind him.

"Who are you? What are you doing here?"

"Brasidus. Lieutenant, Police Battalion of the Army. Take us to whoever's in charge here."

"Oh, I recognize you—that painfully shy workman who strayed in from the warehouse . . . But *who* are you?"

"I'm from the ship."

"What I thought." The blonde stood there, juggling absently with her knife. *And she'll be able to use it,* thought Brasidus. "What I thought," repeated the woman. "So, at long last, the Police and the outworld space captain are arriving in the nick of time to save us all from a fate worse than death."

"I'm afraid not," Peggy Lazenby told her. "Our respective lords and masters have yet to dedigitate. We're here in our private capacities."

"But you're hung around with all sorts of interesting-looking hardware, dearie. And I can lend Brasidus a meat chopper if he wants it."

Brasidus said that he did. It was not his choice of weapons, but it was better than nothing. The Arcadian went back through the door, through which drifted the sound of excited, high-pitched voices, returned with the dull-gleaming implement. Brasidus took it. The haft fitted his right hand nicely, and the thing had a satisfying heft to it. Suddenly he felt less helpless, less naked.

"And what's your name, by the way?" the blonde Arcadian was asked.

"Lazenby. Peggy Lazenby."

"You can call me Terry. Short for Theresa, not that it matters. Come on."

With her as a guide, they found their way to the vestibule without any delays, bypassing the wards which the infants were making hideous with their screams. But the noise in this entrance hall was deafening enough; it was like being inside a lustily beaten bass drum. Furniture had been piled inside the door, but with each blow of the battering ram, some article would crash to the floor.

There were doctors there, white-faced but, so far, not at the point of panic. There were nurses there, no braver than their superiors, but no more cowardly. They were armed, all of them, after a fashion. Sharp, dangerous-looking surgical instruments gleamed in tight-clenched fists, rude clubs, legs torn from furniture, dangled from hands that had but rarely performed rougher work than changing a baby's diaper.

"Heraklion!" Terry was calling, shouting to make herself heard above the tumult. "Heraklion!"

The tall doctor turned to face her. "What are you doing here, Terry? I thought I told you women to keep out of harm's way." Then he saw Brasidus and Peggy. "Who the hell are these?" He began to advance, the scalpel in his right had extended menacingly.

"Lieutenant Brasidus. Security."

"Looks like a helot to me," muttered somebody. "Kill the bastard!"

"Wait. Brasidus? Yes, it could be . . ."

"It is, it is!" One of the nurses broke away from his own group, ran to where Heraklion was standing. "It is. Of course, it's Brasidus!"

"Thank you, Achron. You should know. But who are you, madam?"

"Doctor Margaret Lazenby, of the starship Seeker."

Heraklion's eyes dwelt long and lovingly on the

weapons at her belt. "And have you come to help us?"

"I let myself get talked into it."

"I knew you'd come," Achron was saying to Brasidus. "I knew you'd come." And Brasidus was uncomfortably aware of Peggy Lazenby's ironic regard. He said to Heraklion, more to assert himself than for any other reason, "And what is happening, Doctor?"

"You ask me that, young man? You're Security, aren't you? You're Captain Diomedes' right-hand man, I've heard. What is happening?"

Brasidus looked slowly around at the little band of defenders with their makeshift armament. He said, "I know what will happen: massacre, with ourselves at the receiving end. That door'll not hold for much longer. Is there anywhere to retreat to?"

"Retreat?" demanded Heraklion scornfully. "Retreat, from a mob of hoplites and helots?"

"They—the hoplites—have weapons, sir. And they know how to use them."

"Your Doctor Lazenby has weapons—real weapons."

"Perhaps I have," she said quietly. "But ethology happens to be my specialty. I've studied the behavior of mobs. A machine gun is a fine weapon to use against them—but a hand gun, no matter how deadly, only infuriates them."

"There's the birth-machine room," suggested somebody. "I've heard said that it would withstand a hydrogen-bomb blast."

"Impossible!" snapped Heraklion. "Nobody here is sterile, and to take the time to scrub up and break out robes at this time . . . "

"The birth machine won't be much use with nobody around to operate it," said Brasidus.

Heraklion pondered this statement, and while he was doing so a heavy desk crashed from the top of the pile of furniture barricading the door. Half-heartedly, three of the nurses struggled to replace it, and dislodged a table and a couple of chairs. "All right," he said suddenly. "The B-M room it is. Terry, run along and round up the other women and get them there at once. Doctor Hermes, get along there yourself with all these people."

"And what about the children?" Achron, in his agitation, was clutching Heraklion's sleeve. "What about the children?"

"H'm. Yes. I suppose that somebody had better remain on duty in each ward."

"No, Doctor," said Brasidus. "It won't do at all. Those wild animals out there hate the nurses as much as they hate you. To the hoplites, they're helots who live better than soldiers do. To the helots, they're overprivileged members of their own caste. Those nurses with the villa outside and the crèche have all been killed. I saw it happen."

"But the *children* . . ." Achron's voice was a wail.

"They'll be safe enough. They might miss a meal or a diaper change, but it won't kill 'em."

"And if there's no other way out of it," put in Peggy Lazenby, "we'll make them our personal charge." She winced as an uproar from the nearer ward almost drowned out the heavy thudding of the battering ram. "I sincerely hope that it never comes to that!"

One of the nurses screamed. The pile of furniture was tottering. The men below it tried to shore it with their bodies, but not for long. A spear probed through the widening gap between the two valves, somehow found its mark in soft human flesh. There was another scream, of pain, this time, not terror. There were other spearheads thrusting hopefully and not altogether blindly. There was a scurrying retreat from the crumbling barricade. Suddenly it collapsed, burying the wounded man, and the great valves edged slowly and jerkily inwards, all the pressure of the mob behind them, pushing aside and clearing a way through the wreckage. And through the widening aperture gusted the triumphant howling and shouting, and a great billow of acrid smoke.

The mob leaders were through, scrambling over the broken furniture, their dulled weapons at the ready. There were a half dozen common soldiers, armed with swords. There was a fat sergeant, some kind of pistol in his right hand. He fired, the report sharp in spite of the general uproar. He fired again.

Beside Brasidus, Peggy Lazenby gasped, caught hold of him with her left hand as she staggered. Then her own pistol was out, and the filament of incandescence took the sergeant full in the chest. But he came on, still he came on, still firing, the hoplites falling back to allow him passage, while the Arcadian fumbled with her gun, trying to transfer it from her right hand to her left. He came on, and Brasidus ducked uselessly as two bullets whined past his head in quick succession.

Then he fell to his knees as Achron shoved him violently to one side. The nurse's frail body jerked and shuddered as the projectiles thudded into

him, but he, like the sergeant, refused to die. He
lifted the table leg with which he had armed himself, brought it smashing down with all his
strength onto the other's head. The wood splin-
tered, but enough remained for a second blow,
and a third. No more were necessary. The sergeant
sagged to the floor, and Achron, with a tired sigh,
collapsed on top of the gross body.

"He's dead." muttered Brasidus, kneeling beside his friend. "He's dead."

But mourning would have to wait. Hastily he
shifted Achron's body to one side so that he could
get at the sergeant's pistol. And then he saw the
face of the dead man, recognizable in spite of the
blood that had trickled down it.

It was Diomedes.

He got to his feet, ready to use the pistol. But he
did not have to. Firing left-handed, Peggy
Lazenby had shot down the other mob leaders,
then used the weapon to ignite the tangle of
wrecked furniture and the floor itself.

"That should hold 'em," she muttered. "Now
lead us out of here, Doctor."

"But you're wounded," Brasidus cried, looking
for telltale patches of wetness on the dark material
of her clothing.

"Just bruised. I'm wearing my bulletproof un-
dies. But come on, you two. Hurry!"

Chapter Twenty-Three

SUDDENLY THE SPRINKLERS came on, saturating the air of the vestibule with aqueous mist and choking, acrid steam. But this was a help to the retreating defenders, a hindrance to the mob. Frightened, the rioters drew back. They had been ready enough to charge barefooted through and over blazing wreckage; now (but too briefly) the automatic firefighting system instilled in them the fear of the unknown. *An acid spray*, they must have thought, *or some lethal gas*. When their shouts made it obvious that they were inside the crèche, Heraklion and his party were already halfway along the first of the lengthy corridors.

The Doctor, it was obvious, knew his way. Without him, Brasidus and Peggy Lazenby would have been hopelessly lost. He turned into cross alleyways without hesitation, finally led them up a ramp, at the head of which was a massive door. It was shut, of course. Heraklion cursed, wrestled with the hand wheel that obviously actuated the securing device. It refused to budge.

Peggy Lazenby pulled out her laser pistol. Heraklion stared at her ironically. "Sure," he said. "Go ahead—if you've all day to play around in. But long before you've made even a faint impression, you'll wish that you'd kept the charge in that weapon for something more useful."

The mob was closer now. They did not know the direction their quarry had taken, but they were spreading through the vast building, looting and smashing. Sooner or later some of them would stumble upon the ramp leading up to the room housing the birth machine. *Sooner*, thought Brasidus, *rather than later*. He examined the pistol that he had taken from Diomedes. It was a standard officers' model Vulcan. One round up the spout, four remaining in the magazine. He regretted having dropped the cleaver that Terry had found for him.

"Here they are," announced Peggy unemotionally. She fired down the ramp, a slashing beam that scarred the paint work of the walls at the foot of the incline. There was a scream, and, shockingly, here was the rapid, vicious chatter of a machine carbine. But whoever was using it was not anxious to expose himself, and the burst buried itself harmlessly in the ceiling.

"I thought that only your people were allowed firearms," said Heraklion bitterly to Brasidus. Brasidus said nothing. If Diomedes, armed, had been among the mob leaders, how many of his trusted lieutenants were also involved?

Still Heraklion wrestled with the hand wheel, and still Peggy and Brasidus, pistols ready, kept their watch for hostile activity. But everything was quiet, too quiet—until at last, from the alleyway that ran athwart the foot of the ramp, there came an odd shuffling, scraping sound. Slowly, slowly the source of it edged into view. It was a heavy shield mounted on a light trolley. Whoever had constructed it had known something about modern weaponry; a slab of concrete, torn up from a floor somewhere, was its main component. Of course, it could not withstand laser fire indefinitely, but long before it crumbled and disintegrated, the riflemen behind it would have disposed of the laser weapon and its user.

There was a small, ragged hole roughly in the center of the slab. Brasidus nudged Peggy, drew her attention to it. She nodded. Suddenly something metallic protruded from the aperture, something that flared and sputtered as the laser beam found it. But Brasidus, at the last moment, switched his own attention from the decoy to the rim of the shield, loosed off two hasty but accurate shots at the carbine that was briefly exposed, at the hands holding it.

Then Heraklion cried out. Under his hands the wheel had moved, was moving of its own accord. The enormously thick door was opening. The Doctor grabbed his companions, pulled them through the slowly widening gap, pushed them clear of the narrow entrance as a deadly hail of bullets splattered around it. Then he turned on the colleague who had, at last, admitted them. "Shut it! At once!" And, as the man obeyed, he demanded coldly. "You were a long time opening up. Why?"

"We had to be sure that it was you. We couldn't get the closed-circuit TV working."

"Even on this primitive planet," commented Peggy Lazenby, "one can find oneself at the mercy of a single fuse."

The little crowd of refugees, with their nervous

chatter, seemed out of place in these surround-
ings. There was an air of mystery—of holy mystery, even—that could not be dispelled by the
intrusion. Tier upon tier towered the vats, empty
now, but spotlessly clean and gleaming. Mile after
convoluted mile ran the piping—glittering glass,
glowing plastic, bright-shining metal. Bank upon
bank stood the pumps, silent now, but ready, in
perfect order, awaiting the touch of a switch to
carry out their functions as mechanical hearts and
lungs and excretory organs.

"There's no place like womb," remarked Margaret Lazenby.

"What was that, Peggy?"

"Never mind. You're too young to understand."
Then, crisply official, "Doctor Heraklion, what
now?"

"I . . . I don't know, Doctor Lazenby."

"You're in charge. Or are you?"

"I . . . I suppose that I am. I'm the senior doctor
present."

"And Brasidus is the senior Security officer
present, and I'm the senior Interstellar Federation's Survey Service officer present. And what
about you, Terry? Are you the senior anything?"

"I don't know. But the other girls usually do
what I tell them to."

"So we're getting some place. But where?
Where? That's the sixty-four-dollar question."
She took two nervous strides forward, two
nervous strides back. "I suppose that this glorified
incubator is on the phone, Doctor Heraklion?"

"It is, Doctor Lazenby. Unluckily the main
switchboard for the crèche is just off the vestibule."

"A pity. I was thinking that you might get through to the military. Or even to the palace itself."

"We tried that as soon as we were warned that the mob was heading our way. But we got no satisfaction. In fact, we gained the impression that the top military brass was having its own troubles."

"They could be, at that," contributed Brasidus. "That sergeant who was leading the rioters, the one with the pistol—it was Diomedes."

"What!"

Heraklion was incredulous, Margaret Lazenby was not. She said, "It makes sense, of a kind. This wouldn't be the first time that an ambitious, comparatively junior officer has organized a coup. And I think I know what makes him tick—or made him tick. There was the lust for power, of course. But, with it, there was a very deep and very real patriotism. I'm a woman, and I had to meet him officially. I could tell, each time, how much he hated me and feared me. No, not personally, but as a member of the opposite sex.

"There are some men—and he was one of them—to whom a world like yours would be the ultimate paradise. *Men Only.* There are some men to whom this stratified social system of yours—cribbed, with improvements, from the *real* Spartans—would seem the only possible way of running a planet.

"But . . .

"But, Doctor Heraklion, there are other men, such as you, who would find the monosexual, homosexual setup rather unsatisfying. And you, my good Doctor, were in a position to do something about it."

Heraklion smiled faintly. "It's been going on for a very long time, Doctor Lazenby. It all started long before I was born."

"All right. The doctors were able to do something about it. I still don't know how this birth machine of yours works, but I can guess. I suppose that all approved Spartans make contributions of sperm cells."

"That is so."

"And the most important contribution—correct me if I am wrong—will be the annual shipments made by the aptly named *Latterhaven Venus* and *Latterhaven Hera*. Venus and Hera were Greek goddesses, by the way, Brasidus. Women—like me, and like Terry and the other playmates. How did the ships get their names, Heraklion?"

"We have always suspected the Latterhaveneers of a warped sense of humor."

"I wonder what the mob is doing?" asked somebody anxiously.

"We're safe enough here," said Heraklin curtly.

Are we? thought Brasidus, suddenly apprehensive. *Are we?* It seemed to him that the floor under his bare soles had become uncomfortably warm. He shifted his stance. Yes, the floor *was* heating up. He looked down, saw a crack in the polished surface. Surely it had not been there before. And if it had been, there had not been a thin wisp of smoke trickling from it.

He was about to tell Heraklion when a device on Peggy Lazenby's wrist—it looked like a watch but obviously was not—buzzed sharply. She raised her forearm to her face. "Doctor Lazenby here."

"Captain here. What the hell are you doing? Where are you?"

"Quite safe, John. I'm holed up in the crèche, in the birth-machine room."

"The crèche is an inferno. Admiral Ajax requested my aid to evacuate the children and to restore order in the city. We're on the way now."

The floor tilted, slightly but sharply. One of the vats shattered loudly and the piping dependent from it swung, clattering and tinkling, against the vessels in the tier below, breaking them. The smell of smoke was suddenly very strong.

"Is there only one way out of this place?" demanded Peggy sharply.

"No. There's a hatch in the roof. Through the records room." Heraklion told her.

"Then that's the way that we have to go to escape from this alleged H-bombproof shelter of yours." Into her wrist transceiver she said, "You'll have to pick us off the roof, John. And while you're about it, you can send a squad of Marines down to save the firm's books. No, I'm not joking."

Luckily the hatch was clear, and luckily the ladder was readily available. Through the little room they passed—the women, the surviving nurses and doctors, then, last of all, Heraklion, Peggy and Brasidus. Brasidus had almost to pull her away from the shelves of microfilmed records, and from the glass case in which was displayed the big, flat book on the cover of which, in tarnished gold, were the words, *Log of Interstellar Colonization Ship DORIC. First Captain Deems Harris.*

They were on the roof then—the tilting, shuddering roof, swept by scorching eddies and black, billowing smoke. The night sky above them was alive with the noise of engines, and from below sounded, ever louder and more frightening, the roar of the fire. Cautiously Heraklion made his way down the listing surface to the low parapet. Brasidus followed him. The two men cautiously peered over, flinching back when a sudden gust of flame seared their faces, crisping their hair and eyebrows.

Grimes had sent down a landing party. Disciplined, uniformed men and women were handling chemical fire extinguishers, others, in a chain, were passing the children out of the blazing building. And still others had set up weapons to protect the rescuers; the rattle of heavy automatic fire was loud and insistent above the other noises.

Peggy Lazenby had joined the two men. "Intervention," she murmured. "Armed intervention. Poor John. He'll be in the soup over this. But what else could he do? He couldn't let those babies burn to death . . ."

"As we shall do," stated Heraklion grimly, "unless your captain does something about it, and fast." As he spoke the roof tilted another few degrees.

But the peculiar, irregular throbbing of the inertial drive was louder now, was deafening. Directly overhead, the glare of the fire reflected from the burnished metal of her hull, Seeker dropped through the vortex of smoke and sparks. Lower she sagged, and lower, until men and women cried out in fear and ran in panic to escape from the inexorably descending pads of her vaned landing gear. Lower she sagged, and lower—and from her open main airlock the boarding ramp was suddenly extruded, the lower end of it scant millimeters only from the heaving, cracking surface of the roof. Even Brasidus knew that he was privileged to watch an exhibition of superb spacemanship.

Down the extended ramp ran six men. Peggy Lazenby met them, cried, "This way!" and led them to the still open hatchway. And a vastly amplified voice was booming from the ship, "Board at once, please! Board at once!"

Heraklion hustled his people into some sort of order, got them onto the gangway, the women first. He stayed with Brasidus, making sure that the evacuation proceeded in an orderly manner. Still the two men waited, although the loudspeaker was blaring. "Get a move on, there! Get a move on!"

At last the six men and Peggy Lazenby were emerging from the hatch, she last of all. They were heavily burdened, all of them, and she, clasping it to her as tenderly as she had clasped the rescued child, carried the antique log book.

"What are you waiting here for?" she demanded of Heraklion.

He said, "We have no spaceships, but we have read books. We know of the traditions. This crèche is my ship, and I shall be the last to leave."

"Have it your own way," she told him.

She and Brasidus went up the ramp after the six marines. Heraklion followed them. Just as he reached the airlock, a geyser of flame erupted from the open hatch and the once flat surface of the roof cracked and billowed and, as *Seeker* hastily lifted, collapsed.

"That *was* my ship," whispered the Doctor.

"You can build another," Peggy told him.

"No," he said. "No. No longer do we have any excuse not to revert to the old ways."

"And *your* old ways," she said, "are not the old ways of Diomedes and his party. That is why he hated and feared you. But can you do it?"

"With your help," he said.

"That," she said, "is a matter for the politicians back home. But let's get out of this damned airlock and into the ship, before we fall out. It's a long way down."

Brasidus, looking at the burning building far below, shuddered and drew back hastily, It was, as she had said, a long way down.

Chapter Twenty-Four

THE NIGHT OF the Long Knives was over, the Night of the Long Knives and the four action packed days and nights that had followed. The power had fallen into the streets, and Admiral Ajax, warned by his own intelligence service of the scheduled assassinations of himself and his senior captains, had swooped down from the sky to pick it up. The birth machine was destroyed, the caste system had crumbled, and only the patrolling airships of the Navy kept Sparta safe from the jealous attentions of the other city-states. Cresphontes—a mere figurehead—skulked in his palace, dared make no public appearances.

Grimes and his *Seeker* had played little active part in quelling the disturbances, but always the spaceship had been there, hanging ominously in the clouds, always her pinnaces had darted from one trouble spot to another, her Marines acting as ambulance men and firemen—but ambulance men and firemen backed by threatening weaponry to ensure that they carried out their tasks unmolested.

Brasidus had rejoined his own police unit, and, to his surprise, had found that greater and greater power and responsibilities were being thrust

upon him. But it made sense. He knew the spacemen, had worked with them—and it was obvious
to all that, in the final analysis, they and the great
Federation that they represented were the most
effective striking force on the planet. They did not
strike, they were careful not to fire a single gun or
loose a single missile, but they were there, and
where they had come from there were more and
bigger ships with even heavier armaments.

The universe had come to Sparta, and the Spartans, in spite of centuries of isolationist indoctri-
nation, had accepted the fact. Racial memory,
Margaret Lazenby had said, long and deep-buried
recollections of the home world, of the planet
where men and women lived and worked together
in amity, where the womb was part of the living
female body and not a complex, inorganic machine.

And then there was the last conference in John
Grimes' day cabin aboard *Seeker*. The Lieutenant
Commander sat behind his paper-littered desk,
making a major production of filling and lighting
his pipe. Beside him was Margaret Lazenby, trim
and severe in uniform. In chairs facing the desk
were the rotund little Admiral Ajax, the tall,
saturnine Heraklion, and Brasidus. A stewardess
brought coffee, and the four men and the woman
sipped it appreciatively.

Then Grimes said, "I've received my orders,
Admiral. Somewhat garbled, as messages by
psionic radio too often are, but definite enough. I
have to hand over to the civil authorities and then
get the hell out." He smiled bleakly. "I've done
enough damage already. I fear that I shall have to
do plenty of explaining to my lords Commissioners."

"No, Commander." Heraklion's voice was firm, definite. "You did not do the damage. The situation, thanks to Diomedes, was already highly explosive. You were only the . . . the . . ."

"The detonator," supplied Ajax.

"Just how explosive was it?" inquired Grimes. "I'd like to know. After all, I shall have a report to make." He switched on a small recorder that stood among the litter on his desk.

"Very explosive. Some of us at the crèche had decided to make women, not only for ourselves, but for every man on Sparta. We had decided to revert to the old ways. Diomedes knew of this. I still think that he was actuated by patriotism—a perverted patriotism, but patriotism nonetheless."

Peggy Lazenby laughed scornfully. "Fine words, Doctor. But what about the female baby who was exposed, the one that Brasidus and I rescued?"

"Yes, the Exposure. *That* was a custom that we intended to stamp out. But the unfortunate child, as well as being female, was mentally subnormal. She'd have been better off dead."

"So you say. But you forget that the planets of the Federation have made great strides in medical science during the centuries that you have been stagnating."

"Enough, Peggy. Enough," said Grimes tiredly. He put his pipe into a dirty ashtray, began to sort his papers. "As I told you, my orders are to hand over to the civil authorities. Who are they? The King? The Council?" The Spartans smiled scornfully. "All right. I suppose that you gentlemen will have to do. You, Doctor Heraklion, and you, Admiral Ajax, and you—just what rank *do* you hold these days? I've rather lost track, Brasidus. But before I hand over, I want to be sure that the Admiral and friend Brasidus know what it's all about. Heraklion knows, of course, but even the most honest of us is liable to bend the facts.

"This ship, as you know, is a unit of the fleet of the Federation's Survey Service. As such she carries, on microfilm, a most comprehensive library. One large section of it is devoted to colonizing ships that are missing. We're still stumbling upon what are called the Lost Colonies, and it's helpful if we have more than a vague idea as to their origin. This Sparta of yours is, of course, a Lost Colony. We've been able to piece together your history both from our own reference library and from the records salvaged from the crèche.

"So far, the history of colonization comes under three headings, the First Expansion, the Second Expansion and the Third Expansion. The First Expansion was initiated before there was a practicable FTL—faster than light—drive. The Second Expansion was carried out by vessels fitted with the rather unreliable Ehrenhaft Drive, the so-called gaussjammers. The Third Expansion made use of timejammers, ships with the almost foolproof Mannschenn Drive.

"The vessels of the First Expansion, the deep-freeze ships, went a long way in a long time, a very long time. They carried at least three full crews—captains, watch-keeping officers, maintenance engineers and the like. The colonists, men and women, were in stasis, just refrigerated cargo, in effect. The crews spent their off-duty months in stasis. But there was, of course, always one full crew on duty.

"As a result of some incredible stupidity on

somebody's part, the crews of many of the early ships were all male. In the later ones, of course, the balance of the sexes was maintained. *Doric*—the ship from which this Lost Colony was founded—had an all male crew, under First Captain—he was the senior of the four masters—Deems Harris. This same Captain Harris was, probably, a misogynist, a woman hater, when the voyage started. If he were not, what happened probably turned him into one.

"Third Captain Flynn seems to have exercised little control over his offiers—or, perhaps, he was the ringleader. Be that as it may, Flynn decided, or was persuaded, to alleviate the monotony of his tour of duty by reviving a dozen of the more attractive colonist girls. It seems to have been quite a party while it lasted—so much so that normal ship's routine went by the board, vitally important navigational instruments, such as the Very Long Range Radar, were untended, ignored. The odds against encountering a meteoric swarm in deep space are astronomical—but *Doric* encountered one. Whether or not she would have been able to take avoiding action is doubtful, but with some warning *something* could have been done to minimize the effects of the inevitable collision. A collision there was—and the sphere in which the female colonists were housed was badly damaged, so badly damaged that there were no survivors. I should have explained before that these deep-freeze ships didn't look anything like a vessel such as this one; they consisted of globes held together by light girders. They were assembled in orbit and were never intended to make a landing on any planetary surface.

"Anyhow, Captain Flynn aroused Captain Harris and the other masters and their officers after the damage had been done. Captain Harris, understandably, took a somewhat dim view of his junior and formed the opinion that if Flynn had not awakened those women the collision would not have occurred. Oddly enough, as his private journal indicates, he blamed the unfortunate wenches even more than he blamed Flynn. He despised Flynn for his weakness and irresponsibility — but those poor girls he *hated*. They were thrown into some sort of improvised brig.

"Meanwhile, *Doric* was far from spaceworthy. Apart from the slow leakage of precious atmosphere, much of her machinery was out of kilter, the automated 'farm,' upon which the crew depended for their food and their atmospheric regeneration, especially. Although the world that you know as Sparta was not the ship's original objective—oddly enough, long-range instrumental surveys had missed it—*Doric's* quite excellent equipment picked it up, made it plain to Captain Harris that he could reach it before air and food and water ran out. So, putting all hands save himself and one officer back into stasis, he adjusted his trajectory and ran for this only possible haven.

"His troubles were far from over. The shuttles — relatively small rocket craft used as ferries between the big ship in orbit and the world below—had all been ruined by that meteoric shower. Nonetheless—it was a remarkable feat of spacemanship—he succeeded in getting that unhandy, unspaceworthy and unairworthy near wreck down through the atmosphere to a relatively soft landing.

"At first glance, the survivors were not too badly off. The planet was habitable. The fertilized ova of various animals—sheep, pigs, cattle, dogs and cats, even—had all been destroyed by the crash landing, but the local fauna was quite edible. And the ship had carried a large stock of seed grain. There was a decided imbalance of the sexes—the only women were Captain Flynn's hapless ones, and there were all of five thousand men — but even that would right itself in time. The ship—as did all ships of that era—carried equipment that was the prototype of your birth machine, and there were supplies of deep-frozen sperm and ova sufficient to populate a dozen worlds.

"But . . .

"Twelve women, and five thousand and forty-eight men.

"Rank, said Captain Flynn and some of the other officers, should have its privileges. It most certainly should not, said the colonists—among them, of course, the twelve men whose wives the women had been.

"There was trouble, starting off with a few isolated murders, culminating in a full-scale revolt against the officers and those loyal to them. Somehow the twelve girls were . . . eliminated. Deems Harris doesn't say as much in his journal, but I gained the impression that he was behind it.

"Now, this Deems Harris. It is hard for us in this day and age of quick passages to get inside the skins, the minds of those old-time space captains. Probably none of them was quite sane. Most of them were omnivorous, indiscriminating readers, although some of them specialized. This Deems

Harris seems to have done so. In history. By this time, with his colony off to a disastrous beginning, he seems to have hankered after some sort of culture in which women played a very small part—or no part at all. One such culture was that of Sparta, one of the ancient Greek city-states back on Earth. Greek women were little more than childbearing, housekeeping machines—and the Spartan women suffered the lowest status of them all. Sparta was the state that specialized in all the so-called manly virtues—and little else. Sparta was *the* military power. Furthermore, the original Spartans were a wandering tribe called Dorians. Dorians—*Doric*–See the tie-up? And their first King was Aristodemus. Aristodemus—Deems Harris.

"The first Aristodemus, presumably, kept women in their proper place—down, well down. This latter-day Aristodemus would go one better. He would do without women at all." Grimes looked at Margaret Lazenby. "At times I think that he had something."

"He didn't have women, that's for certain. But go on."

"All right. Aristodemus—as we shall call him now—was lucky enough to command the services of like-minded biochemists. The sperm, of course, was all neatly classified—male and female being among the classifications. Soon that first birth machine was turning out a steady stream of fine, bouncing baby boys. When the adult populace started to get a bit restive, it was explained that the stock of female sperm had been destroyed in the crash. And somebody made sure that the stock *was* destroyed."

"But," Brasidus interrupted, "but we used to reproduce by fission. Our evolution from the lower animals has been worked out in detail."

"Don't believe everything you read," Peggy Lazenby told him. "Your biology textbooks are like your history textbooks—very cunningly constructed fairy tales."

"Yes," said Grimes. "Fairy tales. Aristodemus and his supporters were able to foist an absolutely mythical history upon the rising generations. It seems fantastic, but remember that there was no home life. They—like you, Brasidus, and like you, Admiral—knew only the Spartan state as a parent. There were no fathers and mothers, no grandfathers and no grandmothers to tell them stories of how things used to be. Also, don't forget that the official history fitted the facts very neatly. It should have done—after all, it was tailor-made.

"And so it went on, for year after year, for generation after generation, until it became obvious to the doctors in charge of the birth machine that it couldn't go on for much longer. That bank of male sperm was near exhaustion. This first crisis was surmounted—ways and means were devised whereby every citizen made his contribution to the plasm bank. A centrifuge was used to separate X-chromosome-bearing sperm cells from those carrying the Y-chromosome. Then the supply of ova started to run out. But still the race was in no real danger of extinction. All that had to be done was to allow a few female children to be born. In fact, this did happen now and again by accident—but such unfortunates had always been exposed on the hillside as defective infants. Even so, the doctors of those days were reluctant to admit female serpents into this all-male paradise.

"And now Latterhaven comes into the story. I'm sorry to have to disappoint you all, but there never was a villainous Admiral Latterus. And, apart from the ill-fated *Doric*, there never were any spaceships owned by Sparta. But while Aristodemus was building his odd imitation of the original, Terran Sparta, the First Expansion ran its course. Then, with the perfection (not that it ever was perfect) of the Ehrenhaft Drive came the Second Expansion. Finally, there was the Third Expansion, and there was the star ship *Utah*, commanded by Captain Amos Latter. It was Latter and his people who founded the colony—one run on rather more orthodox lines than yours—on Latterhaven, a world only a couple of light years from this one.

"The Latterhaveneers made explorations of the sector of space around their new home. One such expedition stumbled upon Sparta. The explorers were lucky not to be slaughtered out of hand—the records indicate that they almost met such a fate—but they were not, and they dickered with the Spartan top brass, and all parties eventually signed a trade agreement. In return for the spice harvest, Latterhaven would send two ships each Spartan year with consignments of unfertilized ova.

"The situation could have continued indefinitely if we hadn't come in—or if Diomedes hadn't found out about the doctors' secret harem."

"The situation would not have continued," stated Heraklion. "As I've told you, Commander, it was our intention to introduce a reversion to the normal way of birth."

"That's your story and you stick to it. It could be true, I suppose; it would account for the way that Diomedes hated you." He refilled and relit his pipe. "The question is, what happens now?"

"What does happen?" asked Admiral Ajax.

"To begin with, I've been recalled to base. I shall have to make my report. It is possible that the Federation will replace your birth machine—although, come to that, you should be able to import materials and technicians from Latterhaven. You might even be able to build a new one for yourselves. But . . .

"But the Federation is apt to be a little intolerant of transplanted human cultures that deviate too widely from the norm. Your monosexual society, for example—and, especially, your charming custom of Exposure. This is your world and, as far as I'm concerned, you're welcome to it. I'm a firm believer in the fifth freedom—the freedom to go to hell your own way. But you've never heard a politician up on his hind legs blathering about the Holy Spirit of Man. If you want to reconstruct your society in your own way, in your own time, you'll have to fight—not necessarily with swords and spears, with guns and missiles—for the privilege.

"I advise strongly that you send a representative with us, somebody who'll be able to talk sense with my lords and masters, somebody who'll be able to take a firm line."

"There's Brasidus," said Peggy Lazenby softly, looking directly at him. *You and I have unfinished business,* her eyes said.

"Yes. There's Brasidus," agreed Grimes. "After all, he knows us."

And he'll get to know us better. The unspoken

words, her unuttered thought, sounded like a caressing voice in Brasidus' mind.

"But we need him," said Heraklion.

"A first-class officer," confirmed Ajax. "He has what's left of the Police eating out of his hand."

"I think that one of *my* colleagues would be a better choice as emissary," said Heraklion.

"So," murmured Grimes. "So . . ." He looked steadily across his desk at the Spartans. "It's up to you, Lieutenant or Colonel or whatever you are. It's up to you. I'm sure that Admiral Ajax will be able to manage without you—on the other hand, I'm sure that Doctor Heraklion's friend will prove a quite suitable envoy.

"It's up to you."

It's up to me, Brasidus thought. He looked at the woman sitting beside the space commander— and suddenly he was afraid. Diomedes' words about the frightening powers wielded by this sex lingered still in his mind. But, in the final analysis, it was not fear that prompted his answer, but a strong sense of responsibility, of loyalty to his own world. He knew—as the aliens did not, could never know—how precarious still was the balance of power. He knew that, with himself in command—effective if not titular—of the ground forces, peace might be maintained, the reconstruction be commenced.

"It's up to you," said Peggy Lazenby.

He said firmly, "I'd better stay."

She laughed, and Brasidus wondered if he alone were aware of the tinkling malice that brought an angry flush to his face. "Have it your own way, sweet. But I warn you, when those tough, pistol-toting biddies of the Galactic Peace

Corps get here, you'll wonder what's struck you."

"That will do, Peggy." Grimes' voice snapped with authority. "That will do. Now, gentlemen, you must excuse us. We have to see our ship secured for space. How soon can you get your envoy here, Doctor Heraklion?"

"About an hour, Commander."

"Very good. We shall lift ship as soon as he's on board." He got to his feet, shook hands with the three Spartans. "It's been a pleasure working with you. It's a great pity that it was not in pleasanter circumstances."

This was dismissal. Ajax in the lead, the three men walked out of Grimes' cabin. Brasidus, bringing up the rear, heard Peggy Lazenby say softly, "The poor bastard!"

And he heard Grimes reply, in a voice that held an unexpected bitterness, "I don't know. I don't know. He could be lucky."

For a long while Brasidus wondered what they meant, but the day came at last when he found out.

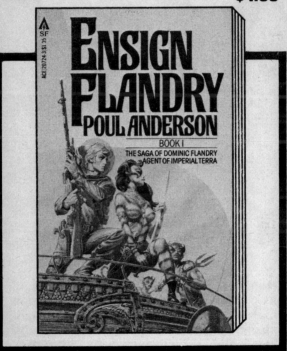

A magnificent new illustrated novel by the author of RINGWORLD and co-author of LUCIFER'S HAMMER!

$4.95 *Cover illustration by Boris*

Here is a science-fantasy novel such as only Larry Niven could create. And to make this magical tale even more so, it is stunningly and profusely illustrated with black and white drawings by Esteban Maroto in this special over-sized (6" x 9") edition.

 Ace Science Fiction